Infamous

ALSO BY LEX CROUCHER

Reputation

Infamous

A NOVEL

Lex Croucher

ST. MARTIN'S GRIFFIN
NEW YORK

First published in the United States by St. Martin's Griffin, an imprint of St. Martin's Publishing Group

INFAMOUS. Copyright © 2023 by Lex Croucher. All rights reserved. Printed in the United States of America. For information, address St. Martin's Publishing Group, 120 Broadway, New York, NY 10271.

www.stmartins.com

Designed by Meryl Sussman Levavi

Library of Congress Cataloging-in-Publication Data

Names: Croucher, Lex, author.
Title: Infamous : a novel / Lex Croucher.
Description: First U.S. Edition. | New York : St. Martin's Griffin, 2023. |
    Identifiers: LCCN 2022051599 | ISBN 9781250875655 (trade paperback) |
    ISBN 9781250875662 (ebook)
Classification: LCC PR6103.R673 I64 2023 | DDC 823/.92—dc23
LC record available at https://lccn.loc.gov/2022051599

Our books may be purchased in bulk for promotional, educational, or business use. Please contact your local bookseller or the Macmillan Corporate and Premium Sales Department at 1-800-221-7945, extension 5442, or by email at MacmillanSpecialMarkets@macmillan.com.

First published in 2021 in the United Kingdom by Zaffre, an imprint of Bonnier Books UK
First U.S. Edition: 2023

1   3   5   7   9   10   8   6   4   2

I wrote this book out of love and spite.
To those it's for: you know who you are, respectively.

Infamous

Chapter One

WHEN THE BELL RANG FOR SUPPER UP AT THE HOUSE, EDDIE and Rose were practicing kissing.

"Your mouth is too slack," Eddie said, slightly muffled against Rose's lips.

"What?" said Rose, pulling away, her face very flushed despite the fact that they were sitting in a rather half-hearted tree house on the first chilly evening of a London September.

"Your mouth. It's just sitting there, a bit wet. Sort of akin to a mollusk. I don't mean to dictate, but as you were the one who wanted to get in the practice, I thought you ought to know."

"Oh," said Rose. She had one hand on Eddie's shoulder, and her fingers tightened on it as if she were reluctant to let go. "Sorry."

"Put your hand on the back of my neck again," Eddie instructed, pleased to be in charge of the operation, where she felt she belonged. "Yes, like that. It was nice before, when you were really digging your nails in."

"You are so odd," said Rose, but her mouth was already very close to Eddie's, which softened her words somewhat. Her fingers were tentatively exploring the hair at the nape of Eddie's neck, and it eased the transition from talking to kissing; Eddie leaned in first and felt Rose's lips part at once. Whatever deficiencies Eddie may have noticed during their previous attempt had already been vastly improved upon, because she found herself relaxing into this kiss, with a warmth not unlike the burn of purloined whiskey spreading slowly through her chest.

"Well, that's more like it. I think it's working this time," Eddie said. "You should try with your tongue. Just to see if you're any good at it."

Her friend sighed as if she were going to protest, but after a few seconds Eddie felt Rose's tongue ghost hesitantly against her bottom lip, her eyelashes fluttering against Eddie's cheek like moth's wings against the glass of a lamp.

They had been sitting apart, leaning across the space between them, but it suddenly occurred to Eddie that it might make more sense, logistically speaking, to press her body closer to Rose's—so she did. *That* certainly improved matters even more. She could feel the swell of Rose's chest pressing into hers now, smell the faint scent of lilac in her hair. It all seemed to be going swimmingly until Rose shifted against her and let slip a breathy, half-restrained *gasp* into her mouth.

Eddie broke away and stared at her. "What the hell was that?"

"The . . . what? What was what? I don't know," Rose said, flushed and red-lipped and looking mortally embarrassed.

"Well, I suppose it's a good job we're practicing. When it comes to the real thing, you might want to keep that sort of thing in check. Oh—hang on." Eddie cocked her head to listen as the bell rang out, interrupting the velveteen quiet. "That's supper."

The bell was ringing quite insistently already, with the sort of urgency that indicated an imminent fire or that the French might be coming. Eddie disentangled herself from Rose, got to her feet, and held out a hand; Rose hesitated, looking dazed, and then took it and allowed herself to be hauled upright. There was the matter of the lantern to be dealt with, but Eddie had recently innovated a particularly ingenious method of scaling the ladder with it swinging festively from her mouth. Rose, who seemed very concerned with telling Eddie which materials were and were not flammable, did not approve.

Once they had alighted safely on the ground, it was just a

quick sprint across the lawn to reach the house, skirts flying up behind them as they cast long, ungainly shadows in the lamplight. All four floors of the narrow house were lit up from within, the glow spilling out onto the patio as Eddie reached the back door and flung it open.

A few steps into the hallway, a small girl with her dark hair gathered on top of her head so that she resembled a very angry pineapple was focusing too determinedly on her task to notice that they had entered.

"You can stop ringing the bell now, Trix," Eddie said, ruffling her youngest sister's alarming hair as she walked past her in the direction of the dining room.

"Father said I'm doing a *damn good job of it!*" Beatrice shouted, over the sound of the ongoing peals. She was seven, and enthusiastic to a fault about any task she was delegated.

"Oh, you *are*," Eddie heard Rose say. "It's just that . . . Well, we're here now, aren't we? I'll follow your lead, of course, but . . . I'm quite hungry."

"All right," said Beatrice magnanimously, followed a second later by the loud metallic thud of something heavy hitting the floor. "You look *very* red in the face. Were you and Eddie having a fight?"

There was a short silence.

"Yes," Rose said eventually, and then Eddie heard her hurrying to catch up.

The large dining room already seemed rather full. Mr. and Mrs. Miller sat at either end of the table, and between them in varying states of patience sat their three middle children. Simon, who was twelve and perpetually disappointed, was staring morosely down at the table as if he suspected supper might never come. Amelia, who had just recently celebrated her fourteenth birthday by campaigning for her own horse and crying for an impressive six days when she only received one made of wood, was humming under her breath. Lucy-Anne, who fancied herself the eldest and most mature of them all, even though she decidedly was not on either count, was glaring openly at Eddie from across the room.

"You're really very late," she said, as Caroline the housemaid appeared with the roast duck. "We shouldn't have to ring a bell to fetch you in, like you're *livestock*."

Eddie ignored her and took a seat next to her father; Rose sat down next to Simon, who solemnly offered her his hand to shake.

"They were wrestling in the tree house," Beatrice said helpfully, scrambling into her own seat, which had been pre-cushioned to ensure maximum height and a greater sense of authority over proceedings.

"Oh, *Edith*," said Mrs. Miller, sounding tired but unsurprised. "You are a woman of two-and-twenty. Don't you think you're a little old for that sort of thing?"

"I wish you'd told me you were going to wrestle," added Simon. "If I'm really not to have any brothers, you ought to think of me and extend an invitation to any horseplay, don't you agree? *Think* next time, Ed."

"Did you get in any good right hooks?" said Mr. Miller, sounding interested. "Are you keeping your thumbs out, like I showed you?"

Eddie looked up and surveyed them. For some reason they were all looking at her expectantly. She glanced at Rose, bemused, and then picked up her fork and pointed at the spread in front of them.

"If you're quite finished with the interrogation," she said, "this bird is not going to eat itself."

After supper they gathered in the drawing room, as was customary, although their approach to the whole ceremony was noticeably lax. In other houses across London, men would be huddling to discuss war, finances, or recent sporting endeavors, and ladies would be laughing from behind their fans or preparing to entertain with a jaunty tune on the pianoforte; at the Millers', Beatrice was clinging on to Simon's leg like a limpet as he walked, and Eddie was holding a piece of cake in her mouth, shedding crumbs as she led them into the room.

"What's the latest story about?" Rose asked Eddie once they were settled.

The heavy blue drapes were closed, the smell of her father's pipe smoke filling the air, and Lucy-Anne had started playing her harp with a sense of grandiosity and an excess of flourishes that did not quite match the occasion. She kept shooting them all furious, narrow-eyed looks every time they were too loud; juxtaposed with the angelic piece she was playing, it was starting to feel like a very surreal performance about the duality of man.

Eddie unfolded the rather ink-stained and crumpled wad of paper from her pocket and smoothed it out on the polished walnut table between them.

"Do not get ink on my polished walnut table," Mrs. Miller said from her customary chair in the corner. Eddie rolled her eyes.

"This one," she said, leaning in close to Rose with a dangerous grin, "is about *lady pirates*."

"They don't let ladies be pirates," Simon said from underneath the table. "They are bad luck, and bad omens, and their arms are too small to put hooks on the end. Imagine how silly it would look, to have a spindly little arm and a big great hook at the end of it."

"*Simon!*" Beatrice shouted. "They'd just get smaller hooks. There isn't just one size of hook, you *ninny!*"

"I am having a private conversation," Eddie said, although she knew it was futile. Their house was generously proportioned and should have been more than big enough for all seven of them—eight, if Rose was to be included, as she almost always was—but no matter which room she entered in search of some much-needed privacy, there always seemed to be at least one sibling in there, ricocheting off the walls or demanding help with their dress or asking if she thought their fingernails had grown a suspicious amount since last inspected.

"Go on," Rose said, nudging Eddie's foot with hers underneath the table, and narrowly avoiding kicking Simon in the ear.

"These were *real* lady pirates," Eddie said loudly, mostly for Simon's benefit, but also to encourage Beatrice, should she have aspirations of a piratical nature. "From just a hundred years ago. Anne Bonny and Mary Read. They dressed as men and they pillaged the Seven Seas and *then*, when the time came for them to face the noose, they pleaded their bellies so they wouldn't swing."

"God," said Rose, looking fascinated and a bit sick. "Is that what your story is about, then?"

"No," said Eddie. "My version imagines them as young academics, disguised as men so they can study at university. They meet for the first time in a teahouse, both reaching for the last piece of gingerbread. A tense argument ensues."

"Which one of them gets it on their hook first?" said Beatrice, already entranced, if slightly confused. Amelia, who had been lying facedown much too close to the fireplace, flopped gracelessly onto her back. Even their father had lowered his book and was waiting expectantly for Eddie to speak.

"You'd all better be quiet if you want me to read it," she said sternly. There were general noises of assent, except from Lucy-Anne, who only played the harp more loudly.

"All right. *It was a cold, misty morning in March when Anne Bonny opened the door to the Jelly Roger Tea House—for all intents and purposes a morning like any other, although the events that were about to transpire were to change the course of her life forever . . ."*

Chapter Two

WHEN EDDIE FIRST MET ROSE LI, THE LATTER HAD BEEN standing in the Millers' garden clutching one of their kitchen cat's two-week-old kittens. Rose had been black-haired, pink-cheeked, and pleasantly chubby; after she had deposited the kitten back into its box with its harried mother, she had wiped her furry palm on her dress and solemnly stuck out a hand to be shaken. Eddie had been immediately fascinated, and had announced that Rose was staying for supper.

It had been pointed out to her that as she was eight years old, she had no business announcing exactly who was staying for supper, even if they *were* children of her father's business associates; luckily the Li family had already been planning to join them for their meal, and Eddie had ushered Rose to the seat next to her as if she were the owner of a fine dining establishment seating her most important customer.

"Our cook is very dreadful," she said to Rose in an undertone. "Mama says we mustn't take it personally, and that if she really meant to kill us, she'd have done it years ago."

"Can I please have a kitten, if you have one to spare?" Rose had replied, apparently unbothered by the quality of the upcoming victuals.

Eddie had struck a bargain—a kitten in exchange for Rose returning the next day to continue their friendship. She hadn't factored Lucy-Anne into this particular negotiation, who had screamed as if she had given birth to the kitten herself when she saw it being borne away in the arms of a stranger. She had never particularly warmed to Rose, and Eddie suspected it was entirely due to that kitten, who had disappointed them anyway by ignoring their plans to take him marauding and include him in various criminal activities and deciding to become a prissy little lap cat instead.

Rose lived only two streets away, in one of the more modest terraces, and was present at dinner at least three times a week for the next fourteen years. At one point she and Eddie had attempted to calculate how many dinners that added up to, but they had given up on the mathematics after five minutes and had to open a bottle of wine to recover. Over the years their interests had matured from exploring the wilderness of the small garden to swapping horror stories and snatches of poetry by candlelight in the attic; from standing at the window, throwing stones at passing boys to see how many they could hit, to lurking in the corner of their parents' dinner parties, throwing grapes at passing boys to see how many they could hit.

At thirteen Rose had had the better arm, but Eddie was entirely unafraid of being caught.

Eddie had always loved to invent stories, lengthy plays for her siblings to perform and short dramatic tales of daring starring herself and Rose in the main roles, but it was in her early teens that she started to write what she thought of as *proper* stories—all of them written exclusively for the entertainment and delight of her best friend. She was relentlessly prolific; there was an entire trunk full of her work at the foot of her bed, a treasure trove of great loves and gruesome deaths that she would dip into regularly so that she could present Rose with a story as one might give a bouquet of flowers.

"I am going to be a famous writer one day," she told Rose once, when they had spent the evening giggling over her latest. She had decided that this was to be her fate only moments before.

"I know," said Rose, immediately and without an ounce of doubt.

Eddie had become accustomed to feeling as if she and Rose weren't really two separate people at all, but some many-limbed creature with a shared neural center. They didn't exactly look alike, but they weren't *unalike*, either; Eddie was tall and Rose of average height, Eddie all sharp angles and gangle where Rose was soft, Eddie pale and hollowed-out next to Rose's light gold skin. They both had dark hair—Rose's was very long and straight and black, Eddie's shorter, wavy, darkest brown—and when they sat ensconced somewhere together at the end of an evening, their heads meeting in the middle, the differences fell away. Rose was certainly friendlier and far less impudent, but otherwise they were so alike in humor and temperament—so aligned on almost everything they encountered in their shared existence—that it was an enormous shock when sixteen-year-old Eddie had called round to Rose's house, flopped onto a chaise and started complaining about the evils of being forced to come out into society, and found herself alone in her misery.

"Oh, I don't know. I think it'll be nice," Rose had offered, her face pink. "Don't you like parties, really?"

"No," Eddie said, sitting up very straight and staring at Rose in genuine horror. "They're terrible! They're monstrous! The only absolutely minuscule shred of joy to be found in them is that I can attend them with you, and as I can attend *anything* with you, that leaves them with no redeeming qualities whatsoever."

"Well, I'm looking forward to it," said Rose. "And besides—my parents are *so* proud. Not everybody is guaranteed a grand coming out, Ed. It's a privilege. If you do anything to ruin it for me, or them, I'll throw you overarm into the Thames."

It was the very first sign that Rose did not in fact coinhabit Eddie's brain, and it was extremely jarring.

Their coming out itself had gone mostly without incident.

They did not have to present themselves to the Queen herself due to her ill health, which Rose said was a blessing, as "Eddie would have undoubtedly done something so heinous and inappropriate that she'd have been executed right then and there in the middle of the ballroom."

Rose had been asked to dance many, many times, and Eddie only a few; she hadn't minded *that* at all, although she had resented the fact that she had to watch Rose line up again and again, her painstakingly fashioned ringlets flying as she was whirled and courted by all manner of eager, pink-faced gentlemen.

Toward midnight, they escaped up some stairs and out onto a balcony to be alone, crashing through the doors in a rush of silk and lace. London spread out before them, an intricate puzzle of rooftops partially obscured by chimney smoke.

"If I were queen, I'd abolish all this. Balls. Coming out. Suitors."

Rose snorted into her ivory glove. "If you were queen, everything would be burning down around us. It would be the sequel to the Great Fire of London—the even *greater* fire of London. And anyway, mad genius, you'd have had to marry the King to become queen."

"Hmph."

"I'm sorry you sat out some of the dances."

"Dear God, not at all—I'm sorry you sat *in* them."

Rose laughed and leaned her elbows on the stone balcony, her eyes drifting across the horizon.

"That does not make even half a jot of sense."

"You didn't *like* any of those boys, did you?"

Rose paused for too long a moment; Eddie felt herself on the verge of a gentle fret.

"No. I did not."

Eddie breathed a little easier. She came to stand next to Rose, leaning her head on her friend's shoulder. Ordinarily she would have been batted away, but instead Rose just closed her eyes.

"Sixteen is a terrible age," Eddie said seriously.

"What are you pontificating on about now?"

"I feel like I could do anything and nothing, all at the same time. London is enormous! But it's too small! I want to write something great, but I fear I am far too young—I am not a child, but dagger to my heart, I never want to be a minute older."

"How much wine did you have to drink?"

Eddie shifted against Rose, tilting her head up to look at the stars.

"Nash Nicholson published his first poem at sixteen. It was one of the only cheerful ones."

"Which one is he?"

"You never listen to me, do you?"

Rose reached up to pet her clumsily on the head. "All I *do* is listen to you. London is big, it's small . . . Daggers . . . Er . . . Famous poets."

"I am destined to be tragically misunderstood."

Rose laughed quietly. There was a brief silence, an oasis between the bustle of the city and the distant strains of music from the ball below them.

"You are right about one thing, though. I don't know how I'll get on with being an adult, full grown."

Eddie straightened up. "We ought to make a solemn pact."

"Ought we now?"

"Yes," said Eddie, taking Rose firmly by the shoulders and turning her so that they were facing each other head-on. "I mean it. We must swear that things will never change between us. That we will be like this always. And . . . and that we will *never* marry."

"Eddie . . ."

"What? Are you so eager to be rid of me?"

Rose frowned, her eyes searching Eddie's face. "No. But . . . be reasonable. I can hardly say I'll never marry. It wouldn't be fair to place that burden upon my parents. How would I take care of them? And whatever would I do with myself?"

"Anything! Look, you *can* say it. I certainly can. I mean it. To hell with the lot of it—I am quite determined to do exactly the opposite of what the world wants from me. We should clasp our hands. We should cut them, and join our blood."

"I'm not having any of your blood. I've seen how many potatoes you eat. I shall stick to my own, thank you very much."

"Fine, fine, not the blood—but the pact. Come on, swear it."

She took up both of Rose's hands in hers and squeezed gently.

Rose wavered for a moment. Her hair was coiling loosely around her shoulders and her eyes were dark and intent in the moonlight; Eddie was desperate, suddenly, to know that she would never lose her. Rose sighed.

"All right. I swear it."

With the reckless, implausible optimism that belonged entirely to girls of sixteen, Eddie had believed her.

Chapter Three

To EDDIE'S UTTER DISMAY, ROSE *LOVED* BEING OUT IN SOCIETY.
Her parents treated her to not one but *three* new dresses.
She went for tea. She accepted party invitations, and sometimes
dragged Eddie along with her. She actually *blushed* when Sophie
Newport, who was the pale, insipid cousin of some duke and
therefore far outranked them both, had complimented her hair.

"I like your hair, too," Eddie said fiercely when they were
walking to their carriages afterward, "but you don't start *blushing*
about it."

Rose had turned toward her in a flurry of muslin and dark
curls and fixed her with a very penetrating look.

"Perhaps that's because you never say it," she snapped, before
hurrying away, leaving Eddie speechless on the steps of the assembly rooms.

They had made up quickly, but it had been the first real rift
between them that hadn't been about who was allowed to hold
the frog they found in Mr. Miller's boot, or which poem by Pope,
Byron, or Nicholson they should take turns reading aloud, and
from that day forth there was a frisson of tension in their friendship that had never existed before. Eddie had always felt as if she
could say absolutely anything to Rose, and had assumed Rose felt
the same way, but now she found herself holding her tongue—or
at least attempting to, and occasionally succeeding—when it
came to the subjects of parties and society and *ladylike behavior*.

"You didn't really want to stay, did you?" she had asked one night, when she had succeeded in begging Rose to leave a particularly dismal party early. They were sitting in the tree house with their hair half-undone and gloves off, enjoying the cool breeze after a long and stuffy day, a bottle of wine and half a lemon cake stolen from the kitchen between them. Rose had just turned eighteen, and was getting alarmingly beautiful.

"You know I did, and you also know that I am not interested in bickering with you when there is cake to eat instead."

"That boy was lurking. Barker? Baker?"

"He was hardly *lurking*. If you must know, I think he's got half a mind to marry me."

Eddie choked on quite a large mouthful of wine. "*What?* Well, I certainly hope the other half wins, poor thing."

"My mother is getting quite worried. She sees me putting people off. She keeps having hushed conversations with my father about it, when she thinks I'm not listening."

"Let them mutter. *We* made a pact."

Rose rolled her eyes. "But it wasn't . . . it wasn't *real*, was it, Ed?"

"Of course it was," Eddie said firmly.

"But we were children when we said that. We said a lot of things. It's like when we were fourteen and you were convinced you were going to run off with that poet you love, Nash what's-his-name. Or when we were twelve and we said we were going to eschew society and live in this tree house. You changed your tune rather quickly when that big moth fell on you," Rose said, licking icing off her fingers. "Someone is actually going to get up the courage and ask me, eventually."

"Well, they can't have you!" Eddie said, outraged. "You're not free for the taking!"

"Well, *you're* hardly going to marry me, are you, Ed?" Rose said lightly, dabbing ineffectually at a smear of cake on her skirts.

"Obviously not. Just . . . stay here with me, and things will be as they've always been. I hardly care what your parents think. I hardly care what *anyone* thinks. You promised—you cannot back down now. It would be cowardice."

Rose wrinkled her nose and picked up the bottle of wine, taking a deep swig from it as she stared straight ahead at the house, where the lamps were starting to go out in the upper rooms as the Miller family took themselves to bed.

"That's not fair," she said eventually, so quietly and with such a noble air of suffering that Eddie had been quite lost for words.

From that evening on, she spent a lot more time actually *looking* at Rose than she had ever done before. Rose had become as familiar as the coat hooks in the hallway or Lucy-Anne's cat perpetually slumbering by the fire: the sort of things you never spared a second glance simply because they were always there. Eddie had always assumed that their friendship was permanent, their pact not to be wed as strong and everlasting as any marriage, but now things felt precarious. She wanted to get a good look at Rose, just in case. Eddie noticed the little things about her that had become invisible: the fact that her hair was simply too soft and too straight to keep a curl, and always ended up halfway down her back by midnight; the lopsidedness of her smile, one corner of her mouth always crooked up and inviting a dimple; the fact that she had many different laughs on hand for every possible occasion, but that Eddie's favorite was the undignified, goose-like honking that occurred when she had truly lost her head.

She watched as Rose became a woman, taking to it far more easily than Eddie did. It suited her.

Rose still called for Eddie on her way to parties, and sometimes managed to convince Eddie to come with her, but when they arrived she had *other* friends. High society ladies who had been thoroughly charmed and had accepted Rose into the fold; who squealed with delight at the sight of her and handed her drinks and enveloped her in a whirlwind of gossip and jokes about events and people that seemed, to Eddie, about as scintillating as twisted ankles and taxes. Mostly, Eddie stayed at home, and tried not to sulk when Rose sent a note or dropped by to say she wouldn't be joining the Millers for dinner that evening as she had another engagement. She usually failed very miserably at not being miserable, and spent the evening arguing with Lucy-Anne, who was only four years her junior and therefore her natural sparring partner.

The time they spent together after the dinners Rose *did* attend—crashing from the house with pilfered libations in hand, Rose never hesitating for a second when it came time to climb the wizened oak tree even if she was wearing her finest dress—became sacred.

A week after Eddie had recited her story about Anne Bonny and Mary Read as strangely violent female academics, Rose committed a cardinal sin: she willingly invited a man into their tree house.

Not literally, of course. If she had done, Eddie would have kicked him right back out, and wished him luck on his way down.

"I met him at Ava Forester's house," Rose said, shivering as autumn threatened. "Do you know William Rednock?"

"*William Rednock?*" Eddie said disparagingly. "Is he not about sixteen? Is he not the one completely obsessed with model ships? He's only got half a mustache, Rose, and it's not even the good half."

"Yes. But it's not him," Rose said, dropping her chin onto her hands. "It's his uncle Albert."

The only appropriate reaction to this was extensive swearing, and Eddie did not waver in her duty to deliver. Rose raised an eyebrow and waited patiently for her to finish.

"He's only eight-and-thirty. He's still got full use of all his parts. He's very kind. And besides—you've never even met him."

"Yes I *have*," Eddie said indignantly. "I met him when I was ten, which means he was already . . ." She had to pause to do the mathematics, and Rose waited politely. "*Six-and-twenty*, ugh. It was at a picnic, and he gave me his hat to get me to stop fighting with Lucy-Anne."

"Well, there you go, then. I told you he was kind."

"He's a good *babysitter*. So that'll certainly come in handy."

"Oh, stop it. Sixteen years is nothing. My mother is twelve years younger than my father, and you don't heckle them every time you see them."

She was, of course, entirely correct—but Eddie felt very strongly that there was a world of difference between *other people* marrying men over a decade their senior and *Rose* considering doing the same.

"I don't like it," she said unnecessarily.

"Well, you don't like anything," Rose said, which was unfair. Eddie liked lots of things. Rose. Writing. She was sure there were others; she just couldn't recall them at the moment. "I saw him at the Foresters', and Ava's father introduced us. We ended up spending a very pleasant evening together."

"What?" Eddie said scathingly. "*Dancing?*" She managed to make "dancing" sound as horrifying as "frolicking in your own excrement," as she had intended.

"No, actually, even worse—*talking*," Rose said, wiggling her eyebrows suggestively. "He breeds rabbits in his spare time. He was telling me all about it. Apparently, they're actually very complicated creatures."

"Just because he's good at animal husbandry," Eddie said, already smirking as she worked her way to her punch line, "doesn't mean—"

"No," said Rose. "Sorry, but you are not permitted to make that joke. It's low-hanging fruit. I did all the setup for you."

"Oh, fine," said Eddie crossly. "But if you're allowed to tell me that you might be considering signing your entire life away to a man because he thinks rabbits are *thrilling and complex creatures*, I have to be allowed to make jokes, too."

"I'm not joking," said Rose.

Eddie's brain came to a grinding halt. "You're serious? This is real?"

"It's real."

All manner of childish rebuttals flared in Eddie's mind, but she knew they were futile. She took a breath, feeling slightly sick. This day had been coming for a while; she had just tried very hard to ignore it. Almost all of Rose's friends were now married or betrothed. It had been like watching a huntsman pick off game birds one at a time, until only Rose was left, the best and the brightest . . . and for some reason now flying directly toward the smoking barrel.

They had put it off for six miraculous years, but Rose had been winged.

"Oh God," Eddie said suddenly, trying to keep her tone light. "Is that why you were so fixated on *kissing*? You're planning on kissing this . . . this *desiccated prune* of a man?"

Rose glanced away, and then looked back at Eddie with a shrug.

"Well, as you've so tactfully pointed out, he's quite a few years my senior. He'll probably have *lots* of experience."

Eddie swallowed down the bitter dread that had threatened to overwhelm her and then laughed too loudly and pressed a hand to her chest in a facsimile of a swoon.

"Whereas *we* are innocent young maidens who have never so much as caught a glimpse of ourselves nude in a looking glass."

"Well—I don't stand around staring at myself naked in the looking glass," Rose said, frowning. "Have you been staring at yourself naked in the looking glass? Because I think that might be a sure sign of—"

"I want to go to bed," Eddie said. She was suddenly very tired.

Rose squinted at her with a strange, sad little smile on her face and then shrugged, as if she didn't mind at all.

"Edith Miller. Only two-and-twenty, and with all the party stamina of her sister's elderly cat. What *are* we going to do with you?"

Chapter Four

⸻

IT HAD BEEN SAID ON A NUMBER OF OCCASIONS THAT THE way the Millers ran their house and raised their children was a little unorthodox. To Eddie, it had on the whole been a blessing.

Her mother, it was whispered, had been exposed to far too many *books* from a young age, and it had engendered in her a curious mind and a lack of respect when it came to propriety for propriety's sake. This deficit of character was excused only because her husband had been particularly prosperous over the past decade—enough so that Mrs. Miller never had cause to look with horror upon her four daughters and wonder how, exactly, she would be profitably rid of them. She had taught all her children herself rather than engage a governess, assisted by Mr. Miller when he was not off merchanting, with a focus on expanding their minds rather than teaching them pristine manners. It was only when Eddie reached her teenage years that Mrs. Miller had been confronted with the true extent of the independent, freethinking horror she had wrought.

Lucy-Anne had rebelled by caring very deeply about decorum, talking often of marriage and loudly lamenting the Miller children's prospects with Eddie at their helm, more an interfering grandmother than a younger sister. It had befuddled Mrs. Miller almost as much as her eldest, who was prone to carrying things about the house between her teeth and putting her feet up on the furniture, like some sort of upright Labrador.

Eddie's mother *did* insist on a certain level of decorum when leaving the house, not wishing for them to be cast out of polite society altogether, and more than once had stopped Eddie in the hallway on her way out of the door and demanded that she go and wash the ink from her fingers, or at least attempt to do something with her hair that did not resemble an explosion in a textile mill.

"Edith," Mrs. Miller said now, touching Eddie on the arm as she tried to slink past. "You have a pine cone on your head."

Eddie—who had been writing in the tree house all morning, meaning that arboreal debris was entirely possible—patted the back of her head and then frowned.

"That is just my hair, Mother. I did it myself."

"Good God," said Mrs. Miller. "Yes—you did, didn't you? Hold still a moment."

Holding still was not Eddie's forte, but she filled the time by tapping her foot impatiently as her mother fetched a comb and some ribbon and attempted a coordinated attack.

"It was very nice of Mr. Rednock to invite you to his party," Mrs. Miller said, eliciting a hearty scoff from her daughter.

"He is attempting to ingratiate himself with me, in order to win favor with Rose."

"Well, honestly, Edith. Would you rather he spurned you and made it clear you were never to darken his door?"

Eddie shrugged. "At least I would respect him for his honesty."

"You are speaking as if you are still a child," said Mrs. Miller, tugging too hard on a lock of Eddie's hair and making her wince. "Oh—sorry. I did tell you to stay still. I know it all seems dreadful now, but you would do well to befriend this man, if you think Rose does intend to marry him. You do not want your friends' husbands as enemies. They tend to hold the keys to the front door."

"Then I shall use the window," Eddie said, wriggling free of her mother's grasp. "Farewell, Mother. If I do not return, assume

I have committed murder and taken on a new identity to escape prosecution."

"I assume that whenever you leave the house," said Mrs. Miller.

When Eddie reached Rose's door, she had barely lifted her hand to knock when it opened.

"Oh," said Rose. She was wearing pink, her gloves immaculate, her curls behaving for the time being. "You look . . . lovely."

"Liar," said Eddie. "*You* look like a strawberry shortcake."

"There are far worse things to be," Rose said, stepping forward to try to pick up where Mrs. Miller had left off and attempt to fix Eddie's hair. "Now, don't get yourself into a temper, but I did promise that we would stop in on the way—"

"Oh, God. Who is it? Not the Foresters?"

Rose's hand stilled on Eddie's parting. "The Feldmans."

"I shall stay in the carriage and watch out for brigands."

"You will do no such thing—she's been asking after you."

Eddie was about to protest, but Mr. and Mrs. Li were stepping out of the doorway, so she instead tried to express her agony through the medium of mime. She continued this performance all the way into the carriage, through the darkening streets of London, and into the Feldmans' front hall.

Eddie had likely been in this house before, but at this point, all the houses of the merchants of London had blurred into one nightmare of bright new wallpaper and recently purchased antique furniture; it wasn't unlike her own house, aside from the fact that it was filled to the brim with people she felt she had no obligation to speak to under any circumstances.

The newly married Mrs. Hannah Feldman came rushing over to meet them, pale but for the vivid pink of her cheeks, wearing a confection of marigold silk.

"Good evening, Mr. Li, Mrs. Li, Miss Li . . . gosh, and Miss Miller! What a surprise. I thought you had perhaps died."

"Sadly not," said Eddie, as Rose's parents went to greet their own friends. She noticed that both Rose and Mrs. Feldman were standing with impeccable posture, and attempted to comport herself less like a collapsed umbrella.

"You always were so witty. Well . . . what do you think of me, Rose? A married woman!"

Rose exclaimed obediently and launched into congratulations; Eddie smiled briefly like an ape under threat and then eyed Rose warily out of the corner of her eye, thinking that marriages seemed a catching disease.

"Well, I must introduce you," said Mrs. Feldman, and then they were off on a tour of excruciating introductions, starting with her husband. Eddie's curtsies quickly became half-hearted, and barely quarter-hearted by the end. Smiling at strangers made her face hurt. Wearing gloves made her itch. Having to watch her tongue was even worse. She felt she had been tricked into attending this party; she had only agreed to be part of this evening at all because the thought of the elderly Mr. Rednock as Rose's potential suitor had whipped her into a panic and made her want to hold on to Rose a little tighter, but good God—at what cost?

At one point she drifted away to find a drink and came across Hannah Feldman's younger brother, Jacob, standing with his hands clasped behind his back by the refreshments as if he were part of some sort of wine garrison.

"Evening, Jacob," she said; he immediately went very red.

"We have not been introduced," he said out of the corner of his mouth, as if afraid to be overheard.

"Do not be ridiculous," said Eddie, requisitioning some alcohol. "I know who you are. You fell over that dog last Easter, it was an outstanding piece of physical comedy."

Jacob was turning puce. "Miss Miller, you are not allowed to speak to me until we have been formally introduced."

"Aha! So you do know who I am."

Jacob darted a desperate glance at the nearest group of guests, and then firmly trained his eyes on the ceiling.

"I cannot hear you."

Eddie stared at him. He seemed to be perfectly serious. She waved a hand in front of his face, and although he blinked, his gaze did not waver.

"Oh dear," Eddie said, picking up a napkin and wafting it over a candle on the table. "I seem to be about to start a small fire."

She had the satisfaction of seeing him twitch. The edge of the napkin was starting to look a tad sooty; she was just wondering if he would actually need to smell smoke before he acknowledged her when a hand closed over her wrist, neatly moving it aside and squeezing until she was forced to relinquish the napkin.

"Arson?" Rose said quietly in her ear. "Really?"

"I thought of it more like sending smoke signals," Eddie said, as Rose steered her across the room and out into the empty corridor. Down the hall, she could hear the jovial clatter of servants at work.

"Was this some sort of cry for help?"

"No," said Eddie, slumping against the wall in relief. In the other room, there was a burst of applause as a pianist and a violinist struck up a tune—it could only mean *dancing*. "It was an experiment. He insisted he would not speak to me until we had been *formally introduced*. I honestly don't know how you do this every other night."

Rose looked unimpressed. "You realize that *you* are the outlier here? Everybody else manages to follow the rules of decorum perfectly well without looking as if they have one foot trapped in a mangle all the while. It's not that difficult, Ed—just try to imagine that other people are actually worth your attention and respect, as a starting point, and the rest follows."

"I was being perfectly polite to Jacob," Eddie said, crossing her arms.

"Before you tried to set his house on fire."

"Yes, before that."

Rose sighed. "I wish you would just allow yourself to have the tiniest bit of fun."

"Fun begins at home," said Eddie. "And it ends there, too."

"You don't want to make new friends at all, now that you're supposedly grown up?"

"Not with any of *these* people."

Rose folded her arms crossly, glancing toward the door to the party. The music was in full swing, accompanied by the sounds of shuffling feet, laughter, and off-beat clapping. She worked her lip between her teeth for a moment and then looked back at Eddie.

"Would you like to dance?"

It was so far from anything Eddie might have expected her to say that she just laughed.

Rose raised her eyebrows. "Well? Or have you promised the first dance to Jacob?"

"Nobody ever asks me to dance," Eddie said. "Nobody would dare."

Rose shrugged, uncrossing her arms and then prising Eddie's apart, too.

"I'm asking. I dare."

"Are you trying to *waltz* with me, you brazen harlot?"

Rose laughed quietly, one hand coming to rest on Eddie's shoulder blade.

"It's the *only* dance for the discerning ne'er-do-well."

It wasn't much of a waltz; neither of them was particularly good at it or knew how to lead, so they just swayed in lazy circles, Eddie feeling a little disarmed by their proximity and almost tripping over herself despite their slow progress. The music in the drawing room came to an end and the next song started up, leaving them hopelessly out of step. Rose sighed and let her head fall forward onto Eddie's shoulder.

"I suppose . . . we should leave soon. I don't want to be late for Mr. Rednock's."

"I suppose so," Eddie said into Rose's hair, closing her eyes. The party suddenly felt very far away, where it belonged.

"Not just yet, though," said Rose.

"No," Eddie agreed. "Not just yet."

Chapter Five

"I DON'T LIKE HIM."

"Oh, come off it, Ed. You've hardly given him a chance."

"Five minutes is more than enough time to make an impression. Do you remember the first five minutes of our acquaintance?"

Rose sighed. "Yes, but . . . we were children."

"Precisely! He's had his entire, *very* long life so far to work on his personality, and this is all he can come up with!"

"Hm," said Albert Rednock, who was standing right next to them, peering into his wineglass. "For some reason, I find I quite urgently need another drink. Miss Li?"

"Thank you, Mr. Rednock," Rose said, watching him walk away with a frown on her face. As soon as he was out of earshot, she turned back to Eddie. "Vile creature."

"That's what I've been saying!"

"Not *him*—you! I cannot believe you'd be so unconscionably rude to the poor man's face—it's only the fact that he's so sweet that's saving you from social disgrace—"

"I like being a disgrace," Eddie said, grinning in the manner of a child who has secretly put ants in your bed. "He's old, he's dreadful, I don't like him."

Actually, if the circumstances of their meeting had been different, Eddie thought she *might* have liked him just fine. He was generally inoffensive; of medium height, pinkish all over and balding at the temples, slightly jowly and with a pair of thin gold spectacles perched on his nose. He had a lot of laugh lines, and he seemed ready and willing to produce more.

Rose's parents didn't seem to object to him one bit. In fact, the only thing they *did* seem to object to was Eddie herself; they had been darting rather concerned looks at her all evening, which Eddie had decided not to take personally, until she'd been lurking near the drinks table partially hidden by a large vase and heard Mrs. Li say, "Oh, dear, I wish she hadn't brought her. She can be so rude."

Still, Eddie had reasoned, she could have been talking about somebody else—until Mr. Li had said, "Who, dear?" and Mrs. Li had said, quite distinctly, "Edith Miller."

For some reason Mr. Rednock had seemed very nervous as Rose's parents introduced him to Eddie, and had busied himself with directing the taking of coats, et cetera, but Rose had firmly steered Eddie back over to him a while later and subjected her to all manner of banal niceties that left her with no real impression of the man whatsoever.

He was returning now, a glass of wine in each hand. Eddie expected him to hand his spare to Rose, despite the fact that she was still holding one that was mostly full; instead, he had the audacity to hand one to Eddie, and she had no choice but to say thank you.

"Miss Li tells me you're a writer, Miss Miller. It is so rare and wonderful to come across a woman who writes prose!"

"I suppose you think I ought not do it," Eddie said, narrowing her eyes at him as she took a begrudging sip of wine.

"Not at all—I dearly love to read. I have many friends in the arts, in fact, and I have been known to write the occasional piece for newspapers and pamphlets. All utter rot, I'm sure. Do you write novels? If you'd do me the honor, I'd love to read your latest."

"Well," said Eddie, feeling her neck flush. "I don't . . . That is, I haven't—"

"Edith writes short stories," Rose said quickly, touching her fingers to the back of Eddie's arm. "They're wonderful. So clever, and funny! She is going to be a published author."

"Ah. Lovely. A story, then. Whenever is convenient."

"I haven't got any copies," Eddie said stiffly. "Only the originals, and I shouldn't care to hand those out in case the recipients were careless with them."

"Don't be silly, Eddie," said Rose, her smile strained. "He's a grown man, he's not going to get sauce on them."

Eddie smarted a little at the mention of sauce; Lucy-Anne had once "accidentally" managed to get enormous globs of beef dripping all over a story she had spent weeks on, and all because the prissy blond antagonist named *Mary*-Anne had fallen to her death trying to impress a passing man on a horse.

"You might think they're just *funny little stories*, but I'm not going to start parceling them out willy-nilly to anybody you choose—"

"Eddie, you know very well that is *not* what I meant."

"I don't mean to put you out," Mr. Rednock said, somehow still smiling. "Honestly! The last thing I want to be is a bother. Perhaps instead you could do a reading? That way you need not part with your stories, and we can all enjoy them without risking a saucing. I should love to be present at one of the first readings of someone who I am sure will one day be a great and accomplished author."

Eddie could find no logical reason to object to this plan, and so settled on an illogical one.

"I don't have the right sort of voice for reading to so large a room." Rose's fingers on Eddie's arm went the way of pinching. "But I'll—*ow!* I suppose I'll consider it."

"Good. Good!" said Mr. Rednock, visibly relieved. "Actually, there's an acquaintance of mine you might like to meet, an old friend . . ."

Eddie was no longer listening to him. She was instead giving Rose a Meaningful Look. They had been friends for so long that it was very easy for them to communicate without words—up until very recently, Eddie thought ruefully, she wouldn't have needed to employ a Look at all, as Rose would have known her well enough not to drag her to such a party—but even though she was entirely sure that Rose understood her meaning, they did not seem to be running full tilt for the door. In fact, Rose was pointedly not meeting her eye, and was instead smiling at Mr. Rednock as he continued to prattle on.

Rose and Eddie were by far the youngest guests invited for dinner, and when they sat down at the dining table Eddie kept looking around at the others with barely concealed horror. Were these the sorts of people Rose wanted to spend her time with? Miss Higgons, a spinster of five-and-thirty who looked as if she had never been acquainted with a washbasin in her life? Mr. Carter, who lived one street over from the Millers and could often be seen pushing his snaggletoothed dog in a perambulator? The man sitting opposite Eddie had been introduced as the editor of a newspaper, which would have piqued her interest, but he had immediately started talking at great length about *sailing*, which had not. The chair next to him was empty, and Eddie found herself staring at it, finding it far better company than any of the ones that were filled.

"Pass me that cranberry sauce," Eddie whispered to Rose as they were presented with the main course. "And I shall fashion myself a nosebleed."

"You shan't need to fashion one if you carry on like this," Rose whispered back, her tone entirely at odds with her genial expression. "I shall punch you in the face and you'll bleed a merry trail all the way home."

"Oh, gosh, please do. Perhaps I'll be knocked out entirely and you can just revive me when it's time to leave."

"Stop being such a toad, Edith."

"Don't call me Edith, Rose."

Eddie sensed that she was pushing Rose too far and that they might be on the brink of a proper bout of hurt feelings, which simultaneously made her feel rotten to the core and even more inclined to dig her heels in, but there was a commotion in the hallway that caused all conversation to cease immediately.

It sounded as if a very large dog or a very small bison had just entered, ricocheting off the walls as it went; when the door opened, quite a few people actually inhaled sharply, and the newspaper editor, Mr. Edwards, paused with his knife in the air as if he might be about to fend off whatever was about to descend upon them.

The tension was broken when a tall, mustachioed man walked in backward, dusting off his sleeves as he turned toward them. He was all elbows and knees, with wild dark hair sticking up in all directions and an irritated expression on his pale face. A moment later, a very large dog entered, rather more politely than its owner had.

"Bloody hell, sorry, Christ, it's the . . . Well, of course, *now* it's all butter-wouldn't-melt, but I swear to God, a minute ago she was channeling the spirit of her ancestors and trying to make sausages out of me—evening, Jonathan, Albert. Evening, all. You haven't got any whiskey, have you?"

If he was at all aware that this had been received by a stunned silence, he didn't seem to mind a bit; Mr. Edwards, the editor, broke it by getting to his feet and going to clap the newcomer on the back, while Mr. Rednock went in search of whiskey. The dog walked straight over to Rose as if she had called it and immediately leaned its enormous head against her leg, looking up at her through thick, wiry tufts of fur while Rose visibly struggled not to stroke it.

"Who *is* that?" Eddie said to Rose, who was distracted by the dog and needed a light poking to draw her attention.

"Oh? I don't know—a friend of Mr. Rednock's, I suppose. He knows all sorts of odd people, he used to write bits and pieces for quite a radical pamphlet. Oh, you are *gorgeous*, aren't you, you darling thing . . ."

The dog responded by thumping its tail so hard against the leg of Eddie's chair that she could have sworn she was shifted a full inch to the right.

Mr. Rednock returned with whiskey, and the newcomer thanked him profusely before taking the entire bottle from his hand and returning to his conversation with Mr. Edwards, which was accompanied by many dramatic gestures and exclamations. He seemed to find his seat by accident, half falling into it and only acknowledging that he had arrived by groping for a glass to decant some alcohol into. His cravat was loose, his collar was falling open, and he was wearing a waistcoat that Mrs. Miller would have politely described as "courageous."

Conversation resumed around the table. Rose was trying to mutter something to Eddie, but Eddie was staring in rapt fascination at this new man, who had managed to swallow half of his whiskey in one graceful gulp.

"The fellow who sold her to me said she was some sort of cutting-edge hybrid, you know—one-third mastiff, one-third boarhound, one-third ancient warhorse—she's clearly a deerhound, but she has got the sense of a Pomeranian and she's the size of a frigate and it's a bloody lethal combination." He turned very suddenly to look at Eddie, who jolted backward in her seat and then tried to give every impression that she hadn't. "Who are you?"

"My apologies, Miss Miller, the man's not got a courteous bone in his body," said Mr. Edwards fondly. "Miss Edith Miller, this is Mr. Nash Nicholson."

"No it's not," Eddie said, so loudly and with such force that quite a few people turned to look.

The man who purported to be Nash Nicholson, the young poet whose works had been carefully cut from newspapers and plastered across Eddie's walls—the man whose latest collected works had been a twenty-first birthday present from Mr. and Mrs. Miller to Eddie last spring—looked down at himself, shrugged, and then met Eddie's eye and laughed delightedly, as if he had not been so entertained in quite some time.

"Well. All right. I'm fairly certain that I am, but I'll gladly hear your arguments in opposition."

"My apologies," Eddie said, feeling suddenly very sweaty. "It's just . . . I didn't . . ." She could feel Rose staring at her—could sense that Mr. and Mrs. Li farther down the table were also looking at her, with even more concern than they had earlier, as if all their fears about her ruining the evening might be coming true—but she was floundering. "I didn't know you had a mustache."

"Oh, Christ, do I?" said Nash Nicholson, finishing his whiskey and languidly reaching for the bottle. "Well, it can't be helped, I suppose. Jonathan . . ." He smacked Mr. Edwards on the arm with the back of his hand to get his attention. "That bloody critique in the *Review*—have you read it? Don't, if you haven't. You'll be tempted to put both your eyes out with rusty spoons . . ."

He kept talking to Mr. Edwards about the various failings of a newspaper writer Eddie had never heard of, but she hung on his every word as if he were performing some of his poetry. She only realized that she had been openly staring, her chin resting in the palm of her hand as she leaned impolitely on her elbow, when Rose cleared her throat. Eddie turned, dazed, to see Rose frowning at her. The dog, its head resting fully in Rose's lap now as she continued to try desperately not to stroke it, seemed to be frowning, too.

"Are you having some sort of breakdown?" Rose asked quietly. "You don't seem to be breathing."

"I'm breathing a bit," Eddie said breathlessly.

"Your elbow is on your plate," Rose pointed out. "It's covered in cranberry sauce."

"Haven't you got anything better to do than stare at me?" Eddie said, removing her elbow from its bed of sauce and wiping it on a napkin. "Aren't you trying to *court* that secondhand sofa of a man down at the end of the table?"

"Keep your voice down," Rose hissed, glancing over at Mr. Rednock, who was currently talking to her mother. A man had appeared to remove the plates, and Eddie noticed distantly as he whisked hers away that she had forgotten to eat her turkey. "Who is he?"

"Nash Nicholson. The poet," Eddie said, trying to move her lips as little as possible; as a result, Rose clearly didn't hear a word of it, and she had to repeat herself. "You know. The *poet*. I used to read his poems to you. He wrote . . . he wrote 'To the Lady of London' and . . . and 'The Death of Beauty.'"

Rose's nose wrinkled in a way that Eddie knew she found mortifying.

"I can never tell them apart. Did he write the one about the pilgrimage?"

"God, no, that was Byron—do *not* mention Byron," Eddie said, glancing furtively at Nash Nicholson, who was too engrossed in his own story to notice that he was being discussed mere feet away. "I can't *believe* he's here. Were you aware that Mr. Rednock knew him?"

"He said he knew a poet," Rose said, wincing as a bit of dog drool dripped down her hand and trying to wipe it surreptitiously on the tablecloth.

"He's not *a* poet, he's *the* poet—"

"I thought Lord Byron was *the* poet—"

"Christ, Rose, I told you *not* to mention Byron."

Eddie could tell that Rose was about to query this, no doubt drawing Nash Nicholson's attention and ire and ruining any chance that he might consider Eddie worth talking to again, but luckily they were interrupted by the precipitous arrival of pudding.

Rose was dancing with Mr. Rednock. It was dreadful, but there was no way around it: they looked *happy*. She kept laughing at things he was saying—a real laugh, not her society one—and he was smiling so much that his eyes had almost disappeared into the depths of his face.

Miss Higgons, the spinster, had proven herself very adept at the pianoforte and had been playing lively tunes to accompany the past twenty minutes of dances, all of which Eddie had sat out, nursing a drink in the corner of the drawing room and watching Nash Nicholson smoke his pipe, with the intensity and focus of a hawk pursuing a particularly voluptuous rabbit.

She had just resolved to concoct a good excuse to cross the room to sit next to him—some invented draft, perhaps, that risked a chill, although she did not wish to appear fussy and unrobust in front of him—when she glanced up from her lap and saw that he had vanished, leaving only pipe smoke behind.

Eddie got to her feet immediately, looking around to see where he might have gone. Mr. and Mrs. Li were nearby speaking with Mr. Carter, of dog-perambulator infamy, and she saw Mrs. Li's eyes slide from where her daughter was still giggling on the dance floor to where Eddie was standing stricken by indecision.

"I'm going for some air," Eddie said, not addressing anybody in particular, before plowing through the dancers and escaping into the hallway beyond. The front door was open, and she followed the scent of smoke to find Nash Nicholson standing on the dusky doorstep without his jacket on, his shirtsleeves rolled up to his elbows. She stilled, with no idea what to do now that she'd caught up to him. Luckily, he spoke first.

"Do you smoke?" he said, as if they had already been mid-conversation, turning and offering her his pipe without looking at her.

"No," said Eddie.

He glanced up at the sound of her voice, and Eddie realized that he hadn't known who she was at all, and had simply not minded who he was offering his pipe to.

"Aha! Miss Miller. Not dancing?" Eddie shrugged. "No. No, well, it's not really for me, either—two left feet. *Eight* left feet. Like a well-soused spider, with no command of my . . . Anyway. The weather's turning. I thought for certain we had a few more weeks, but look at *this.*" He raised his arm for Eddie to study. "Goose-flesh. Bloody gooseflesh! You'd better go back in, before you freeze, or before . . . Well, I suppose they might call for the constable, to have me clapped in irons for showing you my forearm."

Eddie snorted, and Nash Nicholson grinned, with a softness about his eyes that was entirely unexpected. She thought he'd look away again, but he held her gaze, tilting his head to one side like a quizzical dog.

"Albert said you're a writer."

This was simultaneously the best and worst thing that could have possibly come out of his mouth. Eddie spent half a second luxuriating in it and then the other half feeling her veins flood with panic.

"I'm . . ." She paused, her protests dying on her tongue. He was looking at her expectantly, and she knew there was only one correct answer. "Yes. Yes, I am a writer."

"Very well, then. And what do you write?"

"Everything. Nothing. Er . . . It's silly, really."

"Is it, now?" He continued to appraise her with immense focus. His nose was very slightly dented, as if it had been broken on some grand adventure. It only added to his general rakishness. "I shouldn't think it is. Albert said it was your dream to be published. You should not be so quick to sell yourself short, Miss Miller. If you are serious, there will be plenty of people willing to do that on your behalf."

"What do you mean?" Eddie said, noting as she did that she sounded breathy, like a knight-struck maiden of yore.

"Oh, only that you must be your own champion in this sort of business. To everybody else, your writing will be . . . a commodity, or a passing curiosity. A horror. A punch line. *You* must love it fiercely, and take pride in it regardless." His gaze had drifted out across the street, but he shook his head and then smiled bashfully at her. "God, listen to me. Eight-and-twenty, and yet I sound ancient. And miserable. It ages you, writing. Or . . . not the writing, but all the rest."

Eddie could not agree. From the moment he had crashed into the dining room, she had been stunned by his vigor, his spirit; even if it was subdued now, he still looked as if he might gather himself any minute and shoot off again like a greyhound.

He straightened up, giving her a very gentle nudge with his elbow. Eddie felt the shock of even such a brief contact skitter down her arm.

"*You* ought to come to my salon. My wife and I, we hold a . . . Well, it's a silly old thing, really, always ends in spilled drinks and tantrums and tears, and that's just me—but there are a lot of fascinating, *artistic* types who've become quite the regulars. You'll fit right in."

"I . . . Thank you," said Eddie, her heart beating embarrassingly fast as she did. "Yes. I will."

"Good, good." A door shut loudly inside the house and he startled, then craned his neck to find the source of the noise, frowning as if he'd been interrupted doing something nefarious. Seeing that nobody was coming to accost him, he gave Eddie a solemn salute. "I'll see you back inside, then, soldier."

"Oh. Yes, Mr. Nicholson."

"Fuck, don't call me that," he said, laughing. Eddie hoped he hadn't noticed just how hard she had to press her lips together to stop herself from gaping at him. "Christ. Just . . . Nash. Call me Nash."

"Nash," Eddie said, as if it were the most natural thing in the world. "I'm Eddie."

"Eddie," he said slowly, one side of his lip quirking upward, as if her name tasted good in his mouth. "I'll see you back inside, then. Eddie."

Chapter Six

"So he invited you to dinner?" Rose said. She was lying on the sofa with her head hanging off one end, so she was upside down when she said it, and it came out high-pitched and strangled.

"No," Eddie said, walking to the table with an armful of books and depositing them in a messy pile that immediately threatened to topple. "It's not *dinner*. It's a literary salon. It's a lot of very creative, very clever people sitting around having stimulating conversations about . . . about life, and art, and politics—"

"And then you'll eat dinner," Rose finished.

Eddie frowned at her. She didn't seem to be grasping the most important part of all of this.

"Well, perhaps. I don't know!" Eddie pulled up a chair, picking a book from the top of the pile and flipping it open to the contents page.

"And you have to study this mountain of texts before dinner because . . . ?"

"Because I don't want to sound like a half-wit," Eddie said, chewing on her lip as she thumbed through the introduction, barely registering a word.

"Are you having a crisis of confidence?" Rose said, wriggling back up the sofa and then turning herself the right way up. "You are, aren't you? Stay still, I must make a sketch—it's never happened before, and never shall again."

"Stop your mockery and *help* me. Actually . . . Wait." Eddie glanced up at her. "Come with me."

"Come *with* you? Oh, honestly, Eddie. What am I going to do at a *literary party* hosted by *Nash Nicholson*?"

"I haven't run it past Mother yet. His wife will be there, it's all aboveboard, but I can't very well go alone. In fact . . . what about Mr. Rednock?" Eddie smacked her hand on the table and then pointed at Rose, the idea solidifying. "He knows Nash."

Rose raised her eyebrows and slumped against the cushions. "Listen to you. *Nash.*"

"I'm serious, Rose. Come with me."

"I don't actually understand why you want me there. Surely I'll just dilute your brilliance. And you don't even like Mr. Red-nock, as you've made *abundantly* clear, although you'd do well to remember that it was Albert who talked you up to Mr. Nicholson in the first place. Why don't you go alone, and make all sorts of fabulous new friends, and I can quietly hate them for taking you away from me?"

She was laughing, as if this were all a bit of light fun to her. It made Eddie feel *silly*, which was perhaps the worst feeling she could imagine, excepting appendicitis.

"Fine," she said stiffly. "You're right, I don't want you there at all. Perhaps you can go and have dinner with Mr. Rednock and the man who thinks his dog is his baby, or visit Ava Forester or Sophie Newport for a round of cards, and Sophie can give you a list of every man she's seen recently in descending order of income and remaining teeth—"

"I yield," Rose said.

"What?" Eddie was momentarily baffled. They hadn't used the phrase for years; it had been a mainstay of their childhood years, during games of tag and high-speed chases around the gar-den, and then had been occasionally employed when they were teenagers, always by Rose, when Eddie was pushing her too far. The last usage, by Eddie's estimate, had occurred during a game of Truth or Commands, when Eddie had asked Rose to confess the identity of the most attractive person she had ever laid eyes on. "You can't yield. I was only halfway through berating you."

"Berate no more, your dueling partner has retired in disgrace."

Eddie looked at Rose properly. Unless Eddie was much mistaken (unlikely), she looked sad around the corners of her mouth.

Abandoning the books, Eddie strode to the sofa and dropped heavily into the space next to Rose, accidentally sitting on quite a lot of leg. Rose squeaked and looked indignant; Eddie dismounted and flung an arm around her, and Rose sighed and allowed her head to drop onto Eddie's shoulder.

"I don't want to go alone because I'm nervous," Eddie said into Rose's hair, which today smelled like grass and something sweet and smoky. "All right? I'm nervous, and if you're there, and bloody Albert Rednock is there, I'll *know* people."

"You're going to be a triumph," Rose said. Eddie could feel Rose's mouth moving against her neck, and it was a little distracting. They had been touching casually like this a lot recently; the night in the tree house had broken down some physical barrier between them, even as the rift over the puzzling Mr. Rednock grew. "I'll come if you need me to. You know I always will. If anything, you clearly require someone to keep a *very* close eye on you."

"I need you to," Eddie said, at the exact same moment the door was flung open and Beatrice sprinted in, her arms blackened up to the elbows.

"Oh, Trix! What on earth have you been doing?" Rose said, sitting up quickly and putting out her hand to stop Beatrice from colliding with her legs.

"It's coal dust," Simon said from the doorway, following at rather a leisurely pace for somebody who was clearly supposed to be intercepting his little sister. "She tried to climb up the chimney again."

"There are pigeons in there," Beatrice said to Rose confidentially, grinning. She had a dot of soot on her front tooth. "They're nice."

"What are you going to do with a pigeon if you catch it?" said Eddie, watching as Beatrice wriggled in Rose's surprisingly strong grip. She ceased wriggling to consider.

"Ride it to China."

Rose rolled her eyes at Eddie, who snorted. Beatrice had become so fascinated by the fact that Rose's family was from Guangzhou, a port city in China, that she had been inventing all manner of schemes and criminal enterprises to transport herself there. She asked Rose unceasing questions about it, despite Rose's protestations that she had never *been* to China, and was not going to ask for her mother's help to write to her grandparents and ask if they liked the same sort of sandwiches as Beatrice.

"Well, good luck and Godspeed," Eddie said, as Beatrice managed to get loose and sprinted for the opposite door into the dining room.

Simon looked at Eddie, who still had one arm around Rose, and sighed.

"Nobody ever asks me if I'd like a hug," he said, before sloping out of the room, following a trail of small, black footprints.

"This is *Nash Nicholson's* front door."

"Yes, and it's in desperate need of a repaint," said Mr. Rednock jovially. "Also, I think he may have woodworm."

Eddie shot daggers at Rose, as if she had been the one to speak. She had immediately regretted asking Rose to invite Mr. Rednock when he'd stepped out of his carriage just thirty seconds after their arrival looking so distinctly *ordinary* that it made Eddie's jaw hurt. She was trying to ignore him as much as possible now; no further nonsense from him could be allowed to detract from the fact that she was standing on *Nash Nicholson's* doorstep, awaiting admittance into one of his famed salons.

Well . . . awaiting admittance implied that she had already knocked, which she certainly had not.

"Perhaps we ought to go home," Eddie said. She could hear laughter from within, the sound of many people crammed into too-small rooms, and suddenly she wanted to be at home in her bed, or in the tree house with Rose, dreaming of literary salons instead of having to actually attend one. "Perhaps . . . I don't feel well, so perhaps if we just take a turn around the—"

She was cut off by Rose, who had gently pushed past her and knocked. Eddie stared at her, frozen in place, half hoping that she might not have been heard over all the noise inside. Ten long seconds passed; Rose was just preparing to knock again, and Eddie was preparing to tell her not to, when the door opened abruptly.

"Good evening!" said a tall, fair, ice-blond person sporting a men's waistcoat over a dress of pale pink muslin. "What business?"

"Oh," said Eddie, momentarily lost for words. "We're . . . I'm . . . That is, we were just—"

"Mr. Albert Rednock," said Mr. Rednock, leaning past Eddie to offer his hand, clearly intending for it to be shaken; instead, it was kissed in a perfunctory manner. "Ah. Yes. This is Miss Rose Li and Miss Edith Miller. Mr. Nicholson's guests."

"*Mr.* Nicholson, is it? Who are you? His accountant?"

"He breeds rabbits," Eddie said, for no particular reason.

"Well," they said, sighing. "I suppose that's something. Come in, come in, you're letting all the good air out."

Inside, Eddie immediately noticed that it wasn't just the front door that needed repainting. The wallpaper in the hallway was faded, dark patches in some corners suggesting either creeping damp or a strong aversion to cleaning. There was an enormous bouquet of flowers on an ornately carved side table, dahlias

spilling out of a cracked vase in every direction. A stack of un-
opened mail sat in a pile on the windowsill, and Eddie's fingers
twitched without her permission, as if they might be about to
produce a letter opener and tear into Nash Nicholson's private
correspondence at his own party. There was what looked like a
brand-new waistcoat, hand-painted silk in duck-egg blue, tossed
carelessly over the banister of the stairs.

"Liza has been away," said their makeshift host, waving an
arm at the odd combination of opulence and squalor as they
turned right and down a short corridor. "He's been living like a
feral badger. Here we are."

The door was shoved unceremoniously open, and the sound
of the party spilled out to meet them.

The room was small, but somehow four sofas had been
crammed into it, facing one another to form a square; an assortment of people were packed onto every inch of furniture, with
more propped up against the walls or leaning their elbows on a
sideboard covered in numerous bottles of uncorked liquor. Nash
Nicholson was holding court, everybody around him leaning in
to listen, with a blond woman Eddie supposed must be his wife
almost sitting in his lap; when he looked up and saw them enter,
he threw his arms wide, almost relieving the blond woman of
her nose.

"Valentine! You've delivered friends!" he said, not getting up.

None of the gentlemen got up, which struck Eddie as rather
odd for a moment—but of course, she reminded herself, these
were *true* nonconformists. Radicals. Not standing when a woman
entered probably did not even register on their list of regular so-
cietal transgressions.

Nash flashed her a grin and then gestured to the sofas.

"Sit, sit."

There was nowhere *to* sit; Mr. Rednock offered Rose the only
patch she could reasonably occupy, next to a couple of middle-

aged ladies passing a pipe back and forth, then went to fetch her a drink. Eddie tried to lounge nonchalantly against the back of one of the sofas, but instead found herself listing to one side with all the grace of a scarecrow in a hailstorm, so instead stood up straight, her hands clasped behind her back. She had never been particularly conscious of the arrangement of her limbs; usually they just got on with things. Now they were rather letting her down.

Eddie had expected Nash to make introductions, but he had immediately been drawn back into his story, stretching out some detail with evocative hand gestures and causing the gentleman to his right to choke on his drink. The person Eddie assumed was called Valentine—although whether this was a first or last name she was entirely unsure—had been fetching a drink, but returned to see her standing there and looked aghast.

"Has nobody offered you a drink? Or a seat? Good Lord, these *radicals* and *artists*—get *up*."

A gentleman with his shirt hanging open who had been sitting near Nash, was forcibly ejected from his seat, and Eddie shot him an apologetic grimace before sitting down.

"Thank you," she said to Valentine, who handed her a glass of wine and then disappeared into a corner of the room.

Eddie tried to make eye contact with Rose on the sofa opposite, but she was speaking to Mr. Rednock at her shoulder, leaning back in her seat. They made absolutely no sense together—him practically middle-aged and portly, her radiant with youth as she sipped at her drink and twisted her fingers through the strings of her reticule—but nobody could look at them and think they weren't thoroughly enjoying each other's company. It made Eddie want to pinch someone, so she settled on pinching herself on the knee through the fabric of her dress.

"He keeps telling me," Nash was saying to the lady next to him, "that a *novel* is nothing but a very long poem and you don't even have to concern yourself with rhyming, and then he throws his hands up like he's just solved the whole damn thing for me, the bastard. As if it's that simple just to *write* a *novel*."

"It tends to be simpler if you actually put pen to paper, darling," said a woman's voice from behind Eddie; she turned to see a very tall and thin woman with an olive complexion and thick, dark waves of hair, holding a glass of wine in each hand. She leaned forward to offer one, and Nash took it from her, looking slightly dazed by her appearance. A pleasant, musky perfume wafted over Eddie as the woman withdrew.

"Somebody keeps hiding all my pens," he said, and she laughed.

"*Hiding* them in the pen drawer."

"Well, I didn't say it was a particularly inspired hiding spot. Say, Liza, you haven't met Miss Miller, have you?"

"Obviously not," said the woman who must have *actually* been Nash's wife. "Have you done *any* introductions, Nicks?"

Nash froze comically before his face fell, and he turned to Eddie, looking anguished.

"I can only apologize, sometimes I just . . . *Right*." He cleared his throat, and to Eddie's mortification, everybody in the room ceased speaking to listen. "Everybody, this is Miss Edith Miller, a young writer. Her companions are Miss Rose Li and Mr. Albert Rednock here, whom some of you have already met."

"He breeds rabbits," said Valentine from behind a very full glass of wine, barely concealing a smirk.

"He— Do you now?" Nash said, swiveling around in his seat to look at Mr. Rednock, who shrugged amiably. "I didn't know that, Albert."

"I have told you quite a few times," Mr. Rednock replied.

"Well. Fantastic. Miss Miller, Miss Li, this is . . . everybody."

There were general noises of greeting and a couple of raised glasses; Eddie raised hers in response and shot a look at Rose, who looked as mortified by the attention as Eddie felt.

"Liza Nicholson," said Nash's wife, offering a hand to be shaken.

"I hope you aren't too scandalized by the goings-on in my house. Usually, I'd have been here to see it cleaned, and I certainly would have insisted on proper introductions, but I arrived back from visiting my sister only an hour ago." She let out the tiniest of exhalations, looking very tired, and then fixed a pleasant smile on her face. "This gentleman to your right is Oluwadayo Akerele, writer and abolitionist. Mr. Akerele, as I'm sure you heard, this is Miss Miller."

The short, Black gentleman who had been speaking to a lady on his other side inclined his head in greeting.

"Call me Dayo. A pleasure to meet you. What do you write, Miss Miller?"

"Oh," said Eddie. "Short stories?"

"You do not seem entirely sure," said Mr. Akerele, but he was smiling at her, so Eddie smiled back.

"I'm not," she answered truthfully, and he laughed.

"Well, I shall be interested to hear more once you are firm in your decision. This fine lady," he said, nodding to the woman he had been speaking to, "is Miss Catherine Stuart."

"God!" Eddie exclaimed before she could help herself. "But you're . . . not the *artist* Catherine Stuart?"

"If you believe the rumors," said the large, lightly tanned woman of about five-and-thirty. She had green eyes and dark curls, most of which were falling loose down her back. "And Kitty, please. None of this *Miss Catherine* hell."

"You are just the most *wonderful* painter," Eddie said, aware that she was gushing but unable to stem the flow. "I saw one of your portraits a few years ago, and I've been desperate to see your more recent work—I read the descriptions, of course, in the papers."

"Ah, yes," said Kitty Stuart, raising an eyebrow. "Effusive in their praise, were they?"

"They said you were an affront to God and man, and that had

it been but a couple of hundred years ago, you would have been burned as a witch," Eddie said reverently. "They seemed quite disappointed that burning was no longer considered a proportional response to art they didn't like. Art that's . . . *courageous*."

"'Courageous' wasn't the word they used, though, was it?"

"No," said Eddie. "They said 'dangerous.'"

Dayo Akerele snorted quietly. "When was the last time one of your paintings put somebody in *danger*, Miss Kitty?"

"Actually, my latest fell on my assistant last week," said Kitty. "It's about six feet in length and height. He nearly lost his kneecaps, but he's expected to make a full recovery."

Eddie laughed, which luckily seemed to be the expected reaction, and then listened with almost religious fervor as Kitty Stuart went on to explain the inspiration behind her latest painting.

"It's a family portrait, but it's meant to convey this sense of decay, of the legacy crumbling . . . I thought I'd cracked it, but then my assistant pointed out that the little spaniel at their feet that I had thought looked subtly ominous actually seemed to be grinning, and I'd accidentally given him human teeth . . ."

Eddie forgot about Rose and Mr. Rednock entirely, and only vaguely registered some slight movements in the corner of her vision until Rose—having clearly been attempting to get her attention for some time—managed to inch her leg far enough over to stamp on Eddie's foot.

"Excuse me," she said to her new companions.

Rose communicated through a series of small glances that she wished to step to the back of the room, and Eddie reluctantly followed.

"What is it?" she said, as they tucked themselves into a window, Eddie becoming briefly entangled with the drapes before managing to get the better of them.

"These people are dreadful," Rose whispered, putting a hand to Eddie's wrist.

Eddie was startled; Rose so often strove to think the best of people that this was a shocking indictment after just half an hour or so in their company.

"Are they?" said Eddie.

Rose laughed bitterly. "A man asked me what I *created*, and when I said nothing at all, he looked at me as if I'd just shot the head off his dog. He asked how I find *meaning* in my life if I am not producing art, and when I said that I found friendships, family, and various social connections to be meaning enough, he clearly felt very sorry for me indeed. He all but said so."

"Well," Eddie said, glancing over at the back of Nash Nicholson's head. "They're *artists*, aren't they, and thinkers—they cannot imagine any other way to be."

Eddie was inclined to agree with them, but didn't think it quite the right thing to say to Rose.

"Who separates a great thought from all the ordinary ones, I wonder?" Rose said, raising her eyebrows, her fingers still encircling Eddie's wrist. "Is it impossible to have one if it concerns *domestic* drudgeries and things so low and common as *companionship* and *friendship*?"

Eddie frowned, and Rose looked taken aback.

"I have never known you to be so . . . so cynical, and unkind," Eddie said. "We've been invited here among all these important people, we are in *Nash Nicholson's* drawing room, and I intend to make the best of it even if you are determined to ruin it for me."

Rose's mouth dropped open, and color flared high in her cheeks as she let go of Eddie's arm. She was just about to speak when Eddie felt something brush her elbow; when she turned, she saw that Nash himself was standing there, looking conspiratorial.

"I fear I've been neglecting you."

"Oh, no, not at all," said Eddie.

It was warm in the drawing room with so many bodies

crammed into it, and Nash was glowing with perspiration, his hair curling attractively over his brow before he pushed it away.

"It's a nightmare in here, we're packed in like swine and only half as polite—come and see my study and breathe the free air again."

"Eddie," Rose said forcefully, but Eddie was already following Nash from the room with a spring in her step.

Chapter Seven

Nash's study was an oddly crooked room on the first floor of the house, lit by a single lamp. It seemed to slope to one side, giving Eddie the impression that if she dropped a handful of marbles, they would flee westward, never to be seen again. There was a large, ancient desk in front of the window, with ornate carvings of cherubs and gods and fat bunches of grapes twisting up the legs. Books and drifts of paper were stacked on every available surface; Nash tripped over a pile on the floor on his way into the room, and swore very graphically before kicking them aside. A decanter of wine sat on the desk, next to a partially filled glass that had left dark, wet rings in the oak.

"The first person to spot a rat," said Nash, pushing some writing detritus aside, "wins a shilling. You're not afraid of rats, are you?"

"No," said Eddie firmly. "In fact, we raised them. Rose and I, one spring. It was her idea—she loses her head over animals. We didn't realize quite how many there would be after such a short time. My parents discovered them when they escaped the trunk under my bed and all came streaming down the stairs and into the dining room during dinner. My mother said it was like we had been visited by one of the plagues."

"Ah, well. At least it wasn't . . . . you know. Boils. Rivers of blood."

"I think that day they would have preferred death of the first-born," said Eddie.

Nash snorted. He collapsed into his desk chair and then looked around, as if he were surprised that another chair hadn't materialized for her.

"Are you above sitting on a trunk?"

"Depends if the previous occupant was a large family of rats," said Eddie.

"Oh, *indubitably*."

Eddie located the trunk in question, gave it a quick once-over for inhabitants, and then sat down on the very edge. There was an odd little sculpture on the floor next to her: some kind of pagan goddess, in the throes of dark magic.

"Can I pour you a drink?"

Eddie nodded. Nash turned in his chair and rooted around behind him until he arose triumphant with a dusty flute in hand, which he cleaned with his sleeve before filling it to the brim with wine. He handed it to Eddie, and then topped up his own abandoned glass.

"Cheers. To . . . Well, to rats, I suppose," said Nash, raising his glass in her direction and then knocking back quite a lot of wine. "Not bad company, if you can get it. You are, of course, marginally better company than a rat."

"Well, thanks," Eddie said seriously.

"Now," said Nash, straightening up and matching her tone, leaning forward across his desk. "It's all very well and good, this talk of rats, but this is a room for conducting business, as you can see by the . . . the very businesslike paraphernalia all around you."

"There's a pipe carved to look like a naked woman next to your elbow."

"Christ, is there? That must be Liza's, she's an infamous bawd. Anyhow—*don't* change the subject. You claim to be a writer, yes? Tell me what you've written."

Eddie leaned back, momentarily forgetting that she was sitting on a trunk rather than a chair and risking her gown as her glass threatened to spill.

"I've written one hundred and thirty-five short stories."

Nash looked taken aback. "How short is short?"

"Most of them are around five pages, front and back. The shortest was one page, and the longest, I think . . . thirty pages. So far."

"So *far*? I think somebody may have misled you about the typical length of a story. Either that or you're terrible at mathematics."

"Oh, I *am* terrible at mathematics. But it is around thirty pages, I'm sure of it. It's the only thing I've ever written where I can't see the end yet—I know it's there, but I haven't quite hit the bottom."

"Like one of those country wells that dogs and babies are always falling down," said Nash. "Or . . . something nicer, I suppose. The ocean? A lake? I always think there's something a bit ominous about lakes, although I certainly spent enough time around them as a boy. All right, so you've written a hundred and . . . well, an *indecent* number of short stories. What are they about?"

"All sorts of different things. Some of them are about pirates, or kings . . . I've written quite a few just about ordinary people living their lives . . . wayward nuns, hauntings, murderers, criminals . . ."

Nash raised an eyebrow at her, looking thrilled. "Wayward nuns?"

"Yes. They hold up some bankers with muskets. I fancy that when the most devout and well-behaved among society go astray, it must be a *thing* to behold."

"Oh, well, I'm sure of it. But I mean . . . Pirates, kings, nuns—those are your characters. But what are the stories really *about*?"

Eddie paused. "Well, I don't know. People, I suppose. People and how they get on, and how they don't, and how they . . . relate to one another."

"So, you're telling me that your story about nuns on a crime spree isn't a comment on organized religion, or the place of women in society, or . . . or the criminal justice system?"

"Oh, well, I think it's sort of about that. But overall . . . it's just about love, and friendship. Conversation and human nature. People."

Nash took another large gulp of wine, and then left the glass resting there, pressed against his chin, as he studied her.

"Organized religion is about people. Who exactly do you think's being organized?"

"They're just silly stories," Eddie said quickly. "I write them to make Rose laugh."

"Ah. So they're funny, are they?"

"Well, she usually thinks so." Eddie was suddenly completely mortified to have proclaimed herself a *writer*, to have had Nash announce her as such in the company of actual writers and artists, with so little to shore up her claim. "The . . . Well, the longest story is about a lady called Delilah Fortescue who accidentally kills her husband, and decides to impersonate him. That's the one I haven't finished yet. It's funny, but in quite a dark and miserable way . . . Rose can hardly bear to listen to it, but she always tells me to keep reading, even when she's clapped her hands over her ears."

"Goodness, Miss Miller. They'd have you bound for the jail for even thinking about such a thing, let alone writing it down. God help the man who eventually becomes your husband. I'll advise him to keep a sturdy hammer beside the bed."

Eddie was irritated to discover that she was blushing, at both the mention of *husbands* and of anything being kept beside some future *bed*. She stuck her chin out in an attempt to distract him from it.

"I *told* you to call me Eddie."

He waved a hand in dismissal. "I can't call you *Eddie* with a straight face, I'm afraid. That's a little boy's name. And you are . . . very much *not* a little boy. Can't we compromise? Strike a deal?

I can pay you off, as long as you don't mind being compensated in . . . God, what do I even have in here? Bawdy pipes and rat droppings. Oh, look, there's half a rotten poem here . . . I'll give you a stanza, and you'll let me call you *Edie*, instead."

"Edie?" said Eddie, wrinkling her nose. "It sounds . . . I don't know. Girlish."

"You *are* girlish, even if you claim otherwise. Don't look like that, there's no shame in it! Edie it is. And I owe you a poem. Here you are."

Girlish or not, it gave Eddie a thrill to hear him using a pet name—a name that she could guarantee only *he* would use, as she would not countenance it from anybody else. She took the poem with slightly shaking hands and thought about casually folding it and tucking it into her reticule, as if famous poets were always handing her precious unpublished excerpts of their work, but her enthusiasm won out and she unrolled the crumpled parchment eagerly on her lap, bending low to read it in the soft glow of the lamp:

> Look no longer, fore or aft,
> The sea scanned for that blooded foam,
> She smites you true, that winged shaft,
> The hunger and the limbs below,
> 'Tis a shrewd and wicked craft,
> Struck down before you feel the blow—

"You can keep that one," said Nash, leaning back in his chair and squinting up at the ceiling. "Hideous. It's been reworked a thousand times since, and it'll all come to nothing."

"I like it," said Eddie, suddenly feeling strangely protective of this scrap. "It's about . . . love?"

"Love, sex, Aphrodite, Eros, death . . . It might as well be an instruction manual about how to build a ship, I spent enough time studying vessel plans to eke out horrible little metaphors and turns of phrase that made me want to vomit." He rubbed his thumb over his dark mustache, and Eddie watched its journey, strangely fascinated. "Byron is squirreled away in Europe writing an epic. It's supposed to be a secret, so of course everybody I know keeps bloody *asking* me about it. You know—where's *my* epic? Where's my . . . ? Well, I suspect it'll be his magnum fucking opus, and I'm still fussing around with frothy descriptions of *love* and pictures of ships."

"But you're a genius!" said Eddie, forgetting that she had promised herself she'd stay cool and collected. "You're brilliant, everybody thinks so. I can barely move for people recommending you, passing around your work—whatever you write next, it'll be wonderful."

Nash seemed to smile despite himself, but then he shook it off, put down his wineglass, and scrubbed a hand through his already quite disorderly hair.

"Certainly not everyone."

"You have a whole house full of admirers here!"

"Ha! You'd be surprised. Liza, for one, is *not* best pleased with me. In fact, she's sick of me—my writing, my moping—and frankly, who could blame her."

"What?" said Eddie, genuinely stunned. "*Surely* not."

She had known that Nash was married—had discovered it years ago after reading some of his early poems, and had felt momentary but crushing disappointment, long before she thought she'd ever actually share a *room* with him—and had just assumed that whoever had the honor must have been as fiercely glad of it as she would be herself.

"I am most certainly *not* mistaken, but don't cry for me, Edie—I'm sure the slow, agonizing affliction of love gone putrid will do wonders for my work."

He said it lightly, but Eddie was gripped by an urge to reach across the desk and touch his arm in an attempt to be comforting. She was just working herself up to actually do it when Nash clicked his fingers and pointed at her.

"Aha! Diversions, distractions, misdirection. I want to read your writing."

"You can't," Eddie said reflexively. Then she paused and looked down into her wine, which had a speck of dust floating on the surface. "Yet, I mean. It's not ready."

"If you had to put an estimate on it," said Nash, "when do you imagine it *might* be ready? Come on, I showed you my dreadful stanza, please respond in kind."

"Give me . . . Give me one month," said Eddie, plucking the number from the air and then wishing she could put it back. "It won't be great in a month, but it might be . . . readable."

"That's all I ask," said Nash. "That'll be, what . . . a week or two after Michaelmas?"

Eddie nodded. She had been so caught up in surviving this one evening and making an impression that she hadn't thought beyond it, and the idea that Nash was making plans with her for four weeks hence filled her with scorching terror and anticipation.

"God," said Nash, wincing as something seemed to occur to him. "Nearly Michaelmas. I've been in town for too long. I don't know if I can survive another week in London, let alone another month."

"Oh, but you must stay!" Eddie said, once again letting the words burst forth before she'd had time to consider how stupid they might make her seem.

"Must I, indeed?" said Nash, still looking grave. He considered her, and she felt her posture stiffen under his attention, trying to keep her head up and her back straight—to look as if she deserved to be here, sitting on his dusty trunk. Drinking his wine. "I suppose it would be a shame for us to part, when I've gone so long without meeting anybody truly interesting. You are . . . *truly interesting, Edie*."

"Am I?" said Eddie, in barely a whisper, not daring to believe it.

The stillness of the moment that followed was shattered by the sound of something falling to the ground in the hallway outside, preceding the scramble of paws on wood and some exasperated shouting. They both listened as many footsteps came rapidly up the stairs, and then the door was flung open by Liza, who had Nash's enormous dog by the collar.

"She ate about half of Kitty's coat," Liza said, looking out of breath and extremely unamused. "Fur-trimmed, Nicks. Sent from Switzerland."

"She probably thought it was a very large squirrel," said Nash, making eye contact with the dog rather than his wife and raising his eyebrows playfully. "Or a very flat bear. Didn't you, Juno?"

"It's not *funny*, Nash! You *said* you'd attempt to train her, after what happened to my cousin's walking stick." She seemed to notice Eddie for the first time and looked startled before recovering herself. "What are you *doing* up here, anyhow? You're being unforgivably rude to your guests—who *you* invited, need I remind you."

"You need not," said Nash, in a singsong tone. Eddie thought he might be mocking her, but then he got abruptly to his feet. "All right, I'm here. I'm there. I'm coming. Go forth, and we'll . . . you know. Be there forthwith."

Liza left, Nash following her; the dog had broken free, and as Eddie approached the doorway, it pushed its nose into the back of her leg to politely herd her from the room.

Chapter Eight

"For the love of god, lucy-anne, i'll give you ten shillings to stop playing the harp."

"Go and sit somewhere else," Lucy-Anne said, with a snide smile that made Eddie want to shove her head through the aforementioned instrument. "This is where my harp is, and I must practice."

"I *can't* sit somewhere else," Eddie said through clenched teeth. "Father is in the study, Mother is in my bedroom fussing with my clothes, and all of the others are in the dining room playing Carriage Crash."

"No, they're not," said Lucy-Anne, playing the harp even louder. "Trix is in her tree house."

"It's *my* tree house."

"*You* are two-and-twenty! Are you not embarrassed to still have a *tree house*? I would be. But then, if I were you, the list of embarrassments would start and never stop . . ."

Eddie's head was pounding; she had stayed too late at Nash's party, feeling emboldened by his singling her out and at ease among his friends after some more wine, and she was experiencing the sort of hangover that makes one long to be put into a comfortable drawer somewhere and then shut away in the dresser for at least twenty-four hours. Instead of crawling into any of the furniture, she had brought out her story—it was thirty-three pages on second count, a number that when announced aloud always prompted Simon to say "That's the age Christ died" in a sad little voice—and she was now endeavoring to pick up the threads of it and see how she might carry on. Spending the evening with somebody who had been published many times over, surrounded by all his similarly accomplished friends, had kindled the spark that had always burned in her chest into something far more incendiary.

This could be her *chance*. After so many years of proclaiming her future as a published writer, that mad dream might finally be within her grasp. She wasn't going to let it slip through her fingers.

Unfortunately, the only good light for writing that wasn't inhabited by family members was in the drawing room, and she had not been there twenty minutes before Lucy-Anne had flounced in and taken a pointed seat at the harp stool.

"Lucy-Anne, I asked you politely the first time—just give me the last half an hour of daylight and then you can play enough of your silly harp to save the Argonauts for all I care."

"I want to practice now," said Lucy-Anne, punctuating her words with a twang of high C. "You don't *own* the drawing room. I know you're feeling very high and mighty because that horrible poet invited you for dinner, but I'm afraid that doesn't particularly impress me."

"You *followed* me in here and took up the harp because you could see I was busy!" said Eddie, clenching her fist and then swearing softly when she realized she'd crumpled the page in her hand. "All I want is a *moment* of peace in this house, something I *rarely* ask for—"

Lucy-Anne finally stopped playing. "Peace! You're the one always inviting Rose over, so there are even *more* people around the dinner table, and at least you're *out* and get to go to parties and dinners whenever it takes your fancy—I'm stuck here in this house! When do *I* get any peace? I wish you'd just hurry up and get married and leave, so I never have to see your hideous face again—"

"Eddie," said Simon, who had just appeared in the doorway, looking rumpled. "Is Trix under your table?"

Eddie sighed, but then pushed her chair back and ducked her head under to have a look. She hadn't seen Beatrice for hours, but it was always worth checking.

"No."

"Damn," said Simon. "I mean . . . oh, dear."

"Isn't she in her tree house?" said Lucy-Anne, with too much emphasis on "her" for Eddie's liking.

"No," said Simon thoughtfully. "In fact, she doesn't seem to be anywhere at all."

"Oh, God," said Eddie. "Are you sure? Have you checked the fireplaces?"

"Do you think she could actually climb a chimney?" said Lucy-Anne, chewing on a piece of her hair, as she did when thinking. "I don't think she'd really have anything to hold on to, and she's too small to shimmy."

Mr. Miller walked in, reading glasses balanced on the end of his nose, looking around for something.

"Father, have you seen Trix?"

"Beatrice? No, no, I haven't. Have you seen my newspaper? Perhaps they're together. The last time I saw Trix she told me she was packing a bag for China."

Lucy-Anne and Eddie exchanged a grimace.

"So she's finally done it," said Simon, sounding impressed. "I didn't think she had it in her. How far is it? To China?"

Eddie got up, shuffling her papers into a pile, just as Lucy-Anne rose from her harp stool.

"Simon, she's seven years old, she doesn't even know the way to Marylebone. Has she told you anything about where she thinks China is?"

Simon looked thoughtful. "South."

"I'll get your mother," said Mr. Miller. "We'll search the house and then look farther afield."

"I'll get Amelia," said Simon, "although we were playing Carriage Crash and she was the unlucky soul this time, and you know she does commit to her roles, so we might have a tricky job getting her up from the floor."

It was looking decidedly dusky by the time all six of them left the house, and although Eddie had reprimanded Simon for spending too long rummaging around in the kitchen with Caroline the maid, she was glad of the lanterns they had managed to unearth; all hopes that Beatrice might be hiding very well in the garden or that she had only made it a short way down the road were dashed quickly, and Eddie started to feel an uncomfortable swell of panic in the vicinity of her lungs as they decided to split up and search in smaller groups.

Eddie was partnered with Simon, both of them calling out Beatrice's name as they journeyed southeast. As they walked, he grew increasingly frantic in a way that only those very close to him would recognize.

"Did you know that bees actually have four wings, not two?" he said, as Eddie peered over a stranger's gate to see if Beatrice might be hiding among the shrubbery.

"You told me that last week," said Eddie. Simon had an excellent memory; if he was forgetting the facts he had already dispensed, he must have been feeling truly wretched. "Chin up, Simon. We'll find her. She's not *trying* to be lost, after all."

"Well, did I tell you that some people think bees communicate by dancing?" said Simon, rolling up one of his sleeves and then unrolling it again. "I didn't tell you that, did I?"

"Yes," said Eddie, moving on to the next house and appraising what she could see of the exterior. "She couldn't fit inside a barrel, could she? I mean, she could, but I don't know why she'd . . . unless she thinks all barrels end up on ships, and that all ships end up in China . . ."

"No," said Simon. "She knows some barrels go in cellars. I don't think she'd risk ending up in a cellar, do you?"

Eddie did not. Beatrice didn't thrive in any situation where she was forced to stay still, or without diversion, for more than approximately eight seconds.

"She's so friendly," she said suddenly, her hand gripping tight around the handle of the lantern. "I wish she weren't quite so *friendly*."

"D'you mean . . . you think she may have just gone off with the first person who told her good afternoon?" said Simon, his brow furrowing.

That was *exactly* what Eddie thought, but she had momentarily forgotten that she was supposed to be repressing her own fears to keep Simon's at bay, so she perked up and started marching down the street again.

"She's not a fool," she said, somewhat untruthfully. "And she wouldn't go with anybody who said they were bringing her home, not when she thinks she has a ship to catch."

Simon offered up a few more half-hearted facts, but after a while they lapsed into silence, only opening their mouths to call Beatrice's name. When they reached a busier thoroughfare with shops and traders closing up for the night, Eddie went from person to person describing her sister, and receiving only shaken heads in response. There was an acidic tightness in the back of her throat, her voice coming out strained and croaky as she asked the last few with little hope—and then she turned to Simon, who was on the verge of tears.

"No matter," she said, pausing to clear her throat. "We shall just go back in the direction we came, but we'll take a different route. All right, Simon?"

"All right," he said miserably.

They were almost home again and it was nearly truly dark when Eddie saw a figure rushing toward her from the opposite direction, holding a bundle in her arms; as they drew closer,

Eddie realized with a leap of joy that it was Rose, and the bundle in her arms was none other than—

"Beatrice Elizabeth Miller, you absolute *weasel!*" Eddie cried, as Rose placed her on the ground looking harried and Beatrice ran to Eddie's skirts and grabbed two fistfuls of them. Eddie ducked to squeeze her by the shoulders, hard, and then gave her a small shove. "What on earth were you thinking, running off like that? The whole family has been out looking for you—Mother may have called for the constable by now!"

Beatrice only grinned up at her. "I'm hungry," she said. "Forgot my provisions. Do you have a biscuit? And then I will be on my way."

"You most certainly will *not*," said Eddie, grabbing her by the back of her dress to prevent any sudden attempts to escape. "Thank you so much, Rose."

"She came to ask my father the best route," Rose said, pushing a few damp tendrils of hair away from her face—she clearly hadn't trusted Beatrice not to do a runner, either, and had carried her not inconsiderable weight all the way to make sure. "She almost gave us a heart attack—we were sitting in the drawing room and then suddenly there was this *face* at the window, with the most demonic grin. We brought her in for some milk and tried to send a messenger, but I suppose none of you were at home to receive him."

"She hasn't been to your house for ages," said Eddie, mildly impressed despite herself. "It's a wonder that she remembered the route."

"I'm very quick-witted," grunted Beatrice, trying to pull herself away from Eddie's iron grip and failing.

The rest of the Millers appeared at the end of the street, and there were cries of joy and relief upon seeing Beatrice wriggling like a determined fish in Eddie's grasp; Amelia came running and picked her up, immediately bursting into tears, before Mrs.

Miller gently took Beatrice from her and led them in a procession the rest of the way home.

Only Eddie stayed behind, waiting until they were out of earshot before she spoke.

"Thank you, truly. I know she's not the easiest to catch, or to keep caught."

"It's all right," said Rose. "I told her I was taking her down to the docks to catch a ship."

"Wise," said Eddie. There was a small and uncomfortable pause. "How are you? You didn't seem particularly . . . pleased, last night."

When Eddie had returned from her tête-à-tête with Nash, Rose had seemed out of sorts; she had shot Eddie a deeply questioning look, which Eddie had only met with a shrug and a smile. Rose and Albert had announced their departure at the rather early hour of eleven o'clock, and Eddie had quickly said her goodbyes before going back to the conversation she was having with Kitty Stuart. It had only occurred to her half an hour later that Rose had probably expected Eddie to go with her.

"I just don't think they're particularly nice people, Eddie."

"Because your friends are so *nice*," Eddie said, immediately riled, thinking of every society party she'd sat through at Rose's behest. "How many times have they made pointed little remarks about my dress, or made it clear that they'd rather I had stayed at home?"

"Never!" said Rose, looking shocked. "They were trying to be sweet, Eddie! They were actually complimenting your dresses!"

"My dresses are hideous. Nobody with eyes could ever compliment them in good conscience, and therefore they must have been making fun of me."

"One of Mr. Nicholson's friends, a political writer, asked me all these questions about politics in China," Rose said, quite red in the face now. "And when I said I didn't know, he acted as if I'd let the side down. As if it's *my* job to be his emissary to the East. He was talking to me like I was some sort of curiosity for him to examine. Somehow Trix manages to have better manners when she asks questions, and she's seven years old."

This gave Eddie pause.

"Damn. Which friend? We won't speak to that one."

"I don't know, Eddie, because they were all practically the same—"

"How could you say that? That was a room full of some of the most interesting people I've ever met in my life, horrible political writers excluded, and if you can't see that—"

"We're interesting," said Rose quietly, stopping Eddie in her tracks. "You and I. We don't need some horrible gentleman with a half-written manuscript about the revolution in France to tell us that."

Eddie looked over her shoulder at the house, where all the lamps were now lit and Beatrice was probably being given a very angry bath.

"I know that, Rose. *You* don't have to tell me that. Look, I am truly sorry, I didn't realize . . . but you cannot write them *all* off, simply because of one ill-mannered ogre. *Nash* would never say such a thing. I promise if you spoke to him properly, you'd understand."

Rose snorted. "He's not going to speak to me, Eddie. He doesn't want anything from me. I have nothing to offer."

"What do you mean? You have lots to offer! You're wonderful!"

"That's not what I . . . Never mind," said Rose, shaking her head. "I just think you ought to be careful. That's all."

"Careful is my middle name," said Eddie, smiling tentatively. "Edith Careful-How-She-Goes Miller."

Rose rolled her eyes but smiled back. "Your middle name is Hortensia, and if you think I'm likely to forget that in a hurry—"

She had to stop speaking because Eddie had grabbed her and

put a hand over her mouth, laughing. Rose didn't bother with violence, simply going slack against her and then biting gently at Eddie's palm until she was released.

"Let's not quarrel," Rose said. "I can't bear it. It feels like everything stops making sense when we do."

"All right, you poor sentimental creature," said Eddie, stroking Rose's hair fondly until she sighed. "Let me walk you home."

"Then who's going to walk *you* home?"

"It's ten minutes, Rose. I'm not going to get into any trouble in ten minutes."

"If anyone can," said Rose, lifting her head and looking at Eddie with genuine consternation, "it's you."

Chapter Nine

NASH HAD NOT EXACTLY INVITED EDDIE TO HIS READING later that week, but he *had* mentioned it within her earshot at his house, which felt almost the same. The subject of poetry (and those who wrote it) was enough of a sore spot between her and Rose that Eddie did not immediately launch into aggressive negotiating tactics in an attempt to get Rose to accompany her; it was, unbelievably, Mr. Albert Rednock who proved himself useful on this particular occasion.

"He asked if we wanted to go with him to this *reading*, or whatever they call it. All their old friends from the pamphlet they wrote for are going," Rose said reluctantly as they walked with the Millers in the park one morning, watching as Amelia attempted to lure a duck to her by whispering what might either have been sweet nothings or an attempt at some sort of occult enchantment. "*Amelia*, darling, I don't think that duck wants to be stroked."

Mr. and Mrs. Miller were both preoccupied up ahead, trying to chase Beatrice while maintaining a somewhat dignified pace; Beatrice, who had never spared dignity a thought in her life, was on a firm trajectory toward the pond and showed no signs of slowing down. Lucy-Anne and Simon were doing their family proud simply by walking along the path like ordinary human beings.

"I still cannot picture Albert Rednock as a writer," Eddie said, trying to keep the distaste out of her voice just this once.

"Do not be such a hideous snob," said Rose. "He has a lot of thoughts on the state of the world, you know. He and Nash worked together, when Nash was just starting out—I think Albert tried to take Nash under his wing for a while, steer him right, not that it had any effect whatsoever. I imagine . . . you want to go. To the reading."

"Excellent guesswork," said Eddie. "Though I imagine you'd rather embrace Amelia's duck."

Rose pulled a face. "Albert said there would be some people there he'd like me to meet. So I suppose I shall go, for him. Perhaps I can just tune out the poetry."

"Should be no problem at all, at a poetry reading," said Eddie. "Perhaps you could stick your fingers in your ears and hum, like Trix does whenever Lucy-Anne sings. Damn, speak of the devil . . ."

"Edith," Mr. Miller called, quite red in the face, "could you catch her, please?"

Beatrice had made an about-face, dodged between her father's legs, and come sprinting back toward the rest of her family; Eddie tried to meet her, spreading her arms wide as if she were defending a net at some sort of sporting event, but at the last minute Beatrice pirouetted away with surprising grace and sprinted toward Amelia. Eddie didn't quite understand what happened next, but she heard twin shrieks of triumph and despair, and a second later Beatrice was holding a very perturbed duck aloft like a trophy.

"That's *my duck*!" Amelia wailed. "Don't *hurt* it, Trix!"

Beatrice seemed so overcome that she could only gaze up at her prize, which was now flapping its wings violently in protest; Mr. and Mrs. Miller were shouting at their youngest daughter to *drop it, please, Beatrice, it likely has all* manner *of diseases*, which only seemed to strengthen her resolve.

"It's *mine*!" she shouted, her voice taking on an alarming resonance, as if she might be possessed by some bird-fancying devil.

At that precise moment, the duck lifted its tail feathers and defecated on her.

The reading was to take place at Woolton's, a club that restricted its day-to-day patronage to gentlemen but was apparently willing to make exceptions for celebrated poets. Eddie was torn between her perpetual outrage that places such as this existed, and an undeniable sense of wonder at being allowed to see behind the curtain—*two* curtains, in fact, which were opened wide so that she, Rose, and Mr. Rednock could step inside. The club was a tall, narrow building in the classical style, sandwiched between two similar but less imposing neighbors; the entrance hall was flanked with marble columns, and from the morning rooms on either side Eddie could hear the grumble and bark of many overlapping male voices.

The man who had allowed them entrance seemed mortified to be aiding and abetting the admittance of two ladies, and hurried them through to the stairs in the manner of a hound helpfully escorting a fox. They passed a group of frowning gray-haired gentlemen, who seemed to inflate with indignation at the sight of them; Eddie was glad when they reached the card room, which contained some five or ten other ladies and was so stuffed with people that nobody noticed them enter. Guests were crowded around card tables, calling to one another as they weaved through the crush, leaning against the ornately molded walls with glasses of wine in hand. All were laughing and talking and contributing to the most unbelievable din. It seemed impossible that they would find a place to sit, but Mr. Rednock spotted a middle-aged gentleman he knew and was waved over to a half-full table to the right of a small platform.

They bowed, curtsied, and attempted introductions, but it was simply too loud for banal niceties. Eddie left Rose to it and settled back in her seat instead to gaze around the room at the menagerie of people who had been drawn here by the promise of port and poetry. She was convinced she recognized a few faces, although she could not quite place them; the lady in forest-green silk with an entire bottle of wine in her hand was perhaps an actress, the gentleman in the beautifully cut rose tailcoat with his hand on her elbow potentially a famous orator who had featured in the paper. It was almost more thrilling *not* to know, and to aggrandize them in all directions.

"Mr. Nicholson's friend Valentine is over there," Rose said in Eddie's ear as Mr. Rednock poured them glasses of wine; Eddie craned her neck until she spotted that Valentine was indeed standing near the door, dressed rather more traditionally than the last time Eddie had encountered them. As she watched, Nash appeared through the doorway, clapping Valentine on the back; when the crowd spotted him he was greeted with raucous cheering, and he held up his hands in sheepish greeting with a roll of his eyes before making a dash for the stage. Somebody let out a long whistle as he ascended, and he shook his head disapprovingly and scrubbed a hand through his hair as the audience cackled.

"Please calm yourselves, this is *not* that sort of establishment. Christ, is that Grimaldi in the second row? In that case, I am gravely mistaken . . . it *is* in fact that sort of establishment, and I am honored that you would all besmirch your good names for the love of a lowly *poetizer*."

More cheers; Rose tried to say something in Eddie's ear again, but she was entirely drowned out, and Eddie could not tear her eyes away from Nash. He seemed superhuman, like some gilded god of chaos; he certainly had *far* more energy than a normal person could expect to generate. It was practically coming off him in waves as he grinned wickedly around at the crowd, drawing them all in. Somebody stood up to pass him a glass of wine,

and he gave a small bow of thanks and then downed half of it in
one gulp.

"In all seriousness . . . No, no, I mean it, you must all join me
in looking grave for a moment . . . Do not *laugh*, Miss Watkins, I
can see you behind that fan . . . You may recall that the last time
I entertained you all here, there was a brief and very polite altercation with another member, during which some poor bystander
called for the constable. Yes, you may well boo—I booed, at the
time—but really, a moment of silence for my worthy adversary
on that occasion, who has gone to *extreme* measures to avoid a
repeat by leaving the country altogether. I believe that particular
poet is currently terrorizing the poor people of Italy—so please
join me and drink to this." He raised his remaining wine, looking
at them all expectantly, and glasses were raised all around the
room to match. "Thank *God* we aren't Italians. Cheers!"

There was an explosion of laughter and applause—
accompanied by a few good-natured shouts of protest, which
Eddie could only assume had come from any Italians present—
but Eddie was too enchanted to do more than grin up at Nash
like a fool. She thought she saw his eyes dart in her direction, but
then he was off, eliciting more riotous laughter from the crowd
as he worked himself up to the main event. He had his audience
in the palm of his hand; when his easy patter finally gave way to
a reading of his longest and most famous poem, "The Death of
Beauty," everybody listened in rapt silence.

Eddie forgot she was in a gentleman's club; she forgot that
Rose was sitting next to her, or that she was breathing the same
air as Mr. Rednock. She was on a windswept parapet; she was
at the bow of a ship; she was on a battlefield, listening to Nash
lament the death all around her. She felt speared through with
feeling, pinned to her chair by the force of it. It was a magical
enough thing to read poetry lying with Rose in the tree house,
or alone by the light of a candle in the middle of the night, but

somehow this felt just as personal and more besides. It was as if he were reading directly to her; as if every word he spoke had been written to appeal to the most private and burning parts of her heart.

Nash read two more, but they flew past far too quickly, and suddenly he was being dragged off the stage by the many people who wanted to buy him a drink and shake his hand. Eddie watched as he was swallowed up by one group and then another, everybody trying to touch him as much as possible, as if some of his magic might rub off on them; she didn't realize that she had half stood out of her seat until Rose gave her a gentle yank downward.

"He was *wonderful*," Eddie said, regaining her senses. "Do you not think?"

"He is a very gifted public speaker," said Rose flatly.

Eddie shot her a brief grimace and then went back to tracking Nash across the room. His smile never faltered; he seemed glad to see everybody, although she noticed that he paid only the briefest of attention to each of them out of necessity before moving on to the next person, like a roving spotlight in constant motion.

"Do you wish to go and speak to him, Miss Miller?" Mr. Rednock asked; Eddie felt immediately horrified, imagining herself as part of the throng, tapping him on the shoulder so that he might smile and say good evening and then move on to the next adoring fanatic.

"Good Lord, no. He has far too many people to speak to as it is . . . Let us just finish our drinks quickly, and then we can go."

"Nothing would please me more," said Rose. "I mean . . . it is *dreadfully* stuffy in here, isn't it?"

Albert said something inane in reply about the lack of open windows. Eddie ignored them both. She could see Nash speaking to Valentine now, the two of them conversing properly even as the crowd around them refused to abate, and she realized that she felt heavy with disappointment; she was almost *sure* that he had seen her, and had hoped that he might make a point to greet her—and yet of course it was foolishness to imagine that he would make a beeline for her when he had a whole room full of admirers to entertain, as if she were an important or noteworthy guest.

Her heart sank a little more; she drank her wine quickly, wishing to slip away as hastily as possible so that she could tell herself that his lack of attention was entirely due to the fact that she had exited too soon.

"Steady on," Rose said, noticing that she was draining her glass at an alarming pace and putting a warning hand on her arm. "You are in danger of drowning."

"Come on. It *is* too hot, you're right, I think we ought to . . ."

Eddie was already standing, and Rose scrambled to join her. Mr. Rednock had to say very rapid farewells to his friends at the table; Eddie was already pushing her way across the room before he'd managed to get his hat back on. He was waylaid again halfway across the room by some more acquaintances, but Eddie did not wait—she ducked her head and pressed on until she reached the lavishly carpeted hallway outside, where the air was far more breathable.

"My God, Eddie, are you trying out for a sporting event of some sort?" Rose said, upon eventually catching up with her. "A twenty-yard dash, perhaps?"

"I just want to go home," Eddie said, glancing impatiently back at the doorway to see if Mr. Rednock had yet appeared. "I wish he would—"

"*Christ*," said an unfamiliar voice. "What the bloody hell is this?"

A group of young gentlemen had just crested the stairs; they were staring openly, and it took Eddie a moment to recollect that she and Rose were two ladies standing unaccompanied in the hallway of a gentleman's club.

"I'm sure I was told upon joining," said one of the men, a blonde with a plummy voice, "that guests of this sort would *not* be tolerated. It seems I have been missing out, all these years."

They all laughed, but there was something very unfriendly about the manner in which they did it.

"Guests of what sort?" Eddie said indignantly. Rose's hand closed around her wrist.

"He is implying that we are working women," she muttered.

"Oh," said Eddie. "Well, we are not."

An older man stepped forward, inspecting Eddie with open disdain. "We ought to have you arrested, you know. It isn't *decent.*"

"Arrested for attending a poetry reading?" Eddie snapped back, ignoring Rose's warning tug on her hand. "It is not yet illegal to have an interesting thought, sir, although even if it were, you would certainly be in no imminent danger."

The man bristled with instant affront. "I *beg* your pardon?"

"Oh, let her off, Archie," said the first man. "She has simply never been taught how to behave. Sad, really. I shall tell you what—come with me, *young lady*, and I shall give you the first of a few very important lessons—"

"Sir," Rose said. She was very pink in the cheeks. "There is no need to speak to us that way. We were just leaving."

The blond man smirked, turning his attention to Rose; Eddie wanted to break his nose, to put an immediate stop to this leering.

"I save my manners for those who deserve them, madam. And I know a *whore* when I see one."

"Excuse me," came a furious voice from behind Eddie. "What the *hell* did you just say?"

It appeared that Nash had just exited the card room, a clutch of hangers-on in tow. He looked utterly incandescent with rage, but the sight of him lightened something in Eddie's chest.

"Women! In the club!" the man said, gesturing at Rose and Eddie as if this would get Nash on side.

"They are my guests," Nash said in a very dangerous tone, stepping in close to him; he was at least two inches taller, and the blond man seemed to shrink slightly. "If you should like to insult them again, we can see how you manage it without any teeth."

"Nash," said Valentine, pushing people aside to reach them. Eddie could see Mr. Rednock attempting to do the same. "Brawls. Constables. We have been over this. I believe short prison sentences were bandied about."

"Now look here," said the older gentleman, seeming on the verge of a bluster.

"Apologize," Nash snapped, his gaze still fixed on the blond man.

"When *they* are the interlopers at *our* club?" the man scoffed, glancing back at his friends, although he was visibly unsettled. "I think not."

"*Our* club, is it?" said Nash, narrowing his eyes. Valentine's words must have had some sort of impact; he no longer seemed about to do any punching. "Well, we shall see about that. I happen to have some very good friends here, I'm afraid. I do not recognize you, sir—what name shall I give, so that they might strike it from the book?"

The man looked at a loss for words. He seemed to have noticed the rather large crowd of Nash's friends and supporters, who were still spilling out into the corridor behind him; his eyes were moving rapidly, as if he were doing some very quick calculations.

"Well . . . it seems . . . I suppose apologies are in order," he said brusquely.

Nash crossed his arms and cocked an eyebrow. "I'm afraid that wasn't particularly convincing."

"I am sorry," he said stiffly, looking at Rose and Eddie properly now. "I apologize. It was . . . I was mistaken."

"Run along now," Nash said, as Mr. Rednock reached Rose and put a protective hand on her elbow. "If I am ever unfortunate enough to encounter you again, we shall revisit the subject of urgent dental extractions."

The man and his cohorts scuttled away to muted laughter and scattered applause from those watching. Rose was saying something to Mr. Rednock in a low voice, her face still very red; Nash turned to Eddie and took her gently by both shoulders, his gaze roving around her face as if to ascertain if she had been somehow injured in this exchange.

"Inciting skirmishes in the halls now, are we, Miss Miller?"

"*They* did all the inciting," said Eddie, trying and failing not to feel lit up from within by his attentions. "I am surprised you were able to see that we were under attack at all, over the heads of *quite* so many adoring admirers."

"Oh, don't start," Nash said, giving her a bracing little shake and a fond smile. "Come on, trouble. Let's fetch you a drink."

Chapter Ten

$\mathcal{B}$ACK WHEN EDDIE AND ROSE HAD BECOME SUCH FIRM friends that even a day or so apart felt like a deeply painful separation, Mrs. Miller had at first rather half-heartedly tried to enforce the rules of decorum, which dictated that visits from the Li family necessitated a visit in return. Eventually, when Rose had started mysteriously arriving by herself and Mrs. Miller quickly ascertained that Eddie had bribed the cook's son to send Rose notes of invitation that did *not* extend to her parents, an agreement had been struck up between the two families: as Mr. Li was so often away from the house or locked up in his study on business, and Mrs. Li often suffered from maladies of the stomach, Rose would visit the Millers for dinner whenever she wished, and Eddie would eat with the Lis every other Sunday.

Eddie looked forward to these Sundays enormously—even more so since Rose had insisted on transforming into a butterfly so social that her dinners at the Millers' home were reduced to perhaps only one or two a week. No matter how busy she had become, no matter how many other social engagements she had or letters of thanks she was duty bound to write after said engagements, Rose never once suggested that they postpone or cancel their fortnightly meals at her house.

The Sunday after the poetry reading, Eddie emerged from her bedroom, where she had been curled over her manuscript for hours, barely human, and scrubbed as much of the ink off her fingers as was possible without resorting to sanding them down like woodwork. Then she removed her bonnet from Beatrice's head, where she had been wearing it like a lampshade, and set off for dinner.

The Lis' maid, Jemima, answered the door and ushered her into the modest house, taking her hat and cloak.

"Profitable week, was it, Jem?" said Eddie. Jemima winked.

"I know how to pick 'em," she said. "Want me to put one on for you, next time?"

"My mother has only just about recovered from the shock of having a daughter who's unreasonably tall and frequently forgets the purpose of a hairbrush," said Eddie. "Let's give her a few years before I add gambling on horses to the list, shall we?"

"Your loss," said Jemima.

All three of the Lis were in the small, beautifully kept drawing room: Mr. Li sitting by the window, frowning over a pile of papers and ledgers; Mrs. Li bent over the low table that currently contained at least sixty miniature porcelain figurines of animals; and Rose pretending to read on the sofa while in reality looking over the top of her book at her mother.

"There's a horse missing," said Mrs. Li. A lock of dark hair had escaped from its pins and she blew it out of the way, not even seeming to notice that Eddie had entered. "Isn't there? Little Rosie, help me count the horses again."

"I am not helping you count the horses again," Rose said gently. "If a horse has gone astray, perhaps Jemima moved it when she was cleaning."

"Or perhaps she put it out to pasture," said Eddie. "Have you checked the garden?"

"Good evening, Edith," said Mrs. Li. Eddie thought she could have put at least ten percent more effort into not sounding audibly disappointed to see her. "You haven't seen my horse, have you?"

Eddie raised her eyebrows at Rose. The insinuation that she

might have stolen one of Mrs. Li's prized ornaments—she collected them, and on the whole seemed to find counting and personally polishing them very soothing to her nerves—would have been deeply offensive if it weren't for the fact that it was exactly the sort of thing Eddie might have done between the ages of eight and twelve.

"Eddie hasn't taken your horse, Mama. What would she even do with it?" said Rose, giving up the pretense and closing her book.

"Sell it?" ventured Mrs. Li. "They're very valuable, Rosie."

"I wouldn't do anything quite so ordinary as *selling* it," said Eddie, sitting down heavily next to Rose and making her squeak as they collided. "I'd hold it for ransom. Send you little notes in blood that said 'pony up, or you shall face your worst nightmares . . .'"

Rose tried not to laugh and mostly succeeded. She side-eyed her mother quickly, looking rather sheepish, before muttering to Eddie, "No stalling."

Eddie burst out laughing, and Mr. Li put down the ledger he was holding and considered Eddie with mild disappointment. His employment—managing lodgings and other necessities for seamen recently arrived from China—took up so many of his waking hours that it was rare to see him without a bundle of papers in hand, or stacked so high he was barely visible behind them.

"A pleasure to see you as always, Edith," he said, his tone intimating the exact opposite. Eddie wondered, not for the first time, if he or his wife had ever gently suggested to Rose that it might be time to end their long tradition of shared meals under his roof. "Mr. Rednock tells us you have been hard at work on a novel."

"Has he been here?" Eddie said, trying not to sound as horrified as she felt. "For dinner?"

"Oh, yes," said Mrs. Li, finally forgetting about her lost horse in favor of Albert Rednock. "And for tea, and we all took a walk with him yesterday."

Eddie had long ago stopped asking Rose what she did on the days their paths did not cross, entirely out of a selfish desire to pretend that Rose's life began and ended when Eddie walked into it; she couldn't escape hearing about the parties and dinners she had not attended entirely, but Rose knew these stories rankled her, and kept them to a minimum. The discovery that Rose had apparently been spending her free time with Mr. Rednock made Eddie's stomach cramp violently.

"You didn't tell me that," she said to Rose.

Rose shrugged, as if it were immaterial, but she had gone slightly pink. "You didn't ask."

The whole thing left a bitter taste in Eddie's mouth that she couldn't rid herself of all through dinner, not even soothed by her favorite pork buns; she knew she ought to at least attempt to be winsome and likable, to try harder to ingratiate herself with Rose's parents even if *that* particular horse had bolted the stables long ago, but she found herself even more curt and ornery than usual.

Afterward both Mr. and Mrs. Li excused themselves, rather than spend another minute in her company, and Eddie barely noticed them go.

"You could at least try to be pleasant," Rose said as they sat at the dinner table, watching Jemima clear it. "You were downright rude tonight, and you know they already think you're a terrible influence—you're not doing yourself any favors, Ed."

"Yes, but they know I make *you* happy, and so they are forced to tolerate me out of love for their only daughter," Eddie said, pointing at Rose with her chopsticks before Jemima plucked them from her hand. "Look, I'm sorry, I'm not trying to be any more dreadful than usual. I just think . . . they've known me for fourteen years. If they don't like me by now, I don't see what I could possibly do to gain their good opinion, other than grow a new personality."

"You know it doesn't require an entirely new personality to simply be polite and cordial and watch your tongue sometimes, rather than just saying whatever it is you get into your head without a moment's consideration."

"Excuse me," said Eddie, sitting up straighter in her chair and glowering at Rose, who didn't flinch. "Just because, unlike some people, I don't pretend to be somebody else whenever it suits me—it is a sign of a lack of character to simply cast off your true self like an old shawl whenever it might inconvenience *society*, or—"

She broke off because Rose had pushed back her chair with a sudden scrape of wood on wood and abruptly left the room. Eddie sat for a moment, drumming her hand on the table, before deciding that it was no good being furious without an audience; she followed Rose upstairs and into her bedroom, letting the door slam shut behind her.

Although the Lis' home was far smaller than the Millers', they only had one daughter to share it with, and had given Rose the finest room in the house. It was just as large as Eddie's, the furniture a little more worn than hers but carefully chosen and meticulously polished, a vase of marigolds placed neatly on the windowsill. Rose was sitting on the end of her bed, not bothering to pretend she was doing anything in particular except looking past Eddie at the wall.

"Go on," said Rose. "Open fire."

"What do you *see* in him?"

"Who?"

"Albert Rednock!"

"Oh," said Rose. She looked down at her hands, which were twisting in her dress as if trying to wring something out of it, and then back up at Eddie. "Well, I've already told you. He's kind. He's patient. I enjoy talking to him."

"But you're not in love with him!"

"No," said Rose. Eddie was surprised how easily she admitted it. "No, I'm not in love with him. But I think I'll like being mar-

ried to him. You know as well as I do that my father's income isn't
half what it should be. My parents worry, they want to see me
happy and married—and Albert's position is very comfortable.
I'll like keeping my own house. I like his friends, and he lives not
far from here, so I'll be able to see all *my* friends, too. I'd have
thought you'd be happy that I'm not being whisked away to the
country somewhere."

"How can I be happy about any of this?" said Eddie, folding
her arms. She felt immovable and resolute, taller than ever, filling
the doorframe. "The society parties I could just about stomach,
but suddenly you're going to marry this man we hardly know,
because it's *convenient*? It doesn't make sense!"

Rose sighed. "Do you ever think about what I might want,
Eddie?"

"Well . . . surely not *this*. You said it yourself, you don't *love*
him. I can only assume that this is all just some . . . some part
you're playing, so that you'll fit in with the rest of them. It's a total
overreaction!"

"Stop it," said Rose, lifting her chin to meet Eddie head-on. "I
don't want to be your punching bag over this anymore. I know
you don't approve or understand, but it's my *life*, and this is what
I have decided. If you can't make your peace with it, then maybe
it's . . . I don't know. Maybe we just have to accept that what's between us is something we've grown out of."

Icy panic rose in Eddie's chest. "That's not . . . I haven't grown
out of anything. You haven't, either, Rose. You're just pretending,
you're playing along so that—"

"*Eddie*," Rose said, exasperated. "I am not the same person I
was when I was a child. I want different things. I am not *pretending* to enjoy people and parties and dancing—I actually do enjoy
them. You always knew who you were. Who you were going to
be. A *writer*. God, you dragged me and your family into book-
shops enough times, to show us *exactly* where your name would

be on the shelf. That's how certain you were about your future. You could quite literally point to it. I didn't know what I wanted, it took me a long time to realize, and then I . . . Well." She made an abortive movement with her hands and then paused for a second before continuing, more in control of her tone. "There are many things I can't have, but I *can* build a place where I feel at home. Where people like . . . people like Albert and me . . . can feel truly welcome. This is me being realistic about *my* prospects. The sort of life I might hope to lead. And, on balance . . . I think a life with a nice gentleman like Albert and a home that's a haven will be quite enough for me. I would love for you to be part of that life. But not if you're going to be dreadful to me every day because you're angry that I've grown up, and you want to be eight and covered in mud and holding hands in that tree house forever."

The silence that followed this felt impressively awful. Rose was looking at her evenly, as if she'd said something completely reasonable, which was obviously *insane*; Eddie wanted to argue, to attempt to take apart every word Rose had said and show her exactly how wrong she was—but she didn't want to appear to be as dreadful as Rose had made her out to be, even if she sometimes suspected that she was.

The bell rang downstairs. It felt entirely irrelevant to the two of them in this room, having *this* conversation, but a moment later they heard footsteps on the stairs and then there was a quick rap at the door.

"Miss Li?" said Jemima. "Rose? Mr. Rednock has come to have a nightcap with your parents."

"Thank you, Jemima," Rose called, her voice steady.

"Please don't go down there," said Eddie. The stakes felt strangely high, all of a sudden. "We aren't finished talking."

Rose looked at her quizzically, her dark eyes shining in the low light. "What would you have me do instead?"

"I don't know," said Eddie. "Stay here. With me. I need to . . . I need to get things straight, I don't want us to quarrel—"

"I am going downstairs," said Rose. "You are welcome to join me."

She got to her feet and smoothed down her dress, walking to the mirror to check her hair, which needed re-pinning. Eddie wanted to do it—wanted to gather up handfuls of that long, dark silk and carefully slide the pins back in, feeling Rose relax back against her chest, knowing that she was the only one who could touch Rose like that for the time being—but she couldn't move. She wondered why it felt so much like her heart was breaking.

"I'm sorry if I've disappointed you, Ed. But you've disappointed me, too. It was silly, I suppose, but I really thought that after the initial shock, you'd be happy for me."

Eddie didn't say anything. She didn't say anything as Rose kept putting up her hair, or when she noticed that despite how calmly she had spoken, her hands were trembling so that she kept fumbling the pins; she didn't say anything when Rose turned around to look at her quickly, the briefest of glances from under her eyelashes, and then left the room.

It was only when she heard Rose reach the bottom of the stairs, when she heard Mrs. Li's voice rise in greeting and Albert say something in a low, amiable grumble, that she felt able to move again. She sat down on the bed and stared at the back of the door.

"I'm sorry," she said, to the only audience she could bear to hear it.

Chapter Eleven

EDDIE TRIED TO SNEAK OUT WITHOUT NOTICE—SHE WAS sure that even if Mr. and Mrs. Li *had* seen her, they would have pretended not to rather than being forced to invite her into the drawing room for a drink—but she hadn't reckoned on Albert wanting to speak to her.

"Miss Miller," he said, as she tried to flit across the doorway and only succeeded in looking like she was performing in some sort of pantomime. "Good evening! I have just been at Mr. Nicholson's, I wondered if I had missed you there."

"Oh," said Eddie, trying to do a convincing impression of a friendly person. "Good evening, Mr. Rednock. Why might I have been there?"

"Ah," said Albert. "I take it you didn't read the papers."

"Edith was just leaving," Mrs. Li said hopefully, but Albert had produced a folded newspaper from somewhere about his person, and Eddie came forward to take it from him.

"But . . . this is . . ." Eddie said, her eyes quickly scanning the page.

"An attack on Mr. Nicholson on all fronts, yes," said Albert grimly. "It's hardly a *review*, although it certainly purports to be one. I imagine it was paid for by somebody with a rather potent grudge who doesn't have the courage to challenge him, and decided to throw down in the papers instead."

"But it says here that he's washed-up, and he'll never write again," said Eddie, horrified. "Good God. Poor Nash."

"I'm sure he's weathered worse," said Rose.

Eddie hadn't dared look at her since she'd entered, and she didn't try now.

"I was there for an hour or so," said Albert. "He's not in the best shape."

"Of course, he must be in need of comfort, friendly faces—I shall call in on him at once," said Eddie, dropping the newspaper onto the table and turning to go before remembering her audience. "I mean . . . I shall go home, of course. And . . . pray for him. And see him at a later date, when I am properly accompanied. Good evening, Mr. Li, Mrs. Li! Thank you for having me for dinner."

Where anybody else might have been highly offended, Rose's parents just looked relieved.

Five minutes after her arrival at the Nicholsons', Eddie was trapped between the artist Kitty Stuart and another woman she'd never met before in her life, the stranger's hands firmly cupping her head as her eyes raked all over Eddie's face.

"Excellent bone structure," she said, pressing her thumbs quite forcefully into Eddie's cheekbones. "You're all skull."

"Iss tha' good?" Eddie said, her voice slightly distorted due to being so violently compressed.

"Claire is a sculptor," said Kitty, providing the context that would have been very useful a minute or so ago. "She collects heads."

Eddie's eyes widened.

"I don't disconnect them from bodies," clarified Claire the sculptor, but her wistful tone wasn't entirely convincing, and Eddie decided it was high time she wriggled free. "God, all that dark hair and those eyebrows, you look positively—"

"I must find Nash," she said, and Claire watched her back away with a hungry expression in her eyes.

"Come and see me some time," she called, as Eddie turned and started shouldering her way through the crowd.

Based on Albert's description of Nash's mental state, Eddie had expected to arrive at a quiet, solemn house, and perhaps discover Nash deep into a bottle of wine. In reality, she hadn't been able to locate him or ascertain just how soused he was, due to the fact that the house was absolutely full to the rafters with people. The party was so loud that she had been able to hear it from all the way down the street, and she had almost given up on trying to summon somebody to the door to let her in when she had simply pushed and it had swung open, revealing at least thirty people packed into the hall.

The society parties she had attended with Rose had sometimes been loud; there had been a certain amount of visible drunkenness, and occasionally somebody had bucked decorum and done something really quite saucy, like walking from room to room unaccompanied by a chaperon, or eating a lemon ice in a manner that could have been described as lascivious.

Nash's house this evening looked like the after-party of a circus on the outskirts of Sodom and Gomorrah in comparison—and Eddie was completely enchanted.

Dayo Akerele was moving through the riotous, heaving crowd in the opposite direction, and they met in the middle of the room.

"Good evening, Miss Miller!" he shouted.

"Good evening, Mr. Akerele! Have you seen Nash?"

"He was in the garden, the last I saw of him," he said, his nose wrinkling. "He was attempting to drink an entire bottle of wine while the crowd sang 'God Save the King.' When I left, there was only one verse remaining, and not much wine."

"Oh dear," said Eddie. Somebody tried to walk between them, and they were jostled apart, Dayo waving to her as he was swept up in the momentum and started to move away. "Thank you!"

Getting to the garden was no mean feat; Eddie had to dodge and weave as if she were playing some sort of mad contact sport, trying to avoid elbows to the chin and spilled wine as it flew through the air. Eventually she found a door that led to the outside world, and she tumbled through it, the cool air an instant relief.

Nash was leaning against a mossy stone sculpture of the god Pan. There was a small crowd assembled around him, but things seemed to have cooled since the drinking contest that Dayo had witnessed; an empty bottle of wine lay at Nash's feet, and he had one hand pressed politely to his mouth, as if he might be considering vomiting.

"Nash?"

His companions didn't seem to notice her—they were preoccupied with laughing and clapping him on the shoulder, their voices overlapping as they all talked at him—but after a moment Nash's eyes found her, and he removed his hand from his mouth so that he could beckon her over.

"Edie! Where did you come from?"

There it was again. That glow in her chest; the feeling that she had been divinely selected for companionship. *Now* Nash's friends turned, appraising Eddie as she walked forward to greet him. She ignored them, taking Nash's hand when he offered it, and then just holding on to it awkwardly as he neither shook hers nor kissed it.

"Where's Mrs.—Where's Liza?"

"Out," said Nash. "Well, she was in, but then she saw how many people were heading up the garden path and she fled. Really, I don't know how word spreads like this, you'd think I'd put an advertisement in the paper."

There was a very brief pause, and then he winced. Clearly, he had inadvertently reminded himself of the review, and Eddie quickly attempted to change the subject.

"I met a sculptor in your hallway," she said brightly. "She said I had good bones. She seemed disappointed that she couldn't remove them from my body for further study."

Nash didn't laugh, but he did tilt his head to one side in that very puppyish fashion of his and look at her face quite intently, which made Eddie smile self-consciously.

"They are good," he announced. "As is the rest of you. Come on, I want to show you something."

The crowd around him seemed perturbed that he was leaving, and a few of them broke off and attempted to follow, but he put his head down as if battling through a rainstorm and pushed on into the house and through the hallway, leading her to a room at the very end of the corridor. He turned to her with an expression of mock severity and put a finger to his lips, and then produced a small key; it took him two attempts to unlock the door, and once it was open he pulled Eddie inside as if they were running from some ravenous beast, shutting the door behind him and immediately locking it again.

"You can't *lock* it," Eddie said, shocked despite herself. "What will people think?"

"How are they going to form thoughts about us if they can't *see* us?" said Nash, tapping his nose as if he'd just said something very clever, which he hadn't. He left the key in the door and then threw himself onto a small, neat, green sofa, sighing with evident relief. The whole *room* was neat—far cleaner and more organized than any other corner of the house that Eddie had encountered so far. It smelled pleasantly of polish, and the waxy white roses in a vase by the window.

"It's Liza's private parlor," Nash said, loosening his cravat. "She doesn't like me to come in here for some reason. Locks it when we entertain guests."

"Er . . . Somebody might have noticed us coming in here, even if they're unable to see through walls," said Eddie, still standing halfway between the door and the very inviting-looking armchair opposite Nash.

Nash waved her away. "They're all foxed up to their eyeballs. Nobody around here notices anything."

Eddie knew he was wrong; they all noticed *him*, eyes following him wherever he went. She could only hope that nobody had glimpsed the face of his accomplice as she ran along in his wake.

"How's this?" said Nash, reaching into his jacket and pulling out an engraved silver flask. "I'll exit through the window, and then you can go by the door, and nobody will ever know of our various crimes."

"Oh, fine," said Eddie, finally giving in and sitting down. "You are ridiculous."

"Catch," said Nash; Eddie's hands went up without thought, and she caught the heavy flask as it flew toward her face. "Oh, *excellent* catch. Liza is always furious at me when I do that, but she's got no . . . you know. Brain-to-hands. Whatsit. Reflexes."

"I have four siblings," said Eddie, uncorking the flask. "I'm used to people throwing things at me from all directions."

"I shall remember that and test you at a later date," said Nash, rolling his head back until something in his neck clicked. "Drink up, I'm drying out over here."

"Incredibly unlikely," said Eddie. She took a sip from the flask and then handed it back to him. The alcohol slid quickly down her throat, seeping into the corners of her at once. "Are you all right? Mr. Rednock said—"

"Alas, poor Albert. He's not quite built for bacchanalia. He came to dish out condolences and give friendly pats on the head with those enormous hands of his, but balked when somebody started handing out cups of laudanum like it was tea."

"So you *are* all right," Eddie said.

"All right. Hmmm," said Nash, fingering the neck of the flask as he considered a spot on the ceiling. "After some thought, no. All wrong. Very, very, very wrong. Can't be helped, though, can it? Can't win them all, or even . . . any of them, lately."

"Don't be silly," said Eddie. "You just seem to be in a little bit of a . . ."

"Hole?"

"I was going to say a period of reflection."

"Reflection? No, no, it's *stagnation*, if we're talking bodies of water."

"I don't believe we were."

"Oh, Edith," Nash said, suddenly tilting his head backward over the edge of the sofa in order to catch her eye. "How terribly pathetic. I must be a great disappointment in person. Nothing like a poem."

"People are never like poems," Eddie said, although for some reason she immediately thought of Rose; Rose was at least *somewhat* like a poem, even when she was being unreasonable.

"Sit with me," Nash said suddenly.

"I am sitting with you."

"You are sitting *adjacent* to me." He hauled himself upright and then patted the resulting space on the sofa. "I promise to behave perfectly. Or at least as perfectly as a . . . a well-trained dog."

"I've seen how well you've trained your dog," Eddie said, but despite her misgivings, he *had* visibly wilted during their conversation; it felt only polite to attempt to cheer him up. She came to sit next to him, noting that he was careful to keep a courteous amount of distance between them.

"I shall tell you what the trouble is." He paused to hand her the flask, still draped ridiculously over his side of the sofa, and Eddie took a drink and then handed it back. "It follows thus—I believe I have said all I have to say, in all the ways I wish to say it. I have set a certain precedent with the work I've done so far—not to say that it's so *great*, you understand, that I can't possibly top it—but I cannot stray from the narrow parameters I've drawn for myself, because then what I produce won't be a *Nash Nicholson* poem—or indeed a *Nash Nicholson* novel."

"A novel?" said Eddie, sitting up straighter. "But you never told me you were seriously working on a *novel*."

"Well. Yes. I ask you, Edie, what fool writes poem upon poem, *only* poetry, poetry for breakfast and luncheon and in the middle of the night, and then wakes up one morning and says, 'Ah, yes, I know exactly what I'll promise my editor on pain of death—something I have thus far never even attempted.'"

"It'll be a triumph. I know it will."

"Well, there have been no signs of triumph so far. Writer's block is so very *boring*—very pedestrian. But I've cracked it. Blown the whole thing wide open. The problem was that I was spending *all* my time with the same people, having the same conversations, pacing around this bloody house, breathing in this fetid London air—I just needed some fresh perspective. New faces, new voices. You," he said, poking Eddie very gently on the arm, "have come to *rescue* me from a fate worse than death."

"What fate is that?"

"*Obscurity*," said Nash, smiling at Eddie in a way that made her feel warm from the tips of her fingers to the base of her spine.

"And how exactly am I to be your means of rescue?" said Eddie, hiding behind the flask so he couldn't see her blush. "I am nobody, with nothing to my name but a hundred or so stories and a manuscript that, as of this morning, is covered with jam."

"You need not do anything but be exactly as and who you are," said Nash. "Just having you here, sitting in my parlor—well," he amended, "sitting in *a* parlor—is a greater source of inspiration to me than I've found all summer. The novel will flow out of me like a river." This brief, sparkling moment of hope seemed to gutter out almost as soon as it had begun. "If only I can remember who the hell I am, and what the devil I have to say about literally anything."

"*I* know who you are," said Eddie.

She really felt she did after years of reading his poetry, of following his career in the papers. She had grown up with him. He had guided her, without knowing, and now he was looking at her as if she might be able to return the favor.

"Please, tell me," said Nash, leaning his head on the back of the sofa and looking up at her through dark lashes. He had shaved badly, or perhaps hadn't shaved at all, a roguish scattering of stubble decorating his sharp jaw, and he smelled like a pleasant mix of musky perfume and sweet alcohol. "Sometimes I truly cannot remember. You're a writer. Tell me the story of Nash Nicholson."

"You are simply setting me up to embarrass myself," said Eddie, but Nash waved away her protestations. "Fine, fine. Nash Nicholson. Nash Nicholson is a young—"

"I'm eight-and-twenty," he said mournfully, rubbing his forehead against the sofa and then looking back up at her with wild hair and wincing eyes. "*Young*, indeed. Almost in middle age. No wonder my brain is rotting."

"Nash Nicholson," Eddie plowed on, "is a *relatively* young poet, who writes with . . . with heart, and spirit, and candor, about the many great and terrible facets of life on this earth and beyond—"

"Can a facet be terrible?" Nash said, nudging Eddie's arm with his elbow. His whole body was curled toward her now, like a neglected bloom reaching toward the sun, and Eddie was acutely aware of their proximity.

"A facet can be anything I like," said Eddie. "You cannot stop yourself from interrupting, can you? Go on, then. Tell it yourself."

He didn't even pause to draw breath, letting his hand trail along the back of the sofa as he spoke.

"Nash Nicholson is a washed-up hack approaching middle age, slowly suffocating to death in an airless house, in a loveless marriage, suddenly deaf to a thankless calling. And *what's more* . . . he's run out of gin."

"Well," said Eddie, "you're wrong about one thing."

"Am I?"

"There is plenty of gin to be had outside the confines of this room."

"That's all very well for the rabble, but *I'm* disinclined to leave the confines of this room," said Nash.

He had been running his fingers lightly along the upholstery, back and forth in mesmerizing laps, and it took Eddie a moment to realize that they had jumped ship; his fingertips were now brushing featherlight along her arm before returning to the sofa. She didn't move or speak, didn't acknowledge it, and he kept going, his face and demeanor entirely unchanged, as if he hadn't noticed he was doing it at all.

"Rose and Albert Rednock are to be married," Eddie said suddenly. "It's not been made official yet, but I fear . . . it's only a matter of time."

"Rose?" Nash said, frowning. "Well . . . Albert's a pleasant enough chap, I'm sure she could do worse. He doesn't have the spirit of a true revolutionary, but I have known him for a very long time, and he's never done anything remotely horrible. Or interesting."

Eddie shook her head miserably. "You don't understand . . . She doesn't even *love* him, and nobody is forcing her into it—I have no earthly idea why she's marrying him. Things have been difficult between us lately, and she doesn't understand any of . . . this." She waved around at the room, as if that would somehow convey the enormity of her feelings.

"People *don't* understand," he said, his face softening. "Those of us who live to create, who throw ourselves upon the altar of art and bleed and bleed for it . . . how could we ever really inhabit the same world as those who simply dress for the day and read the paper and never dream that they could be the god of something new?"

"I don't even know if that's who I am," Eddie said, wondering why her voice had gone so strangely quiet and husky. Nash's hand landed on her arm and then stayed there, the pads of his fingers tracing slow circles at her wrist.

"Of course it is, Edie," Nash said. "Why else would you be here? How would we have found each other?" His voice was no more than a murmur, and Eddie's eyes closed briefly like a soothed child, focusing on the sound of his breath and the feeling of his fingertips lingering over her pulse. "Listen, I'm getting out of here. London is killing me. The whole damned city is sitting on my chest, and I'm not quite sturdy enough to bear it. I'm absconding to my accursed little country estate—it's upon a lake. You should come. Write, walk, cultivate genius. I shall invite Albert and your friend to accompany you—one last jaunt before marriage claims them. I'm going to drag Dayo and Valentine with me, and perhaps Kitty, if she soaks in turps for a few days to get the oils off her."

"And Liza," Eddie added. It wasn't a question, although perhaps it should have been. Nash's fingers had paused, and he removed his hand from hers to ruffle it through his hair.

"Oh, yes. Well. That's a given."

There was a scattering of loud bangs that made Eddie jump in her seat; somebody was hammering on the door in drunken earnest, and Nash rolled his eyes, but got up to answer it anyway.

"But . . . you said you'd leave by the window," Eddie said, jumping up and putting a hand to her hair as if it might have somehow been salaciously disheveled.

"Nobody will mind," Nash said, ignoring the fact that *Eddie* certainly minded.

He unlocked the door as Eddie tried to shuffle inelegantly out of view, and then paused for a second.

"Edie. Do come to the house, won't you? And when you've finished that novel of yours I'll have a read of it and send it to my editor, and see if we can't do something about getting your name in print."

The door swung open.

"There you are, you miserable bastard," said an unfamiliar voice. "Half the party is looking for you—come on."

Nash glanced back at Eddie with an apologetic expression on his face—as if he had anything to apologize for, when he had just spoken the most beautiful words Eddie had ever heard in her life—before being dragged quite forcefully from the room. She heard cheers go up from the corridor, and then Nash's voice, raised to meet them.

"All right, all right—tell me, who here wishes to be rid of the idea of God?"

Eddie was too elated to mind his sudden departure. Nash wanted to show her book to his *editor*. Nash thought she might actually be *published*, and soon. It was too much to comprehend; too much feeling to contain. Eddie had to find someone, tell someone—shout it from the rooftops. She forgot to be clandestine as she left the room and made her way to the hall, but luckily nobody was looking in her direction now that Nash was out in the crowd. Watching him go, Eddie's eyes alighted on a familiar face deep in conversation, with an even more familiar head of glossy dark curls just visible at his side.

Eddie pushed her way toward Rose and Albert Rednock, her heart brimming over with her news. She was irritated by the number of people who seemed determined to hamper her progress, but when she finally neared her friend, she stopped dead.

One of Albert's acquaintances was talking to him, his wife leaning in to listen, and when Albert responded to his query, the man cheered and clapped him on the shoulder. His wife took Rose's hand and was clearly bestowing congratulations on her; for her part, Rose looked quietly pleased, her smile tentative but genuine.

Suddenly Eddie didn't want to be there anymore. She knew why they had come; what Rose would tell her when she saw her. It was childish, ridiculous, but maybe if she could just postpone the moment she heard those words, then for a while longer they wouldn't be true. Time would stand still. Rose would still be hers.

Eddie turned to leave, hoping the crowd would suck her back in and swallow her whole, ignoring Rose calling her name. It was only when she felt a hand on her shoulder that she did finally stop, a reluctant grind to a halt to allow herself a moment to arrange her face before turning.

Rose's chin was lifted defiantly, braced and ready. She had to raise her voice to be heard.

"Well?"

"What do you want me to say?" said Eddie.

She was knocked sideways by somebody passing with a bottle of wine in each hand, but managed to stay upright, looking down at Rose and biting her tongue harder than she ever had in her life.

"You could at least congratulate me."

Eddie could hear cheering somewhere behind her, and wanted to disappear into the wall of sound. But Rose had her pinned at the boundary, and no matter how fast or far she ran away from this moment, the facts remained: Rose would go on being engaged. Their childhoods would be over, forever. Nothing would ever be the same again.

Eddie nodded, and let the hurt come flooding in.

"Congratulations."

Chapter Twelve

"AMELIA, HAVE YOU SEEN MY WINTER HAT FROM LAST YEAR?"

Amelia looked up from where she was sitting cross-legged on the floor reading a book and considered.

"Trix was using it for a boat."

"She can't fit inside it," said Eddie, dropping the pelisse she was carrying onto an armchair and frowning. "And it doesn't float."

"It wasn't for her. And I think she found that out quite quickly," Amelia said, returning to her book and turning the page without reading the one she had abandoned, as if she might prefer what she found on the next one anyway. "She also discovered that frogs can swim, although I could have told her that . . ."

"Couldn't she have used a bucket? Or . . . *anything* other than my hat?"

"A bucket would not have befitted the occasion. You can borrow *my* winter hat, if you'd like."

Eddie couldn't restrain herself from ruffling Amelia's hair.

"Thank you, Ames, but then whatever would you wear when it gets cold?"

Amelia had dropped flatly to the floor to avoid any further hair-ruffling.

"Bucket?" she suggested, picking up the book again and holding it over her head like a shield.

"Edith?" Eddie followed the sound of her mother's voice out into the hallway. "Oh, there you are. Here—mittens. I couldn't find that pelisse anywhere—"

"It was in Lucy-Anne's room," Eddie said. "As was that shawl from last Christmas. Honestly, in future I shall look there first before I bother opening my own wardrobe . . ."

"I can hear you!" Lucy-Anne shouted from the dining room.

"Good," said Eddie. "Now hear this—stop taking my things and hoarding them like a fashionable dragon."

"*Fashionable*," Lucy-Anne scoffed, just loud enough for Eddie to hear, but muted enough for plausible deniability. "Your clothes are hideous."

Perhaps sensing that disaster was looming, Mrs. Miller forced two slightly misshapen pairs of mittens into her eldest daughter's hands.

"*Must* you go? I am not at all sure about this."

They had been having some variety of this exact conversation for a week, since Nash had written to Mr. and Mrs. Miller extending a formal invitation for Eddie to join him in his family's house in the country for a month or so. Eddie had been quite impressed that he was capable of doing something so polite and tedious; he had written all about the house, the lake it resided on, and the other guests who would be joining them. He had made the whole thing sound so utterly dull and proper that even Lucy-Anne had wrinkled her nose and said that it sounded like a waste of a good autumn.

"Of course I must," Eddie said now. "Rose and Mr. Rednock are going, and it might be my last chance to spend time with her now that she's to be married."

"Married people are allowed friends," said Mrs. Miller.

"Then why don't you have any?" said Amelia earnestly, walking past from the drawing room to the dining room; she stopped abruptly when she saw that Lucy-Anne was in her intended destination and made an about-face, heading for the stairs.

"Amelia, that's very rude," Mrs. Miller called after her. "Your father and I have plenty of friends. You see them all the time."

"No, you don't," Amelia said, pausing on the stairs. "You aren't truly *friends* with them, you're just a bunch of people going around to each other's houses!"

"That's what friends are when you're older, darling."

"Goodness," said Amelia, looking stricken. "How dreadful."

"I think this time away from London will be the best opportunity to finish my manuscript," said Eddie, barely listening to them. "And Na—Mr. Nicholson said that he's going to show it to his editor. He thinks it might be good enough to publish."

"Has he read it?" said Mrs. Miller. Eddie bit her lip.

"Well, no. But I think he has a feeling about it."

"Hmm," said Mrs. Miller. "It's not usually wise to trust men who have *feelings* about things."

"Warning noted," said Eddie. "But you know Rose will take care of me, don't you?"

Mrs. Miller sighed again. "I suppose so. And I also know that there's not much point trying to stop you."

"No," said Eddie, smiling and kissing her on the cheek. "Thank you, Mother!"

Mrs. Miller looked very weary as Eddie made for the door.

"I have too many children."

"Well, whose fault is that?"

"God's."

"He hasn't read a word of what you've written," Lucy-Anne said, appearing in the doorway with a pinched expression on her face. "Not a single word! How do you know he won't just have one note for you—'Please stop writing'?"

Eddie had been attempting to rise above her sister's prodding, but at this her resolve snapped.

"Just because you've never done anything interesting in your life, and likely never *will*—"

"Edith!" said Mrs. Miller, pressing a hand to her chest. "That is *quite* enough."

"You heard what she said, Mother!"

"I'd think that you'd be old and wise enough to know that your sister is only needling you."

Lucy-Anne *was* only trying to get a rise out of her—but Eddie's fear that Nash would indeed find her writing wanting had been keeping her up late into the night, poring over her manuscript, crossing out lines and phrases and rewriting them in the margins until the entire thing was almost indecipherable. Her protagonist, Delilah Fortescue, was proving difficult to pin down. Eddie felt as if she were skittering over the surface of what she truly wanted to say, as if there were hidden depths beneath her writing kept at bay by a thick sheet of ice; no matter how hard she pounded, she could half glimpse them but she couldn't quite reach them.

"You should read to him," Lucy-Anne said suddenly. "From your story. When he comes for dinner. And then we shall see how he really feels about your *genius*, before he's gone to the trouble to have you to stay."

"Dinner?" said Eddie, completely blindsided. "He's coming for dinner?"

Mrs. Miller looked flustered. "Yes, Edith, I'm sorry—I did mean to tell you but I only got the note today, and I had to run straight out for your things. He's to join us for Michaelmas, the evening before you set off. His wife is busy, and he was going to be by himself, so your father invited him. Rose and Mr. Rednock will be dining with the Lis, so there's room at the table. I do think it best we meet him, anyhow."

Eddie couldn't think of anything more horrifying—*Nash*, in her terribly ordinary house, meeting her frankly rather bizarre family? Would Lucy-Anne hold her at knifepoint until she recited a few pages of her half-baked story? Would Simon treat him to a half-hour lecture on steam power? Trix would, undoubtedly, try to put something alive down the back of his trousers; *that*, she thought, he would bear with good humor, but as for the rest of it . . .

"Well . . . this is going to be a very interesting sort of disaster."

When the evening came, it was as if a whirlwind had entered through the front door; Nash shook hands enthusiastically with Mr. and Mrs. Miller and then very solemnly with Simon, as if they were two business associates meeting at a funeral, and then kissed both Lucy-Anne's and Amelia's hands as if they were society ladies in a ballroom. Eddie noticed that Lucy-Anne blushed, and felt a strange sort of triumph; not even her sister was immune to his charms, now that she was meeting him in person. When he reached Beatrice, who was almost hopping on one leg from her impatience to be greeted, he surprised Eddie immensely by crouching down into an undignified squat.

"All right, then. Hop on," he said; she did immediately, throwing her arms around his neck so that she could be borne aloft on his back.

"Good evening, Miss Miller," he said, bowing to Eddie and causing Beatrice to howl with delight as she was almost pitched forward to the floor. Mr. Miller, looking bemused, pointed him in the direction of the drawing room, and he carried an ecstatic Beatrice in as the rest of them trailed after him.

He sat down carefully on the sofa so that Beatrice could perch atop the back of the seat and stay a head and shoulders above the rest of them as they arranged themselves around him, Eddie taking a chair opposite and watching with barely restrained fondness as he reached into his jacket and then handed his pocket watch to Beatrice for her to examine.

"Careful," said Eddie. "She'll have it taken apart and put back together entirely wrong within five minutes."

"Well, perhaps she'll improve on it," Nash said, accepting with a brief flash of a smile when he was offered wine. "Gosh, there are rather a lot of you, aren't there?"

"I hope you don't mind," said Mrs. Miller. "We eat as a family, even the youngest. I know it's unusual—try not to be too shocked by our indecorous ways."

"I was born only recently," said Beatrice, putting the pocket watch down on top of Nash's head so that she could open it.

"Absolute rubbish, you're obviously the eldest. What are you, five-and-twenty?"

Beatrice considered this. "Yes. About that age."

"Well, I'm never wrong," said Nash, glancing over at Eddie, who couldn't help but smile back. "You are far too kind to invite me to join in your feasting, but I'm very glad you did—I'm afraid it would have been yesterday's beef and a few mushy potatoes for luck back at my house."

"Oh, you poor thing," said Mrs. Miller. "We're very happy to have you—and to meet you, at last! Eddie's been talking of little else for the best part of a month."

Eddie's expression soured; she caught Nash's eye and shook her head, trying to convey both her utter mortification and the fact that her mother was obviously exaggerating. Nash seemed to find the whole thing very amusing.

"It has been a delight to meet her! Liza and I are so set in our ways, we practically swoon from the shock when we meet some-body young and lively who wants to entertain us at our table."

This was hardly an accurate representation of what her eve-nings at Nash's house had been like so far, but there was no need to let her parents know this.

"It's very good of you to have Edith to stay in the country," said Mr. Miller. "And Rose and her fiancé, too."

"I suppose they wish to spend some time together, to get to know each other before they marry," said Mrs. Miller, ignoring Eddie's dour expression. "And what better place to do it! Gosh,

I used to love my trips to the country. My sisters and I would all hike up our skirts and go running about the place like wild, leggy beasts."

"*Mother*," said Eddie, but Nash only laughed.

"Edith, the knowledge that I have legs cannot be such a shock to you, you have seen them many times yourself. Do stop glaring at me. Mr. Nicholson, has the house been in the family long?"

"Oh, since before recorded time," said Nash. Beatrice patted him on the shoulder and then held out her hand; he took something that looked suspiciously like a tiny, integral cog from her and then placed it on his knee for safekeeping. "Owned by all manner of dastardly ancestors of mine over the years. Apparently, it's cursed. It's certainly haunted to the rafters."

"Ghosts?" said Simon.

Eddie noticed that all of her younger siblings were suddenly paying far more attention than they usually did to anything at all.

"Stuffed full of them. You can hardly move without walking through strangely frigid patches, or glimpsing an apparition in the next room. I'm convinced there was somebody else sitting in my chair at dinner once—it felt frightfully rude to eat my chicken in some poor dead fellow's lap."

"Have you spoken to one?" said Amelia, gazing at him with enormous eyes from under her unruly fringe.

"On occasion," said Nash.

Simon's mouth had fallen open. Beatrice tapped Nash on the shoulder again, and when he held out his hand, she dropped so many pieces of metal into it that some of them bounced off and scattered onto the floor.

"Ah," said Mr. Miller. "Sorry about that. Family heirloom, was it?"

"You know, I have always found linear time to be very restrictive," said Nash cheerfully, as Beatrice handed back what had once been a watch with an expression of impish glee on her face.

Dinner was much of the same. Eddie would have been horrified by her family's behavior, but Nash seemed genuinely thrilled by it all; he managed to hold a long conversation with Simon about different types of tree nut without looking the least bit bored, provided Amelia with a long list of every horse he had ever encountered and their merits, gave Beatrice all of his pudding when he caught her eyeing it up, and even managed to engage Lucy-Anne in a lively discussion about music.

"I play the harp, myself," she said, fluttering her eyelashes at him in what she probably imagined was a coquettish fashion and instead looking as if she had grit in both eyes.

"I should dearly love to hear you play," said Nash.

He was treating her like an adult, like he would any other lady around the table, a clear distinction between how he spoke to her and how he spoke to the *children*, and Eddie could tell that she was completely intoxicated by it.

After dinner his wish was granted; they all sat in the drawing room while she played piece after piece, only looking up from the harp to ensure that Nash was watching. Eddie sat on the floor with Simon, attempting to put Nash's watch back together, Simon getting increasingly frustrated with her lack of technical know-how, while Nash smoked a pipe with Mr. Miller—the two of them were united in their disdain for a particular newspaper, and were very content to sit and complain about it at length.

"Stop flirting with my sister," Eddie hissed when she got the chance, handing him another glass of wine while her father tried to placate an overtired Beatrice.

"Who *should* I flirt with, then?" Nash muttered back. "I did try your father, but he's very hard to read . . ."

Eddie snorted and then tried to turn it into a cough when she saw her father watching them.

By the time Nash bade them all farewell, Eddie was halfway convinced that he could have told them that he was whisking her away to perform satanic rituals in this apparently very haunted house of his, and her mother and father simply would have shaken his hand and wished him well on his commune with Satan. To Eddie's horror, Lucy-Anne *giggled* when he kissed her hand in farewell, and then stood at the window watching him walk away down the street.

"You do know he's married," she said, when the rest of the family had either naturally dispersed or, in Beatrice's case, been carried, struggling, up to bed.

Lucy-Anne, who had clearly been in another world entirely, turned to face Eddie with a scowl on her face and crossed her arms tightly over her chest.

"*I* know that," she bit out. "But I am not entirely convinced that *I* am the one who needs reminding."

Eddie could only gape incredulously at her sister as she raised her eyebrows, clearly feeling very pleased with herself, and then turned and flounced away toward the stairs.

Chapter Thirteen

When Nash had described the house as being "upon a lake," Eddie had conjured visions of a large and comfortable estate tucked into the curve of a glorified pond, perhaps with a pretty wooden sailing boat moored at the end of a jetty for afternoon jaunts around the water. It hadn't seemed important to dig for more details, the fact of her invitation being all that truly mattered, and she only realized halfway through their first day of traveling that she had absolutely no idea what she was getting herself into.

The party had been divided between two coaches. At first Eddie had been glad that she had been allocated a place with Dayo Akerele, the Nicholsons, and Juno the dog, far from eager to spend two days sitting opposite Rose and her fiancé with her heart a gaping wound, but it had quickly become apparent that Nash and Liza weren't really speaking, which added a palpable frisson of awkwardness to their journey.

"Have you been to the house before?" she murmured to Mr. Akerele, once Nash was either asleep or doing a good job of pretending. Liza was staring expressionlessly out of the window.

"No," said Dayo. "Decamping to the countryside to stay in a haunted house with friends of Nash is usually the sort of thing I stay away from at all costs."

"Why did you decide to come this time, then?"

Mr. Akerele pulled a face. "I have a deadline," he said. "I need to write, and Nash said . . . Well, he said a lot of things, but primarily that it would be a good place to get my head down and work uninterrupted."

Nash had said the same to Eddie, but she had heard the rattling of many bottles of liquor when their trunks were deposited into the back of the coach, and was starting to have doubts.

"At the merest hint of a ghost, or nonsense of that sort," Dayo said, pulling his hat down over his face and crossing his arms so that he might nap, "I will be on the first boat out."

First *boat*? Eddie wanted to interrogate this, but resisted the urge to draw him back out from under his hat to ask more questions. Liza hadn't reacted to anything that had been said; she had been perfectly polite to Eddie for the first hour of their journey, asking her the usual sorts of questions that could maintain a tentative back-and-forth between two people who were not yet at ease with each other, but once they had lapsed into silence neither of them had attempted to break it again.

They were staying for the night at a small inn, at the center of a town that was really only a handful of buildings that had sprung up on either side of the road; everybody was so exhausted from the strangely wearing task of sitting still for eight hours that they drifted away from one another without making plans for dinner. Rose and Eddie were to share a room, and once they had made it up to the narrow, comfortable attic lodgings, each sat down on a bed and considered the other.

"Thank you for coming," Eddie said, her throat dry. "I sort of . . . didn't think you would."

Rose sighed. "Neither did I. But then my mother said it might be a good chance to get to know Albert away from London before we marry—she thinks we're heavily chaperoned, of course, she has no notion that these people are as likely to keep a proprietary eye on us as they are to renounce their vices and turn back to God—and . . . if you must know, I kept thinking about you squirreled away in some mysterious house with Nash Nicholson, and

I thought that if I didn't come to keep an eye on you, you might end up drowned in the lake or sacrificed upon an altar after too many drinks."

"And now that you're here," said Eddie, "at least you might reap the benefits of the sacrifice. Buy favor with the gods."

"Exactly," said Rose. She looked just as tired as Eddie felt. "I suppose you were having some riotous party in your carriage, while we were making polite conversation and reading?"

"Something like that."

A silence stretched between them, populated by all manner of unsaid things, but Rose broke it by asking if they ought to go and see about some supper, and Eddie agreed that they ought indeed. Eddie sat at one end of the table opposite Nash, Rose sat at the other opposite Albert, and everybody in between ate and talked sleepily, unaware that they were being employed as social buffers.

The next day Nash was clearly in better spirits; instead of collapsing into a corner to sleep the day away, he opened a bottle of wine at ten o'clock in the morning and engaged Mr. Akerele in a lively discourse about parliamentary reform, rubbing Juno the dog behind the ears as she smacked her tail enthusiastically against the inside of the carriage. This time it was Eddie who pretended to be unconscious, to prevent herself from being dragged into a conversation about politics that was sure to reveal her as a nincompoop of the highest order.

Pretending to be asleep quickly gave way to *actually* being asleep, and she was only awoken when somebody tapped her on the arm; opening her eyes, she saw that it was Liza, and that she was now pointing out of the window.

"You can just about see the house from here," she said.

Eddie sat up and peered out of the window, at first confused about what she was looking at; after a moment it started to make sense, and she realized that the vast, glittering sheet of gray that had been confounding her was in fact the lake.

It was *enormous*, more like a sea than a lake—if she squinted, Eddie could just make out the far shore, bordered by a thicket of evergreens. Hills swelled on either side, also crowded with trees and topped with pale crags that were almost the same color as the silvery sky, looking wilder than anything Eddie had ever seen in her life. She half expected a dragon or a very large eagle to come swooping across the vista to make it complete.

The one thing she *couldn't* see was a house.

Nash noticed her looking.

"God. Dreadful weather for it. When it's sunny you can almost imagine that it looks inviting."

"Don't be ridiculous," said Liza.

Clearly there *was* a house, and Eddie simply wasn't trying hard enough to see it; she practically pressed her nose against the glass, and after a moment she realized what she had missed.

The house wasn't hiding among the pines at the shore; it wasn't on the shore at all. There was a small, lopsided island rising out of the lake to the east, almost completely camouflaged due to the thick covering of trees that made it near-identical to the woods on the mainland.

"The isle is St. Bede's," said Nash, "and the house is named for it, too—apparently the poor fellow was never canonized, but he's saintly enough for us."

Eddie was only able to eventually spot the house because it had been built in light gray stone, so that it loomed palely out of the greenery, the roof and top two stories visible for a moment before the road turned and it slipped from view. From their vantage point as they followed the curve of the lake, Eddie could see that one side of the island ended abruptly in sheer cliffs, the land falling away dramatically. A few white birds were circling, buffeted by the wind.

"And therein lies our doom," said Nash dramatically, causing Mr. Akerele to sigh in a pained sort of fashion.

"How many times a week does the boat come from the mainland?" he said, his voice grim with apprehension.

"Oh, once or twice," said Nash, sounding all too pleased to deliver this bad news. "Although I rigged a system to signal them, should we all be driven mad by faces in the mirror and figures in the wallpaper and need to flee."

"Do you not have your own boat?" said Eddie, eyeing the unfriendly-looking lake and shivering at the thought of being adrift on it, tiny and insignificant in the face of all that menacing water.

Liza made a disapproving noise. "We *did*."

Nash reached down and groped about until he found the mostly empty bottle of wine, and then took a fortifying pull from it.

"Apparently there is no limit to the amount of times a man can apologize for a boating accident—"

"Shipwreck," said Liza. "A maritime disaster, precipitated by gross negligence and obscene quantities of alcohol—"

"Maritime means *ocean*, Liza," Nash said acidly. "Were we at *sea*?" Eddie glanced at Dayo out of the corner of her eye, and saw him press his lips together in grim solidarity. "We are unfortunately between boats. I meant to . . . Well, I haven't been here for quite a while. Five years? Six?"

"I suppose it's too far to swim," said Eddie.

"Yes," said Liza. "It is not the distance, although it is far—I think a strong swimmer could make it without too much trouble. It is the currents. People don't expect lakes to have them, but they do. And when the wind gets up, conditions become dangerous very quickly."

"I've swum most of the way," Nash said dismissively. "It just requires a sort of deranged fortitude of spirit and the unwavering belief that you'll survive."

"Deranged is right," said Dayo, also gazing out at the lake.

"When Nash sets the house on fire I shall save you a spot on the boat I will fashion out of tree branches, Miss Miller. But be warned, I shan't wait around for long."

They were traveling through dense forest now, the shoreline only occasionally visible in flashes, until suddenly the road ahead of them opened up to reveal a large farmhouse. It backed onto fields that looked hard-won from the landscape, and liable to be swallowed up by root and branch again at any moment. Eddie could see more buildings in the distance, smoke rising from the chimneys—the suggestion of a small village, which did little to abate how remote it all felt.

The coachman pulled the horses to a stop. Eddie felt as if her limbs had calcified; she managed to unfold them with a disconcerting chorus of quiet clicks and crunches, and then half fell out of the carriage, righting herself in time to see Liza step out with easy grace. The dog bounded out, beside herself with delight that their travels were nearly over. The second coach arrived a moment later, but Eddie didn't wait to see them disembark; she was already walking toward the lake, wrapping her arms around herself as a chill breeze blew in from across the water.

In front of her there was a narrow, dilapidated jetty, which seemed to be doing its best; moored at the end of it was a small boat, nudging against the dock every time a wave caught it. It looked antique, and big enough to fit perhaps six people at most. It did not fill Eddie with hope.

An elderly man who had seen them pull up exited the farmhouse and walked toward them, wiping his hands on his breeches.

"Here you are, then," he said, nodding at Eddie. He glanced over the rest of the party and frowned, apparently not at all convinced by what he saw. "How many of you can swim?"

"Rose and I have gone sea-bathing," Eddie offered.

The furrows between the old man's brows deepened.

"Never fear," said Nash, stepping forward to greet the man

with a thoroughly shaken hand. "If we go over, Liza and I will float on our backs and carry you on our bellies like otter pups, for we are *excellent* swimmers. Good afternoon, Mr. Perkins! You're looking hale."

"And the same to you," said Mr. Perkins, seeming keen to get this transaction over with as soon as possible. He was already walking away toward the dock before he'd finished his sentence. "Mrs. Hall sends her apologies, but she and the rest are making ready. Hard going, with such a small staff."

"Ah," said Nash, momentarily stumped. "Well! I suppose we'll just have to make do." He turned to his guests and gave a small, apologetic shrug. "I'm afraid everybody is going to have to . . . grab a trunk."

"Is that thing seaworthy?" Valentine said, looking quite rumpled from the journey and none too pleased to be there.

"That thing has a *name*," said Nash, "and it's Mr. Perkins. Wait, no . . . *Captain* Perkins. Right-ho. Heave to and . . . you know. Avast."

He strode over to the carriage and picked up his own trunk, which did involve a certain amount of heaving to, and then walked determinedly away toward the dock with it. Eddie attempted to lift her own and almost knocked all of her teeth out when it slid toward her at alarming speed; she was saved by an elegant, familiar hand.

"Is it really going to float with the nine of us and all our luggage?" said Rose. She looked artfully disheveled from travel, unlike Eddie, who probably looked like a broken broom.

"It has to," Eddie said, as they each took one end of the trunk and began to walk with it, slow and crab-like, toward the jetty. "Not that I care if you all drown, of course, but my manuscript is in here."

"Ah," said Rose. "Has it been going well?"

Rose had read the first twenty or so pages as they'd been written, but this new and unsettling distance between them meant she was now rather behind. Usually she read absolutely everything Eddie wrote; it was either handed to her as she and Eddie said goodbye so that she could read it before bed at her leisure, or performed aloud by Eddie herself, which often led to on-the-spot revisions and edits as she realized how foolish certain sections sounded with an audience. On many occasions Rose had, with permission, taken a pen to the margins to leave Eddie little notes of encouragement, or queries, or critiques that were tantamount to heckles.

What on earth does this mean?? she had written next to a line that described somebody's personality as "foaming."

"You know," Eddie said indignantly later. "Sparkling! Effervescent!"

"Eddie, if you write that she's *foaming*, everybody is going to think the poor thing's gone rabid."

She had been right, of course, about that and a great many other things. Eddie hadn't meant to keep her current project a secret; it had just suddenly felt so much bigger than the ones she usually wrote—the ones she handed off to Rose without a thought or a care—and then this business with Albert had frayed what usually came so easily between them until she didn't feel like sharing it.

If she was honest with herself, Eddie also couldn't bear the thought of seeing disappointment or hesitation in Rose's eyes once she had read it. They had always been perfectly forthright with each other about these things, and Eddie had felt strong enough to withstand any criticism Rose threw her way, not that it was ever particularly damning. This manuscript, written not just for her eyes, but now for Nash's, too, and perhaps even some glamorous editor in London with the power to change Eddie's life, felt raw and a bit fragile, as if it might fall apart under too much early scrutiny.

"It's . . ." Eddie said now, not entirely sure how to finish her sentence. She was interrupted by Albert, who had come to rid them of the trunk that was drooping between them. "We can carry it," Eddie said a little too sharply; he gave her a slightly frightened-looking smile and quietly insisted.

"Oh, don't be silly, Eddie," Rose said, letting go of her end and forcing Eddie to relinquish the rest of the weight into Albert's arms. "If you're so determined to break your fingers, you can go and fetch mine."

They all managed to get into the boat in the end, although it did seem to be sitting quite low in the water once all the luggage had been dispersed evenly around under the watchful eye and rather spittly directions of Captain Perkins. Valentine sat down next to Eddie and wordlessly offered her a drink from a flask, which she declined; it was then offered to Kitty, who gazed at it with utmost reverence and then drank half the contents down in a few gulps. The dog almost sent them all overboard, having little understanding of the need to keep the boat balanced, and had to be hauled into Liza's lap, where she sat panting excitedly.

"I don't like boats," Kitty said, as Valentine wrestled the flask back from her. She was wearing jewel tones from head to foot, peacock-green and amaranthine velvet, with turquoise in her ears and on her fingers, contrasting dramatically with her dark curls; apparently, this was what counted as traveling clothes when you were Kitty Stuart. "Man is fallible, therefore boat is fallible. This is just somebody's best attempt at keeping us afloat."

"And that doesn't soothe you?" said Eddie, watching as Nash helped Captain Perkins spool rope with great enthusiasm, while the captain looked as if he'd quite like to keelhaul his employer.

"Good *Lord*, no," said Kitty, shuddering. "Just close your eyes and pretend you're half to three-quarters sprung, swaying safely on dry land in liquor's sweet embrace."

"Er . . ." said Eddie. "All right."

When Valentine shook the flask at her again, she thought it wisest to take it.

Chapter Fourteen

THE JOURNEY WAS NOT QUITE AS HARROWING AS KITTY HAD made out it would be.

For one thing, it only lasted fifteen minutes, aided by the stiff breeze that was apparently blowing them in just the right direction, if Nash's knowledge of sailing was to be believed. Eddie had just become used to the rocking of the boat and the particular deafening quality of the bracing wind when Captain Perkins turned the vessel in readiness to dock it and Eddie got her first proper look at the island.

There was a small jetty, twin to the one on the mainland; it, too, looked ancient, and a bit nervous about the job it had been given. There had clearly been some other wooden structures next to it in the water but these had long rotted away, leaving only dark, jagged stumps rising up above the shallow breakers. A squat, gray stone building with overly decadent arched windows sat behind them—it must have been some sort of boathouse, although there was no obvious way for any boats within to reach the water. Beyond, endless trees and no sign of the house, although Eddie thought she could make out the start of a well-worn path through the woods.

Five pale figures were standing on the shore, clearly not keen to advance onto the jetty itself. As the boat drew closer, Eddie saw an elderly man and woman, standing close enough together that she presumed they might be married, a lady of about five-and-fifty in a very severe dress, a housemaid, and a young, broad man of around eighteen, who stood head and shoulders above the rest.

"That cannot be young *Henry*," said Nash, leaning so far out over the edge of the boat that Mr. Akerele had to grab him by the back of his jacket lest he urgently acquaint himself with the lake bed. "Good God, I think it is. Liza, wasn't he a . . . a shrimpish sort of thing, the last time we saw him?"

"He would have been only thirteen or fourteen then," Liza said, shielding her eyes with one hand to get a better look at the shore. "He was already taller than you."

"Well, yes. He's shrimp, I'm krill."

"Mr. Nicholson," Captain Perkins said in his gravelly voice, nodding to the rope in his hand. "If you don't mind."

Nash clearly didn't mind one bit—in fact, it had become obvious that he thought of himself as a seasoned sailor, even if Captain Perkins's eyebrows vehemently disagreed. He was all too willing to roll up his shirtsleeves and grab at various ropes and pulleys until Mr. Perkins forcefully put the correct ones into his hands. The young, robust man on the shore—Henry—bravely half jogged down the dock to receive them, and Captain Perkins clapped him on the back in a surprisingly good-natured way as he climbed up out of the boat.

"Miss Li," said Albert, offering Rose his hand; he managed to look only briefly surprised and then rearrange his face into pleasant neutrality when Kitty reached him first and took the proffered hand instead, stepping up onto the dock and sighing with obvious relief.

"When we leave, I'll thank you all to knock me out first with either a gallon of laudanum or a large mallet, whichever happens to be closer to hand."

Once they had all clambered out of the boat and the staff had done a lot of bowing and curtsying, there was a brief silence as they considered the luggage-to-servants ratio. Henry, who seemed to be imbued with the strength and pectoral muscles of ten men, somehow managed a trunk in each hand, and strode off up the path through the trees with a promise to come back for the rest. When Albert tried to pick up Rose's trunk, Nash held up a hand to stop him.

"You can't do that and rob him of his sport, the poor fellow lives for it. What else has he got all those muscles for? Leave it here. It's hardly going to be stolen. We're the only living creatures on this island apart from a few spare owls and lost voles."

So it was sans luggage that they all followed Nash and Liza up the path, which sloped gently until it reached the tree line and then became rather steep. Somebody had recently cut back some of the undergrowth—Henry, probably, making use of his enormous biceps—but they were still under constant threat of being jabbed with stray branches or tripping over the roots that had encroached onto the track. The dog loped on ahead, frequently vanishing and reappearing in unexpected places, her nose to the ground. Daylight had already been dwindling when they stepped onto the boat, and the thick canopy of branches overhead made things even murkier.

"Have you brought us here to kill us off one by one?" Kitty asked Nash, sounding not the least bit worried, as if this might in fact be quite an interesting and entertaining outcome. She had hiked up her skirts, revealing pink stockings, and was marching determinedly at the front of the pack.

"If that had been my plan, don't you think I would have elbowed one of you off the boat midway across and blamed it on the boom?"

Kitty did have a point; the whole thing was starting to feel quite ominous as they trudged through the gloom with no signs of civilization in any direction. Eddie lengthened her stride, trying to catch up with Rose so that she could mutter so in her ear, but as she drew nearer Albert offered Rose his arm and she took it, smiling gratefully at him. Eddie let herself fall back, and stayed resolutely silent for the rest of the walk, listening to the sound of the birds and the soft crunch of leaves and sticks underfoot.

Eventually the ground beneath them started to level out. They turned a corner and suddenly the house was right there in front of them, framed neatly through the opening in the trees.

Eddie's first thought was that it was less a house and more a *castle*. It was three stories tall, with small square turrets protruding at each corner, one of which was flying a couple of flags that had been so shredded by the elements that they looked like proudly displayed rags. The house felt strangely hollow, perhaps because almost all of the windows on the uppermost floors were shuttered, and the ones that weren't were dark. Only the lower floors were lit; there was a small stone porch housing the front door, which was ajar and spilling yolk-gold light out onto the worn steps. As they approached, the wind picked up, and one of the flags gave up the ghost entirely and tore itself free, fluttering away across the short lawn and into the trees.

"I love a bad omen," said Valentine.

Dayo laughed resignedly.

"It is not an augury—the house is simply informing us that it knows we are entirely ungovernable," Nash said brightly.

Henry stepped out of the front door, not even slightly out of breath. The rest of the servants were still a little way behind the main party, struggling through the woods with as much luggage as they had been able to carry.

"The fires are lit, sir."

"Very good, Henry," said Nash. "God, what have you been eating? Lesser men?"

"Er . . ." said Henry, nonplussed. "Eggs?"

"I shall have whatever you've been having," said Nash. "Tell your grandmother."

Liza was clearly impatient to get inside, and touched Nash firmly on the arm.

"Stop torturing the poor boy."

"It's not torture!" Nash said, raising his hands to demonstrate his innocence. "It's eggs!"

"Yes. Eggs, sir. Well . . . I will, sir," said Henry, before hurrying away, clearly far more keen on dragging mountains of very heavy luggage uphill than having to continue this conversation about the particulars of his diet.

"Come in, everybody," Liza said, and they all trooped obligingly after her.

The hall they entered was clad in floor-to-ceiling dark wood paneling, with a dramatic bronze chandelier presiding over faded portraits and a hunting tapestry in which a deer was coming to an unfortunate and sticky end. Everything had clearly been recently cleaned, but polish and elbow grease weren't enough to disguise the fact that nothing in the room had been updated since the Stuart era. Eddie could smell something promising roasting in the far reaches of the house, and pressed an admonishing hand to her abdomen when her stomach betrayed her and started gurgling ostentatiously. Nash was speaking to the austerely dressed woman, who appeared to be the housekeeper, the other staff having already deposited some bags and turned around to go and fetch the rest, but he clapped his hands together to call them all to attention.

"We shall have an early dinner shortly, I know everybody is starving. Rooms . . . Well, there is something I need to tell you about the rooms, but you must all put on your bravest faces." Nobody did. "Excellent. Now, the house has suffered some . . . water damage in the past couple of years. There was an absolute rager of a storm, and then a much smaller and more pathetic one, but the two of them compounded to sort of . . . wipe out the top floor."

"Wiped out?" said Valentine. "It looked thoroughly unwiped from out there."

"Do not tempt me into ribaldry with your phrasing," said Nash. "It is still *standing*, but there is quite a large . . . hole. In the roof. I am told."

"You are told, or you've seen it?" asked Dayo.

"It is impossible to miss," said Liza. Her tone indicated that she had perhaps raised, many times, that it was unwise to leave an unmissable hole in the roof of one's home.

"Regardless of the size of the hole—*watch* it—we are now in a very peculiar position. Mrs. Hall tells me that some of the rooms on the first floor have been repurposed as additional bedrooms. Liza and I sleep in the Gold Chamber, but there are three more, as long as nobody takes issue with sleeping in the billiard room."

"Has it still got a billiard table?" Mr. Akerele inquired.

"No, we've had it moved to the long gallery," said Liza.

Valentine raised a hand. "How long is the long gallery?"

"Long," said Nash. "Dash it all, now I've lost count."

"Five on the first floor, yourself and Mrs. Nicholson included," Albert supplied.

"Ah! Yes. Now, on the second floor, I'm afraid the plot thickens. The majority of the bedrooms are not in use due to water damage, but there are three still mostly intact on the north side. Two are just damp around the edges, and one is . . ."

"Birthing new life," Liza said dryly.

"Well. Yes. We could squeeze three of you into the two drier rooms. I think that would do."

"I'll take the billiard room," Valentine said.

"Very good. I thought that perhaps Dayo could take the room next to it, and then the room next to ours . . . Miss Miller?"

"Miss Miller and Miss Li can share the larger second-floor room," Liza said immediately. "They have been close friends since childhood, have they not? I think there is no pair more suited to share. Besides, Miss Stuart is their senior and should certainly not be subjected to the damp air on that floor."

"I will happily share with Mr. Akerele, if he'll have me," said Albert. "And I certainly do not mind taking one of the wetter rooms."

"You and Mr. Akerele are grown men," said Liza. She had the

beginnings of a tic starting up at her temple. "Anyway, ladies like to share rooms. It gives them the chance to be in each other's confidences away from unfriendly ears."

"We don't mind," said Rose. She rarely spoke for Eddie unless committing her to being nicer than Eddie ever would have been herself. "Honestly. You are right, of course, Mrs. Nicholson. We are the best suited."

"Excellent," said Nash, now seeming a little bored of the whole thing. "In that case, we shall have Kitty in the Yew Room next to us, then Mr. Akerele. Valentine has already bagged the billiards. Edie and Miss Li in the Ivy Chamber on the damp floor, and Albert, you can take the Naval Room down the hall. It features the most upsettingly vivid painting of a ship going down in the Channel I have ever beheld, so that ought to give you something bracing to think about as you fall asleep."

The second half of their luggage was brought into the hall and, after a brief recess to divvy it up and a near scuffle when Kitty and Valentine both insisted that a trunk was theirs, the party were led along a narrow passageway to the east stairs, which creaked and groaned at regular and almost musical intervals as they ascended.

"Mrs. Morris will show you to the second floor," Liza said, when the inhabitants of the floor that Eddie was already beginning to think of as "the dry floor" went to find their lodgings.

Mrs. Morris, the elderly cook, seemed put out by them being there at all. She showed Eddie and Rose to their doorway—it was directly adjacent to the stairs, so did not really require much in the way of showing—and then exited immediately with Albert in tow. He gave Rose a cheerful, frilly wave farewell, which made Eddie want to chop his hand off so he might never do it again.

Eddie wasn't sure which had come first—the decor or the name—but the Ivy Chamber certainly lived up to expectations. It was decorated in shades of green and brown—floral green paper on the walls that had gone dark and started to curl in the corners; a matching walnut bed, wardrobe, and dressing table with chipped gold detailing—and there actually seemed to be ivy pushing through the gaps in the window frame, although somebody had recently pruned it. There was a fire lit in the grate, but Eddie could still smell that particular odor that accompanied damp—a gently fetid greenish hum that could not be entirely overruled by the much more pleasant scent of woodsmoke.

"This is nice," Rose said, tentatively sitting down on the edge of the stool at the dressing table.

"You didn't have to volunteer us so willingly for the moldy rooms," Eddie said, marching over to the dresser beside the bed and opening the top drawer suspiciously. The liner was stained, but otherwise it contained nothing offensive.

"Oh, don't gripe at me," said Rose. "Although I must say, this isn't quite what I pictured when I accepted this invitation."

"Don't be a snob. It's an adventure."

"Of course—*I'm* the snob, at your new friend's ancient family estate in the country."

This once could have passed as nothing more than gentle banter between them, but given that Eddie had been struggling to meet Rose's eye with a genuine smile since she heard the news of the engagement, it instead came across as a little barbed.

"Look," Rose said hesitantly, talking into her lap. "This is your scene, not mine. I'm glad of the chance to spend time with Albert, but you and I had better make this trip worthwhile together, too, because I nearly went overboard when Mr. Nicholson pulled on the wrong rope."

"I thought you were here to keep an eye on me and to giggle with Albert," Eddie said bitterly. "Not to make fond memories with me before you become the mistress of Rabbit Manor."

"I'd like to do both," Rose said, with more edge to her voice, "but you're certainly not making me feel very fond of you so far."

The jut of her lip as she pouted was strangely distracting; Eddie was assailed, suddenly, with the memory of running her tongue over it that night in the tree house. It had felt as soft as it looked.

"One last hurrah, then, is it? Before your life is over."

Rose rolled her eyes. "I can assure you that your disapproval has been duly noted. Now will you please stop sulking? It makes me sad."

She really did look quite downcast. It made Eddie feel somewhat monstrous.

"I reserve my right to sulk, but you know I never wish to cause you pain."

"Good," said Rose. "You will remember what I said about being careful, won't you, Ed? I mean . . . I know you never are, but—"

There was a rap at the door. It opened a crack, and a small portion of Nash's face became visible.

"Are you decent?"

"Never," said Eddie, making him laugh. She thought she saw Rose roll her eyes again in her periphery, but decided it must have been a trick of the light.

"Well. True enough. Coming for the house tour?"

"We need to freshen up before dinner," Rose hissed to Eddie, who had immediately jumped up. "And you really shouldn't go *alone* with him, Ed."

"You look plenty fresh to me," Nash said, opening the door fully. "Come on, I'll show you all the ghost's favorite haunts."

Eddie had felt briefly torn, but all was lost at the mention of a ghost.

Chapter Fifteen

"BRACE YOURSELF. I HAVEN'T LOOKED IN HERE FOR YEARS, and I'm told it's frightful. You're not going to faint in horror, are you?"

"No," said Eddie. They were starting their tour at the end of the second floor corridor, outside an ominously dark door. "Are you?"

"I might. Be ready to catch me," Nash said as he turned the handle.

It was very stiff, and he had to shoulder the door hard to get it to move at all. Once it was open, the cloying, damp smell intensified, and Eddie covered her face with her hand as they stepped over the threshold.

The room was cold and dark, the drapes drawn shut, although light was creeping in through the places where the fabric had simply rotted away. One of the windows was clearly broken, its forlorn curtain billowing in the breeze; as they watched, it spat out a scattering of small, dark leaves onto the rug, which may have at one point been blue but was now a mottled sort of black.

Somebody—Henry, Eddie supposed—had mostly stripped the room of furniture, but there was an enormous bed frame up against the east wall that had been left to fend for itself and was slowly giving in to the inevitable. Sprawling mold was feasting on the wallpaper, separate colonies that had started in corners and by window frames and had merged to form new, exciting colors and patterns.

"This is delightful," Eddie said dubiously, and Nash laughed.

"The bed was too big to get out of the door without dismantling the whole thing, and apparently I was asked many times if I consented to them taking an axe to it and did not provide an answer. Ah, well. It was my grandmother's. May it rest in peace. Oh—I wouldn't go much farther, if I were you." Eddie had taken another step into the room; she froze, feeling the floorboard beneath her feet sagging alarmingly. "You might end up in the long gallery by accident."

"What happened?" Eddie said, carefully returning to drier land.

"A very enthusiastic tree took out the window, and the rain seemed to have been coming in sideways. A branch got the roof, too, although it didn't completely collapse in here. Next door is a different matter and is a very alfresco sleeping experience, but we can't investigate further because the door is now warped shut."

"So this is where the ghost lives?"

"Ha!" Nash said. "Good God, no. He takes his breakfast in the South Parlor, like a gentleman."

They passed the Naval Chamber on their way to the west stairs, which were dark and cramped, turning back on themselves dramatically as they descended—"would usually just be for the servants, I suppose, if we were doing anything properly"—and came out into a central corridor like the one on the floor above.

"Now this is the silliest room in the house," Nash said, "but I've found that it does have its uses, especially on rainy days."

He showed her into the long gallery, which was indeed very long. The walls were fitted with paneling that had been painstakingly carved into lush trees, lusty animals, odd symbols, and demonic-looking faces before they gave way to a dingy white; there were light, rectangular patches at intervals where paintings had clearly once hung, and a similar strip on the floor that indicated the previous existence of a rug. The billiard table had been tucked politely into a corner with a sheet over it, as if it were slightly embarrassed to be discovered here.

"What do you do in here?" Eddie said, peering at something abstract carved into the wood and wondering if she was missing the symbolism before realizing that it was a deer whose head had been chipped off.

"Running wild when the weather is poor," Nash said. "Dancing, if we can get it. And our very own version of shuttlecock. I'll teach you, if you're any good with a racket."

The ground floor contained the dining room, which was currently being prepared for their dinner, and the South Parlor, which was light and airy, with so many windows that it almost resembled a greenhouse. The Oak Parlor down the hall was the primary drawing room; it was indeed very oaken, with deep red walls and furniture to match, a grand pianoforte pushed into the corner, and a small sculpture of Hercules wrestling his lion on the windowsill.

Next door was a strange, narrow room that was in use as an armory; it contained row upon row of ancient weaponry bolted to the walls, swords and daggers, maces and axes, a selection of bows, and even a small cannon on its own table.

"The men in my family collect them," Nash said, pulling a face as he fingered the handle of an ornate dirk. "Really disturbing stuff. Ought to just throw them all in the lake and see if some lucky local fellow fetches one out and announces himself king, but I suppose one or two of them might be worth some money if I could bring myself to have them valued."

He ushered her across the corridor to the last room and opened the door with a flourish. Eddie actually almost gasped.

The library was enormous; two stories tall, the second floor a balcony that wrapped around the entire room. The shelves were full of cracked leather spines in navy and maroon and forest green, the titles picked out in faded gilt. The very last of the eve-

ning light filtered in through the high windows, slanting across
the books and armchairs and painting geometric patterns on the
rug. It had the air of a cathedral, something venerated and quietly
holy—until Nash sneezed very loudly and then said, "For *fuck's*
sake."

"This is *amazing*."

"Apparently it is where we store all of our dust."

"But you must get so much *writing* done in here," Eddie said,
walking over to a desk by one of the windows, freshly polished
and with a new pot of ink waiting in the well. She ran a hand over
the mahogany inlay, imagining herself sitting there in glorious
silence with hours ahead of her and writing her only obligation.

"You would think that, wouldn't you?" Nash said lightly. "If
you look out of the window here you can see the terrace, or what
passes for a terrace—you can sit out there and drink your breakfast in the morning when the weather is fine. We might have a
few more good weeks in us before it turns for good. This time
of year the island is really only good for brooding—quick stomp
around, kick a few trees, back inside for whiskey by the fire."

"It is so beautiful," Eddie said, watching as a neat formation
of geese flew across the darkening sky. "I don't know why you
ever leave."

"God, you're easily won," Nash said, grinning warmly at her.
"You're positively swooning. I had no idea that a hovel with a
hole in the roof in the middle of a pond would be the way to your
heart."

"I'm not *swooning*," said Eddie, but she was a bit, in the wake
of the house and its owner. It was all so romantic—the magnificent sweeping vista, the isolation, the estate with all its quirks
and foibles. She wanted to disappear into it and not emerge for
months or years, imbued with the mystery of the place. She
wanted to write in the faded chair by the South Parlor window,
at Nash's antique bureau, on the floor under the cannon table

in the armory. She was jealous, she realized, of the fact that this place belonged to Nash, and Nash to it—that their histories were intrinsically tangled, a legacy and an inheritance that were much bigger than him.

She could tell why he talked it down, why he picked at it and called it a hovel; it was the antithesis of everything he stood for. A yoke around the neck of the revolutionary poet who put no stock in familial wealth and lineage.

It was a very *nice* yoke, though. Not a yoke to be sniffed at, in Eddie's opinion.

"Lord," said a voice from behind them; Dayo had walked in, dressed for dinner, Juno the dog at his heel. "These are a lot of fine, unread books, Nash."

"How do you know I haven't read them?"

"Just based on my knowledge of you as a person," said Mr. Akerele. "Are you giving a tour? Or is it . . . private?"

"No, no, not private," said Nash cheerfully. "But it is over, I'm afraid. I'll show you around after we eat, Dayo, it'll all look a lot better after a few bracing drinks."

"Nicks?" Liza put her head around the door, looking irritated, as if she'd been seeking him for a while. "They're calling us to dinner."

"Excellent!" said Nash. "Follow that woman and she will lead you to the promised land."

The dining room was too cavernous to be cozy, but with the fire lit and the table aglow with candles, it felt as if they were all huddled together in a very atmospheric cave. Eddie found herself sandwiched between Liza and Valentine, the latter of whom kept topping up her wineglass and smoking a pipe between mouthfuls of soup. Kitty told a wild story about a sitting gone wrong—an attempt to paint a member of the nobility that had almost landed her in prison—and it kept them all entertained through the entire first course and well into the main.

"You know Donne went to prison," said Nash. "And Thelwall. And Chaucer. All great thinkers should."

"Oh, well, what's good for Thelwall and Chaucer," Kitty said, rolling her eyes. "*I* don't believe one must suffer for one's art, Nathaniel."

"Not my name," Nash said good-naturedly.

"Nashaniel—"

"Oh, come on. Now you're just being silly."

"I *enjoy* making art. I don't have to storm off into the wilderness to stub my toe and have a weep about it just to rustle up some inspiration. This idea that everything must come from pain, that even poetry about love and joy must be tinged with the exquisite agony of mortality . . . it's all very sad and morbid."

"But you make some truly depressing art sometimes," Valentine countered. "I have seen your portraits of men returned from war—they were harrowing."

"Oh, God, yes, when the mood takes me. But I don't *manufacture* the mood. All I am saying is, if I make something out of joy, if everybody who beholds it feels that joy and their life is improved, however fleetingly, because of it . . . is that not worth merit?"

Eddie cleared her throat. "I agree with Miss Stuart."

"Kitty," said Kitty.

"All right, I agree with *Kitty*."

"Expand," said Nash.

"What?"

"Oh, you don't have to turn every dinner party into a debate in the House of Lords, Nash," Liza said despairingly, accepting another glass of wine from Mr. Akerele opposite her.

"Defend yourself," Nash said, ignoring his wife, waving his knife at Eddie as if he were about to use it to spar with her.

Eddie glanced at Rose, who was studying her with a carefully neutral expression.

"Well, I think . . . I think that, as Kitty says, if you try to dictate the precise emotions that can result in great art, you will only restrict it. And . . . no good art ever came from imposing arbitrary restrictions. Even if those restrictions are imposed by so-called artists themselves."

Valentine cheered and clapped her on the shoulder; Kitty laughed and raised her glass. Eddie went pink, pleased with herself for holding her own but trying not to let it show. Down the table, she saw Rose say something quietly to Albert; for some reason it prompted a spike of unease in Eddie's stomach—the worry that perhaps Rose thought her pretentious and was telling Albert so behind her hand.

"I'd be perfectly happy for you to go to prison, Nash," said Mr. Akerele. "Happy indeed, if you were to do it in pursuit of the betterment of this country and the freedoms of your fellow man, and not because you are so afraid of your editor that you would rather be starved and beaten and set upon by rats than simply sit down at your nice comfortable desk and finish writing your novel."

"All right, all right. You've all made your points. You villains can stop tormenting me now and eat all my food, warm yourselves by my fires, sleep in my comfortable beds . . ."

"Comfortable?" said Valentine. "I think mine is made out of old shipping crates. I sat down on it and almost fell through to the floor."

"Would you prefer to sleep on the billiard table?"

"Is it structurally sound?"

"If you're a billiard ball."

"Valentine, if your bed is not to your liking, we'll have the servants make other arrangements," Liza said firmly. "Or you can sleep in ours."

"I'm flattered, but really, Liza, I think of the two of you like siblings. *My* siblings, not each other's siblings . . . although actually, if you're mine, I suppose you're each other's, too . . ."

Liza sighed. "We would, of course, no longer be occupying the bed."

"You know, she was being very nice to you," Nash said, raising his eyebrows at Valentine. "What a thing to squander so early in the trip."

It went on in this fashion right through to pudding. Eddie noticed that Rose and Albert continued to be comparatively quiet, preferring to confer with each other down at the end of the table or listen silently to all the rest while they ate their food. Nash and Valentine steadily drank their way through quite a lot of claret and ended up trying to converse in what sounded like an odd form of Greek, leaving Eddie and Liza trapped between them.

"I feel I should apologize for the state of the house," Liza said, as Valentine dragged a chair around them to sit closer to Nash. "Unfortunately, my husband does not feel particularly inclined to manage it, and barely gave the staff notice that we were returning. The poor things probably haven't slept for days."

"Nonsense, I think it's wonderful," Eddie said earnestly. "It's the best place I have ever seen. I should like to hole up here forever."

Liza looked at her as if she were more than a little deranged.

"Oh . . . you are too kind. You and Miss Li should let me know if your room becomes unbearable. I don't imagine you want to sleep on the billiard table, but I'm sure we could—"

"Here, Edie, you look like a pagan at heart—have you read Homer?" Nash said, leaning across the table and lightly tapping Eddie's wrist with his fingers.

"Let's go through to the drawing room," said Liza. "It is far more agreeable there. Lingering in here like cave bats, we are all liable to catch a chill."

The party obliged. The Oak Parlor was indeed much more homely than the dining room; once the eight of them had situated themselves around the fire, Eddie could almost forget that somewhere above them, the roof looked as if a giant had attempted to use it as a bowling green.

Eddie had tried to follow Nash, Kitty, and Valentine over to the window, where they were lighting their pipes, but had somehow found herself steered toward the fire by Liza, who had similarly ensnared Rose. Juno the dog came with them, collapsing into a large heap by the hearth with a contented sigh. Eddie listened to Rose and Liza discuss the furniture, the weather, and Rose's engagement—at this point Eddie started trying to wrestle with Juno rather than have to listen, and received a rather perplexed look from the dog in return—and tried to think of ways to extract herself, so that she might go over and join the smokers.

She had just managed to get to her feet when Nash stretched, put down his glass, and yawned indulgently.

"I'm half-dead. Let's retire so that we can seize tomorrow rather more firmly by the scruff."

In the darkness, lit only by smoldering coals, Rose and Eddie's room looked almost stately. The bedclothes had clearly been freshly changed, two warming pans slid into them to stave off the cool, damp air. With no maid forthcoming, they took down their hair and undressed quickly in silence, and then both half ran to get under the covers, Eddie swearing under her breath and laughing at the shock of the cold. She felt a very frigid foot brush against her leg and yelped in indignation, making Rose giggle into her pillow. The odd atmosphere that Eddie thought she had felt between them broke as abruptly as a dropped egg.

"Now I remember how dreadful you are to share a bed with," she griped. "Like a fish at a dance, wriggling all over the place."

Rose was silent for a moment and then laughed to herself.

"What?"

"A fish at a ball would dance . . . the cod-rille."

"I am going to suffocate you with this pillow," Eddie said serenely. "Hold still, will you? Otherwise I shall find it quite upsetting."

She rolled over and tried to press the promised pillow to Rose's face while Rose squeaked her protests, laughing and trying to slide out of Eddie's grip; Rose succeeded in batting the pillow away, knocking it onto the floor, and Eddie seized her wrists instead.

"I don't know why you won't just take it on the chin and die quietly," Eddie said.

Her face was rather close to Rose's; once again she found her gaze involuntarily dropping to Rose's lips. Rose didn't say anything. She just looked up at Eddie from under the sweep of her lashes, slightly out of breath, her hair a mess against the pillow. It took a moment for Eddie to realize it was odd that she still had Rose pinned; she released her abruptly and then leaned over to collect her pillow from the floor.

"Oh, wonderful, it smells like damp wood now and has likely become a haven for silverfish."

"*You* try to kill *me*," Rose said, still sounding a bit breathless, "and somehow *I'm* the one to blame."

Eddie just ruffled her hair and then retreated to her own side of the bed, pulling the covers up to her eyes for warmth. She fell asleep listening to the strange creaks of the house, the sound of the wind moaning ominously overhead, and Rose's soft, comforting breathing in the dark beside her.

Dear Mother and Father,

We have arrived at the house after two days of travel, and Mr. and Mrs. Nicholson have made us very welcome—our every need is catered for, and we are already residing in great comfort, for the house is beautiful and well kept. From my bedroom on the second floor I can see out over the lake; it is the perfect place for inspiration to take me by the hand and force me to write.

The other guests are very genial, and I have already had a number of scintillating conversations with them about literature, politics, the construction of boats, and the like. I imagine we shall be very happy here for however long the Nicholsons will have us.

Rose also sends her best, and adds that Amelia should check the _Gazette_ dated from the day we departed from town for a fascinating story about horse psychology that she read on the carriage ride here. Apparently horses hold grudges!!

Yours,
Eddie

Chapter Sixteen

THE FIRST WEEK AT BEDE HOUSE WAS A DREAM.

The weather bucked up its ideas and the house was almost permanently lit by soft, syrupy autumn sunshine that made them all feel indulgent and lazy. The days settled into a pattern; those who were awake early would drift about the house or convene quietly in the parlors to drink tea and warm up by the fires, and then Nash would emerge just before noon and they would eat a breakfast that was logistically more of a luncheon and lasted hours. This was followed by a walk around the island, an expedition that Nash led with military enthusiasm while Liza entertained those who remained in the Oak Parlor. Everybody went their separate ways in the afternoon, bedding down in various corners to read or write or nap, until it was time to dress for dinner. Kitty set up in the South Parlor so that she could stand at an easel looking out over the lake and paint; as a result it constantly smelled like oils, and anybody who sat down on the furniture was liable to come away with flakes or smudges of paint somewhere about their person.

Rose expressed an interest in expanding her reading on the subject of abolition, and she and Mr. Akerele took to sitting out on the south patio in the bright afternoons engaged in long, involved discussions about his work; sometimes Eddie joined them, but mostly she used the time to write, sitting either at Nash's desk in the library—which, to her knowledge, he hadn't used once—or curled up in the corner of the South Parlor in a patch of sun, watching Kitty paint, her gaze often wandering to the backs of Dayo's and Rose's heads through the window. Albert ambled through every now and then, complimenting Kitty on her work or asking Eddie how things were going before disappearing again. He seemed to enjoy being in a constant state of motion, going for walks by himself in addition to the scheduled daily afternoon excursion. By contrast, Valentine always seemed to be stationary, taking long naps whenever possible in odd places and remonstrating loudly when roused from them. They only seemed to come fully alive in the evenings, and would often entertain the others with snatches of songs and enthusiastic performances on the pianoforte, somehow managing to keep a pipe or a drink in one hand the entire time.

It was as if Eddie had opened a door and stumbled into a world that she had always longed for, but never quite dared believe existed: a world where tradition and propriety were practically obsolete, and ladies and gentlemen treated one another as equals, without any of the usual daily fuss or pointless rituals to maintain acceptable standards. Nobody bothered standing when she entered a room; equally, nobody batted an eyelash when she came to breakfast with her hair unpinned or with ink smudged the lengths of her fingers. At Bede House, Nash was king—and he was extremely lenient with his subjects.

It was almost like the freedom of childhood, except that people kept handing Eddie glasses of wine.

"The thing about the island," Nash said to Eddie the first time they set out for a walk, "is that it looks both smaller and larger than it is. If you whiz around it by boat on a windy day, it looks minuscule, barely big enough to hold the house. But the woods tricksy and quarrelsome, and even the best of men might find elves lost in them."

ntine, who only attended this first walk and then declared business unsavory, snorted. "You mean *you* get lost in o many drinks or one of Kitty's special pipes."

Eddie discovered on this walk that the woods encircled the island almost completely. The only bare patches were the rocky outcrop that led to the cliffs and the stunted, sloping lawns around the house. Various genres of waterfowl inhabited the underbrush and the stony beaches that poked out from the trees. When they reached the boathouse, Eddie peered through the cobwebby window and discovered that it did in fact contain a rowing boat, which looked as if it had been made for a child, and all manner of other miscellanea: an old kitchen table; a stained and torn chaise; a broken bathing machine with only two wheels; a net and bucket; and a half-sanded rocking horse.

"Well," Dayo remarked, "this looks rather cursed."

Eddie enjoyed their walks, primarily because Liza always stayed up at the house. She was beginning to notice that Liza liked to insert herself into conversations between Nash and Eddie, or to call Nash away to some task whenever they snatched a moment of privacy. It seemed that her desire to be ever-present did not overpower her aversion to walking loops around the island. In fact, after the first two walks, the participants narrowed down to only Eddie, Nash, Albert, and Dayo, the latter of whom were happy to lag behind, going at an ambling pace rather than a brisk trot. It was not in Nash's nature to amble or to make accommodations for those who did, which came as somewhat of a surprise to Eddie, who had seen him engage in quite an impressive amount of lounging. The dog took their walks very seriously; she gave Nash baleful looks when Eddie tried to induce her to chase a stick or a pebble, as if Eddie were embarrassing herself.

"She's far too high-minded for that sort of thing," Nash said at the end of the week, watching as Eddie tried to make a bit of tree branch look more enticing with a seductive wiggle. "Not for her the baser joys of dirt and twigs. Recite poetry for her instead. She loves a bit of Pope, don't you, Juno? *Why dimly gleams the visionary sword?*"

He had raised his voice to a shout, and in response the dog

wagged her tail and barked; Nash was delighted, giving her a firm rub about the ears and then slipping her something from his pocket.

"What on earth was that?"

"Ham," he said, as if it were the most natural thing in the world.

"You have pocket ham?"

"Everybody should have pocket ham when setting out on an expedition," he said seriously. "You never know when you might fall and twist your ankle and be at the mercy of whatever you thought to pack. Oh, look there—a nest!"

There was indeed a very crude bird's nest in one of the trees ahead; when they approached it, they found two perfect, smooth eggs.

"You see," Nash said triumphantly. "I would now have a perfectly good breakfast of ham and pigeon's eggs in my pocket, and what would you have?"

"No pockets," Eddie said, holding up her empty hands.

"You would starve, unless we had *both* fallen and twisted our ankles, in which case I suppose I should give you half my provisions."

Nash reached into the nest.

"Oh, don't," said Eddie. "Leave the pigeons be."

"Nonsense, they'll only lay more. Listen—we shall take them up to the house and candle them to check for occupants. If they're empty, we have provided for ourselves magnificently. If not . . . I suppose we'll have to train them to race, and carry letters, and defecate on debt collectors and newspaper editors."

He pocketed the eggs along with the ham and they stomped companionably on through the woods, the sound of Albert and Dayo talking reduced to a gentle murmur behind them.

"How's the writing going?" Nash said, as he held out a hand to help Eddie traverse a large log.

"Very well! I cannot help but be inspired here. My heroine is currently emboldened by her victories, throwing herself headlong into her new life, the obstacles as yet unseen."

"You must let me read some. My curiosity is piqued, and I cannot unpique it until I have imbibed the words of the great Edith Miller."

"Oh," said Eddie. "Well. It's not quite ready yet."

"Nonsense, Edie. I can hardly write to my editor without knowing what I'm recommending. I'm sure it will be marvelous already. Let me have a peek, when we get back."

"No," Eddie said quickly. She *had* thought that things were going rather well, but the prospect of Nash as a reader made her feel as if she ought to pitch everything into the fire and begin anew. She took a breath, and found herself able to be slightly more reasonable. It probably wasn't a total disaster. It might even be quite good. "Well. All right. Tomorrow."

"Tomorrow, aha! Then I shall be scrupulous in my nagging."

"Are *you* finding time to write?" Eddie said tentatively.

Unless he was doing it somewhere between the hours of two o'clock in the morning and midday, she thought she already knew the answer.

"Here and there," Nash said, shrugging. "I'm in my reading phase. Just devouring everything, pulping it for nourishment, hoping inspiration blooms. I'm feeling very Homeric at the moment—you know at Harrow I was quite the little Greek scholar, really just a complete bore about the whole thing . . ."

As they emerged from the trees near the house, Nash giving some meandering speech about the many potential meanings of the word "polytropos," Eddie gazed out over the lake and spotted something on the far shore.

"What's that?" she said, shielding her eyes and pointing. "In the water."

Nash tried to follow her gaze, frowning, and then arranged

himself very close to her so that he might see from her perspective. His cheek briefly brushed against hers, a quick rasp of stubble and warm skin, and Eddie flinched, immediately feeling foolish when he didn't react at all.

He smelled rather nice. Pepper and musk. Eddie hoped that her face was already ruddy enough from the wind that he wouldn't notice any additional blushing.

"Kingdom Animalia, class Mammalia, species . . . *Persona loci*. They live in one of the nearby villages. I suppose it's one of the last sensible days for swimming."

Eddie watched as the pinkish shapes splashed about in the shallows, and then realized with a start what she was looking at.

"Are they *naked*?"

"I certainly hope so," said Nash. "You know, they make a good point—we should swim soon, before the rain comes in."

"Naked?" Eddie said, before she could stop herself, sounding prudish and horrified.

"*You* may do as you like, you rapscallion—I shall avert my eyes like a proper gentleman. Ah, here come the strollers—let's get inside and have some tea, and then we can enlighten everybody with our proposition. Don't tell them you wish to do it in the nude, though, Edie—best to ease them in gently, in my experience."

Eddie was still red and choking out denials as they walked into the South Parlor, where Rose now seemed to be sitting for Kitty, who was making a sketch. Liza was in an armchair by the fire; she frowned when she saw Nash and Eddie enter, closing her book in quite a pointed way.

"You've been gone awhile," she said, but Nash ignored her entirely, shrugging off his jacket and patting down his pockets.

"Kitty, have you got much in the way of snuff? I find myself at a loss."

"In the drawing room," Kitty said, not looking up from her work. "Behind the candelabra."

"Why do you never ask *me* to sit for you? Miss Li has been here for five minutes and you have already talked her onto your stool."

Kitty rolled her eyes. "You know I would dearly love to paint you. I always say that a subject in turmoil makes for the most exquisite art, and there is nobody *ever* in more turmoil than you—but alas, you are incapable of sitting still."

Nash turned to pull a face at her from halfway through the door.

"Oh, fetch a candle," called Eddie.

"Whatever for?"

"The eggs!"

"Oh, Christ." He picked up his jacket, which he had tossed unceremoniously onto the side table, rummaged in the pocket, and then grimaced. "Well. Just ham for us, perhaps, next time we're stranded."

He held out a hand to show Eddie the sad remains of the eggs: one entirely broken, the contents drained away, and the other stoven in at the top, leaking a single blood-pink tear into his palm.

Swimming had been arranged for the following day if the weather held, and it did. Nash emerged unusually early, scruffy-haired and beaming, and announced that they should go before luncheon and then come back up to the house to eat and revive themselves by the fire.

"Nothing better for the appetite than swimming," he said, flicking Valentine on the head as he walked past. Valentine just scowled at him.

Mrs. Hall was sent to find the linen towels, and then parceled them out to the guests, looking grim.

"Mrs. Hall, we are not going to drown," said Nash.

Mrs. Hall did not seem convinced. Based on her general demeanor, Eddie rather thought that it was the prospect of the amount of administrative work required if they died that was making her glum, not the idea that they might lose their lives.

They all gamboled down to the dock in high spirits, the promise of doing something foolish lending an air of hysteria to the proceedings. Juno bounded along ahead of them, barking madly; Albert and Valentine, who had announced they were not to swim, were the only two to keep level heads. When they reached the water, the reality of the plan slowed all but Nash in their tracks.

"Bunch of bloody cowards and shit-sacks, the lot of you," he said, already yanking off his stockings. "Now look away or live with the image of me in a state of undress forever. I don't mind which."

"Ladies," Liza said, gesturing toward the trees. "If you'll follow me."

"You're going in, then?" Eddie said to Rose, holding a branch out of the way for her as they followed Liza into the woods. "Good Lord, what would Ava Forester say if she could see you now?"

"Yes," said Rose. "Well . . . If there is any place to behave like a fool, it's here, where nobody with better sense can see us. And . . . well, we did have such fun that time in Brighton."

They all began undressing, hanging their dresses from the branches and then standing around laughing and shivering in their shifts.

"If you get into trouble," Kitty said, shaking out her hair, "just scream as loud as you can, and I shall come and fish you out. I am a very strong swimmer."

Eddie shot a wide-eyed look of alarm at Rose, who laughed.

When they made it back down to the shore, Nash and Dayo were already in the water.

"How is it, Mr. Akerele?" Liza called, perhaps suspecting that Nash would not give an accurate report of the temperature.

"Cold," he said. "But bearable once you are submerged."

"Listen to the man and submerge yourselves at once!" Nash shouted, before launching himself into a spirited backstroke. Where his shirt was open, Eddie could clearly see his pale chest, covered in whorls of fine, dark hair; she looked away quickly and was greeted by the sight of Rose, her hair swinging loose as she dipped a toe in the water and shuddered.

"Oh, hell," said Eddie; she grabbed Rose by the hand and dragged her into the water, both of them gasping and shrieking. There were sharp stones beneath their feet, and going slowly just made them hurt all the more, so they pushed on until they reached the carpet of soft, muddy sediment instead. The water was up to their waists now, rendering their shifts completely transparent; for decency's sake they plunged fully into deeper water, Eddie misjudging the velocity required and ending up completely submerged. She came up choking and spluttering, shaking her head like a dog.

"You look like some . . . some creature from the deep," Rose said through gritted teeth, kicking vigorously to stay warm, her hair still mostly dry. "Limbless kraken."

"Some sympathy would be nice," Eddie said, clumsily wiping dark tendrils of hair away from her face.

"Behave less foolishly and you will receive more compassion."

Kitty and Liza entered the water with much less fanfare; they simply strode out and in, no screaming or splashing, and then started swimming leisurely laps. Eddie attempted to emulate Kitty, who was employing big, sweeping strokes, and immediately almost drowned again. She backed up until she could stand on the bottom, just her head and shoulders above the surface.

Rose suddenly gave an earsplitting shriek and rocketed toward Eddie, flailing about as she attempted to move faster, spray flying.

"Something touched my leg!" she gasped, throwing herself into Eddie's arms; Eddie prepared to be capsized and was surprised to find herself more than capable of supporting Rose's weight in the water. She instinctively grabbed Rose's legs, as Rose threw her arms around Eddie's neck.

"What's this now? Do you not love *all* of God's creatures?"

"Not the ones that brush up against me in the dark," Rose muttered, pressing in closer. It was almost as if neither of them were wearing their shifts at all; Eddie could feel every curve of Rose's body against her, her breath hot against Eddie's now-freezing neck. Eddie shivered, and Rose's fingers curled in her hair.

"This is deeply inappropriate, Miss Li. Ugh—stop wiping your nose on my neck."

"I'm not wiping my nose on anything," Rose said. "My nose is just wet. All of me is wet."

"Lovely," said Eddie, abruptly letting go of her; she fell hard into the water with a satisfying splash and came up with murder in her eyes.

Eddie ducked beneath the waves, feeling as if she needed a moment to collect herself, and then let out a near-silent, bubbly yelp when she felt Rose grab hold of her by the ankle and pull.

They embarrassed themselves for a while longer without doing any real swimming before Eddie found herself too cold to continue; she called up to Valentine and Albert for a towel, and Albert came to the shoreline to give her one, his eyes firmly closed as she exited the water. Rose had swum over to Kitty and was kicking about on her back, listening to instruction. Nash and Dayo seemed to be racing each other; they were much farther out than the ladies, just two dots above the small, choppy waves.

Eddie shook even as she wrapped the towel around her; the day was clear but there was a strong, stiff breeze ridding the trees of their leaves and prickling her all over with gooseflesh. Juno the dog was lying flopped at Valentine's feet; she lifted her head when Eddie joined them, but then sighed and settled it back between her enormous paws.

"I think this will be the last good day," Albert said, sitting back down next to Valentine on the dock.

"What will you do when it's too cold for walks?" Eddie said, rubbing at her arms, trying to keep her teeth from chattering.

"Oh, it's never too cold for walks! I shall walk come rain or shine, sleet or snow."

"Age has addled you," Valentine said, also taking a towel and arranging it like a winter shawl. Albert just laughed.

"You are probably right. Gosh, we are rather exposed here—I wonder how the house will weather it when winter really takes hold."

"It won't," said Valentine. "I imagine the whole rotten lot of it will come down and bury us under it."

"I suppose when the late Mr. Nicholson ran the place they would have been making it ready for the bad weather for months already. He always seemed the practical sort."

Valentine snorted. "*Practical?* The last Mr. Nicholson would have been running about absolutely blind drunk, hunting Nash with a Baker rifle, but yes—I suppose *someone* would have been giving the orders."

"What?" said Eddie.

Albert looked just as startled as she felt.

"He was *not* a pleasant man in private. I suppose he didn't *actually* hunt children, but he certainly liked to threaten it. Just before he died there was some terrible business with a maid here—an argument, an altercation between them. Nash doesn't particularly like to speak of it, but she went over the cliffs. He was the one who found the poor woman washed up onshore."

"*What?*" said Eddie again.

Albert frowned. "He's never told me any of this."

"Close your mouth, Edith. You are not a fish," said Valentine. "It's true, I'm afraid. All sorts of dreadful things have happened here—why do you think Nash is always going on about ghosts and curses? The old man tried to die here, too—his heart—but they managed to get him to shore. I think he ended up passing on in some sort of cart provided by a local. One can only imagine the depths of his horror."

"I don't suppose he minded the cart," said Eddie. "He probably minded the dying more."

"I wouldn't count on it. Terrible snobs, the Nicholsons. Really flagellated Nash for not making more of himself. They hated poetry, which I think is why he took to it. Nothing more embarrassing than having to tell the fellows at the club that your son is a *poet*. Honestly, I think almost everything he's managed in his career is down to spite. It was almost a shame when they died—it mellowed him toward them, and they deserved none of it. I suppose Byron gets the brunt of his ire now."

"Yes, why *is* he so down on Lord Byron?" said Albert. "I have always thought the two of them could have been firm friends."

"Oh, well, that's no mystery. They were at Harrow at the same time, as you know, and I believe they were friendly enough. I don't think they saw much of each other after school. Nash was just working himself up to publish when Byron put out *Pilgrimage* and the whole country went mad for him. Nash's first poem met quite an underwhelming reception—undeserved, in my opinion—and the rest, as they say, is history. They are far too similar in temperament and ambition to have ever been true friends. Irreconcilable similarities. I hear Byron has precious few friends anyhow—even Shelley he calls *the snake* and maligns in select company."

"Goodness," said Albert.

"*Fascinating*," breathed Eddie. She had been hanging on Valentine's every word, her eyes wide; all of her energy was going into staying warm, which left absolutely no reserves for trying to appear worldly and unimpressed by stories of infighting in the ranks of the literary elite.

"Oh dear. Obviously, I have said too much, as Eddie's brain has imploded. You must both be far more discreet than I. Gin?"

Valentine was holding up a flask; Albert shook his head, but Eddie took a nip to stave off the cold. Nash was coming out of the lake, not at all shy about the fact that he was only wearing a shirt down to his knees, and that it was not particularly opaque; Eddie stared fixedly at a pebble the shape of France near her foot as he came to claim a towel and then wrapped it haphazardly around himself like a toga.

"Refreshing, is it not? Warms the blood! Arm-wrestles the mind into submission! Is that gin?"

He took a deep pull from Valentine's flask and sighed in a very satisfied fashion.

"You ought to get out of those wet clothes, Edie—you'll freeze like that."

Eddie just blushed and pulled her blanket a little tighter around her, not wanting to begin the arduous task of traipsing back into the woods and reclaiming her dress. Juno sat up and gave an odd little grunting bark, her eyes fixed on the water; Eddie followed her gaze, scanning for the ladies' impromptu swimming lesson.

"I can only see Kitty and Liza there, and Dayo farther out. Where's Rose?"

Albert leaned forward, squinting. "She can't be far away . . . ah, yes. There she is. She's by herself, closer in."

Something about the way she was moving felt odd to Eddie. She didn't even seem to be attempting to swim, just bobbing in place in the water. Juno seemed agitated; she took a step forward and then stopped, looking at Eddie with urgency, as if to ask what on earth she was going to do about this.

"Is she all right?" Eddie said to Nash, who had turned to look. She waved a hand at Rose, but Rose didn't seem to see her.

"Oh, yes. Just floating about like a duckling. Now, I know just

the thing for getting warm—if I throw down the gauntlet, will
you consent to a footrace, Miss Miller? I know it's not the done
thing for ladies to run, but I think it's a skill best practiced often,
in case of—"

"I think something is wrong," Eddie insisted.

Albert had snapped to attention, and was shading his eyes
with one hand as he attempted to get a better look.

"If something were *wrong*, would she not be shouting and
waving for us to come to her aid?"

"I don't know," Eddie said, starting to feel faint stirrings of
panic. "Perhaps she can't. Will you go in and see? Just to ease
my mind."

Albert got to his feet.

Nash grimaced. "I'm just out! I cannot go back in now, the
very thought of it is repulsive."

"I shall go," said Albert, hurriedly taking off his shoes. Valentine was appraising him with raised eyebrows.

"I thought you said you weren't a particularly good swimmer."

"I don't swim if I have a choice," said Albert as he shrugged
out of his jacket, already on the move. "But in this case—I do not
have a choice."

He ran off down to the shore still mostly dressed, and Nash
laughed after him.

"Albert, don't be ridiculous—you've still got your breeches on!"

Eddie didn't think it was ridiculous at all—in fact, as Albert
plunged into the water and began swimming clumsily toward
Rose, she was starting to feel light-headed with panic. Juno had
followed him and was standing in the gentle surf, keeping watch.
Once he reached Rose, Albert hooked one arm around her and
started towing her back to shore; Eddie's pounding heart was just
beginning to slow when she caught a proper look at the expression on Rose's face. She was immediately up and running down
to meet them, stumbling on the rocks, ignoring the stabbing
pains in her feet.

Eddie reached them just as they found dry land, and Albert laid Rose as gently as possible on a bed of pebbles and pushed her hair out of her face as she coughed wretchedly.

"Bring towels!" he shouted to Nash and Valentine.

Eddie immediately took off her own and laid it over Rose, taking hold of her limbs and rubbing them hard in an attempt to warm her. She was ice-cold to the touch and deathly pale, her eyes wide and unfocused, her teeth chattering despite the sun.

"Rose? You're all right now. We've got you."

"I can see that," Rose said very faintly, her voice thin and scratchy. Juno tried to nose at her face, and Eddie pushed her away.

"What *happened*?" she said, as she and Albert hauled Rose upright so that Eddie could put the towel around her shoulders. She continued to shake; Eddie shifted so that she could pull Rose against her, trying to warm her with her body as she rubbed vigorously at her shoulders, her arms—every conceivable part of her that she could reach.

"I don't . . . I don't know," Rose said through violent shivers. "I was . . . I was fine, but then my foot caught on something, and . . . by the time I got it free I was . . . having trouble staying afloat. I tried to shout for Kitty, but . . ."

She succumbed to another round of chattering teeth just as Valentine arrived with the remaining towels and started heaping them on top of her. The other swimmers seemed to have finally noticed the commotion, and were making their way back to shore.

"It's no good, she needs to be properly warm and dry," said Albert. "Mr. Nicholson, would you run ahead to the house and ask them to prepare a bath?"

Nash looked slightly puzzled by this request.

"Well. I suppose—"

"I'll go," said Valentine, already half jogging away.

Liza, Kitty, and Dayo were approaching; Eddie tried not to

look directly at them, as they were rather indecent, and then realized that since giving Rose her towel she was faring no better.

Liza surveyed the scene in front of her and then took charge.

"We should carry her back to the house—Mr. Rednock? Mr. Akerele?"

Between Albert and Dayo they managed to lift her, and then they all started walking slowly up the hill, Eddie reluctant to let go of Rose's hand.

"If nobody is going to say it, then I am," said Kitty. "We are all just going to have to be *very* grown-up about the fact that every one of us is practically naked."

Chapter Seventeen

WHEN THEY REACHED THE HOUSE, ROSE ASKED IN A VERY small voice to please be put down; when they tried, however, she almost fell over, and had to be righted again by many helpful hands.

"The ladies will take her from here," Liza said firmly.

She and Kitty took a shoulder each and helped her up the stairs, Eddie following. They met Valentine on the landing.

"They drew a bath in my room, as the tub was already there."

The billiard room was wallpapered and upholstered in an assortment of greens from olive to juniper, to match its usual occupant; a bed had been pushed into one corner, and there were hurriedly tidied piles of books and clothes on the chest of drawers. As they sat Rose down on a chair, the middle-aged maid—whom Eddie had come to learn was named Anne—came in with a heavy bucket of water and poured it into the mostly filled tub behind the screen.

"I shall help her bathe," Eddie said. "Thank you so much for your help, Kitty. Mrs. Nicholson."

Liza nodded. As they left the room, Eddie heard her instructing Anne to run down to the beach and fetch back their dresses. Eddie had quite forgotten them in all the confusion. She still had one hand on Rose's shoulder, the other testing the temperature of the water, which was steaming softly in the firelight.

"Just a moment and we shall have you hot as a ham, all right? God, you gave me a scare."

"I'm all right, really," Rose said, her voice insubstantial. "Only . . . I did worry they might insist on helping me bathe, and . . . and I think we've all seen enough of each other today to last a lifetime."

"Ha! The image of Albert coming out of the lake with his breeches all wet and see-through will haunt me until the day I die," Eddie said, helping Rose around the screen and to the tub.

"Oh, don't be horrid, he just saved my life," Rose said, clinging to the edge of the bath for support. "Will you peel my shift off? I'll turn around. Don't look."

"I've seen you naked before, you know," Eddie said, unwrapping Rose from her blankets and then getting to work on her sodden shift, averting her eyes as requested.

"Yes, but . . . but we were fourteen, and it was dark," Rose said, shuddering as Eddie pulled her clothes free. "We were only saplings. *Christ*. Help me in, will you? I don't want to survive the drowning only to . . . to dash my brains out in the billiard room. I'd be so embarrassed."

Eddie laughed and did as she was told, relieved beyond measure that Rose was feeling well enough to make jokes; she let Rose lean heavily on her arm as she climbed carefully into the tub, hissing gently through her teeth as the hot water hit her legs. She sank down fully with a sigh of relief, and Eddie pulled round the chair and took a seat, so that all she could see of Rose was her head and shoulders.

"Better?"

"God, yes. I feel like . . . soup."

"Oh, dear. It seems that almost drowning has made you very stupid."

"I don't care," Rose said, closing her eyes and tilting back her head, her face shrouded in steam. "I am stupid and I am happy and I am soup."

"Well then, I am very pleased for you," said Eddie. She shuffled the chair closer to the fire, suddenly realizing how cold *she* was and trying to be very brave about it. She wrapped both of her arms around herself and pulled her knees up to her chin, precariously balanced. "Valentine was telling us that this place really is cursed, and now I think I almost believe it."

"Not cursed," said Rose. "I was just out of my depth. It was my fault."

"That's just what the curse *wants* you to think," said Eddie. "All sorts of terrible things have happened here, you know. A maid was drowned ... Valentine half admitted that Nash's father had something to do with it. It's a wonder that Nash likes it here at all."

Rose laughed weakly. "God. I don't think it's a wonder. He seems the sort to *love* terrible things. He must be frightfully disappointed that I didn't drown."

"How could you say such a thing!" exclaimed Eddie. "Of course he doesn't want you to *drown*."

"I would not be so sure," said Rose. She opened her eyes and frowned at Eddie, who was shaking despite her efforts. "Ed. You're shivering."

"No I'm not," said Eddie. "I'm just doing a little dance, to lift your spirits."

"Get in the tub," Rose said.

Eddie just frowned at her.

"But *you're* in the tub."

"Yes, shrewdly observed. I shall move up. There's room for two if we sort of ... fold ourselves in half."

"Just a second ago you were telling me to avert my eyes from your maidenly form."

"Yes, well, I'd like you to stay an enthusiastic inhabitant of *your* maidenly form. You're the one convinced we're living under a cursed roof—wouldn't it be just the sort of thing to happen? For you to heroically bring me to safety and help me get warm, and then crawl off into a corner, unnoticed, to die of pneumonia?"

"There wasn't much heroic about it. The others did the heavy lifting, I mostly just panicked attractively," Eddie said, but she was already standing to take off her shift. "All right, fold yourself—I'm coming in."

The water was deliciously hot, almost to the point of pain, exactly how Eddie liked it. She had to crouch awkwardly to get herself situated, and inevitably kept accidentally knocking her legs against Rose's as they worked out the logistics.

"You are far too tall," Rose grumbled, eyes closed, as Eddie finally settled herself, knees once again pulled up around her chin.

"You should not have invited me into your tub if you were just going to gripe about it. I was perfectly happy to die a martyr." It wasn't as strange as Eddie had thought it might be, sharing the bath; they were too bunched up to be revealing, only their feet touching under the water. "Look, your color's coming back. I think you may live."

Rose just smiled, her eyes still shut. They sat in companionable silence for a long while, the only sounds the crackling of the fire and the soft ticking of the clock on the mantel, the warmth seeping into Eddie's bones.

"I like it best when it's just you and me," Rose said, with a tiny, happy sigh that jostled something loose somewhere in the depths of Eddie's chest, making her feel light and easy.

"Me, too," said Eddie. "That's what I've been telling you forever."

"Hmmm," Rose hummed sleepily. "I feel very strange. Bone-tired, suddenly. Bone soup."

"Nearly dying probably does that to a person."

"You know, it was very odd, I felt completely sure I would be all right at first—it didn't even cross my mind that I might be in real trouble. I didn't call for help then because it seemed silly, but by the time I realized I was slipping, I hardly had the air left to do it. I should have said something before it was too late, but I was embarrassed."

"That would be just like you," Eddie said, poking her with a toe. "To die of embarrassment, I mean."

Rose opened her eyes. "Do not poke the patient."

"Oh, so you're the *patient* now, are you? I thought you were a happy little soup."

Rose leaned her head against the edge of the tub, eyes fixed on the ceiling.

"I could see you onshore at first. I could see you and I kept thinking—if I can just reach Eddie, I'll be all right. I don't know *why*, it wasn't like you were being particularly useful, it took you long enough to notice. But . . . I don't think I was even scared of drowning, really. The most frightening part of all was knowing I couldn't get back to you."

Eddie should have laughed, but it didn't seem funny, somehow. Rose was still gazing up at the ceiling, her cheeks flushed from the heat of the bath, the planes of her face cast in dramatic shadow and golden, flickering firelight. Eddie was suddenly so overcome with the knowledge of how badly things could have gone, and so glad that Rose was stewing with her here rather than drifting at the bottom of the lake like a dropped shoe, that she leaned forward with a rush of hot water and kissed her softly on the cheekbone, right where the light was making her glow.

"What was that for?" said Rose.

"Don't know," Eddie said stupidly. Her legs were pressed against Rose's, crowding her back into her half of the tub. "I suppose I'm just very fond of you."

Rose considered her for a moment and then leaned forward, a hand on Eddie's knee for balance, and kissed her very gently on the lips. She was so warm, and Eddie was so warm, it was almost as if she hadn't done it at all.

"What was *that* for?"

"I suppose I'm very fond of you, too. Even if you are a bit of an idiot."

"Am I squashing you?"

"Yes. But I don't mind."

Eddie laughed. Their faces were still so close together that her breath ruffled a damp lock of Rose's hair. It brushed featherlight against Eddie's throat.

"This is odd, isn't it?"

Rose shrugged, droplets of water cascading down her shoulders. Her eyes were intent on Eddie's. "I don't know. It doesn't feel odd to me."

"That's because *you're* odd."

Rose wrinkled her nose at Eddie and then retreated back to her end of the bath. Eddie sat feeling out of sorts and foolish, convinced she had somehow said the wrong thing.

"Hold on," she said. "Close your eyes."

"Why?" said Rose, closing them immediately.

"I am taking my leave of you. I'm plenty warm."

Eddie clambered out of the bath, water sluicing from her and splashing Rose, who kept her eyes firmly closed but looked put out; she went to fetch one of the enormous towels that had been draped over the screen and wrapped it around herself, now feeling pleasantly boiled.

"Don't leave," Rose said suddenly. Her eyes were open now, her expression strangely determined.

"I'm not leaving," Eddie said, sitting down on the chair by Rose's head.

"Good," Rose said, the tension falling away.

It was beautiful to watch: the loosening of her shoulders, the slackening of her mouth, the way the lines smoothed out around her eyes. Her hair was falling in dark, wet sheets and her cheeks were blooming rosy pink and Eddie was completely enthralled. Surely no person could ever actually look this soft, this *warm*. Nobody could be this radiant without heavily applied artistic license.

"Why are you looking at me like that?" Rose said.

She was gazing steadily back at Eddie with a sort of heavy-lidded focus, acute and indistinct all at once. Her mouth was still slightly open. For no reason she could fathom, Eddie wanted to sink her teeth into Rose's lip. The thought flickered, and then caught and ignited.

"I don't know," Eddie lied.

"Liar," said Rose.

"Because you're such a mind reader."

"I am when it comes to you."

"Why even ask, then? If you already know what I'm thinking."

Rose gave a minuscule, one-shouldered shrug.

"I'm only wondering if you'll be bold enough to follow through."

"All right, then," said Eddie, her decision made at once.

She cupped Rose's chin gently in her palm, leaned over the side of the bath, and kissed her. Rose's lips parted at once with a tiny exhalation that could have been relief or surprise; she reached out with both hands to pull Eddie to her, but in doing so almost slipped and risked drowning for a second time that day. Eddie had to take hold of her properly, to pull Rose into her arms and grip her tight, the side of the tub digging painfully into her stomach as she did. She didn't care. Rose's mouth was just as soft as she remembered, but kissing her felt different entirely, incendiary and urgent; she leaned into the feeling, trying to pull her closer and kiss her harder, desperately hungry for something she couldn't quite name. Rose was breathing in little gossamer gasps that Eddie thought might just be the end of her.

They were, she noticed, getting rather carried away; she couldn't get enough of how responsive Rose was being—the catches in her breath, the blistering feeling of hot, wet skin under her palms. If those kisses in her garden had faintly stirred something, these kisses were jolting it wide awake—she was suddenly very aware of just how naked Rose was; the fact that Eddie could run a hand down her neck and into the silken dips of her collarbones, making Rose shudder and press herself desperately into Eddie's hands. She was just considering kissing the extremely danger-ous curve where the corner of Rose's jaw gave way to her throat when she came halfway to her senses and pulled abruptly away instead.

"Wait. Um . . . Wait, just a . . . What are we doing?"

"Er . . ." Rose said, gloriously out of breath, her pupils blown as wide as saucers. "We're kissing."

"Right. But . . . historically, this has been an entirely educa-tional exercise, has it not?"

Rose bit her lip in consternation. Eddie got the impression that her face was being completely honest, rendered incapable of artifice by post-drowning, bath-steamed euphoria.

"Is that what *you* think this is?"

Eddie smiled at her, pushing her damp hair away from her face.

"I think . . . I think that our minds may have been parboiled. Come on, let's get you dry."

Rose looked a little flustered, but allowed Eddie to bring her a towel and help her out of the water. Eddie was just wrapping it around her, her gaze fixed firmly on the floor, when Rose stepped forward and kissed her again, chasing her mouth and gently slid-ing her arms around Eddie until her hands met and interlocked at the nape of Eddie's neck.

Eddie supposed they were abandoning reason for this partic-ular brand of madness, and it seemed foolish to complain when it was all so agreeable; she sat down heavily in the chair and Rose followed into her lap, her fingers curling in Eddie's hair. Eddie was just finally exploring the curve of Rose's throat, fascinated by the way Rose's breath went ragged and her hands fisted when Eddie's lips ghosted over her skin, when there was a knock at the door.

"Ah," Rose said in a very strangled voice, immediately getting to her feet, clutching her towel to herself and looking to the door with wild-eyed panic.

"Miss Miller? Miss Li?" Liza called from the hall. "Luncheon is ready when you are. Shall I send Anne in to dress you?"

"Thank you," Eddie called back, trying not to laugh at the expression on Rose's face. "Yes, send her in. I think we are quite finished."

𝓛uncheon—and the rest of the day, for that matter—was entirely taken up with dramatic retellings of Rose's near demise and heroic rescue from all perspectives; Kitty, who considered herself a swimming proficient, was clearly very disappointed that she had been otherwise occupied when the time came to save an actual victim from the water.

"I still don't understand how you managed to almost drown not twenty feet from the boathouse," she said crossly, as if Rose had done it on purpose.

For her part, Rose seemed horrified by all the attention; she gave polite, perfunctory answers when asked how her nerves were managing or exactly how it had felt when she first realized her predicament, and then excused herself to the bedroom to rest, Albert jumping up to assist her. She glanced over at Eddie, but Albert was already proffering an arm, and she hardly needed *two* people to lean on.

Eddie was actually rather glad that she had gone; it had been impossible to look at her without remembering how she'd felt under Eddie's palms, and she still wasn't sure what exactly she was supposed to do with any of *that*.

After the morning's excitement nobody except Albert could quite rouse themselves for an afternoon walk; they sat around in the South Parlor watching Kitty work on her painting of Rose, adding quite a lot of watery blue where before there had been lush greens and golds. When Albert returned from his constitutional they were all feeling too lazy to even greet him; he sat down next to Eddie and took up his book, and Eddie gave him a gentle nudge with her elbow.

"It was very brave of you to jump in after her," she said quietly. "You saved her life, Albert. What a thing."

"What a thing indeed," Albert said, sighing heavily. "Strange, isn't it, how quickly a day can turn? One moment you're living a very ordinary life, and the next . . ."

Eddie shuddered, again thinking of how different the rest of this day—and indeed, her life—could have been. She felt as if she had glimpsed a ghost of herself: her twin, sitting in this very parlor, knowing that Rose was gone forever and there was absolutely nothing she could do about it. They might have found Rose washed up onshore, like that poor maid from Valentine's story. She felt sobered by the horror of how fragile life really was.

"I suppose I should be kinder to you," Eddie said with a tone of deepest resignation. Albert chuckled.

"Yes. I suppose you should."

Nash came wandering in with a bottle of claret in hand and gently tapped Eddie on the shoulder with it.

"Your time is up, Edie. You owe me one manuscript, ready or not. And do not try to drown any more of our companions to provide further distractions."

"Too soon," said Kitty, muffled by the paintbrush clenched between her teeth.

Eddie's stomach cramped uncomfortably. "All right. It's nowhere near finished, so . . . you'll just have the first half, and it's a first draft, Nash, so you can't expect much from it . . ."

"No excuses," he said merrily. "I expect it on my desk posthaste."

"Actually on your desk?"

"Oh, God, no. Just put it in my hand. Or throw it at me from a height and we'll make a game of it, to see if I can catch it."

When Eddie finally made her way up to bed that night, after a dinner that had dragged on for an age as Nash drunkenly regaled them all with the details of a meeting he'd had with his editor (everybody else had seemed quite bored; Eddie had been on the verge of whipping out a pen to take notes), Rose seemed to be asleep. Eddie undressed carefully in the dark, trying not to disturb her, but when she slipped into bed Rose immediately turned over as if she'd been waiting for her.

"Go back to sleep," Eddie said, petting Rose on the arm as she got settled.

"Don't want to," Rose mumbled. "Come here."

"I am here. I don't know how much more here I could possibly be."

Rose answered by pressing her body to Eddie's side, one arm coming up around her waist as she sleepily lifted her head. Her lips brushed against the corner of Eddie's mouth, and Eddie felt her body respond immediately, yearning to pull Rose closer.

It felt easy. Tender. Thrilling.

But also . . . deeply foolish.

It had all been perfectly safe when Eddie had known exactly what it was for—*practice*, they had simply been *practicing*—but she had to face the fact that it had started to feel like something else, something unfamiliar, something *more*, and it scared the life out of her.

She laughed awkwardly and gently pushed Rose away.

"What are you doing, you mad goose?"

"Oh," Rose said, going very still. "I just thought . . ."

"It might get a little . . . confusing, don't you think," Eddie said haltingly, "if we continue with this kissing business? Not to say

I didn't have a good time, Rose, but . . . I think we've had plenty
of practice by now. I don't want things between us to become . . .
complicated."

She thought she was making quite a convincing point, but
Rose didn't reply for a very long time.

"Yes," she said eventually. "You are right, of course. We
wouldn't want things to get complicated."

Chapter Eighteen

Rose was even quieter than usual at breakfast the next day. Eddie sat down at the opposite end of the table, and found herself laughing a little too loudly at Valentine's jokes to compensate for how out of sorts she felt. The wind had picked up and seemed to be working itself into a tantrum, howling despondently through the upper reaches of the house. Fine sprays of rain kept sporadically and violently hitting the window, making them all jump.

Eddie was very aware of the fact that Nash was carrying her manuscript around the place, reading as he walked. She entered the library thinking of doing some work there, found him leaning against a shelf, pages in hand, and immediately turned and walked right back out, her face scarlet and her heart lurking somewhere around her ankles. She was in a state of intense agitation all afternoon, trying and failing to read in the South Parlor, standing listlessly in the armory staring at a wall full of ornamental knives, and had just resolved to stomp down to the shore and let the rain pound at her for a bit when Nash appeared at her shoulder and said, very ominously, "Come."

She followed him into the drawing room, which was empty. He sat down at the pianoforte and immediately started tapping out a tune with little skill as Eddie pulled up the nearest armchair.

"I finished it," he said, not looking up from the keys.

"And?" said Eddie, in agony.

He laughed. "Your protagonist Delilah isn't very fair on the coarser sex."

"Oh," said Eddie. "No, I suppose not. But her husband *is* very horrible, before she accidentally murders him."

"Mmm," said Nash, playing a fiddly little trill. "It is very funny, Edie. I can hear your voice in it, and you do make me laugh. But . . . do you think it *should* be funny?"

"What do you mean?"

Nash shrugged. "I mean . . . *I* like it, of course. But I can already hear what my editor will say—that there's not really room for everything you're trying to do. Either it's a searing commentary on a woman's place in society, *or* it's a funny little dark comedy about a lady bumping off her unfortunate husband. Either will shock and astound, but both together . . ."

"Well," said Eddie, feeling choked with disappointment. "That's just . . . that's how I write. I don't really know of any other way to do it. I do not think that just because it's light and funny sometimes, that means it can't have something to say . . . If anything, that might make what it's saying more palatable . . ."

"Do you want to be palatable, or do you want to be great?"

This silenced her. She was feeling embarrassingly wounded, and tried to shake it off; he'd said he *liked* it, after all. He was just offering her constructive criticism—a precious commodity from somebody as talented and decorated as Nash Nicholson.

Nash seemed to notice that her feelings had been bruised; he stopped playing the pianoforte and reached for her shoulder to give it a bracing little shake.

"The first critique is always the hardest, Edie. I think you're enormously talented, I always knew you would be, I have a nose for these things. I just think . . . it would hardly be friendly of me to tell you to waste your time on something that isn't your best work, would it? Not when you have it in you to be a serious writer."

Eddie smiled weakly at him.

"You're right, of course. Sorry, I don't know why I'm . . . especially when . . . Well, it was so kind of you to read it at all."

"Nonsense, you could not have kept me from it. If you'd barred me from reading it, you'd have found me sneaking into your room late one night to search for it in my stocking feet."

Eddie laughed unconvincingly. Nash glanced up at the window and then got abruptly to his feet.

"Come on, Miss Miller. I spy a gap in the rain. Let's sneak out of here and go for a ramble and talk about the illustrious career you have ahead of you."

They found Juno curled up in the entrance hall on one of Nash's coats, which had fallen from its hook; he dusted it off, swearing at her half-heartedly, and slung it over his shoulders. The dog burst out of the door when he opened it and loped across the lawn, looking as thrilled as she seemed capable of being, nose to the ground and tail wagging slowly at the gray sky.

"That's better," Nash said, politely ignoring the fact that his dog was now urinating with vigor. "I can't think in there. Doesn't matter how high the ceilings are, they still make everything come to an abrupt stop."

"Oh, I don't know," said Eddie. "The library feels like it goes on forever and ever. I don't think I could ever have enough thoughts to fill it."

Nash grinned at her. "God, I'm glad I brought you. The others are all very well and good, of course, I enjoy their company . . . but with you . . . I don't know. I feel as if I see it all through your eyes. The view, it has to be said, is excellent."

Juno came running back to Eddie and pressed her enormous wet nose into Eddie's palm; there was something gray and crumpled in her mouth, and Eddie bent to inspect it.

"What have you got there, Juno? It looks like half an old cap."

Juno turned and tried to bestow it upon Nash, who grimaced at her and pushed her head away.

"Stop slobbering on my breeches, you hideous beast."

The dog seemed to lose interest, and dropped the filthy, frilly piece of once-white muslin on the ground before plodding away. It looked rather like a servant's cap; Eddie thought again of the poor maid who had supposedly washed up on one of these very beaches, and shuddered. That was the thing with tales of ghosts and tragedy: once the mood had been set, you couldn't help but see ominous signs everywhere, even if the protagonists of said stories always seemed unthinkably ignorant to their inevitable doom.

Instead of walking down toward the shoreline, they circled the house until they reached the south side and the slope that ended abruptly in crumbling cliffs.

"Listen . . . your manuscript . . . it needs a lot of work, Edie, but I think that with my help you could knock it into shape very quickly—what do you reckon? I'll be sending word to my editor around All Hallows, I don't think I can put him off any longer."

"All Hallows? That's very soon."

They stopped a few feet away from the cliffs, looking out over the churning, wind-tossed lake. Juno started whining, low in her throat, and Nash tutted and gave her a mostly friendly whack to the side of the head.

"I know you can do it. Just . . . take out the jokes, give it some more *poetry*. You have such a particular talent, Miss Miller, and it mustn't be kept from the world. You'll be the talk of every . . . every eminent salon and dingy drawing room. Gentlemen will swoon, ladies will pine. Kitty will have to paint you."

"Nash," Eddie said, feeling embarrassed; she gave him a little push on the arm to quiet him, but he seemed to misinterpret her intention, and lifted a hand to trap her fingers and keep them there. The breeze picked up, lifting her hair and ruffling Nash's, the two of them flushed pink and white from the shock of the cold.

"You must know that I mean every word," he said, his voice dipping low. His fingers were cool, the pads of them pressing de-

liberately into the gaps between her knuckles. "God, Edie. I don't
know how to tell you what a wonder you are. I feel . . . I feel finally awake, after so long in darkness."

"You took in too much lake water yesterday," Eddie said, her
heart racing as she stared very determinedly at the dog.

"Oh, you mustn't mock me when I'm being sincere—I
don't have the constitution for it. I must sound utterly mad, I
know, but you are such a . . . a *rarity*. The sharpest mind in the
softest trappings. There's nothing for it, I'm afraid. I am quite
helpless."

He ran a thumb over Eddie's knuckles, making her shiver.

"Don't you think we should go back inside?" she said, in almost a whisper.

"I don't feel particularly inclined, actually . . . but you're so
cold, Edith. Come here."

Eddie knew this wasn't true; she was warm, so warm, and
Nash was the one whose hands were freezing as they stroked her
fingers and pressed against the pulse at her wrist. It felt terrible
and wonderful and completely intoxicating; if Eddie's fifteen-
year-old self could have seen her now, after all those nights
imagining what it would be like to be wanted by the great *Nash
Nicholson*, the longing that had persisted even once she'd discovered that he had a wife—

"It *is* cold," Eddie said suddenly, pulling herself free. "We
should return to the house. The others will be missing us."

It wasn't quite what she meant, but it was good enough for
the present.

Nash stared at her, an unreadable expression flitting across
his face—and then he sighed.

"Ah. Yes. Very well, very well."

Eddie felt an odd, uncomfortable rush of guilt, as if they had
been sharing a joke and she had suddenly ruined the fun. As they
started back toward the house this only doubled as she thought

of Liza, waiting for them in the parlor. It felt very grown-up, to get married—and very childish to flirt with a man with a wife just because he wrote excellent poetry and was as handsome as he was insistent.

If only he weren't quite *so* handsome, Eddie thought ruefully, she might have been better able to control her inclination to swoon in his presence.

"We're to host a party," Nash said the moment they walked through the doors into the South Parlor, as Eddie busied herself fussing over the dog's muddy paws to avoid having to look at anybody. It occurred to her that Liza had been sitting by the window, looking out over the lawns; the cliffs were surely too far for her to have seen anything distinctly, but Eddie was still disquieted at the prospect that she had been watching.

"Christ, Nicks, no," Liza said now. "It is such trouble, arranging the boats, and the people from the village hardly need another reason to think ill of us, they're half-convinced we're raising the dead as it is—"

"Absolute nonsense, Liza, they shall be happy for the work, as they always were," Nash said, clapping her on the back and looking very pleased with himself. "Even if they do think we're all filthy pagans. Valentine, come and take a turn about the cellar with me. I can't for the life of me remember what we've got left in reserve. Liza, call for a summit with Mrs. Hall, and if she goes for your throat, remember she has a bad hip and is easily tripped."

Liza did not look particularly pleased, but she went from the room anyway. Dayo sighed.

"My deadline is in a few weeks. If anybody should need me, I suppose I shall be . . . in the boathouse. Hiding."

The atmosphere at the house changed as suddenly as the weather; where it had felt like a sleepy, cavernous shell, with only a handful of occupants drifting from room to room and bumping into one another in the library quite by accident; suddenly it was a hive of activity, more servants appearing as if from nowhere to do Nash's bidding. At one point, sitting in the drawing room writing, Eddie watched through the doorway as Henry and a gaggle of other fine, strapping young men somehow transported a large Grecian sculpture from the garden into the entrance hall. The sounds of grunting, soft swearing, and various limbs bouncing off furniture carried on long after they had left Eddie's field of vision.

She had asked Nash if his editor might make an appearance—a question that had been met with near-hysterical laughter and a fond pat on the shoulder, which she had taken to mean *no*—but had otherwise tried to steer clear of any party-planning activities.

Valentine wandered into rooms sporadically to offer opinions and instruction. Dayo disappeared completely, having apparently made good on his threat to hide. Kitty refused to acknowledge that servants were rearranging the furniture around her; she simply painted in the South Parlor as she had always done, her focus absolute, undeterred by the chaos. Eddie found herself moving from place to place, clutching her manuscript as if it were a life raft, her fingers and other random, odd corners of her being perpetually smudged with ink. Her interactions with Nash were entirely normal by their usual standards, save for the quickening of Eddie's pulse when he drew near, as if the brief moment of madness on the cliff top hadn't happened at all; her interactions with Rose were decidedly not. They were strange and awkward around each other, Rose unfailingly polite but noticeably distant, Eddie always hyperaware of where Rose was in any room and determined to avoid any dangerous physical collisions. At night this descended into farcical territory, as they undressed on opposite sides of the room and then climbed very carefully into bed, each of them attempting to keep a safe barrier approximately the size of the Thames between them.

It wasn't that Eddie didn't want to touch Rose. Increasingly, she was realizing that she *did*, which was far more troubling than lovely, mindless ignorance had been.

The key to dealing with it was to think about it as little as possible.

She had been closely observing Rose and Albert instead, and had noticed that while they were very comfortable with each other, there seemed not to be an ounce of romantic feeling between them. They never contrived little excuses to touch each other; there were no blushes, no signs at all that either of them was awaiting their wedding day with great anticipation. It soothed her, somewhat, although it remained puzzling.

She discovered their hiding place the day before the party quite by accident, walking into the long gallery and finding them sitting on very uncomfortable-looking wooden chairs, reading by the fire. Juno was slumped on the floor between them.

"They have not yet started in here," Albert said, without looking up. "It's the last bastion of refuge."

Rose didn't say anything. She was wearing a dress of sky-blue muslin and a lacy cream pelerine over her shoulders. The only sign that she had given in to the debauchery of the house was that her hair was only half-pinned, and she hadn't bothered trying to curl it into submission. Eddie found herself staring at the place where her hair touched the hollow of her clavicle, remembering how it had felt to fit her fingers there, and then did the mental equivalent of smacking herself on the nose like one would a bad dog and resolved not to think about it again under any circumstances.

"Room for another on the floor?" Eddie said, watching Rose's gaze flick up and then quickly return to her book.

"Be our guest," said Albert. "Although I would appreciate it if *you* didn't chew on my slippers."

Eddie laughed, surprised. "I'll give you fair warning if I get a hankering."

She set herself down with her back to the wall, using a book propped against her knees as a makeshift writing desk, watching the dog's ears twitch whenever her mind drifted from the task in front of her. It was cold despite the fire, drafts seeking her out and chilling her exposed fingers. It took her a while to fall back into the rhythm of writing, but once she did, a tornado could have blown through the gallery and she would only have tightened her grip on her parchment to prevent it from flying away; she was crossing out jokes, adding footnotes, waxing lyrical about the weather and the stars in a way that she hoped would please Nash and his editor. She started when she felt something soft touch her shoulder, and looked up at Rose with utmost confusion, taking a moment to realize that she had just dropped her shawl unceremoniously onto Eddie's back.

"Your teeth are rattling like game dice," Rose said quietly. "It's very annoying."

"Apologies," said Eddie. "I will endeavor to freeze to death with more discretion, if my passing is going to interrupt your reading."

"Please do."

Rose hadn't looked at her properly, but to joke together felt like progress, and Eddie got back to work in higher spirits, feeling rather productive until the door to the long gallery slammed open and Nash walked in with Mrs. Hall and some servants in tow.

"Oh, look—an infestation of unhelpful pests," he said, as Juno sprang to her feet and lolloped toward him. "Not you, June, you beautiful beast of leisure. All right, Mrs. Hall, what do you think—could we fashion a sort of maze in here? An obstacle course?"

"No," Mrs. Hall said immediately.

Nash sighed. "You do so love to say that. Unfortunately, I either cannot or will not hear you. Henry? Where's Henry?"

"He is helping Mr. Morris and some of the men shore up the

repairs on the second floor. As I have told you, Mr. Nicholson, our priority—"

"Fetch him down here, will you? What the man lacks in artistic vision he makes up for in can-do spirit. And Mrs. Hall, if you see my wife, will you please inform her that she must stop hiding those magnificent Tudor goblets from me? I always find them in the end." He clapped his hands together, making Rose jump. "Right. Edie, drag yourself away from your work of genius. I need you. Have you ever planned a séance before? Well, no matter, there's no time like the present . . ."

Chapter Nineteen

"I FEEL," SAID DAYO, "AS IF WE ARE STANDING UPON THE battlements of a crumbling castle, on the eve of battle."

"I don't know if I'd call it a castle," Valentine said, leaning over and handing him a bottle of wine. "But it's certainly crumbling."

They were sitting on the dock, which had tonight deigned to hold the weight of all six of them: Rose and Albert sitting closest to the shore on the sturdiest wood, Dayo next to them with his shirtsleeves rolled up, Kitty with her head on Valentine's shoulder, and Valentine so close to Eddie that when she adjusted her skirts, their knees brushed.

"Strumpet," Valentine said. "Keep your legs to yourself."

"Valentine," said Eddie sternly. "That dress is so low-cut, I can almost see to your midriff."

"Almost?" said Valentine. "Damn. Kitty, do you have any shears about your person?"

Kitty snorted. "Yes, I always keep a sharpened blade tucked into my bodice, for times such as these."

"You may come to need it yet," Dayo said gravely, nodding across the water to the distant lamps. "Here comes the cavalry."

The pinpricks of light were converging on the far shore; as they watched, more and more seemed to flare up, bobbing gently like indolent fireflies. Dayo passed the bottle of wine down the line, and Kitty took an enormous swig.

"I cannot believe they could find this many boats," said Albert. "Or . . . this many people, willing to lend their boats to such a cause."

"I'm sure they were paid handsomely," said Valentine. "Do you think any of Nash's friends know how much a boat crossing ought to cost? They probably handed over enough blunt to purchase passage to America."

They had all been banished from the house an hour before as Nash put the finishing touches on everything; Liza had disappeared upstairs to dress with a bottle of sherry in her hand and had not been seen since five o'clock.

In the spirit of All Hallows season, they were all dressed in the darkest clothes they owned without actually being in mourning blacks, excepting Kitty, who was in an inky, close-cut gown that Eddie imagined must have caused a few gentlemanly heart attacks at any funerals she attended wearing it, and Rose, who was defiant in Pomona green with a pale yellow ribbon in her hair. In a sea of dark, wintry hues, she looked like the first hope of spring. When Eddie had emerged from her room in muted puce, Nash had been on his way down the stairs; he had stopped, clapped a hand to his heart, and then winked before disappearing back into the stairwell.

Eddie had needed a moment to recall that her own heart was not supposed to be racing in response before she went on her way.

"Albert and I are going back," Rose said, as he stood and then lent her an arm to help her up. "Honestly, all this secrecy... What can he have possibly done to the house in the past hour that we haven't seen already?"

She had a point. Eddie had already seen the nude Greek statue now decorated with climbing vines in the entrance hall; the enormous altars of chrysanthemums and Michaelmas daisies that had been rowed over the lake and installed on every available surface; the alarming and very rusty suits of armor that had been procured from some dark, damp corner of the house and set to guard almost every door. Nash had eschewed lamps in favor of naked candles, and had purchased so many that Eddie had felt slightly faint when she saw them being carried up from the dock, hundreds and hundreds of them, neatly wicked and wrapped in waxy bouquets with pale blue ribbon. They must have been sent all the way from London, last minute and at outrageous expense.

The boats were drawing nearer, and Eddie was suddenly gripped by a wave of foreboding, as if they really were attackers coming to lay siege to the house. Dayo, Valentine, and Kitty passed the bottle back and forth along the line in silence, until a cacophony of shrieks and laughter began to float toward them, the sounds of a party that had already started back on the shore.

Eddie glanced back over her shoulder and saw that Nash had suddenly joined them with an uncharacteristic lack of ceremony, and was standing with his arms crossed, his gaze fixed on the lake. He was wearing a dark, wine-colored justaucorps and a heavily embellished waistcoat, a cocked hat with a large black plume in it balanced jauntily on his head. He looked like a pirate king: regal and dangerous, careless and commanding. Eddie realized with a jolt of pleasure that they were wearing almost exactly the same color. A matching set.

Just as she was about to look back to the lake, he caught her eye and put a finger to his lips.

"You never saw me," he mouthed, and then he turned with a whirl of his coat and disappeared into the darkness.

Not wanting to actually have to greet the oncoming hordes, Eddie and the others turned back for the house a few minutes later, picking their way through the pitch-black woods, drinking (everybody) and shrieking (Valentine) as branches reached out like phantom limbs to pluck at their clothing and trip them on the path.

"I can't see a damned thing," Dayo said, after grabbing for a tree and discovering that it was in fact Valentine he was clutching. "Didn't we have a lantern?"

"Miss Li and Mr. Rednock took it," Valentine grunted. "I thought we would have acclimatized to the dark, like . . . large bats."

When they finally made it up to the house, slightly worse for wear, light was blazing from every ground-floor window; Nash was standing on the doorstep, now with an enormous fur draped over his shoulders. He raised his hands in greeting and then frowned.

"Oh, it's just you. Get inside, will you? You are interfering with the grandeur of the proceedings."

When they did enter, it immediately became clear what finishing touches Nash had been putting on the house in their absence: the dark wood floors of the entrance hall had been chalked all over with an enormous pentagram and various other symbols, glowing eerily in the candlelight.

Dayo stopped abruptly, his foot an inch away from one of the pentagram's points.

"What in *God's* name . . . ?"

"Certainly not in *His* name," said Valentine. "Oh, look, I know this rune . . . it means 'horse.' Do you think that's what he meant to write? 'Horse'?"

"Liza is going to positively erupt when she sees this," Kitty said grimly. "Let's take shelter in the drawing room until we achieve safety in numbers."

An hour later they certainly had numbers, but safety was in short supply—almost immediately upon arrival, a gentleman had discovered the armory and decided to arm himself, and his fellows had followed suit. As a result, it was hard to turn a corner or fetch a drink without bumping into a whole host of people clad in antique pauldrons and helms, clutching priceless rapiers, or with jeweled daggers stuffed into their belts. The theme of the evening, which had been vaguely Hallows-orientated, suddenly seemed to be some ghostly, childish game of knights and soldiers; Eddie was squeezing down the packed hallway after obtaining a glass of wine, searching in vain for somebody she recognized, when Valentine appeared and handed her an ornate dueling pistol.

"What the hell is this for?" Eddie shouted over the fracas.

"Best be prepared," Valentine said, before melting back into the crowd.

Nash's guests were exactly as to be expected. They were mostly young, loud, and very dedicated to the spirit of the evening. Some of them had painted their lips in black or daubed their faces to look like skulls and demons; others were dressed in dramatic, trailing blacks, with lace veils and necklaces of polished jet. The noise was unbelievable. At one point Eddie saw Anne the maid, easily spooked at the best of times, place a tray of food down on a side table and then walk into what Eddie knew to be a small cupboard and close the door behind her.

Eddie was extremely alarmed when she came across two blond women who seemed to be merrily bleeding out all over their dove-gray gowns; it was only when she saw one of them lift a hand to be delicately licked by one of their companions that she realized they were not in fact covered in vital fluids.

"It's beetroot," she heard one of them say, grinning wickedly; the gentleman who had licked her grinned back, his teeth stained lurid pink.

Eddie made her way toward the dining room, feeling more as though she was swimming than walking, having to engage both arms to politely shove people out of the way. When she reached it, she found Nash within, sitting at the head of the table playing some kind of card game. Spectators were crammed around the walls, drinking and whispering; Juno was lying by the fire, looking harried.

Eddie went to pet the dog but found her path blocked by Nash's arm, which had shot out to stop her lightning-fast.

"Edie, Edie, Edie," he said; he sounded solemn, but when she looked down at him, she saw that his eyes were sparkling darkly under his hat. "How are you at vingt-et-un? I foolishly appointed Mr. Crawley as banker, and I suspect he plans to rinse me for all I'm worth."

"I have never played," Eddie said, glancing up at the stern faces of the men sitting around the table. "I don't suppose it would do you any good to have me on your side."

"On the contrary, Edie, I imagine your presence would be *frightfully* good luck."

"Nash," said the man dealing out cards, raising an eyebrow, "either invite the lady to sit upon your knee to entertain us all, or gather your wits and place your bet."

All the joy of being claimed by Nash in front of his friends immediately dissipated. If Eddie had hackles, they would have risen—but Nash just laughed, removing his arm and picking up his card instead. Eddie's jaw worked for a second as she considered a rebuke, but it was too late, and she knew instinctively that the room would be against her; instead, she glanced down at the dog.

"Come on, Juno," she said imperiously; luckily, Juno seemed glad of an excuse to leave, and followed her with her head pressed into Eddie's leg until they reached the busy hallway. The dog seemed to know where she was going from there, and pushed on through the crowd, Eddie using her as a canine battering ram and apologizing vaguely to the people who were knocked aside. Juno led her up the stairs and toward the billiard room, nosing the door open and immediately disappearing within. When Eddie entered, she found that Dayo, Albert, and Rose were all sitting inside on various surfaces, talking quietly to a handful of guests who had also apparently sought refuge from the madness on the ground floor. Some of them were around Albert's age—people who looked as if they had come seeking stimulating conversation and good company, rather than satanic rituals in the entrance hall—and Eddie was surprised to find herself relieved at the relative quiet.

Rose was speaking to a woman a few years older than her, at least five-and-twenty. She had on men's clothes: dark breeches and a waistcoat to match, a cravat hanging loose at her collar. Eddie was immediately struck with admiration and white-hot envy; why had *she* never considered that she might be allowed to wear men's clothes? Not at home, of course, but here at Nash's, where anything seemed possible?

She thought of Nash, shaking his head and laughing and refusing to call her "Eddie," and decided that perhaps it was one impossible thing too far.

"Oh, speak of the . . . This is Eddie," Rose said. She was slightly flushed, an untouched glass of wine in her hand, looking frankly luminous surrounded by everybody else clothed in gloom. "I mean, Miss Miller. No, I mean . . . Eddie, this is Miss Isabella Cliffe—"

"Bella," said the woman, offering a hand to be shaken. Eddie took it, dazed, and was on the receiving end of a strong and enthusiastic shake. "Your Miss Li was just telling me that you're a writer."

"Allegedly," Eddie said.

Bella was leaning against the dressing table that Rose was perched on, her hand on the back of the chair; it was perfectly innocent, but there was something about the sight of this tableau that made Eddie's brain itch unpleasantly. It was all a little too *familiar*, for two people who had only just met.

"Gosh, well, you must tell me more—I am a *ravenous* reader, and I am always in search of more women to read. I suppose you've read *The Modern Prometheus*? It was positively shredded in the *Critic*, and for all the wrong reasons . . ."

"I have," said Eddie.

Both Rose and Bella sat waiting for her to say something in addition, but she just crossed her arms and looked down at Juno, who was sitting faithfully at her feet.

"Well," said Rose into the too-long silence, looking desperate. "I felt dreadfully sorry for the beast. What was his name? Victor?"

"Victor was the doctor, not the creature."

"Well, what was the creature's name?"

"Ah," said Bella. "He was called . . . the creature, mostly."

"I see," said Rose.

There was another silence, during which Eddie watched Albert lean in to listen to the tall, thin, and graying Indian gentleman he was speaking to and then laugh heartily, pressing a hand to his mouth. His cheeks were very red.

Bella slapped a hand against her knee as if she had just recalled something.

"You mentioned a tour?"

"Yes!" said Rose, immediately slipping from the table. She looked far too happy to have an excuse to leave. "Yes, of course. Come with me. Eddie doesn't need a tour, she's been rattling around the place like I have for the past fortnight."

Juno, instantly transforming from comrade to traitor, lifted her head and went with them.

Eddie was left standing by the dressing table looking and feeling bemused, as if some sort of sleight of hand had just been performed under her nose. She considered inserting herself into Dayo's or Albert's conversations, but they both looked engaged, and happily so. Instead, she squared her shoulders and made her way back into the fray.

Chapter Twenty

"All i'm saying," a very intense-looking man was shouting in Eddie's ear, "is that the Corn Laws should concern each and every one of us. I mean, do you not believe in the principles of free trade?"

Two ladies ran past screaming, followed by a third, masked person with two swords raised aloft, a manic glint in their eye.

"Er . . . Yes. I think so?"

"You *think* so?" the man said, looking terribly disappointed. "You're not a *Tory*?"

"Good Lord, I should think not," said Eddie. "But I am . . . I'm afraid I'm very thirsty. Would you excuse me?"

She had managed to get herself entangled in quite a few conversations that had demanded an escape, and had now excused herself to fetch a drink on three separate occasions. She was keeping her glass carefully half-full for any future altercations. Her friends seemed to have vanished entirely, and she was somewhat desperate to find a familiar face. Rose, she thought darkly, was probably still giggling about her with *Miss Cliffe*, somewhere in the far reaches of the house. It stung more than it ever had when Rose was off cavorting with her society friends, because Eddie had never looked at Ava Forester or Sophie Newport and fervently wished to *be* them.

Eddie washed the feeling down with a large sip of wine and then continued on her way.

The trouble with parties full of great, important, and subversive minds, she was quickly discovering, was that they often wanted to have great, important, and subversive conversations with her, when she was simply trying to ask the time, or if any of them had seen their host.

It was with great relief that she finally sighted Valentine and Kitty standing on the west stairs, deep in conversation.

"Oh, thank God," she said upon reaching them. "I have been terribly lost."

"Were you with the pagans?" Kitty said with vague interest. "Apparently they have taken up the chalk and done something truly vulgar in the armory."

"No," said Eddie. "I was with a man who was quizzing me about whether I was a Tory."

"Good Lord, I should think not," said Valentine. "Besides, everybody knows that Tories drink *port*. We Whigs only demean ourselves for claret."

"Brigands!" somebody shouted; they looked down to see that Nash had appeared and was pointing up at them. He was wearing a light daubing of rouge, and had at some point lost his fur; Eddie wondered if the pagans were doing something sacrificial with it. "Knaves! Scoundrels! Charlatans!"

"Oh good," said Kitty under her breath. "We're doing synonyms."

He darted through the crowd and up the stairs toward them, surprisingly nimble for somebody so clearly drunk.

"Come hither and redeem yourselves."

He led them up two flights, to the half-rotten second floor. It was dark and quiet, a single candle burning at the far end of the corridor, a world apart from the rest of the party.

"What are we doing up here?" said Kitty.

"All will be revealed," Nash said ominously, striding ahead; there was a single figure already standing silhouetted by the candlelight, and as they drew nearer, Eddie realized that it was *Henry*, of all people. He looked mortified to be there, and gave the new arrivals little half bows of greeting and cleared his throat twice before staring fixedly down at the assortment of oddities that Nash had clearly assembled on the floor.

There were a *lot* of unlit candles, so many that they looked like a waxy audience, crowding palely around a central bowl that was full of fronds of evergreen. Alarmingly, there was also a human skull, thin and brown with age. Nash sat down right in front of it with no qualms at all.

"Come on. Sit. You have been *chosen*."

"Could you not choose me for something else?" Valentine said wryly. "Nominate me to fetch more libations, perhaps, or to take a nap?"

Nash just smiled pleasantly up at them until they all arranged themselves in a small circle on the protesting floorboards.

"First, we burn the cedar," Nash prompted, pushing the bowl toward Henry, who reluctantly lifted the little bundle of needles and held it over the flame. Eventually they started to smoke and crisp around the edges. "Excellent, very good job, Henry. And now . . . we light the candles."

He took up the candle and lit another with it, which he handed to Kitty; she somberly did the same, and soon their circle blazed with light.

"Oh. Well, that's too many, it's as light as day in here. Hardly scary at all," Nash said, blowing around half of them out. He closed his eyes and composed himself with utmost solemnity. "All right. Esteemed friends—tonight, we are attempting to reach into the beyond . . . to snag the fraying trail of a lost soul and bring them here to commune with us. To whisper secrets and tell us bawdy jokes, et cetera."

"Whose skull is that?" said Valentine.

"Shush, Valentine."

"Well, I'm only saying . . . surely we are just going to bring back the previous inhabitant, and they might not be best pleased that we are all sitting around using their own personal head as a centerpiece."

One of Nash's eyes cracked open.

"It is a family heirloom, all right? Now, please—desist."

Valentine sighed, but didn't speak again.

"Now, you must all close your eyes and hold hands. *All* of you, and no complaining." Eddie took Kitty's hand on her left and Henry's on her right; she watched as Henry, red to the roots of his hair, took Nash's. "Eyes *closed*, Edith."

She closed them.

It seemed strange that she could hardly hear the noise of the party up here, when it had felt all-consuming just moments ago; even Rose and Miss Cliffe felt as if they belonged to some other reality. She attuned herself to the breathing of those in the circle, the sound of the floor creaking below them, the breeze whining through the holes in the roof somewhere above their heads.

"Much better. Now, you must all let your minds go quiet, so that the spirits may enter."

There was a period of quiet, during which somebody fidgeted and then fell still. As the silence stretched on, Eddie found that she was actually feeling a little unnerved.

"Now . . . *is there anybody there?*"

No answer came in any form, even when he repeated the question twice, and Eddie felt herself relax slightly. There *was* something deeply foreboding about this part of the house at night. Her mind went to the bedroom door directly behind her, warped shut, the contents unknown for years. What might have crept in through the smashed windows and the hole in the roof, unnoticed? What might be lurking there now, perhaps awaiting a visitor, or preparing to claw its way out?

Dead leaves, Eddie reminded herself firmly. And potentially a family of damp squirrels.

"Are you finished?" Valentine said finally. "Only, if it's a choice between sitting here with human remains and enjoying a party with those still living, I choose the latter."

"Damn it, no, there must be a . . . *I, Nash Nicholson, son and heir to this house and the land it stands upon, call upon the spirits to hear my voice.* I offer you . . . er . . . my body, as a vessel. My life's blood, to sustain you. Come on, there must be something you want . . ."

"I can feel something," Kitty said suddenly, certain and solemn, her grip on Eddie's hand tightening. Eddie immediately opened her eyes.

"What is it?" she asked.

Kitty shuddered. "I feel . . . cold."

"We all feel cold," Valentine said. "There's a hole in the roof."

"Shut *up*, Valentine, let her speak," Nash hissed. "What do you feel, Kitty?"

"Be quiet a moment," said Kitty. Eddie studied her face, trying to work out if this was all a jest, but she did not seem to be joking. "I think there *is* someone here."

A moment after she spoke, Eddie became aware of a noise she had somehow not noticed—it sounded like a soft thudding, coming from one of the uninhabitable rooms. She glanced around the circle. None of them seemed to have heard it—except Henry, whose gaze was fixed in that direction, frowning. There was a brief sensation like fingers brushing very gently against the nape of her neck, and she felt all of her hair stand on end.

It was probably a shutter, Eddie reasoned. Something loose, banging in the wind. A breeze on her neck. Nothing to be concerned about.

"A woman," Kitty said suddenly, making Eddie jump. "There is a woman here. She is . . . angry. Hungry. *Furious.*"

Eddie looked at Nash, who seemed delighted. He leaned toward Kitty, eager for more. By rights his coat should have immediately caught flame, but the candles closest to him seemed to have gone out.

"Ask her something," Nash urged. "Go on."

"Ask why she's here," said Eddie.

Somewhere behind one of the doors, there was a very loud, distinctive creak. Eddie could no longer pretend that she wasn't genuinely alarmed. She wished it were Rose sitting next to her—calming her, grounding her. Kitty was holding on to her so tightly that her hand was beginning to throb.

"She died here," Kitty said. "On the island."

Eddie thought of Valentine's story of the drowned maid, and felt a chill run up the length of her spine.

"She wants to speak to somebody here." Kitty's eyes opened, and she looked straight at Henry; he stared back in open horror, his mouth slack. "It might be—"

Henry yanked his hands away from both Nash and Eddie, and got to his feet so suddenly that he knocked over a candle; Eddie had to rescue it before it set fire to her dress.

"What the devil—?" exclaimed Nash.

"Did you tell her to say that?" Henry demanded.

His chest was heaving, his hands clenched into fists at his side. Eddie looked from Nash to Henry, baffled by this development, shocked to see Henry displaying such obvious contempt for his employer.

"Henry, please calm down, I can assure you—"

"*Calm down?*"

Henry genuinely looked on the verge of striking him; everybody stood up very abruptly, jarred by the transition from quiet séancing to the brink of warfare.

"Henry," Kitty said slowly, "I have no earthly idea what you're talking about. Nash didn't tell me to say anything at all."

Henry shook his head. His eyes were bright, his face mottled red and white with fury.

"I suppose you think this is funny?"

He was speaking to Nash, who had a very queer look on his face, somewhere between alarm and amusement. It really did seem as if it might come to fisticuffs, but Eddie couldn't think of a thing to say to stop it. Rose would have known what to do. She was the empath. The peacekeeper.

Eddie just gaped at them like a beached fish and wondered if she ought to blow out the rest of the candles.

"Why don't you have a drink, my boy? To steady your nerves."

Henry shook his head. "Liars," he said quietly. "You are all nothing but a bunch of devils and liars."

He stormed away toward the stairs, leaving the rest of them standing there in the odd atmospheric crater left by his outburst.

"Wonderful," Kitty said. "I was really getting something before that little tantrum. I suppose since he broke the circle I am to be possessed with the spirit of this malcontent for all eternity, now."

"Don't fret, Kit," said Valentine. "It would only be an improvement."

Kitty shuddered, seeming genuinely put out. Eddie just shook her head, unable to make sense of any of it.

"What on earth just happened?"

"Nothing," said Nash, with a shrug. "Servants' temperaments, you know. Let us go and recover with a few rounds of the gentleman's sport."

The gentleman's sport turned out to be a game that used the long gallery as a court. It was played by hitting various objects scrounged from around the house with a cricket bat toward a large, frowning portrait of a middle-aged man. A small crowd had already gathered, awaiting their master of ceremonies.

"All right," Nash said, claiming the bat and slinging it over his shoulders. "The name of the game is total ruination."

A strawberry-blond man with very floppy hair and a bad-minton racket in his hand raised an eyebrow.

"I thought it was called 'mutual destruction.'"

"Precisely. Now, all you must do to score points is to hit the portrait—five points for the frame, ten for the canvas, fifteen if you hit the honorable gentleman's chest or shoulders, and twenty-five points for a headshot. I shall demonstrate . . . Edie, fetch me something breakable, would you?"

Eddie took a step forward and peered dubiously into a trunk by his feet; it was full of china and candlesticks, clocks and trin-ket boxes, a vase shaped like a cornucopia and a matched set of porcelain dogs. She settled on a small, inconspicuous teapot, and tried to hand it to him.

"No, no, you hold on to that," he said, stepping up to a chalk cross on the floor and flexing the bat. "Now, the trick is that you want it to survive the initial impact—there's no point to it if your projectile never goes forth into the world at all. When I give the signal, Edie, throw that for me and then take cover. Ready?"

Eddie nodded, wondering how quickly she could go from teapot-tossing to eye-shielding.

"Three . . . two . . . one . . . *clear*!"

Eddie threw the teapot as gently as she could into his path and then darted away, pressing her hands to her face; she heard the bat make contact, heard something break, and then a sec-ond later there was a much louder shattering from the far end of the room.

"Ten points," said the blond man. "Although the handle broke off and hit me, which I think should count as a deduction."

Eddie opened her eyes and saw that the remains of the teapot were now scattered about the portrait, a few chips of porcelain caught in the gilt frame.

"Nonsense," said Nash. "Did I at least get a headshot on you?"

"No," said the man, stepping up to take his turn.

Nash leaned over, dipped into the trunk, and pulled out a bronze and crystal candlestick.

"Three . . . two . . . one . . ."

Everybody in the room ducked; he managed fifteen points, and looked exceedingly smug about it. Somebody else stepped forward to take a turn, and things deteriorated rapidly. Kitty, who had been distant and quiet since the séance, managed to get twenty-five points on her very first go, and then curtsied, put down her bat, and left the room. When Eddie stepped up to bat she put all of her might into it, channeling all of the strange, pent-up frustration that had been plaguing her since she had seen Rose disappear with Isabella Cliffe, and as a result accidentally shattered the little porcelain dog that had been thrown for her immediately. Nash put a hand to his cheek, laughing, and when he took it away again she saw that he was bleeding.

"Oh, God, Nash—I'm so sorry," she said, reaching up to dab ineffectually at his face; he caught her wrist before she could touch him, and then blinked down at her through wine-dark eyes and laughed again, sleepy and off-kilter. It felt strangely intimate, the two of them simply staring at each other and breathing heavily from exertion.

"Would have been twenty-five points, but you hit the wrong Nicholson," he said, releasing her and gently brushing china dust from her shoulder. "Right, Valentine, throw me something solid."

None of them noticed Liza enter until she cleared her throat. Eddie turned to see Mrs. Nicholson with her arms crossed, dressed in sunshine yellow, the expression on her face distinctly overcast.

"Nash," she said, just as he obliterated a serving jug. "*Nash!*"

He finally turned, seeming entirely unbothered by the fact that his wife looked murderous with so many blunt weapons at hand.

"Ah, Liza. Valentine, give Liza your bat. She has a wicked arm on her when she's in the mood—don't you, Liza?"

"Some of this is mine, Nash," she said, her tone dangerous. "Is that . . . ? *Is that my mother's Chamberlain vase?*"

"It was," said Nash, peering down at some of the shards near his feet. "May it rest in peace. As may she, for that matter. I did like that woman—she had such an uncanny nose for sherry, she could smell it being uncorked at two hundred paces."

Liza looked apoplectic. As she advanced, Eddie had the good sense to put down the bat she was holding and make for the exit; she reached it at the same time as Valentine, who put a hand on her back to help propel her from the room.

"Very wise. You're gaining survival instincts at a decent clip, there, Eddie. Keep it up and you may yet last the winter."

Chapter Twenty-one

MIRACULOUSLY, THERE WAS NOBODY IN THE ARMORY. Somebody had attempted to remove the cannon and had only made it halfway out of the door before giving up; there was an empty bottle of wine sitting next to it, as if whoever had done it had needed to fortify themselves after expending all their efforts in the pursuit of heavy artillery. There were chalk symbols all over the walls, some of which looked like the runes in the entrance hall, and some of which were very clearly modeled after human genitalia. People rushed past the open door, laughing and whispering behind their fingers, heading for the stairs that Eddie and Valentine had just descended.

"The herd is on the move," Valentine said, picking up a hunting knife and pretending to aim it at Eddie, one eye closed, before letting it clatter back onto the table. "I imagine the Nicholsons are putting on quite a show."

"Do you think they are actually going to watch?"

Valentine shrugged. "Watch. Place bets. Take sides, when war breaks out. It's all ridiculous, really . . . no matter how much Liza and Nash snap and growl at each other, they always end up united again in the end. They are strangely well matched, although Nash would rather perish than admit it."

"Oh," said Eddie, keeping her gaze firmly fixed on the crossbow in front of her as they continued to make a slow lap of the room. "I thought . . . Well, I don't know what I thought."

This was, of course, a lie. Eddie had been entirely convinced that the rift between Nash and his wife was insurmountable. Hearing the opposite spoken aloud with such authority, she had to admit that she felt more than a little disappointed.

Valentine came to a stop and turned, one eyebrow raised.

"Have you been informed otherwise?"

"Well, they hardly seem like they *love* each other, do they? She seems to disagree with absolutely everything he does. She scolds him like she does the dog."

"That dog could do with more scolding," said Valentine, discovering a mostly empty decanter of what looked like whiskey and raising it aloft in triumph. "As could Juno. Liza is actually a great wit and a delight to be around, when Nash isn't pushing her to her very limits. Care to join me for a snifter?"

"Why not," said Eddie.

Valentine handed it over, and Eddie took a large, wincing swig before handing it back.

"What does your Miss Li have to say about Nash? I sense a distinctly cold front from her direction whenever he enters a room." Valentine took an even larger swig, without a hint of a wince.

"Oh, yes. I suppose she doesn't like him much. I don't see why."

"A mystery," said Valentine, with a small smirk that Eddie could not decipher. "Where is she now? I haven't encountered her all evening."

Eddie grimaced, taking back the bottle. "She was talking to some lady in breeches she's never laid eyes on before in her life as if they were the best of friends. Honestly, I have no idea how she can manage to be so friendly to a complete stranger and so unforgiving toward Nash, who has done nothing to earn her ire! And I don't know what's so special about this woman, that she had to abandon the party altogether to abscond with her to God knows where. She's *my* friend, after all."

Valentine gave her a pitying look. "Isabella Cliffe?"

"Yes. How did you know?"

"Despite the insistence of everybody here tonight that they're radicals and freethinkers, casting off the shroud of respectability, waltzing their way into a new era . . . I'm afraid most of the ladies would still balk at the concept of doing something quite as daring as *putting on breeches*. Miss Cliffe is a notable exception."

Valentine sat down on a side table, ignoring its groan of protest.

"Ugh," said Eddie, also taking a seat. "You know, as soon as I saw her, I thought . . . why didn't *I* think to do that? It hadn't even crossed my mind as a possibility. I suppose it's just evidence that I, too, am waltzing under the shroud, or . . . whatever it was you just said."

"Perhaps," said Valentine. "But you know, Miss Cliffe is a few years your senior. She has had more time on this earth to think about who exactly she'd like to be. And she didn't *invent* the concept of ladies in breeches. She probably saw somebody do it, and thought she might like it, and discovered that she was correct. None of us are true originals, Eddie. We piece an approximation of a person together from finding what we like and eschewing what we hate, and somewhere in that muddle we find ourselves."

"*You* do not seem to have any trouble at all finding yourself."

Valentine choked on a mouthful of whiskey. "Ha! I never found myself, and perhaps I never will. I am uncharted territory. Somebody came up to me earlier and said, 'You know, in the right light, you almost look like a lady!' I think she thought she was being kind and *progressive*. I told her that I am not a lady, or a gentleman for that matter, and that any resemblance to either is entirely coincidental, but she looked at me as if I were speaking a foreign language and almost walked into a wall in her haste to escape."

"Ah," said Eddie. "The shroud."

"The shroud indeed," said Valentine. "God, look at me. Dishing out advice. An elder at the tender age of seven-and-twenty. The *horror* of it all."

Eddie snorted. They sat in companionable silence for a moment, and then she sighed.

"Nash really loves Liza?"

"Without question."

"I see," said Eddie, slipping from the table and finding that her hand-eye coordination left something to be desired. "I'm . . . I'm going to find Rose."

She had given Rose plenty of time to cavort with Miss Cliffe, if that's what she wanted to do, but enough was enough. Eddie was drunk, and she wasn't going to stand another moment apart from her.

"Ah," said Valentine. "I am not entirely sure that's a good idea. She might be . . . preoccupied."

"Nonsense," said Eddie, waving a dismissive hand. "The house isn't *that* big. Her tour must be finished by now."

"They treated Cassandra thus," Valentine said sadly, raising the whiskey in farewell. "Good luck and Godspeed."

It did seem as if the majority of guests had relocated to the long gallery; Eddie could hear the sound of shouts, laughter, and shuffling feet, and she walked in the opposite direction, convinced that Rose would have done the same. There were a few guests still scattered around the ground floor—when she opened the door to the South Parlor, three ladies and a gentleman sprang apart like startled mice and then blinked expectantly at her until she closed it again. There were only three people in the dining room; they were still playing cards, despite the fact that one of them seemed to be asleep. Eddie crept away back down the hall until she reached the library, which she knew had been firmly locked by Liza earlier in the day. The door was slightly ajar now; she pushed it open noiselessly, allowing her to peer inside.

Rose wasn't within, but Albert was. He and the tall man from the billiard room were standing over by the window, a book open on the desk as if one of them had just been reading it.

But they weren't reading now. They were kissing. Albert had both arms around the man and his eyes tightly shut, a surprising amount of passion in his expression. She stared at them for another second and then quietly pulled the door closed.

Drunk as she was, Eddie was entirely certain of what she had just seen. In the odd, ringing shock that followed this conclusion, she realized a few things.

Firstly, that Albert wasn't at all the person she'd thought he was. She had, in fact, greatly misunderstood him. In the muddle of her racing thoughts, she noticed a tiny bud of joy, daring to bloom in her chest; there was something innately *hopeful* to her about what she had just witnessed.

Even if that made absolutely no sense to her. Even though it was Albert.

Secondly, that Eddie had been very, very foolish. A lot of things were slotting into place. Rose and Albert's arrangement, devoid as it was of romantic love. The fact that Albert—a quiet man who seemed, on the whole, rather conventional, if one discounted his obsession with bunnies—felt so at home among Nash's rule-breaking, radical friends.

Finally, and most importantly, she realized that this posed an urgent question: if Albert's reasons for entering this engagement were now very clear, where did this leave Rose?

In the dark? Very unlikely. Rose was one of the smartest and most discerning people Eddie had ever known. Was she doing him a favor, to the detriment of her own happiness? Not impossible, but even Rose would not go so far out of her way to ruin her happiness for Albert's sake.

There was a third option, of course. One that simultaneously made a lot of sense in retrospect and cast Eddie's mind into utter disarray.

She was suddenly walking very, very quickly. She practically leaped up the stairs, and almost crashed into Kitty, who was coming the other way.

"It's all a bit bacchanalian up there," she said, righting Eddie by the shoulders. "If you packed a crucifix, best to locate it now."

"I was looking for Rose. I need to . . . Have you seen her?"

"I have—she was entering her bedroom with that Cliffe character. Now *she's* striking. I may ask her to sit for me, if I catch her after."

"After what?" said Eddie.

Kitty tilted her head to one side and considered Eddie as if she were a small child who had just inquired where the elderly family dog had disappeared to.

"Did I say after? I meant . . . soon. On her way out."

Eddie's chest constricted. *If* her suspicions were correct . . . *if* Rose was marrying Albert because she knew, unequivocally, that there would never be a man who would truly capture her interest . . . and *if* Rose was this very minute holed up somewhere in the house with Isabella Cliffe, she of the unfailing confidence and long legs in breeches . . .

"I need to talk to her," Eddie said determinedly.

Kitty seemed reluctant to get out of her way.

"While I'm impressed by your dedication to foolishness, I think you should give Miss Li her privacy. She asked after you a few hours ago, but I actually thought you were with Nash—I suppose he's gone to drown himself in private."

"Drown himself?" Eddie said, momentarily blown off course. "What? Where?"

"I just saw him sneaking out and making for the dock, looking morose. You honestly never know with that man. He might have taken a boat back to shore instead, that would be just like him."

Eddie felt torn. It was probably nothing, but Nash always

seemed despondent and volatile when he and Liza fought, and after the amount he had drunk . . .

"I'm going to find him, just to make sure he's all right. If you see Rose, tell her I'm looking for her. Tell her to come and see me."

Eddie half sprinted down the hallway and through the front door, briefly doubling back to snatch a lantern. Her shadow stretched ahead across the lawn in front of her, as if reaching for the matching gloom of the woods; they had never seemed quite so eerie as they did just then, as she left the life and warmth of the house behind and started to make her way through the darkly grasping trees. Every time she took a step she felt as if she were intruding; twigs cracked beneath her feet and feathers ruffled furiously overhead, punctuated by the sounds of hidden paws scampering and shrill cries of warning.

When Eddie stumbled and a crow started to caw ominously, she began to wish she had dragged Kitty with her, or that Juno could be loping ahead as usual, stalwart and comforting. She felt as if there were hundreds of eyes on her, and in the dark, with a stomach full of wine, it was hard to be rational and remind herself that they were *prey*, not preying. Perhaps it was said wine muddling her brain, but she was starting to dread what she might find when she reached the shore; she thought of the drowned maid again, of the creeping cold of the séance, and hurried even faster.

"Nash?" Eddie called, when she reached the edge of the woods, her pulse racing.

She spied a figure sitting alone on the dock, feet in the water, a bottle of wine gilded in moonlight at their side. A cold breeze was coming in off the lake, and Eddie shivered, pressing her hands as tightly to the lantern as she could without burning them. She picked her way down to the shore, feeling a rush of relief as she drew closer and recognized Nash. He only turned to glance at her once she had set the lantern down and taken a seat beside him, keeping her feet carefully out of the icy waves. He nodded up at the moon, which was a sliver away from being full.

"Did you know the Ancient Greek calendars were all lunar? The Athenians placed the beginning of the year in July, but plenty of other regions had it starting in autumn."

"That's a strange time to begin the year," Eddie said, wrapping her arms around herself and glancing up at the clear, star-scattered sky. "Just before everything dies."

"Well, I suppose their climate keeps most things alive. Not like here. We're half-dead already and there's still a month until the first frost. If we had any sense, we would be in Greece."

"I would love to see it," Eddie said, and Nash turned to her, looking simultaneously ancient and no older than twenty in the reflected moonlight and the flickering of the lamp. "Greece, I mean."

"I have no doubt you will," he said, his focus suddenly absolute. "I have no doubt you shall see anything you want to, Edie."

"You are being mawkish, and it is *not* becoming," Eddie said lightly, elbowing him in the side. "Why are you out here all alone? You invited everybody to a party, you might recall. They are all up in your long gallery trying to see if they can make it the tall gallery, too, by breaking through the floor."

"Good," said Nash. "No, I mean it. Let them tear it to pieces. I thought this house was the answer . . . When I'm in London, I long for the lake, but when I'm on the lake, I yearn for London. It is almost as if *I'm* the problem, but that cannot be it, so it must be something else." He gave her a rueful smile. "The *company* has certainly never been better."

"Your card-playing friends were very rude."

"Were they?" Nash sighed and rubbed at his chin. "Yes. You're probably right. Sorry."

"And Henry seemed rather upset with you."

"Hmmm. Henry is not one to go seeking ghosts. I think our

wild ways shock him terribly. Very superstitious, these country folk."

Eddie wasn't entirely convinced by this, but there seemed to be nothing more to gain from prodding at it.

"Did you and Liza quarrel?"

Nash snorted. "We are in a perpetual quarrel. It's called marriage. It starts with prickling irritation, matures into a gentle seethe, and then before you know it you've fermented yourself an endless supply of unadulterated loathing."

Eddie picked up the bottle of wine and took a sip. It was freezing—the glass and the alcohol—but it warmed her as it went down and induced a pleasant buzzing in her fingertips.

"Valentine says that is all nonsense, and you love each other really."

Nash snorted again. "Valentine is a romantic. Inevitable, with a name like that. Dreadful thing to be—I'd be ashamed to show my face in public."

"Nash. You're a *poet*."

"Oh, don't start. I will admit, under little duress, that I find romance in the glory of nature. A coaxing glimpse of a new moon. The turn of the leaves. Birds chirping, foxes screaming, the usual guff. But there is little romance to be found in the confines of marriage, Edith Miller. A marriage is a job—a contract with unfavorable terms and little recourse when the benefits begin to wane."

"I don't understand why you got married in the first place, if you're so against it."

Nash winced. "I was tricked."

"By whom?"

"You wouldn't know him. Ruggedly handsome, very good with a pen. What he lacked in common sense, he made up for in gall and vigor."

"Ah. You are right, of course. I have certainly never met such a man."

Nash's laugh trailed off into a sigh.

"Rose is avoiding me," Eddie said. "I have been trying to pretend that everything is all right between us, but I think perhaps I have made a few too many mistakes."

Nash had taken a pipe from his pocket and was frowning down at it by the light of the lamp. He lost a few dark flakes of tobacco, which drifted into the lake and disappeared.

"Ah. Then we are both wifeless and adrift."

"She's not my wife," Eddie said indignantly, before realizing how ridiculous this sounded. Nash lit his pipe and took a deep drag, smoke wreathing his face like the breath of a dragon. "I think she likes this . . . Miss Cliffe. I think she might like her very much, in fact."

"Ah. I see." He put the pipe to Eddie's lips, cupping it as if it were precious, one hand on Eddie's shoulder. "Take some of this, for the pain. Go slowly. There's more than just tobacco in there, and we don't want to lose you overboard."

Eddie did as she was told and inhaled gently. Nash kept his hand on her shoulder, his fingers spanning her collarbone, his thumb hooked into the dip of her throat.

"That's it, good girl. Try it again."

She did. At first, she just felt strange, detached and slow, as if she were viewing the scene in front of her through a window— and then she felt a rush of pure euphoria that knocked all of the breath out of her, leaving her giddy and reeling.

"Oh, *God*."

"I am very pleased to say that we are no longer under His jurisdiction."

"I think I'm going to . . . just . . . lie down for a minute."

The rough wood on the dock felt cloud-soft and welcoming; it was almost as if she were actually floating on the surface of the lake, just Eddie and the water and the endless sky. She ran her hand along it and then felt resistance, a distant sting; she lifted her finger to be examined and found that there seemed to be a large splinter sticking out of it.

"Ouch, I suppose," she said, chewing on her lower lip and re-alizing that she couldn't really feel that, either.

"You have done yourself an injury," Nash said, sounding closer than expected. He leaned over her and took up her hand, turning it toward the lamp. "Look at that. An entire ship's mast has impaled you, and you are being so terribly brave about it."

"A ship . . . for ants," Eddie said, laughing at herself and de-lighting in the way Nash's dark eyes crinkled at the corners as he smiled down at her.

"Stop laughing, I am trying to perform a very delicate surgery to save your limbs from wood rot and . . . you know . . . worms. All right, close your eyes and think of England."

"I'd rather . . . think of . . . Greece. *Oof.* Is it out?"

"It is," said Nash. "But it was acting rather like a stopper, and now you are . . . unstopped."

Eddie opened one eye and squinted through it. There was quite an enthusiastic amount of blood for such a small wound. Nash had been studying her finger intently; he suddenly lifted it to his lips, and slipped it into his mouth. She watched him, dis-tantly appalled and strangely fascinated, as he sucked gently on it and then removed it.

"Had to suck out all the poison," he said, still leaning over her. His cravat was hanging loose. The end of it brushed against her neck, and she shivered. "No harm done. Only that I am a creature of the night now, and can only be sated by the blood of maidens, laid out wantonly in the moonlight . . ."

"Am not wanton," Eddie said, through a strangely dry mouth. "Just resting. You were right about the other thing, though."

"What thing?"

"You know . . . that you're . . . a night beast."

"A *night beast*?" Nash said, outraged and delighted, catching

Eddie by both wrists so that she laughed and squirmed to try to escape him. "A *night beast*, indeed."

"Well, you said something like that . . . It's not my fault I can't think, I am full of wine and pipe and . . ."

"*'Tis the wine that leads me on, the wild wine that sets the wisest man to* . . . laugh, to . . . to dance . . . damn, I can never remember Homer's particulars."

Somehow, in their brief scuffle, Nash had crawled almost entirely on top of her. Eddie was suddenly very aware of the weight and the warmth of him; at the exact moment that it came to her notice, Nash stilled and looked very serious. He unpinned her hands and brushed her hair away from her flushed face, his fingers tracing delicately over her brow and behind her ear.

"*It even tempts him to blurt out stories better never told.*"

Eddie blinked up at him, his mussed hair crowned with constellations, and forgot that there were a hundred reasons why they weren't supposed to be doing this.

"What kinds of stories?"

"Close your eyes and I'll tell you one."

She let her eyes close, and a moment later Nash was kissing her.

It wasn't familiar and natural, like it had been with Rose, the flaring to life of something they had been shoring up and stoking for years; if kissing Nash had been a fire, alarm bells would have already been ringing, such was the disconcerting speed and ferocity of the blaze. He was already pressing her into the dock, one hand clenched at her waist, the other tangling in her hair. He tilted her head back so that he could work her open, sweep his tongue into her mouth, bite down on her lip until she tasted blood. She heard herself gasp and wondered if she should be embarrassed, but he answered with a pained hitch of breath and then ran his fingers down to her thigh, his hand fisting in the fabric of her skirts.

"Ah," Eddie managed, when he broke away from her mouth to kiss her neck, "are we . . . ? Are we *entirely* sure this is—"

"Shhhh, Edie," Nash crooned, sounding even drunker than before, his voice thready and hoarse. "Hush now. You haven't done anything wrong. It's right. It's good, it's so good . . ."

Eddie knew that wasn't true. This was another woman's husband. There were plenty of names for ladies who kissed husbands that did not belong to them, but it was very difficult to recall them at present, what with the cold night air and the blinking stars and the fact that Nash had lowered his head and was now kissing insistently along her clavicle, his hand making little circles just below her hip. The combination was completely disarming, and rendered even more potent by whatever drug was currently racing through her blood.

Nash Nicholson was kissing her. It was unbelievable. He smelled like lake water and wine, tobacco smoke and damp wood. It felt like he was touching her everywhere at once.

"Are you cold?" Nash muttered against her neck, his breath skittering across her exposed skin and making her jump.

"No," said Eddie. "Yes. Hard to say."

"Here." Nash sat up on his knees to tug off his coat; Eddie sat up, too, so that he could put it around her shoulders. He helped her into the arms and then pulled her in close by the collar, kneeling between her legs. Their noses were almost touching. "Come to Greece with me."

"What?" said Eddie, bewildered. "When?"

"Who cares? Tomorrow. Next week. I shall charter us a ship."

"Well, I . . ."

Nash pulled her roughly toward him and kissed her hard, one hand finding its way inside the coat, traveling quickly from the jut of her ribs to her back. The initial rush of elation from the pipe was beginning to wane, and his touch felt less like magic and more like ordinary, slightly cold fingers—fingers that were currently sliding her dress off her shoulder, stroking every inch of skin they uncovered.

Eddie thought of Rose's hands clutching at her back, and abruptly wished she hadn't. It made what she was doing now feel even more wrong. If Nash was betraying Liza, then she rather thought that she was somehow betraying Rose.

Even if Rose would not care in the way that Eddie wanted her to. Even if Rose was this very minute locked in a similar embrace with Isabella Cliffe.

"We should stop," she attempted.

Nash just laughed huskily into her mouth.

"You are thinking *far* too much. It's good, isn't it? Tell me. I just want to make it good for you."

Eddie was just considering the Herculean task of actually pushing him away when light flooded the dock, illuminating them in a damning fresco: Nash kissing her jaw, one hand inside her dress, crouched over her like an animal with a kill; Eddie's hair falling loose, Nash's coat around her shoulders, flushed and kiss-swollen and letting him do it.

"*Fuck*," said somebody. It sounded like Kitty.

The light was too bright for Eddie to see; she shielded her eyes as the lamp was lowered, and she saw to her horror that Liza, Kitty, and Rose were standing on the shore. She couldn't see the expressions on their faces.

She could imagine them, though.

Fuck, indeed.

Chapter Twenty-two

"*L*IZA. LIZA, COME ON. SLOW DOWN FOR JUST ONE MOMENT. *Liza!*"

Eddie, Rose, and Kitty walked in silence, listening to the excruciating monologue from up ahead, where Liza was walking briskly up to the house with Nash stumbling along in her wake.

"Did he . . . ?" Rose said quietly, as Kitty kicked a bit of fallen tree out of the way so it didn't trip them. "Your lip. He didn't *make* you do it, Ed?"

Eddie touched a hand to her mouth, feeling blood and a gentle sting, where it had split against Nash's teeth.

"No," she said miserably.

Her soaring high had dissipated completely around the time she'd had to scramble to her feet without falling in the lake, trying to surreptitiously push her dress back into place and knowing that it was futile. She had managed to avoid looking at Rose at all. At least Breeches Bella hadn't been with them, leaning all over Rose and providing another witness to her shame. Small mercies.

"Oh," said Rose now, sounding even more stricken.

They were approaching the lawn; a couple of partygoers were kissing very enthusiastically against the wall of the house, completely unaware of the funereal procession approaching them. Liza stormed ahead into the house with Nash still at her heels.

Eddie felt a fresh stab of embarrassment. Since the moment they had been illuminated, he hadn't even spared her a glance.

Kitty gave her a bracing clap on the shoulder and then went on inside, too. It was just Rose and Eddie and the enthusiastic couple, who were kissing loud enough to punctuate the awkward silence with upsetting little sighs and slurps.

"Why did you do it?" Rose said eventually.

Eddie pulled back her shoulders, trying to preserve a modicum of dignity.

"Please don't say that like I kicked a little puppy, Rose. *He* kissed *me*, I really didn't *mean* for it to happen—and look, it's not as if we don't all know that he and Liza are deeply unhappy. You wouldn't understand—"

"No," said Rose. "I am glad to say that I wouldn't. I *told you* to be careful."

Eddie glanced up sharply at her. Her jaw was set, but there were silvery tear tracks on both of her cheeks. Eddie wanted to brush them away. She also wanted to scream. Either would have been an improvement on just standing there, feeling like an utter fool.

"*You* are engaged," she said, stubborn and stupid to the last. "And you kissed me."

"For the love of *God*!" Rose exclaimed. In her periphery, Eddie saw the couple spring apart, glance over at them in alarm, and then disappear around the corner of the house. "That's different, and . . . and you *know* it."

"I don't know anything!" Eddie shouted back. "Because you don't *tell* me anything! I have to try to discover it all on my own. Anything I know I find out because I accidentally walk into libraries, or . . . or . . ."

"Libraries?"

"Why are we having another quarrel? Why are we *always quarreling* these days? I feel like I am stumbling around, always operating with less than half the pertinent information. I am tired, Rose, and I have made an enormous fool of myself, and

I suppose I'll be lucky if I'm not put on the first boat home to-morrow to go back to London in disgrace. I need you to be my friend right now. I wish you would just be honest about what you have been keeping from me, because . . . because I know you *have* been keeping something from me."

"Fine," Rose said, her voice hard. Tears were streaming steadily down her cheeks. "Let's have it out. But I will never forgive you for making me say it like this, Eddie."

Her face was the very picture of heartbreak, and Eddie wilted.

"Oh, God. Then don't," she said, feeling as if she were being gutted like a fish. She took a step toward Rose, and then another when Rose didn't move. "I can't stand there being anything truly unforgivable between us. I mean it."

"We should never have come here," Rose said, her voice breaking.

Eddie put both arms around her and pulled her in close, and was relieved beyond measure when Rose pressed her face into Eddie's shoulder and stayed there, crying softly. Tears brimmed over in Eddie's eyes, too, and she felt one of them slide down her face, the fleeting sting of salt on her lip.

"Christ, Ed," Rose said tearfully, her voice muffled. "Are you wearing his coat?"

"Don't," Eddie said, squeezing her tighter.

There was a sudden burst of noise from the doorway, and they both looked up as a small crowd of guests spilled out onto the lawn, laughing and calling out to one another as they went. They parted around Rose and Eddie like a river around a rock and then kept walking, lanterns swinging, in the direction of the woods.

"I suppose they must be going home," Rose said, breaking free of Eddie's embrace.

"Or to do really deranged things with trees," said Eddie. "We should go inside."

Rose nodded, wiping at her eyes and taking a steadying breath before leading the way into the jaws of the beast.

Somebody was knocking softly on the bedroom door. When Eddie opened it, Albert, Dayo, and Valentine were standing in their bedclothes, looking faintly ridiculous. The last of the party guests had departed an hour or so before, and ever since the house had been full of the distant din of two people shouting at each other very, very loudly.

"We aren't dressed," said Rose.

Not so long ago, this would have been delivered with genuine concern about the impropriety of the situation, but her time on the island had clearly worn her down, as her delivery was rather half-hearted.

"Neither are they," Eddie pointed out.

Rose just shrugged and pulled a blanket around her shoulders, so Eddie opened the door wider to admit their visitors. It must have been close to dawn; the sky was still dark outside, but it had a fugitive quality to it, as if threatening to turn at any moment.

"Mama and Papa are fighting," Valentine said in a singsong voice, and Eddie sighed.

"It isn't funny."

"No, it actually isn't," Albert said.

He went to sit down in the only chair and then immediately stood up again, offering it to Eddie, who rolled her eyes.

"Just sit in the damned chair, Albert."

He did.

"Liza threw a vase through the window in the South Parlor," said Dayo wearily.

He pulled a pipe from inside his evening jacket and then patted his pockets, frowning, until Valentine leaned over and lit it for him.

"No," said Rose, stunned. "She did not."

"She did," said Valentine. "I don't care that it wasn't anywhere near that portrait of Nicholson senior, I think she ought to get twenty-five points for it."

"Motion sustained," said Dayo.

"Carried."

Dayo shook his head, puffing on his pipe. "That poor woman."

Eddie knew she had gone scarlet. She sat down on the edge of the bed and carefully studied her hands.

Valentine reached out and poked her right in the divot between her fingers.

"I cannot say you are not in any way at fault, Eddie, but you were not the first and you will certainly not be the last. *You* will not make or break this marriage, so stop looking so pink and cowed."

"We went to the theater once," said Dayo. "*With* Liza. It was just after his first big publication, and everywhere we went, everybody set to muttering. We were seated in a box, and the lead actress appeared and gave a speech from the one adjacent about halfway through the second act. She was only there for around five minutes, but she and Nash caught each other's eye, and during the interval we could not find him anywhere. When the curtain went up again the director walked out of the wings to inform us that the play could not continue as the leading lady had absconded from the dressing rooms."

"No," said Eddie. "With *Nash*?"

"Yes," said Dayo. "And Liza was just sitting up there in the box with an empty seat next to her, apoplectic."

"You have to admit that one was rather funny," Valentine said, leaning back against the wall with a snort. "Honestly, you cannot take any of this seriously, or you get drawn into the charade. Treat it as its own bit of light theater. I'm sure that is the spirit in which it's intended."

"It's not theater," said Albert. "It's her life. I have tried to talk to him about this, but he simply will not listen."

"Well, what sort of life do you think she imagined she would have, marrying *Nash*? And besides, if you must know, quite frankly she gives as good as she gets. She is just much, *much* cleverer about it."

Somewhere far below them, a door slammed very loudly. Rose and Albert winced in unison.

"Hang about," said Valentine, dashing over to the window. "I think that was . . . yes. Look."

Eddie went to look, Dayo at her side. Dawn was just creeping over the hills, a bright and dangerous pink, and in the rosy light she could see Liza walking toward the trees, wearing her traveling cloak. Henry was striding to keep up with her, carrying two trunks.

"Well," said Valentine, "that's that, then. I suppose she called for a boat with smoke signals or whatever the hell it is Nash has rigged up."

There was silence as they all considered this. Eddie watched Liza reach the woods and slow, her head half turning toward the house as if she were considering looking back, but a moment later she was gone.

"Time for bed," said Albert, getting to his feet and stretching. "Good night, Miss Li. Miss Miller. Everybody."

Dayo and Valentine followed him out. Eddie stayed at the window for a while longer, shivering in a rogue draft and watching for the first glimpses of the sun, until Rose sighed from under her blanket.

"I don't suppose you'll change anything by sitting there looking morose."

Eddie rolled her eyes, but got up anyway and went to join her. As she clambered into bed, Rose lifted the blanket and then deposited it over her entire being, so that she looked like a small pink ghoul.

"Well, you look nice," said Eddie, her voice cracking with fatigue. "What's the occasion?"

"I need to say something to you," Rose said quietly, made even quieter by the blanket. "But I don't care to look at you while I do."

"Oh," said Eddie. "Well, fine. But I feel you should know that you look like a lost octopus."

"If only it were still dark," Rose said, ignoring this.

"I shall close my eyes," said Eddie, leaning back against the pillows and letting them fall shut. "Although I cannot guarantee that I won't fall asleep."

"Don't," said Rose.

"All right. Go on, then."

"Well," said Rose. The blanket quivered slightly, as if she were rearranging herself. "Fine."

In the ensuing silence, Eddie actually did almost fall asleep; she was exhausted, and it must have been approaching seven o'clock in the morning.

"I like girls," Rose said, the words coming out of her in a long exhalation. "Romantically speaking. I *only* like girls. Oh, God. I actually just said that, didn't I? I heard myself say it. I wasn't sure how to tell you, before. To be honest, Ed, I thought you might have worked that one out on your own. But there it is. And I hope it helps make sense of some things that I know you couldn't quite understand before."

There it was. The final piece of the puzzle that Eddie had only really begun to put together a few hours before. And it *did* make sense.

Rose was marrying Albert for the same reasons Albert was marrying Rose. It was painful and discomposing, but probably not in the way that Rose feared; Eddie felt bludgeoned by the fact that she had not known something so integral about her closest friend—that she had felt the need to keep it secret from her, probably for years. Had Rose thought that Eddie would judge her? Or perhaps that she might retreat from their friendship, afraid of being somehow tainted? If so, she had monstrously mis-understood Eddie's character.

After all, Eddie hadn't thought twice about kissing Rose in the tree house, or in the billiard room. It had seemed completely natural to her. An inevitable development in their friendship, after spending that many years so very close. It hadn't felt par-ticularly remarkable that Rose was kissing *a woman*, or that this made some grand statement about who she was or who she liked, just in the same way that it had not thrown Eddie into some sort of crisis.

Except that . . . for Rose, it *had* been a reflection of who she was. In fact, any reasonable person could deduce that if one liked kissing girls, this might hint at a romantic inclination toward the same sex. That thing that Eddie had been trying to avoid think-ing about—that she had been avoiding so steadfastly every time she and Rose undressed for bed on opposite sides of the room—was suddenly laid bare before her, where she had no choice but to look at it.

"*Oh*," she said aloud, as the implications of this hit her like a stagecoach.

Perhaps it was not too late for a crisis after all.

There was a worried shuffling under the blanket, and she patted what she hoped was Rose's shoulder, attempting to be reassuring.

"Umph," said Rose. "Did you mean to place your hand on my thigh?"

"Whoops," said Eddie, rapidly removing it. "Er . . . Can I please step into your office for a moment?"

"Well," said Rose. "Fine."

She lifted the edge of the blanket and Eddie ducked under, pulling it firmly over both of them. It was very hot and stuffy, but compared to the chill of the room outside it was actually quite pleasant. Rose looked as dusky and pink as her name in the blanket-light.

"I am still not going to look at you," she said, in such an officious and stubborn voice that Eddie snorted a short, soft laugh into the warm air between them.

"That's all right. I just came in to tell you . . . well, to tell you that you are the very best person I have ever encountered. And that I'm sorry you didn't think you could just talk to me about this—because I know I can be an enormous fool, Rose, but I want to know everything there is to know about you. It only ever makes me love you more."

Rose laughed. It sounded wet. Eddie suspected she might be crying. Something occurred to her, and she frowned.

"That's why you wanted all that practice with me, I suppose. Not to kiss Albert. But to kiss . . . ladies. Being a lady, I suppose I was very well suited to be your stand-in."

Rose was silent for a second. "Yes. I suppose you were."

Eddie thought to ask about Miss Cliffe—to ask about the details of what she was now sure had been a romantic encounter, to attempt to squeal and congratulate her and play the role of the delighted friend—but she found herself unable to do so.

Of course Rose would like Isabella. She was brazen, and confident. *She* certainly would not have been surprised by this revelation from Rose, or caught unawares by her own feelings. Perhaps she and Rose would write to each other. Perhaps Miss Cliffe would visit again to continue their acquaintance. Eddie would have to learn to bear it.

"In case it's of interest," Eddie said instead, "I saw your fiancé kissing a very tall gentleman in the library a few hours ago. But I suspect you already know about that."

Rose smiled down at her knees. "Oh, was he? Good for him."

"Yes, well. I suppose that . . . knowing what I know now . . . I am very glad that the two of you found each other. I still don't entirely understand why you have to marry at all, Rose—"

Rose sighed. "Look, I know you are convinced that you can make your own way in this world, and I certainly would not bet against you—but to us mere mortals, being an unmarried woman is not an attractive prospect. I don't want to be the spinster that the married people take pity on—the one they seat by the fire at parties, to warm her lonely bones and consider her failings. Of course, there are things I have wanted—things I know I cannot have—and it would be *wonderful* to simply live as myself, to be free to make that choice, but in the world outside Bede House, I need to be practical. My position, my family, my prospects—they are not quite the same as yours, you must be able to see that. It might seem repugnant to you, but Albert and I have made the radical choice to be *happy*, in our own way. And we want our home to be a safe place, somewhere we can build a community—I can think of no better use for a house, or for my time."

Eddie considered this. The problem with Rose was that she was always so inclined to be kind to others, over and above how kind she was willing to be to herself. It was hard to tell which this was.

"I suppose I understand. And if you were going to marry any man . . . Albert is very well suited to the position."

"He's lovely," said Rose. "My parents adore him. *I* adore him. I think we shall build a very agreeable life together."

"Do you know, I never thought I would say this, but . . . I think you will."

Rose smiled again, but it quickly gave way to a frown.

"I suppose . . . you must like Nash a great deal, to have taken such a risk in kissing him."

"It's . . . difficult to explain," Eddie said slowly. Somehow, she had almost forgotten, but the shame came flooding back in an instant. "God. It's *Nash*. Obviously he is handsome. Clever. Funny. Far more trouble than he's worth—and you *must* believe me when I say I had no intention of doing anything at all untoward with him. I had been drinking, and he gave me something to smoke, and one thing led to another before I realized the first thing had even begun . . ."

"It's all right," Rose said suddenly. "You don't have to tell me. But you must know that no good can come of this, Ed. I cannot imagine anybody left in our party telling tales back in London, but . . . I suppose Liza might, and who could blame her? The rest of England isn't like this little island. The rules are different here . . . There practically *are* no rules. We can't stay at Bede House forever, and when we go back home you must still have a life to return to."

Eddie sighed. "I wouldn't worry. I think it is at an end. He's hardly looked at me since Kitty very helpfully shone that lantern on us."

"Perhaps you should see that as a blessing," said Rose. "A lucky escape."

"Perhaps *you* should not be casting the first stone," Eddie said, feeling more than a little needled. "Do you not think this is a bit rich, coming from . . . Well, you weren't actually giving Isabella Cliffe a *tour of the house*, were you? You might also have been discovered, had Kitty decided to dangle a lantern in your direction."

Rose pulled the blanket off so that she could lie down properly, turning away so that all Eddie could see of her was dark hair and a glimpse of a fist clenched tightly by her forehead. Eddie sighed and slid down under the covers, wishing that one of them had had the presence of mind to close the drapes and knowing that she didn't have an ounce of energy left in her to get up and do it now.

"No," said Rose, muffled against the pillow, long after Eddie had given up on receiving an answer. "I mean, I wasn't just giving her a tour. But we weren't . . . It wasn't what you think."

Eddie's spirits lifted sleepily as images of Rose and Bella ensconced in some rotting corner of the house kissing passionately were made fiction.

"What were you doing, then?" Eddie said.

She couldn't quite keep her eyes open anymore, and gave up fighting the inevitable, letting them flutter closed. She felt Rose turn next to her, a shifting of her weight that meant she was half leaning on Eddie, an instant comfort.

"If you must know . . . mostly, I was telling her about you."

Dear Mother and Father,

Mr. and Mrs. Nicholson hosted a wonderful party at the house last night, inviting all manner of fascinating guests—we drank punch and danced, and stayed up until dawn so that we might watch the sunrise over the hills. It is the perfect house for a party, as there are so many grand rooms and striking portraits, and even an armory that is a little like a museum, where we can view weapons of historical importance. Lucy-Anne would love it; I have never seen so many ways to maim and injure a person contained behind one door!

I am learning a lot here. I think you will be very pleased with the maturity of my character when I return to London society, and with all the new friends and connections I have made, thanks to the Nicholsons' kind hospitality. I miss you all, of course, but my novel is coming along well. I think this trip will be the making of me.

Yours,
Eddie

Chapter Twenty-three

WHEN EDDIE CAME DOWN TO BREAKFAST JUST AFTER MIDDAY, she found Nash sitting at the head of the table, still wearing his party clothes.

"Good morning," he drawled as she sat down at the opposite end, wincing at the scrape of her chair.

Eddie tried not to blush, and failed. He did not seem the least bit embarrassed to be addressing her as usual, despite all that had happened the night before. He *did* look very tired, dark circles under his eyes, his hair even more of a disaster than usual. She wondered if the fact of their kiss had been overshadowed by the dramatics with Liza; it had certainly been the case for her after her revelations with Rose, although in the cold light of day it was all coming back to her.

Was she supposed to be apologetic? Brazen? Blasé?

If he was going to behave as though it was all only mildly interesting—a lapse in judgment between two equals who had simply had too much to drink—then she supposed she should also aim for such maturity. She certainly wasn't going to let on that being kissed by Nash Nicholson had been a wild dream of hers since she had first read one of his poems, and that despite everything, some part of her thrilled at the knowledge that it had truly happened.

It was slightly difficult to achieve such composure with the imprint of his tooth still red on her lip, but she soldiered bravely on.

"It's the afternoon. Actually."

"Oh, *well*," Nash said, perking up. "In that case, I suppose I might be forgiven more wine. Care for a glass?"

"No, thank you," Eddie said, her stomach roiling in protest at the thought.

Nash leaned back as far as he could without overturning the chair and bellowed for Mrs. Hall. She appeared in the doorway, holding a bucket and a rag, looking extremely harried.

"There you are. Could you bring that '65 up from the cellar? And . . . eggs. Salmon. Do you want eggs?"

It took Eddie a moment to realize that he was addressing her. She shook her head.

"Just some toasted bread with butter for me, please."

Mrs. Hall gave such a tiny nod of acknowledgment that it could have been mistaken for a robust blink, and then marched away in the direction of the kitchens.

Nash sighed. "Insisting on living so modestly only makes me look extravagant."

"It is nothing to do with modesty. It's a precautionary measure against vomiting on your very nice mahogany table."

"Everybody who's anybody has vomited on this table. I would consider it rude if you *didn't* vomit on this table."

"Good to know."

Nash grinned, but there *was* something off about his usual devil-may-care demeanor; it seemed like a performance, a valiant but nonetheless transparent attempt at normality.

"Are you all right? We heard . . . Well . . . And we saw Liza leaving this morning."

"Ah, yes. She was just doing a little redecorating. I thought it perhaps too avant-garde to move half of the furniture onto the lawn via the closed window, but she's just *full* of fascinating ideas like that."

"Nash . . ."

"Please don't look all sad and sorry for me, Edie, it puts me in the mood to kick something," Nash said, with enough vitriol that Eddie believed him. "Speaking of . . . Where the hell is my dog? She wasn't hiding with you and Miss Li last night, was she?"

"No," Eddie said, frowning.

She had last seen Juno following Rose and Miss Cliffe around the party; she assumed that at some point, the dog had taken the only sensible course of action and gone to find somewhere quiet to hide.

"For *Christ's* sake!" Nash shouted, jumping to his feet and startling Eddie so badly that she almost fell out of her chair. "This really is the last straw. I *told* Liza she'd scare the poor stupid beast away if she didn't stop screaming, and now look."

"She probably just went to ground to get away from the party," Eddie said slowly. "I'm sure she will turn up eventually, once she's hungry."

"No, no . . . She hates to be without people, and she always comes when she hears my voice. Damn it all to hell. *Henry?*"

He strode from the room, continuing to shout for assistance. Eddie just sat in her uncomfortable chair, listening to the sound of him raging through the house and the low, reassuring rumble of Henry's responses once he had been located. Eventually she heard the front door open and slam shut again; a moment later Mrs. Hall appeared with the bottle of wine, a platter of freshly toasted bread, and a large pat of butter. When she saw that Nash was no longer there, she looked murderous.

"Sorry," Eddie said uselessly. "Thank you for the bread, Mrs. Hall. I don't suppose there is much point uncorking the wine."

Rain had begun to patter against the window; as Eddie watched, softly crunching away at her toast, a drop managed to squeeze its way through a gap in the frame and make a long, dark trail down the wallpaper until it slipped into the skirting board and disappeared. She stood up and went to examine the leak, and as she reached the glass she saw the distant figures of Nash and Henry, heads and umbrellas bowed against the wind, Henry trying valiantly to keep his lamp alight.

Kitty entered and pulled up a chair, reaching for some toast. She looked surprisingly and irritatingly well rested.

"Have you seen the South Parlor? It looks like a hurricane hit it. And there is a very convincing phallus on the wall of the armory. I suppose they might make it a permanent feature."

"Have you seen Juno?"

"The dog? No. She has the good sense to leave me alone."

"Nash has gone out to look for her. He thinks she's lost."

"She's a dog," said Kitty. "She will come back when she's hungry, or when she feels the urgent need to urinate on something valuable or slather somebody in saliva."

"That's what I said."

"And very wise you are, too. Well . . . about this, at any rate. Perhaps *only* about this, after last night's performance. Aha!" Mrs. Hall had returned with boiled eggs, lurid pink strips of salmon, sliced apples, and soft cheese that turned Eddie's stomach. "This will do nicely, thank you, Mrs. Hall."

Mrs. Hall looked slightly pained. "When Mr. Nicholson comes back and starts calling for his eggs, please inform him that you have eaten them."

"Gladly."

The rest of the house woke up in increments, drifting downstairs and eating whatever they could manage, their dispositions directly proportional to how well or poorly they had behaved the night before. Eddie's insides were still rebelling; when she couldn't stand to be around the food for a minute longer, she took her manuscript to the library and spent a few industrious hours glaring at it, which only came to a close when she accidentally knocked over the inkwell and lost half a page to the flood, leaving her with fewer words than when she had started. She promptly gave up, left her manuscript to dry out, and went to find Rose, who was helping Anne and Mrs. Hall in the armory.

"You don't have to do that, you know," she said, crossing her arms and watching as Rose kneeled precariously on top of a side table and dabbed carefully at the chalk. "It's hardly your responsibility."

"I know," said Rose, wiping her forehead with the back of her hand. She had scraped her hair up messily on top of her head and was wearing her plainest day dress, which was now soggy at the bodice and the knees. There was a bit of chalk smeared prettily on her chin and she was dewy with exertion; Eddie found herself looking for too long, and then glanced quickly away. "I thought I'd make myself useful."

"Juno is missing. Nash has been out there for hours."

"Is she?" said Rose, putting down the rag she was holding and climbing down from the table. "Poor thing. We should form a search party. I shall go and fetch the others. It'll be easier if we sweep the island in sections, so we don't miss anything."

Eddie somewhat doubted that she would be able to muster the entire household to go out in a storm in search of a dog, and was surprised when, twenty minutes later, she found everybody gathered in the entrance hall preparing to do just that. Even Kitty was there, looking confused, as if she wasn't entirely sure how she had been tricked into taking part. It was part of Rose's particular charm, Eddie supposed; she was so proactively practical and inclined to be helpful that she accidentally shamed everybody else into trying to match her.

"Has everybody got some ham or some cheese?" Rose said, patting her pockets.

Valentine coughed. "Miss Li, what if, for example, one became hungry waiting for this expedition to begin and accidentally consumed both ham and cheese? What then?"

"You shall have to cajole her back to you with nothing but

your winning personality," Rose said. "Come on, we shall split up into pairs so that nobody else goes astray in this weather."

Rose assigned them their partners, and inexplicably nobody complained or questioned her authority; Eddie found herself setting off toward the southwest shore with Dayo, with as much purpose as if they had been given military orders.

"I suppose somebody might have taken her ashore," Dayo said, as they walked down the gentle slope and into the trees.

"Stolen her, you mean?"

"Not stolen, no. Or, at least—that is not what any of those people would call it. I imagine they would think it was all part of the grand practical joke of existence."

"Hmph."

Eddie crouched down to look for a stick, and discovered a very satisfyingly sturdy one that split into a Y shape at just the right place, giving it a natural handle. She started poking bushes with it at random, checking that they were dogless.

"How has your writing been going?"

Eddie just laughed.

"Ah. Yes. Unfortunately, I understand completely."

"I was actually getting quite a lot done," Eddie said, whacking another bush, "even with . . . you know. How it is here. All the distractions. But then Nash read my pages and gave me his honest review, and I sort of . . . lost momentum."

"Well, that is not uncommon," said Dayo. "I suppose you will find your way back to it eventually."

"What about you?"

Dayo hummed thoughtfully. "Do you mind if I'm honest?"

"Please."

He sighed. "It is all a bit of a contradiction, for me. My being here. Writing here. I knew it would be, of course, but . . . it is different, somehow, actually living it."

"What do you mean?"

"Hm. Well. Writing articles protesting for one's humanity from the parlor of a country estate purchased with the profits of the slave trade, hosted by the ghosts of a family who built their fortune in plantations, with stolen *artifacts* and *heirlooms* on the walls, and mountains of sugar for our tea, is somewhat . . . jarring. To put it lightly."

"Ah," said Eddie.

"Ah indeed."

"Is it any better in London?"

"In some ways. But it is also worse, in others. I will send this essay to the editor of a journal who has given me nothing but encouragement and praise—but who has previously published those who believe that the trade is the natural order of things. I may soon be invited to speak at Westminster, which is considered an honor . . . and will address an audience made up of *many* whose family names decorate the deeds of plantations on the other side of the world. I am being given a seat at the table, I suppose. Made an exception—an example. But I do not want to sit at their table. I wish—we should *all* wish—to overturn it, instead."

"The sword never runs out of edges."

"Correct. And I cannot pretend that being with Nash and his ilk does not open certain . . . doors. Doors which would otherwise remain firmly closed to me. But everything always comes at a price." He paused. "Ah . . . Not to be crass, but does this or does this not look like dog excrement to you?"

"It does," Eddie said, resisting the urge to poke it with her stick. "And I hope you don't mind me saying that it looks rather . . . freshly laid."

"This hound will make detectives of us yet."

They followed the slope downward, slipping in the dark, wet mud, which had combined with the thick layer of fallen leaves to become a treacherous ground stew. It was impossible to look for footprints in the mire; they simply had to hope that Juno had made some logical choices in her journeying and taken the path of least resistance, rather than following the whims of a passing bird or squirrel.

There was a brief scuffle in a nearby bush, followed by the panicked flight of a fat wood pigeon that set off with surprising speed and nimbleness through the trees; a second later the dog appeared, looking exceedingly pleased with herself, plastered in mud from nose to tail.

"There you are, you mad thing!" Eddie cried, crouching down to greet her and almost being knocked over for her trouble. "Where have you *been* all day?"

"Wallowing in a swamp like a hairy hydra, by the looks of her paws," said Dayo, patting the dog on the head and then wiping his hand on his coat.

Juno harrumphed happily and then, without warning, dived merrily back into the underbrush, causing Dayo and Eddie to swear in unison and then head after her in hot pursuit. They crashed through the trees, through shallow puddles and whipping branches, calling her name and straining to keep sight of the wagging tail up ahead.

"For the love of Christ," Dayo said, sounding like he had a mouthful of miscellaneous detritus. "Whatever demon they called upon last night during their phallic chalk rituals has clearly taken hold of this dog."

Juno only barked happily in reply; Eddie followed her over a small hillock, and when she emerged on the other side, immediately saw that she had been leading them to her master.

The scene didn't quite make sense. Henry was sitting on a fallen tree, bright red and with an oddly evasive expression, eyes fixed on the ground. Nash had been standing directly in front of him, so close that he was almost bracketed by Henry's knees. When Juno barreled into him, even after an entire afternoon spent searching for her in the rain, he looked slightly irritated rather than relieved.

"We found her," Eddie said breathlessly, breaking the strange silence that had greeted her.

Dayo had caught up and was brushing down his clothes, also breathing heavily.

"It looks as if *she* found you," said Nash, giving Juno a cursory scratch behind the ear and grimacing when his hand came back covered in mud. "What on earth are you doing out here?"

"Looking for your dog," Dayo said, sounding very unimpressed. "Miss Li was kind enough to rally the troops to help you."

"Oh," said Nash, rubbing at the back of his head and glancing up in the vague direction of the house. "Very good. Well, as you can see, all present and accounted for, so I suppose we'd better go back."

Eddie felt very deflated after the chase, and perplexed at Nash's understated reaction; they trudged homeward in silence, Henry overtaking them all early on and marching with his head down, Juno keeping pace with him. She looked entirely unbothered by the fuss, clearly thinking that they had all just spontaneously decided to join her for a rainy jaunt and were now heading in for a touch of supper.

Nash proved difficult to track down for the rest of the day. Eddie felt that their conversation that morning had been left rather unfinished, the questions that she had been too tired to articulate now burning a hole in her tongue, but although she kept moving from room to room in the hope of catching him, he remained at large. She did catch a few glimpses of Henry, going about his tasks with a grim expression on his face; at one point, Mr. Morris had to ask him three times to bring a stepladder up to the long gallery, and he shook his head as if he had been sleepwalking before acquiescing.

Kitty had taken up her painting and her supplies and moved right back into the South Parlor, despite the fact that the main feature of the room was now the enormous, jagged hole in one of the windows, which had been hastily covered with a large sheet. It was sodden, the wind making it bend and billow, and was sporadically admitting rain through the gaps. The servants had been hard at work; other signs that a raucous party had taken place, followed by an even more raucous argument, were few and far between. Occasionally Eddie came across a wine stain—or what she *hoped* was wine—or some other piece of more permanent damage that they had been unable to eradicate in just one day. On her way to the drawing room, Eddie realized that somebody had inked little hats onto all the horses in what she was sure was a priceless oil painting of a grand battle. Valentine had gone back to bed, Dayo was likely bent over a desk somewhere making the most of the peace to write, and Rose had sat and sketched with Kitty for a while until the cold overcame her, and was now playing cards with Albert in the drawing room, Juno happily asleep with her head resting on Rose's left foot. Eddie sat in the corner, listening to the soothing sound of their game, writing in unproductive little bursts and frequently finding herself distracted watching how the two of them were together.

She supposed that in some ways it must have been easier than a romantic attachment: knowing the limits and parameters up front, clearly stating their hopes and expectations and making an agreement that was mutually beneficial. It was so unlike regular courting, during which the realities of long-term cohabitation and people's true natures were so often secondary to putting best feet forward in the hope that prospective partners found said feet easy on the eyes.

Eddie tried to imagine herself feeling so at ease with

somebody—knowing she would wake up with them every morning, pass the newspaper back and forth, watch them brush their hair and take medicine for their headaches and forget their hat when leaving for parties—and could only see Rose. There was nobody else she wanted to share these ordinary and wonderful mundanities with. In an instant she was there, handing Rose the brush and the medicine, waiting outside on the path as she fetched her hat, and then taking her arm with a smile as they went on their way.

Despite what she knew about Rose and Albert's attachment, she could not help but feel jealous of the life they were planning together; of the fact that Albert would get to claim Rose above all others; of the way they laid out their cards in silence, content, wanting nothing more from each other than that they were happy to give.

Albert had Rose's hand in marriage, and Isabella Cliffe had her attention. What did that leave?

"Eddie," said Rose, glancing up briefly before going back to her hand. "Please stop staring at us, you'll give me a complex."

Unable to commit to this, Eddie decided to take her manuscript for another walk, hoping that inspiration might strike if the temperature in some part of the house felt more amenable, or the light caught her quill just right. Instead she walked right into Nash, who was exiting the kitchen with fruitcake stuffed into his mouth, half of which fell out when he saw Eddie.

"Ah," he said, having removed the other half. "Well met, Edie."

Eddie grimaced at him. "I have been meaning to catch you all day."

"Right," said Nash. "Of course. Shall we . . . ?"

He gestured down the corridor in the direction of the library, and they made their way there in silence.

"Are you trying to avoid me?" she blurted out as the heavy door shut behind them, regretting it at once.

Nash sighed, pulling out a book and flipping it over briefly before returning it to the shelf.

"Avoid you? Why on earth would I? And, for that matter, *how* could I? We are all trapped here on this minuscule island together, are we not?"

"Well . . ." said Eddie. "No, actually, we are not. As Mrs. Nicholson just so aptly demonstrated, we are in fact free to leave at any time, weather and lakeworthy vessels permitting."

Her tone was enough to get Nash to finally look at her properly. He looked slightly sheepish, although it was a degree of guilt that would have better suited the pilfering of fruitcake than adultery with an audience.

"Do you want me to leave?" Eddie pressed on, now being openly churlish. "I feel rotten, and everybody keeps looking at me with such *pity*, and honestly if you are going to ignore me on top of all that, then there hardly seems any point in my staying."

"No, God, Edie—Christ, why must we have all these theatrics?" said Nash irritably, which seemed entirely unfair from a man so given to theatrics that he might as well have sold tickets to his afternoon naps. "Sorry, sorry. I didn't mean that. Look, come here and stop pouting, will you?"

He abandoned the books and reached for her, trying to fold her into his chest.

"Nash, stop it. I wasn't asking for . . . I hardly expected . . . *Stop* a moment, I mean it."

He stopped being quite so insistent, although he kept both hands on her shoulders, holding her at arm's length and looking at her dubiously. Even exhausted and irksome and with a bit of cake in his mustache, he was regrettably handsome, and the magnetic pull toward him persisted. Eddie remembered their kiss, thought of his hand on her thigh and his hot breath on her neck, and felt her resolve waver.

"What the devil do you *want*, then?" he said, not unkindly.

His hands went to her chin, and he stroked both thumbs across her face, following the lines of her cheekbones. Eddie felt her eyes try to close at his touch, and kept them open with a determination that probably made her look like a lunatic owl.

"I want to write," she said firmly. "To finish my story. To see it through. That is what I came here to do. Everything else is . . . a distraction."

It was true, but it was also an egregious lie.

She wanted so much. *Too* much. Rose. Nash. An audience with Nash's editor. But Nash was off-limits, and Rose was out of reach—so the editor would have to bear the full brunt of her desire.

"A distraction, indeed," Nash said, sighing. "Ah well. I have been called worse. Very recently, actually."

"Was she very angry?"

"Hmmm," said Nash, his hands falling to her shoulders again, stroking at her aimlessly. "Best not to dwell. You *have* been writing, though, haven't you?"

"Yes. Some. A lot, I suppose."

"Then it sounds as if you have been sedulous in your efforts and could stand a little . . . distraction."

In a moment of clarity, Eddie understood; his pride had been wounded by Liza's dramatic exit, but he had only needed the day to lick his wounds, and now that his mood was improved, he fully expected that Eddie would be more than happy to kiss him in the library . . . and likely all manner of other places. The entire thing felt so tawdry that Eddie found herself pulling away from him again, shaking her head.

"Nash, please. You're . . . confused. Upset. Let us just be friends—focus on our work, that's what really matters."

Nash had been reaching for her hand, but he stopped. Something flickered across his expression; if she didn't know better, she might say that he looked *aggravated*, although he quickly smoothed it away.

"Friends. Yes. We *are* friends, of course. But if you simply want me for my powers of literary critique, then I shan't hold back. I hardly wanted to put you off, but if you want the truth . . ."

"I do," Eddie said firmly. She offered him her manuscript, thrusting it out in front of her like a sword. "Want the truth. I have no desire to embarrass myself in front of your editor with inferior work, if it is possible to save it. I took your comments on board, I have been making changes . . ."

Nash shrugged and took the papers, turning away from her to flick through them as he walked.

"The thing is, Edie . . . it's all a bit basic and prosaic, isn't it? With this farcical setup, the insistence on all this plot . . . there is barely a glimpse of true beauty."

"You said you liked it," Eddie said, embarrassed by the quavering of her voice and the violent drop of her stomach. "Before, you said . . . You said it was funny, and . . . and *searing*. And I took out most of the jokes, as you asked."

"Cartoons in the newspapers are *funny*. A kitchen pan is searing. I was being gentle with you. I certainly cannot show *this* to my editor yet, even with the changes you have made. You aren't ready. You must know that."

Eddie was trying very hard not to choke on what she could only assume must have been her own saliva and repressed tears; she cleared her throat, her eyes burning, and held out a hand to take the manuscript back.

"Oh, Edith, please don't look at me like that . . . You wanted the truth, and I gave it to you." He had softened, the look in his eyes almost pleading. "You *will* get there, I know it. If you like, I can sit down with a few pages and write some notes for you— how's that? Play at editor, so that you know what needs to change. Don't cry, darling, I thought you wanted to know . . ."

"I did. And I'm not. Crying, I mean."

He handed back the manuscript. She could feel him watching intently as she focused on smoothing down the pages and tried to regain control of herself.

"Please do come here, Edie. I cannot stand to see you look so glum over so little cause."

He didn't wait for her to answer; he just stepped forward and kissed her, his hands finding hers where they held the manuscript and taking hold of them. Eddie was still halfway to crying, frustrated and hurt, and could not reconcile these feelings with *kissing*. She could feel the paper crumpling beneath their hands, and it was all she could think about; his fingers tightened—she supposed in passion, although she had no idea where it could have appeared from—and she felt panic unfurl in her chest at the thought of her manuscript being bent and torn beneath them.

She pulled away, and Nash sighed, that little hint of frustration back immediately. Eddie felt like an enormous disappointment. They were both still holding on to the sheaf of papers between them, Nash's hands overlapping Eddie's.

"I . . . I need to go and fix this," she said. "I will not rest until it's done."

She tugged at the manuscript and felt a moment's resistance before Nash let it go.

"All right. I admire your perseverance. Not about the rest part, though—you *must* rest, or you will become so sick of inventing delightful adjective combinations that you will throw yourself neatly in the lake. Come and find me later and I shall fortify you with whiskey and wine, hmmm?"

Eddie nodded.

The rain had let up, and she walked from the house not really knowing where she was going, the maelstrom of emotions inside her narrowing to a sharp resolve that settled behind her sternum and made her burn with purpose. She found herself at the boathouse, and when she opened the door she discovered that Dayo was sitting inside at a makeshift desk, blankets heaped over his shoulders to warm him.

He glanced briefly up at her and then shrugged one of the blankets off, holding it out for her to take.

"Come in if you are coming in. And take care when you close the door—there is a spider up there the size of Germany just waiting for her chance to strike."

Chapter Twenty-four

BY THE FIRST WEEK OF NOVEMBER, THE RAIN HAD PAUSED. When the early morning fog rolled away the days were bright, grayish-white, a constant thin cover of cloud preventing the sunshine from breaking through.

It was also bitterly cold. All the little quirks and cracks of the house colluded to allow freezing drafts to blast through every room, so that the only way to stay a vaguely healthy temperature was to huddle around the fire wearing every possible layer of clothing. Blankets became currency; they could be traded for the last of a bottle of wine or a nip of good whiskey, or used as payment for being the person to go up and call for one of the servants or fetch something from another room. The damp only made it worse. Even the cleanest bedclothes would succumb quickly to that peculiar, half-rotted smell; Eddie would sometimes catch a whiff of it even on a freshly laundered dress, and could no longer tell if it was real or imagined.

Eddie and Dayo had worked side by side in the boathouse very briefly until it became untenable, and then had taken up residence in the library at opposite ends of the desk. On the first truly cold day, Dayo had come downstairs to discover Eddie vigorously rubbing her hands together in an attempt to regain some feeling in them, and had immediately dragged the desk as close to the fireplace as possible without setting it alight. They worked mostly in silence, although occasionally one of them would ask the other for the correct spelling of a word, or how many sentence clauses constituted a glut. Dayo would sometimes read passages aloud to test the cadence of them, and Eddie would forget about her own work and listen, transfixed, as he carefully unspooled the inner workings of colonialism and the slave trade for proper examination.

The others mostly gathered in the drawing room, which was small enough to retain heat. Eddie thought they also favored it due to the fact that the walls were a deep red, which gave the impression of warmth even before one factored in the fire. The South Parlor, with its gaping hole now boarded over and so much of the outer wall made of glass, had become almost uninhabitable.

At night, Eddie and Rose disrobed as quickly as possible with fumbling fingers, emitting little shrieks and groans of agony as they did; after the first few nights of bitter cold, Eddie had rolled over to Rose's side of the bed while half-asleep, seeking the heat from her body, and Rose had nestled in close without hesitation. After that they slept wrapped around each other like cats, too cold to waste energy on acknowledging this new arrangement as anything other than a necessity, although Eddie often found herself struggling to drift off, guiltily attuned to the feeling of Rose breathing against her in the dark. Sometimes Eddie would open her eyes to discover that her face was pressed into the crook of Rose's neck, or that one of Rose's arms was thrown over her, their dark hair mingling on the white pillows until she couldn't tell which belonged to her anymore. She would lie awake trying to soothe her racing heart and think of Rose's words—*I like girls*—and wonder what, exactly, constituted a *like* so strong and certain that it was worth speaking aloud. She liked Rose right here, pressed against her under a heap of blankets. She liked the smell of her hair, and the odd little snuffling noises she made in her sleep, and the all-encompassing warmth of her.

She had liked kissing her. More than she had liked kissing Nash, in retrospect. That was hard to deny. It was also hard to categorize, in her mind. She could almost place it firmly in the realm of *understandable, kissing is a pleasant physical act, and Rose is very pleasant* . . . but sometimes it got away from her somewhat, and she found herself gently panicking and disentangling herself from Rose's sleeping form. It was no good wondering what might be—or what they could be to each other, if Eddie followed that thread—when all Rose wanted and needed was for Eddie to be her friend.

For her part, Rose had seemed pleased by Eddie's easy acceptance of her blanket revelation, but was still keeping a little more distance than usual during the daylight hours. Perhaps she was still angry at Eddie for kissing Nash. Perhaps she regretted telling Eddie the truth.

There were endless perhapses, and Eddie made sure that she was too busy writing to study them properly.

The heroine in her manuscript, Delilah Fortescue, had now successfully impersonated her husband—with a few near misses—at dinner parties, at Parliament, and even in front of his own mother. She had accidentally begun a new romance with a stranger and was hurtling toward the third act, when all the consequences would come knocking. Eddie felt so mired in all the different threads that she could barely see the path ahead. The only way out was to write, and she barely stopped; she wrote at breakfast, wolfing down the hottest food she could manage before escaping to the library; she spent all day crouched over the desk by the fire, inching closer until she was in grave danger of a singeing; she rarely got away with writing at dinner, but when they all relocated to the drawing room afterward she wedged herself firmly into a corner and put pen to paper again until the words blurred or someone (usually Valentine) threatened to toss the manuscript into the fire and carry her to bed themselves.

She tried to put herself in the mind of a London editor, to imagine what he might want from her. Nash had been strangely and unhelpfully taciturn on the subject, which left her rudderless and unsure, constantly second-guessing her instincts. She was beginning to suspect that she didn't have any at all.

All her hard work seemed to be irritating Nash, who was drinking more heavily than ever, and kept insinuating that Eddie was being absolutely dire company. Truth be told, he seemed sick of all of them. It seemed as if he *had* sent something to his editor, as he had recently received a number of very pointed letters, which Eddie had found half-burned in the grate; from what she could gather, he had missed both a deadline and an extension on a deadline, and things were getting slightly fraught.

As Eddie's chances at publication rested entirely on Nash's continuing relationship with this man, she couldn't help but frown across the room when she saw him not writing in the morning *or* the afternoon. In fact, *any* opportunity to not write was taken up enthusiastically, to the point that Eddie once saw him pick up a quill and then use it to try to wrestle with the dog.

"You have all atrophied," he said one night at dinner, gesturing around at them with an accusatory wineglass. "I only ever discover you sitting in the exact same places. What on earth is the point of being here at all? You might as well be sitting sentry around your fires in London."

"Yes," Albert said to Rose under his breath. "We might as well be."

"I didn't quite catch that, Albert."

Albert cleared his throat and put down his own glass.

"We are, in fact, thinking of returning to London. We are enormously grateful to you for hosting us, of course, but we have intruded on your hospitality for long enough. We have a wedding to plan, and the weather being as it is—"

"Nonsense," said Nash, slamming his glass down so hard on the table that Eddie was surprised it didn't shatter. "You only think the fun has run out because you have ceased to contribute. It is hardly cold enough to warrant an evacuation. We ought to be . . . you know . . . telling ghoulish stories, and roasting things on the fire, and drinking enough that the weather never touches us."

Valentine, who was drinking almost as much as Nash but had been noticeably quieter as the weather had turned, raised a glass in salute.

"See? Valentine understands. Now, if the rest of you could just—"

He was cut off by a very odd noise. It was almost like the groaning of a ship in the wind, the yawning distress of a hull being bent to breaking point. It only lasted a second or so, and then there was an earsplitting crash somewhere above them, so explosive that it sounded as if somebody had actually shot a cannon at the house. Rose gasped, and Kitty jumped to her feet; there was a moment of eerie silence, and then they heard a distant and very furious shriek.

"Bloody fucking hell," said Nash, looking rattled. "Has the sky fallen in?"

The sky had not, but the ceiling of the long gallery had. It appeared that the hole in the roof had worsened, which had in turn allowed all manner of rain and debris into the bedroom above, and that ultimately the ceiling had given in to the inevitable and cracked open, dumping its contents into the room below. Mrs. Hall was beside herself. She had been entering the long gallery at the time of the collapse, and had now been firmly steered away by Henry so that she might politely continue her hysterics in the privacy of the servants' quarters.

They all stood staring up at the hole in the ceiling, watching as scraps of rotten wood and leaves and slow trickles of rainwater continued to fall into the room. Ignoring Dayo's shout of warning,

Nash strode out toward it to get a better look; he peered up, one hand shielding his face from the water, and then swore loudly.

"Well. I suppose . . . Christ. God damn it. If we ever need to land a balloon in the house, we can just . . . *Shit!*"

"I would ask how bad it is," ventured Kitty. "But there only seems to be one answer."

"Don't—!" Nash started, but he seemed to catch himself and broke off, scrubbing his hand violently through his hair. "Do not mock me right now, Catherine. There is an enormous fucking hole in my inheritance."

"I suppose . . . I suppose there might be a way to salvage it," said Rose. "I suspect Henry might know. Although I imagine a lot of the damage has already been done, over time . . ."

"Oh, do shut *up!*" Nash shouted. Rose flinched as if hit, and Eddie's mouth fell open. "I have put up with your mousy presence until now, but even I have my limits. No, I'm sorry—do you think it is the *least* bit helpful to say such a thing now?"

"*Nash*," Eddie breathed, horrified.

"Good God, man," said Albert, his face a brilliant red. "Is there any need to be so unforgivably rude?"

"Oh, please, Albert, we aren't in London now, there's no need to stand on ceremony—I will speak how I wish to in my *own damned house.*"

"She was trying to help," Dayo said firmly, crossing his arms and taking a small step in front of Rose, who was rigid and pale with shock. "And in return, you have insulted her."

Nash seemed to sense that the room was against him. He rubbed at the back of his neck, wilting.

"I suppose . . . I spoke out of turn. As I'm sure you can understand, I have just had an enormous shock, and I . . . Look, Miss Li, I did not intend to—"

"That's quite all right," Rose said stiffly, finding her voice. "There is no apology necessary. If anything, you have just proven to me that I am an excellent judge of character, so for that, I thank you. As for my presence in your house, you needn't worry—Albert and I will depart in the morning."

She turned and left immediately, Albert shaking his head as he followed her out. Dayo wasn't far behind. Valentine went to Nash and gave him a friendly shake of the shoulders.

"Idiot. We shall find a way to fix it."

Eddie assumed that Valentine meant the ceiling, and not any friendship with Rose, which had never really existed in the first place. Nash glanced over at Eddie, who was still frozen to the spot, reluctant to reignite his anger but unable to let his behavior pass without reproach.

"You *really* shouldn't have done that" was all she managed before she went in search of her friend.

"I am not at all surprised," Rose said, picking up a dark pelisse and frowning at it. Juno had found her way into the room and was staring up at her, looking mournful, as if she knew what a trunk was and considered it a dire omen. "Is this yours or mine?"

"Yours," said Eddie. "Could you slow down for one second?"

"No," said Rose, carefully folding the coat and placing it in her trunk. She really did look magnificent when she was angry—and good Lord, was she angry.

"Look, Anne will do that, or Mrs. Hall—"

"Mrs. *Hall*? I imagine the poor thing is having a stiff drink for the shock. I can pack my own trunk, Eddie. Anyway . . . as I said, I am *not* surprised. You know I have always considered him to be a presumptuous, arrogant sort of man. I will be very glad to see the back of this place."

"But you can't mean that. I mean . . . I don't want you to go," Eddie said, sitting down on the edge of the bed. "You cannot leave me here by myself in this room. I shall rot."

"Then come back to London with us," Rose said, shrugging, as if it were that simple. "You can write just as well there— perhaps better, I imagine, now that it's so ludicrously cold here. Nash is not some . . . some magical *conduit* for talent, Ed. You are plenty talented on your own."

"I don't know," Eddie said, utterly miserable. "He said he was going to help me. You know, with all the problems in my writing. Before my manuscript goes to his editor."

Rose snorted. "Problems? What problems?"

"He is a famous poet, Rose, you cannot pretend he is some talentless hack just because he was rude to you—he was *dreadful*, I know, it was unforgivable, but the editor has been harassing him, and his ceiling had just fallen in—"

"He is not without talent, I will grant him that, but he *is* entirely without tact, grace, good manners, or a fully functioning moral compass, and I find those to be key attributes I look for in the company I keep. And . . . and your writing does not have *problems*. None that you cannot work out by yourself, anyhow. You have always done so before."

But Rose didn't understand. If Eddie went back to London now, Nash might never forgive her. All the help he had promised her—the connections, his editor—she couldn't squander it now when she was so close. And besides . . . she didn't actually *want* to leave yet. He was difficult, yes, but Rose was wrong on one point—there *was* a sort of magic to Nash; all things were made possible in his presence. Besides, as Rose herself had pointed out many times, Bede House was its own world apart, and Eddie wasn't ready to return to the harsh reality of London.

"Just stay until Christmas," Eddie attempted. "I shall be returning to town then, and we can go together. I am entirely sure that Nash feels like an enormous ass right now, and is trying to find some eloquent way to apologize profusely."

"If you earnestly believe that, you are in more danger than

I thought," Rose said, pulling her dresses from the wardrobe and setting about folding those, too. "God, everything smells so dreadful. You really will rot if you stay here."

"I know."

Eddie fingered the bedclothes, which were freezing to the touch. The thought of the house without Rose filled her with a heavy sort of melancholy, but perhaps she could convince herself that it was for the best. She supposed it might be a little easier to focus without Rose around.

She might spend less time thinking about kissing her, for one thing.

Rose glanced over at her, and her expression softened; she put down the shawl she was holding and sat next to Eddie on the bed.

"I know this has all been very exciting, Ed. And you do like to get caught up in things like this. Adventures. Schemes. You throw yourself in without looking, wholeheartedly and pigheadedly. But don't you think the fun is over, now? Is it not time to go back to the real world?"

"This *is* the real world. Or . . . it could be. If I take this chance. If I get it right. It's everything I have ever wanted, Rose."

"Really?" said Rose, her nose wrinkling. "*This?*"

"Well, not *this* exactly, but what comes afterward. I don't know how to explain it to you. You are content to just *be*, but I . . . I feel like if I stop trying to make it as a writer, to make something of *myself*, I will simply keel over and die."

Rose considered her, frowning.

"You are a half-wit," she said eventually. "Firstly, because you have been convinced to doubt yourself when you are in fact enormously talented, with or without that man's help. Secondly, because there are *many* other ways to live a life worth living and to share your stories, even if you never end up on anyone's shelf but mine, where you shall always have pride of place. And *thirdly—*"

"I know I am a half-wit," Eddie grumbled. "There is no need to make an itemized list."

"Nash Nicholson is not your friend, Ed. And he did not bring you here because he believed in you as a writer. He invited you without reading a word you'd written, because he liked the look of you, and because he wanted somebody to gaze at him in awe every time he opened his mouth. I know what caring about Eddie Miller looks like, believe me, and this is . . . not it."

"Now you're being cruel."

"*Me*, cruel? Eddie, I have never seen you quite so down on yourself. Can *you* not see it? All that has happened since you came here is that you feel *less* confident in your abilities. You have hardly even picked a fight with me for a week, and that is terribly unlike you." Rose smiled, but it was obviously a strain, and she quickly gave up on it. "I thought this was supposed to be fun."

"It was. It is. It just became a lot more . . . complicated."

"Come home with me, then," Rose said.

This time she did tentatively reach for Eddie's hand. They used to touch all the time, Eddie thought distantly, without it meaning anything at all. It used to be commonplace. Now she felt Rose's fingers interlace with hers and only wanted to pull her closer. The intensity of her gaze was too much, too *loaded* for Eddie to meet head-on.

"The longer you stay here," Rose continued, "the more likely Mrs. Nicholson is to lose her temper and start telling tales about you in London. What if somebody tells your parents? What if they discover what's really been going on? You should come home before it's too late."

Rose had a point, but it was the last thing Eddie wanted to hear; it only reminded her that *polite society* awaited in London, and she could not think of anything worse.

Rose would have a wedding to plan, and Eddie would have to watch her do it. Dinners would now be at Albert's house, likely with a lap full of rabbits. Rose would sit with other married ladies at parties and talk about things like homemaking and upholstery, and even the Millers might raise eyebrows at Mrs. *Rednock* clambering into their tree house for a tipple.

Besides, Eddie could hardly go home and pretend she had never met Nash at all; he, too, would return to London eventually. She already knew that she would be desperate for an invitation to his house so that they could resume their friendship, and devastated if one never came. He had changed her; given her hopes and expectations she never would have dared entertain before. It was dangerous, enticing—and completely addictive. She thought of herself sitting at home, writing stories just to entertain Rose, performing them to her family, and then putting them away in a drawer. It seemed impossible to bear.

"It's already too late," she said eventually.

Rose retracted her hand and got up to continue packing, and all Eddie could do was sit uselessly and watch.

Chapter Twenty-five

"Are you asleep?"

"No."

"Are you cold?"

"Yes. Ugh, your foot is freezing, Ed. *How* is it so cold?"

"My foot is all the way over here. That must be the ghost, touching you. Little ghost toes."

"It is not a ghost, and they are not little. You have feet the size of rowing boats. Besides . . . a ghost would stop fooling about and get on with the business of haunting me."

Eddie tried to find Rose in the mess of blankets. It was difficult; there were so many, and she was thoroughly entangled in them. In the end she discovered and gained entrance to Rose's little pocket of warmth, and laughed quietly when skin met skin and Rose hissed between her teeth. It was certainly not the first time they had huddled together like this, but it *was* the first time they had actually acknowledged that it was happening, and it felt very strange to Eddie after so long pretending she simply hadn't noticed.

"Haunt initiated."

"Cold. Cold, cold, cold."

"God, you are so warm."

"Yes, I know. I have cultivated this warmth. I have been growing it carefully like crops, and now you have come in to harvest it all for yourself."

"You ought to share."

Rose turned over, and when she next spoke her mouth was very close to Eddie's ear.

"You are a blight."

The room felt cozy suddenly, despite the fact that there was an actual breeze ruffling the curtains and lifting the pages of Eddie's manuscript where it sat on the dresser. The fire was crackling merrily, and she imagined she could now feel the warmth of it where before it had eluded her. She thought of the room empty of Rose's things; of the bed cold and too big without her. Of losing these chances to touch her so casually, with the convenient excuse that the house was failing in its primary duty to provide shelter.

"Please stay."

Rose sighed. "Come with me."

"I can't."

Another heavy exhalation. Her breath ghosted across Eddie's neck, and she savored it, feeling a little freakish for doing so.

"Come here, then, you insufferable ghoul. I suppose you might as well be warm for one last night before you succumb to pneumonia and expire."

"Much obliged," Eddie said, but her voice was odd and strangled; Rose had reached out and pulled her close, much closer than they had been consciously since the night they had kissed in Valentine's bedroom. She tucked her face into the curve of Rose's neck. It smelled so comfortingly of *Rose* that she sighed, and as she did she felt Rose's body answer her, pressing in closer. Their chests were flush together, one of Rose's hands holding her gently by the shoulder; it tentatively began to trace the line of Eddie's shoulder blade, and she closed her eyes, breathing into it, feeling as if they were no longer in their freezing bed at all but somewhere far more agreeable. She gave over to the feeling and found herself speaking, mumbling directly into the skin of Rose's throat.

"How do you know if you . . . like girls?"

Rose went absolutely still.

"What do you mean?" she whispered. "You just like them. They don't make you take an examination or get a license or anything to make it official."

Eddie opened her eyes and found herself looking at the delicate shell of Rose's ear.

"Right. Of course. I mean . . . I had never really thought about it before. And I suppose I *have* traditionally liked boys, if I have liked anyone at all."

"You liked that long-haired boy at the assembly rooms two years ago, who asked you what was in the punch," Rose said, with a keenness of memory that left Eddie stunned. "You took a liking to that colleague of my father's, Mr. Chen, when we were eleven. You kept following him from room to room like a puppy."

"Yes. I know. So perhaps I'm wrong. But . . . when you told me how you felt, it made perfect sense. *Too* much sense. I suppose it's not the same as it is with you—you have known for a while, and I have been perfectly oblivious. They won't be giving me my license any time soon."

"You can set up shop without one," Rose said into her hair. "I certainly won't inform the board."

"I would hardly know where to begin," said Eddie. A strangely tense silence followed this. Eddie wished she could see the expression on Rose's face, but lifting her head to look was out of the question. "You can ask Isabella Cliffe. I'm sure she knows."

Rose let out a tiny breath and shook her head.

"Eddie, I am not going to ask Isabella Cliffe anything of the sort."

"But you are going to write to her? And see her again?"

"I am sure we will be reacquainted at some point when she is next in town."

Eddie frowned. This didn't seem right.

"But . . . Don't you . . . ? I thought you might be making plans to fall in love with her?"

Rose made an indignant, huffing sort of noise and then pushed Eddie away so that she could look at her properly. Eddie had been right to try to avoid this at all costs—it was far too intimate, to be scowled at by Rose at such close range.

"Yes. You are right, of course. I came with you to a haunted house in the middle of nowhere, almost drowned, kissed you to the point of madness, and am now lying here holding you in the dark because I love *Isabella Cliffe*."

"Oh," said Eddie. She was starting to suspect that her stupidity knew no bounds. "I thought . . ."

It didn't really seem to matter what she'd thought, at the present. Rose was just staring at her. Her hair was coming free from its plaits, falling forward, obscuring her face. Eddie lifted a hand to push it aside half-heartedly, and then froze when Rose's breath caught. She didn't allow herself to think before speaking again, the words slipping out almost by accident.

"I suppose . . . we could try kissing. Again. *Not* for practice."

Rose laughed disbelievingly, her voice coming out in a strained whisper.

"My God, you are such an idiot sometimes. What on earth is the difference?"

"The difference is . . ." Eddie said, easing herself up. Rose's hand slipped to her waist, seeming reluctant to part with her. "This time, we shall know that it's real."

"Semantics, then, is it?" Rose murmured, blinking up at her.

Their faces were already so close that it required almost no forethought to kiss her; Eddie just shifted her weight very slightly and Rose was beneath her, her lips parting to meet her.

Any doubt that Eddie may have been harboring about her inclinations evaporated in an instant. She wanted all of it: Rose's fingers pressing desperately into her waist as Eddie deepened

the kiss; the roll of Rose's hips; the heat of her breath, broken
up by small gasps. She felt as if she were pleasantly aflame, her
every nerve rewarded, her responsiveness to the friction of their
bodies answering the question that she now felt foolish to have
asked at all.

Of course she liked girls. Or, one girl. *This* girl. She put a hand
to Rose's face, thumbing along her jawline and holding her there,
and Rose responded with an abrupt and urgent repositioning of
her leg, so that they were completely entwined. Eddie realized
she was pressing Rose into the mattress; she pulled back and
tried to be gentle, her tongue ghosting across Rose's lower lip,
but the utterly debauched *sigh* this pulled out of her proved too
much, and Eddie was crowding on top of her again, gathering her
up by her hair and the back of her neck, wanting more of her but
having no idea where to start.

"Ed," Rose said when Eddie next pulled away, her voice ragged. "It *is* real, isn't it?"

"Mmmm?"

Eddie had taken the opportunity to kiss down her collarbone,
and was feeling rather preoccupied with it, and with Rose's little
shudders; the way she kept arching her back to provide further
access to Eddie's mouth.

"It's not . . . *ah* . . . educational, anymore?"

"I am certainly finding this educational," Eddie said, uncover-
ing a little more of Rose's skin so that she could run her teeth over
it. How had she been friends with Rose for so long and never
even considered the fact that her bones were clearly in need of
some gentle biting? It beggared belief.

"Eddie . . . *God* . . . Stop that a moment," Rose said, pushing
her away. "You know what I mean."

Eddie let her head fall onto Rose's stomach as she considered.

"I feel as if I want to eat you alive," she said. "What do you
suppose that means?"

"That you are deeply unhinged?" Rose said, her fingers slipping gently into Eddie's hair. "And . . . and potentially lacking in key minerals, due to your terrible diet?"

"Well, yes, there is that," Eddie said, closing her eyes as Rose smoothed the hair away from her face. "Actually, I'm frightened."

"Frightened? Of what?"

"I have no idea where any of this has come from. But at the same time, I think . . . God, why have we not been doing this all along?"

Rose laughed, which gave Eddie's head a thorough shaking.

"We *have*. I think we first kissed when we were . . . twelve?"

"But it was never like *this*," Eddie said, bringing her hands up to either side of Rose's waist and stroking her there, just to see if she would react (she did).

There was a long silence, during which Eddie briefly wondered if Rose had grown bored of her attentions and fallen asleep. Eventually Rose's hand disappeared from her hair. She sounded as if she were talking through her fingers when she next spoke.

"It sort of . . . *was* for me, Eddie."

Eddie sat up, startled. Rose did indeed have her hands pressed to her face, as if she were horrified by the words coming out of her mouth.

"What—*always*? When we used to fall asleep in each other's arms on your bed waiting for dinner to be ready? When we jumped in the sea that night in Brighton with hardly any clothes on?"

"All of the time, Eddie," Rose said, sounding pained. "I tried not to, I promise. I did a lot of very agonized praying about it. But nothing helped—no god or mortal could undo it. I would wake up in the morning determined not to notice you anymore, but then I would catch my first glimpse of you practically falling down the stairs to greet me for dinner or hear your ridiculous knock on my door and know you were on the other side of it, and . . . all was lost."

Eddie considered her. Her face was still obscured by her fingers, and Eddie reached up to prise them away.

"I am so sorry, Rose. I truly had no idea."

"I know," said Rose, finally looking Eddie in the eye. "I hope . . . Eddie, I hope you understand, then . . . I cannot just kiss you tonight and forget it tomorrow. That's why I need to know . . ."

Eddie took one of the hands she had removed from Rose's face and kissed the palm of it, very gently, at the soft little intersection between index finger and thumb. She still didn't know what it meant, exactly, that she felt this way—but she *did* know with utmost certainty that now she'd had a taste of how things could be between them, she would always want more. How could she not? It was *Rose*.

"It's real," she said, turning Rose's hand over so that she could kiss the back of it, too.

"But how can you say that? Just five minutes ago you were asking—"

"Rose, I will not argue with you that when it comes to certain matters, I can be very, very stupid. Painfully so. It's a wonder I'm still breathing and have all of my original bones. But it is just as you said before—I throw myself into things wholeheartedly. And I could never love you with anything less. I did not see it before, but . . . but now that I do, I don't think I shall ever want to look away. Despite all my failings, I am not *that* much of an idiot."

Rose smiled shakily; there were tears threatening to spill over in her eyes.

"I shall need you to keep saying it," she said firmly, trying to blink them away. "Or I will never believe it."

Eddie smiled at her and brushed away the one tear that had escaped.

"It's real," she said, kissing Rose's wrist. She got up on all fours above her, so that she could reach Rose's throat to kiss her there. "I swear, Rose. It's real."

Rose turned her head away, her lip catching in her teeth, but Eddie took her gently by the chin and turned her back.

"It's—"

Rose kissed her hard, pulling her down so that every inch of their bodies was touching. Eddie felt Rose's hand, bolder than it had been before, slide down her body until it reached the very top of her thigh. Eddie attempted to mirror her, her own hand starting somewhere around Rose's knee and traveling northward under her shift, and smiled into the kiss when she discovered that the graze of her fingernails made Rose gasp helplessly into her mouth.

"You feel so *good*," Eddie said, marveling at the way Rose's breath hitched and her eyes squeezed shut, as if she were completely overcome.

"I . . . I have no idea what I'm doing," Rose whispered, her grip tightening on Eddie's leg.

"Well, nor do I," said Eddie, watching Rose's face with fascination and witnessing a myriad of expressions cross it as she moved her fingers higher. "How do you feel?"

"As if I might die," said Rose, laughing softly and pressing herself harder into Eddie's hand.

"Don't die yet. Not before I've had my wicked way with you."

Rose looked as if she wanted to laugh again, but at the sight of Eddie's expression her eyes went wide instead.

"And what does that entail?"

Eddie kissed her gently, right at the corner of her mouth.

"Frankly, I have no idea. But . . . just tell me what feels good, and between us we shall make sense of it."

Rose's eyes were ink-dark, and they were fixed on Eddie.

"*Everything* feels good."

"Well, then . . . I suppose we'd better try everything."

Chapter Twenty-six

When Eddie awoke, it took her a moment to realize that everything had changed, but her mind caught up very quickly when she registered what her arms were full of: Rose, naked, her mouth pressed to Eddie's shoulder as she slept.

Somebody was knocking politely at the door. They increased their volume, and Rose groaned in quiet protest.

"What is it?" Eddie said, pulling the blankets up so high that Rose's face disappeared completely.

"We sent for the boat," said Albert, muffled through the door. "They shall be here shortly."

"Ah," said Eddie, her heart sinking. "Yes. Thank you, Albert."

She ducked under the blankets to find Rose squinting blearily at her.

"Boat's coming."

"Yes, I heard," Rose mumbled. "The blanket is not the impenetrable shield you think it is. Can you pass me my slip?"

"Well, I certainly haven't any idea where it is."

Rose frowned at her sleepily, looking like a perturbed (but fetching) bulldog.

"*You* are the one who pulled it off and flung it somewhere. You should know its whereabouts. It must be on your side of the bed."

"On the contrary. I cannot be expected to keep track of every single item of clothing I come into contact with, simply because . . . Ah. Here it is."

Eddie located her own shift, which was draped messily over a chair, and wriggled into it; it was so cold upon exiting the bed that she immediately had to pull on an assortment of layers, including a jacket of Valentine's that had somehow made it into her laundry and a shawl of Rose's around her shoulders.

There was another knock at the door; this time it sounded more as if somebody had thrown something heavy at it.

"*Edie.* Come out here, we have urgent business."

It was Nash. Eddie resisted the urge to glance at Rose to see her reaction, and instead went to open the door a crack.

"What is it?"

"What the hell are you wearing? Come on, put some real clothes on and meet me in the library."

He disappeared.

"We don't have much time," Rose said from beside the bed, where she was searching through the clothes in her trunk. She was not trying particularly hard to conceal her disapproval. "I suppose I'll see about some breakfast, as I'm already packed."

"I know," said Eddie. "I shan't be long."

She found Nash bent over the desk in the library, which was covered in stacks of books and a few crumpled maps. It looked rather like one of her sister Beatrice's attempts to plan an expedition. Rain was pattering gently against the windowpane.

"What is all this?"

"Greece!" said Nash, confirming Eddie's fears re: expeditions. There was a strange, frenetic energy to him, as if he hadn't slept. "Fuck this house, fuck the roof repairs, and the Devil take London. I only made it as far as Naples on my tour, and frankly I remember next to nothing—we could make a stop in Rome, for your education, and then onward to Athens. We'll be gone for months."

"Nash," Eddie said slowly, as if she were explaining to Trix that it was not possible to walk to Scotland in an afternoon. "We cannot really go to Greece."

"Of course we can," said Nash, scrabbling on the desk for one of the maps. "See the route marked here?"

"I mean I know it's physically *possible* for us to go, but—"

"Don't worry, I will allow plenty of time for you to finish your novel . . . how long do you need, another two weeks? Three? And then we can sail off into the sunset to celebrate. Wave farewell to merry England, and perhaps throw a few lewd gestures into the mix as we leave port."

Eddie felt she was lagging behind in this conversation.

"But . . . I thought you said my novel was far from ready?"

"I said nothing of the sort," Nash scoffed. "Nothing a little spit and elbow grease cannot fix. In fact . . . look there, under the globe."

Eddie lifted the ancient globe, which had a large illustration of Christ on it implying that He resided somewhere in the north of America, and found a crumpled letter. She lifted it to the light and began to read.

"*An arresting premise . . . send chapters at your earliest convenience . . . readers will be shocked and amused by the misadventures of Mrs. Fortescue . . . but*—" Eddie broke off with an embarrassing little gasp as realization dawned. "You . . . You told him about my novel? He wants to *read* it?"

"Yes, yes. I told you he would, did I not? And I am never wrong."

"Oh, *Nash*."

Eddie was quite overcome. She threw both arms around him and he laughed distractedly, his hands coming up to pat gently at her hair.

"There, there, don't thank me yet—we need to see the damn thing *finished*, and then, as I said . . . celebrations. Athens. I shall fashion us chitons and wreaths of olive leaf, and we can see who falls in the Aegean first."

Eddie nodded, laughing, tears threatening to spill over. Greece—why not? She would have agreed to absolutely anything at that moment, drunk with elation. An editor liked the premise of her book. From what he had written, he seemed almost sure that he wished to publish it. It was all going to happen just as she had always dreamed it would, thanks to Nash.

There was a bark from somewhere in the grounds, and Nash frowned out of the window as he released her.

"Damn. Dog's loose."

It was raining harder now. Eddie peered through the glass and saw that Juno seemed to be cutting a determined path toward the woods.

"Should we not fetch her in? There's nobody with her, and a storm seems to be approaching."

Nash seemed on the verge of shaking his head, but then Juno barked again, and he glanced sharply up at the window, looking concerned.

"Would you, Edie? That would be such a help. Look—I know I was very rude to Miss Li last night. I don't suppose she will forgive me, but I at least want *you* to know that I am quite contrite."

"I think she is in the dining room, if you wish to speak with her before she leaves."

"Is she? Ah. I may just . . . Yes, do fetch Juno, before she falls into a rabbit hole and is slowly nibbled to death."

After the service Nash had rendered her with his editor, Eddie was all too happy to tramp out into the freezing wind and rain in search of the dog. Even the thickest winter cloak she had brought was no match for the particular microclimate that seemed to govern over the lake, but her spirits could not be dampened. Juno had disappeared into the trees, and it took Eddie twenty minutes to discover her rolling in a patch of mud and convince her to go back into the house. It involved quite a lot of miming reaching into her pocket as if it contained ham, and then pretending to rummage.

The past twelve hours had been momentous, and her mind kept flitting back and forth, unable to settle on just one good thing. Nash's editor, calling her book *arresting*; Rose's head thrown back against the pillows as Eddie ran her hands through the cascade of her hair; the thought of her book in the window of her local bookshop in London, *E. Miller* immortalized in gold on the spine; quiet laughter into the crooks of necks and knees, and the all-consuming triumph of discovering exactly how to make Rose *stop* laughing abruptly, and clutch her closer.

She was quite overwhelmed by such an onslaught of successes, and it made her feel giddy and stupid and prone to random, aimless smiling.

When she reached the door she discovered Albert standing on the porch, Henry depositing a trunk at his feet.

"Ah," he said. "Go for a dip in a puddle, did you?"

"Very funny," Eddie said, wiping some of the rain from her forehead with her sleeve and then sighing when Juno shook out her coat and rendered her attempts redundant. Dayo came out behind Albert, carrying a trunk and wearing his traveling cloak. "Oh . . . but you're not leaving, Dayo?"

"The weather has turned," Dayo said, grimacing. "I have done as much work here as I will manage. I will get on far better in London now, I think."

"Oh," Eddie said again, feeling slightly deflated. "Well. That's a shame, but I suppose . . ."

"Ed, what on earth are you doing?" Rose had appeared, rosy-cheeked and dressed to depart, the shawl Eddie had borrowed earlier now neatly tucked around her shoulders. "Why are you plastered in mud? You'd better hurry—the boat will wait, but apparently not for long, there's a storm rolling in. You should see if Anne or Mrs. Hall can bring you hot water for a quick wash, or we shall have to look at you like that all the way back to town."

There was a slight pause while Eddie processed these words.

"But . . . I am not going back to London."

Another pause, punctuated only by the patter of the rain.

"I beg your pardon?"

"We shall give you a moment," said Dayo, exchanging a significant glance with Albert before the two of them ducked back inside.

"I don't understand," Rose said slowly, her brows knitted in consternation. "Yesterday you said . . . I thought you were coming with me."

"What?" said Eddie. She was standing out of the cover of the porch, and as a result was getting even damper by the second. "I told you I couldn't. Not yet."

"But that was before—"

"Rose, listen. Nash wrote to his editor. He wants to read my novel, he wants to publish it, he said—it's all really *happening*." Eddie waited for Rose to smile, to congratulate her—but she didn't say anything at all. "*Rose?*"

Rose did not jump for joy, or pull Eddie into a happy embrace, or laugh with delight. She seemed completely unmoved by Eddie's grin, which faltered and then disappeared.

"So, you're staying here?" Rose said. "With *him*?"

Eddie shook her head, baffled. "Rose . . . did you not hear what I said? Look, if this is about your hurt feelings, Nash said he was going to apologize. Or . . . I think he did. Did he not come to see you at breakfast?"

"What? No, I haven't seen him all morning. My *hurt feelings*?"

The painful disparity between the reception she had expected for her happy news and the reality of Rose's disgusted expression soured Eddie from the inside out.

"Do you really have nothing else to say to me, after what I have just told you? You are just vexed because I won't drop everything to follow you back to London. You want to turn this into some grand choice between the two of you, and I simply won't. You should not have followed me here if—"

Rose stepped out into the rain.

"You think I *followed* you here? What, because I had nothing better to do? I came to look *out* for you, because you do such a poor job of doing it yourself! Because I actually care for you, unlike *Nash Nicholson*. Albert and I would have been married and settled by now, he had no desire to abscond to this damned lake—have you even thought of that? I had my own plans. The life I want to build is waiting for me in London. I can't keep *giving* you so much with so little hope of return. I knew no good would come of this trip. If you weren't so blinkered by Nash's fame and success, you'd see him for what he really is—and what you are to him."

Eddie crossed her arms petulantly. "Go on, then. Impart your great wisdom."

"He's a *liar*, Eddie. He tells you what you want to hear, and expects the same in kind. He has absolutely no use for the truth. You *must* see, after what happened at the party—that was what he wanted all along. I tried to warn you, but you didn't want to hear it. You are caught up in this delusion he's built for you. This *fantasy*. But . . . it's time to grow up."

Eddie took a deep, painful breath, and then let it out again slowly.

"I see," she said. "You're jealous. Jealous of what Nash and I share, because you'll never understand it. Perhaps you don't *want* him to help me succeed, to make something of myself, in case . . . in case I leave you behind. You're not used to being the one left out, it was always me sitting around at home while you went off to live your life, and now it seems as if the tables have turned—"

"Oh, Ed," Rose said, sounding hideously sympathetic. "You already *are* something. And so am I."

Albert popped his head through the doorway, looking nervous. "Are we ready to depart?"

"Just a minute," Rose said, smoothing her hair and lifting her

chin, blinking back her tears. Eddie tried not to stare at her, but
it was impossible; she wanted to treasure this last glimpse before they were separated, as if it might keep her sated all the way
through to Christmas. She looked sad but stalwart, like a general
leading a doomed, righteous last stand. "I . . . I have forgotten
something upstairs."

She disappeared into the house, and Henry and Dayo came
out behind Albert. The former picked up Rose's trunk, and they
all said stilted goodbyes, Eddie promising listlessly to come and
see Dayo speak when she was back in town.

When Rose reappeared, Eddie still hadn't decided what to say
to her—she opened her mouth, unwisely intending to improvise,
but Rose cut her off.

"The wedding is to be just before Christmas. My parents
wrote to say that they have determined an auspicious date, so
that's that. I hope you'll come, even if . . ."

A thousand unspoken things hung in the air between them.

"Of course I'll come," Eddie said indignantly, but the outgo-
ing party was already walking away, Juno trailing them with a
dejected air and a downturned tail. Eddie followed them a little way down the lawn and then stopped, barely feeling the rain,
watching Rose's billowing coat and dark hair flying, keeping her
in sight for as long as she possibly could.

When she looked up at the house she saw Nash standing at a
window on the second floor, also watching them go, his expression impossible to discern from behind the glass.

Dear Mother and Father,

*I am surprised to hear that you saw Mrs. Nicholson the other
day, as you have never managed to bump into her before, what
luck—she is only back in town to see her sister, and will return
very shortly. You need not worry about us being without chap-
erones, as we are always together in a group, and the others are*

older and more mature than I am, so they are taking me under their wings.

Mr. Nicholson, of course, is a perfect gentleman—when people think of poets they imagine them as scoundrels (thanks in large part to Lord Byron!) but luckily he is nothing of the sort. He is helping me greatly with my writing, and has promised to put me in touch with his editor soon.

I hope my brother and sisters are keeping well, and that Trix has not attempted to eat any more shoes. When Mrs. Nicholson returns I shall tell her you saw her—how funny!

Yours,
Eddie

Chapter Twenty-seven

"You know, I think leaving simply because of a little wind and rain shows a lack of character," Nash said at luncheon.

The dining room felt empty to Eddie with four of their original party now missing. It was also somehow less friendly; while Kitty was generally amenable, she did have a tendency to act as if other people's emotions were somewhat beneath her unless they were an interesting study for art, and as much as Eddie had come to be fond of Valentine, they indulged Nash too much for comfort.

"No roof repairs—we die like men," said Valentine, somewhat proving Eddie's point.

Nash snorted appreciatively and then topped up his wine. He topped up Eddie's, too, even though she had hardly touched her glass.

"You ought to move to Dayo's room, Edie. You might be somewhat in the firing line up on the second floor, if any of the rest of my house decides to collapse."

This had not actually occurred to Eddie, but the thought of moving was a blessed relief. The idea of trying to sleep in the bed she had shared with Rose—the bed that they had left rumpled and disorderly, and that was probably this very minute being re-made by Anne until it looked as if nothing of importance had ever occurred there—made her chest ache.

"All right," she said, shrugging, affecting nonchalance. "If Mrs. Hall does not mind."

"Hmm. She does keep quivering like a vexed jelly every time I ask her to go upstairs or suggest that she takes a look at the long gallery."

"Well, you can hardly blame her," said Eddie. "She was almost crushed."

"She was *not* almost crushed. She simply flirted with death, and death said, *Good God, no, thank you.*"

They all laughed except Eddie, who hoped fervently that Mrs. Hall was not currently standing outside the dining room, listening to them mock her near demise.

When luncheon—which had lasted well over two hours, and was more liquid than solid—finally came to a close, Eddie went upstairs to haphazardly throw her belongings into her trunk, so that they could be easily transported downstairs. She found one of Rose's gloves under a cushion and stood holding it for a while like a widow at a window, before shaking the feeling off and tossing it in with the rest of her things. Juno wandered in and stared morosely at the bed, as if expecting Rose to return to it at any moment.

That, somehow, was worse than all the rest of it put together.

It was only when Eddie was on the landing with an armful of her belongings that she realized she hadn't seen her manuscript.

It wasn't on the dresser, where she was sure she had left it. She rummaged through her trunk twice before unpacking it entirely, her panic growing as every possible hiding place came up empty. It wasn't under the bed, or on one of the chairs. She rushed out into the hall, calling for Anne and Mrs. Hall, and when Mrs. Hall came, she was reassured repeatedly that it would never have been thrown out.

"One does not manage Mr. Nicholson's affairs," the housekeeper said frostily, "without becoming accustomed to treating all manner of *scrap paper* like holy scripture."

Eddie asked Kitty and Valentine, who were sitting in the South

Parlor, if they had seen it. They had not. She started searching places she knew it absolutely could not be, in the hope that she might bend the rules of reality and be rewarded for her ingenuity: the library; Albert's old room; her new room on the first floor, which had been freshly turned over. When Nash knocked on the door she was halfway to tears; she almost threw herself at him in her desperation.

"You haven't seen my manuscript, have you? I am so sure it was on the dresser last night, but I cannot find it anywhere."

Nash grimaced and shook his head, extinguishing her last hope. She sat back down on the floor surrounded by the things from her trunk, which she had unpacked for a third time, and pressed a hand to her forehead as tears of frustration streamed down her cheeks.

"Oh, Edie," said Nash softly, coming to kneel next to her. "Perhaps she did not take it on purpose? They were in rather a hurry to catch the boat . . . although I'm not entirely sure what she could have mistaken it for . . ."

Eddie's mind had been free-falling into a void of endless misery, but this broke through. She looked up at him, confused.

"Who?"

"Well . . . I can only assume that it left the island with Miss Li."

Eddie sat with this, unease brewing. Her instinct was instant denial; she could not countenance Rose doing such a thing, even in an almighty snit. But then . . . she *had* seemed deeply hurt, and it had all happened so fast.

If not to punish her—and Eddie could not believe she would stoop so low—she might have taken it to use as bait, to attempt to lure Eddie out of the wilderness and back to domesticity in London. She could picture it now—Rose going upstairs one last time to fetch something she had forgotten, hovering in the room indecisively with their argument still ringing in her ears, and then snatching the manuscript up at the last second and carrying it carefully back to London, the pages stashed somewhere about her person.

"God damn it," Eddie breathed. "She *knew* how much it meant to me. She wanted me to come back to town, but I . . ." She cast about as if the room would provide an answer to this problem, and came up empty. "What on earth am I supposed to do now?"

Nash clapped her bracingly on the arm.

"You stay here and see the damned thing through. You have me on your team—together we will be unstoppable. I am sure she will feel terribly guilty about it and send it back to you shortly, with her tail between her legs. You can still finish it, can't you?"

Eddie clenched and unclenched her fists, feeling as if her heart were miles away in a rickety carriage. *How* could Rose do this to her? And how could she ever expect to be forgiven? It was far easier to just be righteously, deliriously angry than to try to examine the more complicated emotions of their separation, so anger it was.

"Damn it," Eddie growled. "And damn her. I *will* finish it. I will not go running after her, just as she wants. I will stay here, I will get it done, and when it is finished, it will be *despite* her."

"Splendid!" said Nash. "I have always found spite to be delightfully motivating."

His hand slipped off Eddie's shoulder as she got to her feet and brushed down her skirts, now feeling equal parts dismayed and determined.

"I shall start right away."

"Very good," said Nash, who had been left behind on the floor and was now scrambling to his feet. "In fact . . . I'll come with you."

To her great surprise, he did. He sat down opposite her in Dayo's old seat in the library, flicking through a book he had pulled from the shelves, occasionally noting something down on the parchment next to him, and barely interrupted her at all.

Once she had written a few pages, he crooked his finger at her until she slid them over to his side of the desk, and then sat reading them as she started on the next.

"Did you mean to write that the constable looked 'ponderous as an orb' here?" he said, making a small note on the manuscript in his spidery script.

"Ah. No," said Eddie. "That should say 'owl.'"

They continued in this fashion for hours, Juno at their feet. Eddie's feelings were still smarting, her jaw clenched tightly as she tried to keep her emotions at bay and focus on the work, but it helped beyond measure to have Nash at her side. He was a staunch companion for the rest of the day, his attention unwavering, focused in a way Eddie had never witnessed before; she felt a rush of fondness toward him as he frowned seriously down at her latest page, a tiny dot of ink decorating his chin.

When it came down to it, she thought, Nash really *did* understand her. He knew how important this opportunity was to her; he was clearly fighting all of his natural inclinations toward distraction and folly in service of her work, and she was extraordinarily grateful. Here she was, finally on the verge of completing her first novel, publication on the horizon, and Rose had abandoned ship—but Nash was there.

Eddie only realized that it was time for dinner when Valentine stalked into the library, took a book from the shelf at random, and then threw it at her; luckily it bounced off the table leg rather than the back of her skull, and she only suffered a moderate to extreme shock.

"You could have invited us politely, like an adult!" she called after Valentine, who just cackled in reply.

The entirety of dinner was taken up by a good-natured argument that Kitty and Nash were having about Coleridge (Kitty in favor, Nash against). Eddie barely paid attention, scarfing down her chicken, her mind still in the library, her heroine Miss Fortescue tumbling rapidly downhill and now lingering on the cusp of her darkest night. She escaped as soon as she could, ignoring Nash's protests that she deserved a break after the day's work, obtained a few more blankets, and then returned to the library, where she wrote all the way through to the end of her candle. When it gave one last flicker and extinguished, she sat in near darkness for a moment, loath to break her train of thought—but then sighed and gathered up her small stack of papers, heading for bed.

Her new room was far warmer and drier than her quarters on the second floor had been; any misgivings she had felt about staying on the island as the house fell apart around them were temporarily banished by the sleepy crackle of the fire, the blankets that smelled clean and dry, the fact that she could undress for bed without having to then attempt an athletic record in panicked leaping so as not to lose her limbs to frostbite.

She had just climbed sleepily under the bedclothes, wondering if she was smearing ink all over them and then deciding she was too exhausted to care, when she heard a soft knock at the door.

"Who is it?"

"Napoleon Bonaparte. Out on leave. Time off for good behavior."

Eddie sat up, pulling her blankets up to her neck.

"A likely story."

"C'est vrai, you charlatan. Let me in before the British catch sight of my enormous hat and ship me back to die."

The door creaked open. Nash was still dressed, if a little disheveled, a bottle of wine in his hand.

"I am *sleeping*," said Eddie.

"Good Christ, you are. You missed Valentine doing quite an uncanny impression of Shelley's sister-in-law, the poor dear. Move over—I shall bring the party to you."

INFAMOUS   269

"I am not in need of a party. You may have gathered this from the fact that it is bedtime, I am dressed for bed, and I am—what's this?—oh yes, *in bed*."

"There is no need to take that tone with me," Nash said, ignoring her and climbing on top of the blankets as Eddie shuffled out of his way. He settled himself down on the other pillow and crossed his legs, uncorking the wine with his teeth and spitting the cork onto the floor. "I have been very helpful today."

"I suppose you have," said Eddie. "*You* seem in very good spirits."

"In good wine, actually," Nash said, before laughing heartily at his own terrible joke. Eddie hadn't realized quite how drunk he was; it made her feel very sober, and very tired. "Come on, take a swig. It's a nightcap."

"It's a nuisance," she said, but she took the bottle just to shut him up. He winked at her and then lay back and closed his eyes. "You cannot just fall asleep in here, Nash."

"Am not sleeping. Doing some very great thinking, in fact."

"Oh. About what?"

"Mmm? Many things. Although, right now, mostly . . . that this bed is inordinately comfortable," Nash said, stretching languorously so that at least half his limbs came into contact with Eddie. "No wonder Dayo was such a fastidious worker, getting eight hours on this mattress every night. Here—stop inching away from me, I am hardly going to maul you."

"Would it kill you to maintain *some* decorum?"

"Yes, actually, I think it might."

"Well . . . what if I do not want you in my bed?"

"Goodness, hark at you—speaking as if you have never had my tongue in your mouth, which I know for a fact you *have*, as I was attached to the other end of it."

Eddie made a startled sound between a squeak and a splutter, and Nash laughed, reaching out to pat her on what he probably presumed was her arm, but was in fact somewhere around her ribs.

"One could discern from these hysterics that you find speaking of the act to be far more incriminating than actually doing it."

"Oh, I think it was exceedingly incriminating," Eddie said dourly. "I have been mortified ever since."

Nash rolled over onto his side to look at her.

"No, no, Edie, that is simply not on. *Mortified?* I am wounded. I am adrift."

"You are drunk as a wheelbarrow."

"I burn, I pine, I perish."

"You stole that."

"Shakespeare bade me borrow it, to impress upon you how glad I am to have you. Do you know, there is only one thing that could improve this situation . . ."

During this exchange he had somehow managed to get much closer to Eddie; one arm was now flung over her, the other tucked beneath his head as he gazed at her, boyish and hopeful.

"Sleep?"

"Wrong," said Nash.

He took Eddie firmly by the chin and kissed her; Eddie leaned in for just a moment before pulling away.

"There. I have kissed you good night, and now you must go."

Nash let his head fall forward until his brow was resting against hers and sighed.

"Are you really so cruel as to send me back to my empty bed, on a night as cold as this?"

"Don't sulk," Eddie said, turning away onto her back but keeping half an eye on him as she did. "Are you going to leave of your own accord, or am I going to have to call Henry in here to cart you out?"

"*Please* call for Henry. There must be room enough in this bed for three."

"Nash, you are simply saying the worst things you can think of to try to horrify me."

He chuckled, low and throaty. "I just like to see you blush and squirm. Alas, you are so difficult to shock these days."

He had no idea how many times she had truly been astonished at his behavior; she had wanted to seem so calm and collected, so unruffled by it all, and apparently, she had mostly succeeded. She wondered if this was the person he seemed to like so much— *Edie*, the unshockable. A mirage; a person who didn't actually exist unless he was looking directly at her.

"Nash, I'm exhausted. I want to go to bed."

He shifted up onto his elbow, frowning down at her.

"You really want me to leave?"

"I really do."

"Fine. Just indulge me for a minute more."

He leaned over to kiss Eddie again, this time trapping her face beneath his hands. She kissed him back hesitantly and he responded at once, shifting so that he was holding himself above her. He was wearing a silver necklace Eddie had never noticed before; a heart-shaped locket, which was cold against her neck. She found herself unable to relax, discomforted by the fact that they were in her bed with the door closed; there was no chance they would be interrupted this time, and something about that made her feel panicked. She was so tired, and so comparatively sober—and although she tried very hard not to, all she could think about was Rose. How right and easy it had felt with her. The fact that Rose had been so careful not to demand too much too soon, and for no reason at all—Eddie had known she would always find more of herself to give, for as long as Rose wanted to take it.

Nash had already taken too much, and they had only been kissing for approximately ten seconds. One of his hands had started to roam, making its way down to the curve of her waist, and she reached out with one of her own to stop it in its tracks.

"Enough, I think," she said, indistinct against his lips; he sighed another quiet, frustrated little sigh and then released her, getting to his feet. Eddie eased up onto her elbows, frowning after him. "You're not . . . You aren't *angry* with me, are you? For being such a spoilsport."

Nash swiped his bottle of wine and shrugged, giving her a strange little half smile on his way out of the door.

"Angry? No, no. But your skills as a hostess, Miss Miller, leave *much* to be desired."

Chapter Twenty-eight

"YOU LOOK EXHAUSTED. CAN I PAINT YOU?"

Eddie looked up from her luncheon and squinted at Kitty. She *was* exhausted; she had awoken at five o'clock in the pitch-black and immediately rolled out of bed, struck by an arresting turn of phrase. She had attempted to stoke the fire herself and in the end had given up, shivering over her new desk with just the stub of a candle to work by, writing as fast as she could manage while keeping everything legible.

"Why do you want to paint me exhausted?" Eddie croaked eventually, having taken a long time to form the sentence.

"Because you are at your most interesting," Kitty said, shrugging. "Valentine is far too mellow at the moment, it'd be like painting a . . . a fork, or a shrub."

"Thank you *so* much," Valentine said, violently spearing an egg. "You really know how to make a person feel special."

"You are *sometimes* interesting, Val. Just not at this particular moment. If you have another romantic disappointment or fall into the lake, come and see me and I shall paint you in despondent azure and doleful navy."

"Crestfallen cobalt," Eddie said through a mouthful of bread, both sounding and feeling slightly delirious.

"Well, quite."

"Where's Nash?" said Eddie, finally managing to swallow her bread.

"No idea," said Valentine. "He said we'd go shooting."

"What do you want to *shoot* things for?" Kitty scoffed. "Actually, if you do manage to kill anything, would you bring it to me before you pluck it or skin it or whatever you plan to do? So I can—"

"Paint it? So I am a fork, and a pheasant full of shot is a work of art?"

"Now you're catching on. Anyway, he's on another walk with Juno. Or . . . perhaps his walk from this morning never ended, it is hard to tell. He is in a very odd mood again. I would attempt to paint *him*, but I think he might snap my paintbrush in half and run me through with it."

Eddie barely registered getting up from the table and returning to the library. She had expected Nash to join her again, but supposed he must have gone to meet Valentine for their promised jaunt; she could hardly hold it against him, but she did miss his presence on the other side of the table. Before she knew it, the sky was darkening out of the window and she was shivering even in her coat and gloves. She could not understand why she was so cold, until she realized that she hadn't seen a servant for hours— usually they crept noiselessly in to take care of the fire and bring her more candles, not that Eddie noticed when her head was full of Delilah Fortescue, top hat in hand, being held at gunpoint in a churchyard.

It wasn't the cold that eventually stopped her progress—it was the sound of furious barks and raised voices, a cacophony of shouting coming from somewhere below. Eddie frowned and went to the doorway, straining to listen. It didn't seem possible that there were enough people left in the house to cause this much noise. The shouting continued, and Eddie followed it down the hall and to the stairs that led to the kitchens and the servants' quarters. She had never descended into that part of the house, and hesitated for a second—but then she heard something shatter, and her curiosity won out.

The scene that greeted her downstairs was baffling. All the household staff, excepting Mr. Morris, were standing in the doorway to the kitchens. Nash was standing opposite them, holding Juno by the scruff, looking ruffled and furious, the silver locket he had taken to wearing clutched in his hand as if it had been violently removed. Henry's collar was askew, and Mrs. Morris the cook looked scarlet in the face and close to tears; there was a bowl of something, most likely some key aspect of the evening's dinner, shattered on the floor between them, food splattered in every direction. As Eddie approached she saw that Anne was crying; she wiped her eyes on her sleeve when she saw Eddie approaching and then walked quickly away. Juno broke free and followed her.

"Is everything all right?" Eddie asked Nash, perplexed.

"It's all a lot of fuss about nothing," Nash snapped back, smoothing down his hair and attempting to breathe evenly. "If you'll just—"

"I will not stay here a moment longer," said Mrs. Morris, drawing herself up and folding her arms. "I have served this family for forty years, Mr. Nicholson, but this time you truly have crossed a line—"

"This is ridiculous!" Nash shouted. He seemed to reconsider, lowering his voice. "This is an overreaction, Mrs. Morris. Mrs. Hall. I was only—"

"You assaulted the boy," said Mrs. Hall slowly, her eyes grim. "There is no doubt about that."

"Yes!" said Mrs. Morris. "And I won't stand for it. Come on, Henry. We shall fetch Mr. Morris and then we will be away."

She and her grandson departed, Henry looking thunderstruck, leaving Eddie staring between Nash and the housekeeper.

"What on earth happened?"

"Nothing," said Nash bitterly. "She hardly *means* it."

"She does," said Mrs. Hall. "And . . . I am afraid . . . Yes. I will take my leave of you, too, Mr. Nicholson."

She departed, too, and he stormed away after her.

Eddie drifted back upstairs to the library for want of anything better to do, but was completely unable to focus on her work. All was quiet until she heard a lot of quick, neat footsteps in the hallway.

She poked her head out of the door and saw all of the servants dressed for travel, carrying trunks that did not seem nearly big enough to hold all of their possessions; Mrs. Morris was holding her head high, and she hardly blinked when Nash intercepted them at the entrance hall.

"Come on," Eddie heard Nash plead. "Mrs. Morris, I am entirely sure we can come to an agreement that would benefit—"

"I am not interested in making an agreement with you," said Mrs. Morris, with a sniff of indignation.

"Mrs. Hall," Nash said, clearly sensing that Mrs. Morris was a lost cause, "this is a private matter between young master Henry and me, and you need not drag yourself into it."

"I have left my list of local suppliers in the kitchen, Mr. Nicholson," said Mrs. Hall. "Good day to you."

"Henry!" Nash shouted, the end of his tether clearly nigh. "Are you really happy to be the cause of this? Your grandparents out of work, at this time of year? *Say* something, damn you."

"Do not blame this on the boy," said Mr. Morris. "Have some self-respect, man, for goodness' sake."

Eddie waited until the coast was clear and then crossed to the front door to watch them go. Nash was still trailing them, shouting something she couldn't quite hear, although his tone was clear enough; he was back to begging again. Eddie returned to the library rather than be caught spying, and on discovering that the fire had gone out completely, she cast around for a tinderbox, and came up empty. She removed to the drawing room, where the fire was still just about alive, and gave it a light, hopeful stoking before sitting down to work.

Valentine stalked into the room almost immediately.

"Why is it so fucking cold? And why did nobody come when I called? Where on earth are all the staff?"

"Gone," said Eddie.

"What do you mean, *gone*?"

"Apparently Nash and Henry had some sort of . . . altercation. The maid seemed very upset, I did wonder if it was something to do with her."

"Oh, Christ," said Valentine, sitting down heavily on the sofa. "Is that what he said? *Altercation*?"

"Mrs. Hall said Nash assaulted him."

"Did she now?" said Valentine, sighing elaborately. "Jesus. What the hell are we supposed to do? Fend for ourselves? I cannot so much as boil an egg, can you?"

"Yes," said Eddie. "Well . . . I have seen one being boiled, and I imagine I can replicate the process."

"Wonderful, we shall eat the results of your scientific experiments. He really has left us in a fine mess this time. No *staff*? I suppose he thinks he can dally with absolutely anybody who catches his eye, and damn the consequences—"

"Wait—dally with whom?"

Valentine looked slightly guilty, as if once again they had imparted a little too much information.

"Where is he now?"

"Not sure—I saw him going after them, trying to fetch them back, but I don't imagine he had much success. They seemed quite determined."

"Fantastic. I imagine he's swimming after their boat at this very moment."

"He isn't," said Kitty, walking in and striding up to the fire, extending her gloved hands to warm them. She was wearing three furs, heaped on top of one another, which made her look like a very attractive bear. "He has gone to shoot things in the long gallery."

"*Shoot* things?" Eddie said, alarmed. "What things?"

"Well, let's see," said Kitty, cocking her head to listen. They all waited, and after a moment they heard a gunshot, and what sounded like a ceramic extermination. "Plates? Yes, I think that was a plate. I suppose it is no matter—we won't have anything to eat, so why would we need plates?"

"Yes," said Valentine, looking dour, "what *are* we going to eat?"

Kitty shrugged. "That is the least of our worries. What about warmth? Water? We cannot run this house ourselves. They were struggling enough on a skeleton staff."

Eddie looked around at their grim faces and attempted enthusiasm.

"Oh, I don't know! Perhaps it will be like an expedition."

"An Arctic one," said Kitty grimly. "I will stay until I cannot paint anymore, either through starvation or loss of fingers to frostbite, and then I will take my leave."

"I shall stay until we run out of wine," Valentine said, with an air of immense bravery.

"Excellent, well, I'll be back to collect you in the year 1900. I am bringing my painting things in here. Valentine, there's fresh kindling just outside the kitchen—will you . . . ?"

"Ordinarily I would," said Valentine. "But I was just beginning to thaw."

Eddie went instead. She encountered the smashed tureen and the splattered food on the floor and edged around it, before realizing that if *she* didn't try to clean it up, nobody would. She managed to arrange the shards into a neatish pile with some gentle kicking, and then dropped a rag onto the mess, and congratulated herself on a job well done.

Inside the kitchen she was delighted to discover food: freshly baked bread, ham that already seemed to be cooked, and something sweet that had obviously been halfway through stewing when its creator had vacated the island.

At least for one night, they would not starve.

"We will not starve at all," Nash said later, relatively cheerful, fortified by ham and wine. "We have a stocked larder. Plenty to drink. I know how to build a fire."

"I can split wood," Kitty offered, surprising nobody.

"There, you see? That vile woman thought she was stranding us, but she was *liberating* us. I could never relax entirely with her beady eyes watching me, judging my every move. I will signal Captain Perkins upon the morrow and ask him to place my advertisement for new help, and in the meantime—let us see this as an *opportunity*, not a burden. A time for us to let our hair down."

"Your hair was never up," said Eddie, expecting him to laugh. Instead he just raised his eyebrows at her and waggled his knife in her direction.

"This is exactly what I'm talking about, Edith. Moralizing. Judgment. I shall have none of it. Did you not come here to have fun?"

"I came here to write a book," Eddie reminded him, for what felt like the hundredth time.

"That you did, and that you shall. Right! Valentine, would you like to learn the ancient art of fire building?"

"No," said Valentine. "But I suppose you're going to show me anyway."

When dinner was finished, they sat by the fire in the drawing room for a while (Nash really did know how to build one, although whether it was necessary to snap the leg off an antique chair to add to the kindling was yet to be seen), dozing and talking in fits and starts. Eddie excused herself first, and then discovered that of course, the fire in her room was long dead. She thought about going downstairs in search of the tinderbox and some fuel, and then instead just crawled in under the bedclothes, curling in a tight ball like an iced wood louse to try to warm her extremities. She had only been lying there for a minute or two when she suddenly got up, crossed to the door, and pulled a chair in front of it, wedging it under the handle so that nobody on the other side could enter, a trick that had come in very handy against inquisitive siblings at home. She felt silly doing it, but also immediately relieved.

Despite her fortifications, she kept one eye on the door until she fell asleep.

Chapter Twenty-nine

FOR THE NEXT FEW DAYS THE REMAINING INHABITANTS OF the house spent their waking hours together, huddled in the drawing room or eating increasingly odd meals in the dining room. There had been older bread in the larder, but so little of it that they had to eke it out in very small increments; there had also been preserves, but due to the lack of bread, they had taken to eating them as if they were soup or pudding. Eggs, as it turned out, were easy to prepare in a number of ways once they had managed to get the kitchen fire going, and they had quite a few of them as they had evidently been stored for baking. Juno seemed rather fond of them, which was lucky, as they had little else to give her. Nash had offered with much bravado to prepare the brace of birds they discovered, but on further inspection they had clearly been hanging for far too long, and his bluster almost turned to vomiting when they revealed themselves to be populous with maggots.

There were rather a lot of potatoes, so they fried them over the open fire. Eddie didn't mind that part of their makeshift victuals. She felt she could have lived forever on a diet of fried potatoes and slightly runny eggs. It was, however, beginning to wear thin that she could never get comfortably warm. She wasn't sleeping well, either, dogged by a strange, sharp sort of anxiety that serrated all her thoughts and made her feel brittle and irritable.

She felt as if she had been harpooned at the end of a long

length of rope, and that it led all the way to London, where Rose would be starting to make preparations for the wedding: meeting with Albert's family; having the banns read; choosing her dress. She almost imagined that she could feel little tugs in her chest as Rose went about her business, and wondered if she was feeling that same pull, or—far more likely—if Eddie was perhaps inventing it due to being short a few marbles from spending her every waking hour hunched over her manuscript and shivering the night through.

Nash seemed too preoccupied to help much with her writing; he often disappeared from their group huddle and didn't return for hours, although when he did he usually had some new bottle of alcohol to warm them, or some oddity he'd discovered in the depths of the house to show them.

On the third unstaffed day, very abruptly and without ceremony, Eddie finished her manuscript.

She stared down at the last line she had written, sure that there must be more—something she had forgotten or neglected—but nothing came. She got up, so that she could gaze at it from a distance, too tired to even smile. She wandered into the kitchen in a daze in search of something to eat and found all three of the others gathered solemnly around a recently deceased duck, Juno panting at their feet. She thought of announcing that she had finished writing, but something made her hesitate. She wanted to keep it her own private accomplishment for just a little longer; she would tell Nash tomorrow, when she had managed to get some sleep, and they could celebrate together.

The person she really wanted to tell was too far away to hear it.

"Kitty shot it," Valentine said, of the duck. "Now we just have to pluck it and . . . you know. Remove the innards. Decide how the stove works."

"Remember to save the bones for later," Nash said, somewhat ominously.

"What's later?" asked Eddie. "And . . . I know I will regret asking this, but . . . why does it require bones?"

"Not all this again," said Kitty, rolling her eyes and pulling the duck toward her so that she could start methodically plucking it.

"I told you we were going to let our hair down now that we are unobserved, Edie," said Nash. "And tonight is the night. The moon is full. The omens are good."

"You mean you're bored," said Valentine. "And you found the secret stash of pharmaceuticals that you thought you had misplaced."

"That, too," said Nash. "Don your finest garb, for we ride at midnight."

"Ride where?" Eddie asked, still none the wiser.

"To *Hell*," said Nash, spreading his arms wide like a priest gone wrong. He wandered away, humming, and Eddie looked at Valentine, who shrugged.

"We are going to take lots of drugs and likely burn things while Nash screams at the moon and thinks he's communing with Bacchus."

"Wear good boots," said Kitty. "It's terribly muddy out."

"Oh *God*, no," Nash said when he saw Eddie coming down the stairs later that evening. "What the hell is this?"

She was wearing soft buckskin breeches and a dark tailcoat over a shirt and waistcoat; the outfit strained very slightly across her chest, but otherwise was surprisingly comfortable. Valentine had offered a top hat, but Eddie had decided this was one step too far; she had, however, accepted a pair of shiny black riding boots, which were only just too big for her. Valentine had tied her stock for her, and she had grinned like an idiot the entire time.

"I like it," Eddie said, fingering the sleeve of her shirt, her confidence dented. The idea of wearing a dress in this cold had felt repugnant, and when an alternative had occurred to her, she had gone to see Valentine about making it a reality.

"You look ridiculous."

"Nobody said anything about there being a *dress code* for summoning the Devil."

"Well," said Nash. "I should have. You ought to be . . . I don't know. Dancing about in white muslin, barefoot, with your hair down. It's about the spirit of the thing."

"It is November," said Eddie. "*You* dance about in white muslin barefoot, if it suits you."

"Perhaps I will," said Nash.

He did not. When midnight approached, he came to fetch them from the drawing room in his finest dark fur, solemnly broke the seal atop a glass bottle, and indicated that they were each to hold out their hands to receive some of the contents.

Eddie, who remembered her last experiment with questionable substances with some trepidation, hesitated. She hardly wanted to seem like a coward, but she had just enough sense not to put *everything* she was offered directly into her mouth. She automatically began to imagine what Rose would say, and then determined not to care.

Manuscript thieves did not get to have jurisdiction over her thoughts.

"It's dried fungus," said Nash, sensing her hesitation. "A friend of mine procured them abroad. Don't worry, they're perfectly natural. Medicinal! They'll help us relax."

Both Valentine and Kitty took their mushrooms and immediately swallowed them, as casually as if they were grapes. When Nash reached Eddie, she was still wavering; he reached up and cupped her by the chin, causing her to dart a startled glance at the others.

"Receive it like a Catholic, you infidel," Nash said, gently easing her mouth open. He placed the mushroom on her tongue and then released her.

Eddie sighed, and swallowed.

It took a while for everybody to gather their cloaks and for Valentine to successfully manage to light a lamp, but then Nash shut Juno inside the house and they all made their way down into the woods. The wind was picking up, the clouds rushing past overhead, so that the moonlight kept blinking out and plunging them into darkness.

"It's going to rain," said Kitty, frowning up at the sky.

"It wouldn't dare," said Nash.

It was around the time they reached the trees when Eddie began to notice that her mind seemed to have vacated her body. While her feet were undeniably on the ground—she could see them, when the moon came out—she rather thought that her head was elsewhere. Aloft. Adrift. It was only when Nash spoke again that she could convince herself that her brain was where it had always been, tucked safely behind her eyes.

"This'll do nicely."

They were in a small clearing. Kitty had been in charge of soft furnishings, and produced blankets for them to sit on. They arranged themselves cross-legged on the soft ground.

Eddie hardly realized she had pressed her fingers into the mud next to her until Valentine gently prised her hand away and placed it safely in her lap. Kitty and Nash were attempting to light a fire; they had brought dry wood from the house, and it only took a minute or so of fiddling with the lantern to get it to catch.

"Now, we really ought to have a white goat to slaughter, but we're running low on livestock . . ."

Nash produced the duck bones, and lazily tossed one into the fire, where it crackled and spat.

"We are not really attempting some sort of ancient ritual, are we?" said Eddie, surprised by the effort it took to get these words out.

"Of course! We wish to ascend! To dance with Dionysus! To

set out on a noble quest for divine mania, and come back forever changed!"

"Do we indeed?" said Valentine. "I thought we were simply getting foxed outdoors, for a change of scenery."

"Do shut up, Valentine," Nash said, arranging the bones into some sort of pattern in the mud. "Actually—don't. I need you to help me with the Greek."

They conferred, and Eddie let her mind drift again. If she squinted, she could just about see the stars, glittering suggestively through the gaps in the branches when the clouds parted.

"The sky has lights in it," she said to Kitty.

"You're damn right it does," said Kitty, who took a sip from the bottle of wine she was carrying and then handed it to Eddie. "Important to stay hydrated during these things."

"Oh. Have you done this before?" Eddie said, realizing that she *was* thirsty and drinking deep.

"Done what?"

Nash had begun chanting something, Eddie presumed in Greek; he suddenly increased in volume, with a pointed look at Eddie, who abruptly closed her mouth.

It was hard to pinpoint exactly when it all stopped feeling like a ridiculous joke and became something much stranger. Eddie closed her eyes, listening to Nash and Valentine chant, and then, as their voices dragged on, lost all sense of time. She thought she saw Juno, snuffling through the trees toward them, something unidentifiable in her mouth; meanwhile, the chanting blurred into a hum, a frequency in harmony with the sound of the woods, primal and all-encompassing. Eventually she realized that she couldn't have been looking at Juno, because she hadn't opened her eyes at all. When she did, she noted that she also could not have been listening to any chanting, because the rest of the clearing was empty. She was quite alone.

This did not seem on. Eddie didn't know much about pagan

rituals, but she *did* think there was something baked-in about the spirit of togetherness. She managed to get to her feet, smearing quite a lot of mud on Valentine's breeches as she did, and stood swaying indecisively before deciding on what seemed like a likely path and taking it.

The feeling of twigs and leaves brushing against her hands as she staggered through the undergrowth was so heightened that she experienced each one as an odd little zip of static, skittering across her skin. She thought she was making *far* too much noise, the sound of her steps comically loud; she stopped, and in the relative quiet she heard something crashing through the trees toward her.

For a moment she was frozen, her vague interest in her surroundings turning to bone-deep fear, and then she started to run. She only made it a few clumsy paces when something caught her by the arm; she sucked in a breath, intending to scream, but hadn't let out more than a squawk before she felt a hand clap over her mouth.

Chapter Thirty

"For the love of god, it's *me*."

Nash released her, and Eddie sagged against a convenient tree, trying to breathe a little more evenly.

"You left me," she said eventually, when her lungs permitted it.

Nash was staring at her, his eyes so dark they looked completely black. He had the beginnings of a beard, grown out slightly past the point of stubble, and Eddie reached out to test how it felt. It was softer than expected.

"We did not leave you," Nash said. "*You* left *us*."

That did not seem right, but Eddie's hands were in Nash's hair now, and she was thoroughly distracted.

"Rose's hair is soft," she said. It came out in almost a whimper. "So, so soft. Not like a cloud is soft. Like satin. Like drinking chocolate."

Nash sighed. "*Rose.* I thought we had finally been rid of her, and yet here she is again."

"Where?" said Eddie, glancing around, her heart lightening; it took her a moment to realize that he had been speaking metaphorically.

"Do you know what the Greeks and the Romans did when they celebrated these rituals?" Nash said.

His hands had somehow made it to the stock around her neck, which he was slowly loosening.

"Died of exposure?" Eddie ventured. "Or perhaps . . . poisoning?"

"No," Nash said, raising an eyebrow. "They went to bed with each other."

"*Oh*," said Eddie, stunned into silence for a brief moment. "Wait . . . to *bed*, or to . . . soil? I thought these things always took place in the woods?"

"I think you're rather missing the point," said Nash, with a leonine smile.

It turned out that she was; Nash was making a start on the buttons of her waistcoat. The implications of this kicked in with around a five-second delay, and Eddie pushed at his hands ineffectually.

"It's cold, Nash. And I'm on a tree. In a tree? No, on. Definitely on. Could you just—"

He silenced her with a kiss, and then managed to untuck her shirt from her breeches; his hands were freezing on her waist, and Eddie let out a huff of shock.

"You know," Nash said, his voice sounding odd and distant, as if he were trapped at the bottom of a well, "I have wanted to do this from the moment I saw you, gawping at me across the dinner table at Albert's . . ."

Eddie closed her eyes, willing her mind to catch up with the rest of her.

"Wait . . . But you did not invite me to your house because you liked the *look* of me, it was because . . . you wanted to read my writing. You thought I had promise."

Nash laughed quietly into her neck. "Come now. We are both quite grown-up, we can speak plainly to each other. I knew I would not rest until I touched you, and having touched you . . . it seems I only want you more. This is why we're *here* . . . This is what it's all been leading to, Edie . . ."

Addled as she was, Eddie was of sound enough mind to register that she had just been dealt a severe blow. Nash did not seem to realize it—he was kissing her neck, the scratch of his beard no longer soft and pleasant—but she was rapidly going over their earliest meetings in her mind, all of them now cast in much harsher light.

Everybody had tried to warn her. Her mother. Lucy-Anne. Rose—God, so many times, Rose. Eddie had been so desperate to believe that Nash really had faith in her, that he had seen something in her that he would nurture and elevate to greatness, when all along it had been the oldest trick from the most ancient books.

Man meets woman. Man deceives woman. Woman inevitably suffers the insufferable consequences.

"My name is *Eddie*."

"What?" Nash mumbled, still kissing her. One of his hands had dipped dangerously low, thumbing along her hip bone.

"It's *Eddie*, Nash. It's not Edie. Just—get *off* me."

She pushed him away. Nash had the audacity to look wounded.

"Are you really *sulking* because of a name? I'll call you Eddie, if you like. I'll call you whatever you want."

His voice was slow, and slurred around the edges. He was reaching for her again, but Eddie shrank away, feeling a tree retaliate and scratch her hard across the cheek as she did.

"Edie—*Eddie*—you're bleeding. Stop being ridiculous and come here."

"*No*," said Eddie.

She didn't much care if she was being ridiculous. She suddenly wanted to be as far away from Nash as possible, so she didn't have to hear any more of his honeyed words or outright lies. She pushed her way through the branches, aiming for the shore; at first she simply wanted to get some distance from him, but some sort of animal instinct took over when she heard him attempting to follow, and she started running in earnest.

She could hear him calling her name—*Edie* again; was his memory really so short?—and she glanced behind her as she moved, noting that he was no longer in her line of sight. She could

hear odd chattering sounds—angry squirrels, perhaps, or interrupted birds. They seemed to be getting louder and louder, as if
excited by the chase. Somewhere, somebody was laughing.

When she turned around, she slammed immediately into
something warm and solid. All the wind was knocked from her,
and as she gasped and wheezed, she realized who it was: impos-
sibly, *Henry*.

"Miss Miller?" he said, looking concerned. "What are you doing out here? Do you . . . ? Are you in need of assistance?"

"Henry?" Eddie said, dazed.

The effects of the fungus she had consumed only seemed to
be getting more acute over time; the light shifted, and for a split
second she swore she was looking at a rather man-shaped tree,
but then it was Henry again, blinking down at her in consternation.

Nash called out after her from somewhere nearby; it sounded
almost like a howl.

Henry's head snapped up. He narrowed his eyes, and then
glanced back over at Eddie.

"If you'll follow me," he said, unfailingly polite, even as she
stood there with her chest heaving, her shirt untucked, her eyes
unable to focus properly on him.

Eddie did follow him. He led her silently through the trees,
clearly knowing exactly where he was going, holding branches
out of the way so that they would not whip back and maim or de-
capitate her. They emerged onto the stony beach, and Eddie saw
that there was a small boat tied up at the dock, bobbing violently
in the dark water.

Eddie sat down heavily on the rocks.

"Why are you here? *Are* you here?"

"Am I . . . ? Yes, I am here. There was something I needed to . . .
something of mine that I left here. It belonged to my mother."

"That's nice," said Eddie, running her hands over the rough

surface of the rock beneath her and wondering if she was leaving handprints in it, as one would in snow. "It's nice to have a mother."

"Yes," said Henry. "Did Nash—Mr. Nicholson . . . ? He didn't . . . ?"

He gestured generally at Eddie, who looked down at her disheveled appearance and then slowly shook her head.

"Good," said Henry. "That's good. I can take you back to the mainland tonight, Miss Miller. There's a house down in the village, if you need somewhere to stay."

"Back to the mainland?" said Eddie, baffled. "But why?"

"Because you are in danger, Miss Miller," Henry said, as if this should have been obvious. "Mr. Nicholson . . . he's not a good man. He does not particularly like to take no for an answer."

Eddie was struck very suddenly by a crystal clear memory of Nash and Henry, standing much too close together in the woods, Henry's face aflame. Why had they been there at all? Looking for Juno. Yes—they had been looking for Juno, but Henry had been furious. There had been shouting. It had almost come to blows.

But . . . no. That wasn't right. It was muddled, somehow. Eddie just couldn't quite put her finger on why.

"Let me . . . I have a cloak. You're shivering."

Henry vanished from her line of sight. Eddie had absolutely no idea where he might have gone. He had a boat, she knew that much. A boat that would take her across the water, if she asked him. A boat that would take her to Rose.

The moon emerged from behind the clouds. The waves lapped at the shore.

There was something in the water.

Whatever it was out there in the lake, it was pale and drifting, tugged back and forth by the tide.

Now she remembered. Rose was in trouble. Rose would *die*, if nobody saved her. She was out there right now, and she was drowning. This time, Eddie wouldn't just stand there, useless. This time she would do it right.

The cold didn't really hit her until the water was up to her thighs, the wind whipping at her hair; she stopped, recalibrating, looking for the body in the water . . .

But no, she had got it wrong again. Rose hadn't drowned. Rose was alive. The body in the water . . . it was the *maid*. The one from the story. A pale apron. A frilly cap. Eddie could *see* her, as clear as anything.

"Miss Miller?" Henry was back, somehow. He was holding a cloak, looking uncertain. "Miss Miller, you should get out of the water."

"A woman drowned," Eddie said, pointing. Henry looked startled. "A maid. She worked here, at the house . . . It was something to do with Nash's father. Can't you see her?"

Henry waded out to her, and then took her very gently by the elbow.

"It's the moon, Miss Miller. On the lake. It's just the moon."

Eddie couldn't understand why he wouldn't believe her, but when she glanced back out over the water, whatever she had seen had vanished. She let herself be steered back onto dry land and draped in his cloak. He sat down heavily on the beach next to her.

"The woman who drowned," he said slowly. "You said . . . What did Mr. Nicholson have to do with it?"

"I don't know," said Eddie, trying very hard to focus her thoughts. She was feeling the cold now; her legs seemed completely iced over. "Only that . . . there was an argument? He must have hurt her. They found her washed up on the beach. Right here. Nash's father did it, Valentine seemed quite sure . . ."

Henry rubbed at his forehead, looking unexpectedly troubled, and then glanced up at Eddie. If she hadn't known better, she would have said that there were tears shining in his eyes.

"Wait here a moment, Miss Miller, I just . . ."

But Eddie didn't want to wait anywhere, or to be left alone, so when he got up, she followed him. He didn't seem to notice; he forged on ahead, up the path toward the house, Eddie struggling to keep him in view as they tramped through the trees and then approached the open lawn. The wind had picked up, the trees thrashing furiously. She was falling behind. She was falling, full stop.

"*There* you are."

Nash stepped out from the woods. In Eddie's mind, he had become monstrous and terrible, but in reality, he looked just the same as he always did. A little scuffed around the edges, perhaps, and deeply intoxicated, but still just Nash. He was even smiling lopsidedly at her.

"God, but you can run. Come on, I have found the others. They're back up at the house. Valentine has a sprained ankle somehow, Kitty is trying to tend to it ... *Now* ..." His voice changed very suddenly, from warmth to ungodly chill. "What on earth are you doing with that?"

He was talking to Henry, who had turned and come back for Eddie. He was furious and shaking. He was also holding a gun.

One of these facts was not quite like the others.

"Leave her alone," Henry said, his voice trembling slightly, the gun perfectly level.

"Henry," Nash said, laughing, as if this was the most ridiculous thing he had ever seen. The wind was picking at the hem of his long fur, making it flap like great, dark wings. "Put that thing down before you hurt yourself. What in God's name are you even doing here?"

"He killed her," Henry said. "Didn't he?"

"*What?*"

"Don't pretend you don't know!" Henry shouted, the gun wavering. "You know. You've known all this time, haven't you?"

"Henry," Nash said, stepping closer and putting up his hands when Henry lifted his weapon to meet him. "You seem very up-set. Come up to the house, and we can—"

"Stop *talking*. It's always so much *talking* with you, you think you can say whatever you like and make anybody believe any-thing. *Tell me what he did to my mother.*"

Nash looked pitying. "Oh, Henry. I know it must be so very hard. But of all people, *I* understand. This house takes every-thing. But it's like I've been trying to tell you—we are bound by tragedy, you and I."

"Shut *up!*"

The world seemed to slide away. In reality, Eddie had sunk down to her knees on the grass. She couldn't stop staring at the gun. It looked so *real*.

"You're still wearing her locket," Henry said suddenly, his voice perilously quiet. "Damn you, why the *hell* are you still wearing her *locket*—"

In the blink of an eye, Nash had leaped for the gun; Henry, understandably reluctant to relinquish it, was trying to claw it back. There was a brief scuffle, during which time seemed to stand still.

Then a single shot ran out, and Eddie saw Henry fall.

She closed her eyes, but the sound went on and on, a ringing in her ears that wouldn't let up. She pressed her hands to them, trying to block it out, the ground seeming to undulate beneath her. It was all too much. She wanted it to stop. She wanted to be in possession of her own mind again, but until she could, she wanted to be rid of this hideous ringing . . .

It seemed both years and seconds later that she felt an arm on her shoulder, gently shaking her. Eddie dared to crack open an eye.

"What the hell are you doing curled up in the mud?" said Kitty, raising her voice to be heard over the wind. "You look ri-diculous."

"Nash," Eddie said, his name heavy in her mouth. She realized that she was crying, her face a mess of tears and mud. "He shot Henry. Oh, God. Is Henry dead?"

"*Henry?*" said Kitty. "Henry left, Eddie. With the rest of the staff. Christ, how large was your dosage?"

"He's not here?" croaked Eddie, heaving herself up into a sitting position and looking about her, finding only the perfectly ordinary lawn, bordered by heavily protesting trees. She let out a little hiccuping sob, trying to make sense of it, willing Kitty to believe her. "You didn't hear a shot? Nobody is hurt?"

Kitty shook her head. "It's the wind. I think another tree might have gone over. Come on, get up . . ." She offered Eddie an arm and managed to haul her to her feet. "Have you actually seen Nash? He's the last unaccounted for."

"I don't know," Eddie said truthfully, as they started back toward the house, her tears still falling. "To be honest, Kitty . . . I don't know anything at all."

Chapter Thirty-one

HENRY'S MOTHER WHISPERED WORDS OF WARNING TO EDDIE all night long. Sometimes she became Rose again, telling Eddie that the boat was coming, and that they'd better pack quickly so that they could catch it. At one point she had to place a pillow over her head and beg for quiet; it must have worked, because as dawn approached she fell into a few hours of uneasy sleep.

When morning came, there were no ghosts at her window telling her to run. When she stumbled from her bed and looked out across the grounds, she saw no body collapsed and bleeding over by the tree line. Eddie's head was pounding; she had grazes on her knees and a long, thin cut on her cheek, but as far as she could tell, she was mostly in one piece.

She changed slowly, every movement deeply taxing, and then heaved herself downstairs to see if anybody might be up and available to answer a myriad of questions. But when she walked into the dining room she was absolutely astounded to find Liza Nicholson sitting there, dressed in her traveling clothes. There was a newspaper, a brown paper package, and a pile of correspondence sitting next to her. The fire was lit in the grate behind her, a damp cloak hanging from the back of a chair next to it to dry, and Juno was gazing adoringly up at her mistress, her tail wagging slowly.

"Ah," Liza said. "You're still here."

"Er," said Eddie, still staring at her, wondering if she had started hallucinating again. "Yes? I am. Are you . . . ? When did you . . . ?"

"This morning," said Liza, taking off one of her gloves and then clearly thinking better of it and putting it straight back on. "I would have been here yesterday, but as you may have noticed, there was a bit of a storm. What happened to your face?"

Eddie touched her cheek, still feeling as if she were dreaming. "A tree."

"Oh. I see. Good God, this place is absolutely freezing. I could not find Mrs. Hall, or anybody for that matter—"

"They're gone," said Eddie, sitting down for lack of any better ideas. "Apparently Nash . . . er . . . Well. There was a disagreement. And the servants left."

"All of them?"

"All of them."

"And this disagreement concerned . . . ?"

"Henry. It was an argument with Henry." Eddie paused, trying to get things right in her mind before she spoke again, everything flooding back full force. "God, I had no idea. About his mother, I mean."

"Ah. I see," said Liza, looking startled and then recovering herself. "Terrible business. You must understand . . . Nash had no idea what his father had planned to do. He only went to Mr. Nicholson for help. He was eighteen and fancied himself in love with her . . . practically a child himself, not at all ready to become a father, although he certainly wanted to do the right thing. Mr. Nicholson wouldn't stand for it. Nash feels terrible about it, it has haunted him all his adult life. He was actually standing in the South Parlor when it happened. He saw it all from the window. You can imagine how it has affected him since. And Henry was offered lodgings and employment, for as long as he wants it. I trust we can rely on your . . . discretion, Miss Miller."

"My discretion?" Eddie said, trying to catch up, her throat closing up with a slow-creeping horror. "Oh, God. He really did push her? Off the *cliff*? Because she was . . . Because she and Nash . . ."

Liza looked panicked for a moment, clearly realizing that Eddie had known far less than she had assumed.

"No, no, you misunderstand me, it was . . . I shouldn't have presumed to speak . . . I suppose we will never really know what happened. Listen—it is not important now."

Eddie could not disagree more. She was staring at Liza in utter disbelief, thinking of Henry's mother and Nash's father standing on the very cliffs she had walked along herself many times; she had always shuddered slightly when she looked down at the sheer drop below. From the house Nash would have seen two distant figures, indistinct through the glass—and then, very suddenly, only one.

Henry hadn't known, Eddie realized, feeling sick to her stomach. And she had accidentally told him, without even knowing the truth of the matter herself.

If he had really been there at all.

Liza was trying to catch her attention, to divert her from this horrifying train of thought.

"Edith, are you listening to me?"

Eddie blinked at her, feeling close to tears. It was all just too *much*.

"*You're* not in the family way?" Liza said suddenly.

"In the . . . ?"

"There is no need to look quite so shocked, it is a perfectly reasonable question considering the circumstances."

"No," Eddie choked out. "No, that isn't it at all, we have never . . . I would never . . ."

Liza sighed and placed both of her hands flat on the table in front of her, considering Eddie thoughtfully.

"Look, I am well aware of how Nash behaves. I know what sorts of lies he tells about me and our marriage to get silly girls to lift their skirts, but let me tell you plainly—we may quarrel while he is in the process of writing something, but once his work is finished, all is well again. I do not entirely blame him—he is an artist, after all, and he had a difficult start in life with a father like that—but he *had* promised not to go to bed with you, which is why—"

"He . . . ? He had promised . . . about *me*?"

Fresh horrors were dawning. The thought that Nash and Liza had discussed her like this—that Liza had suspected, or even perhaps *expected* that their relationship would be romantic—was utterly mortifying. How long ago had this discussion taken place? When she had been invited to Bede House? Even earlier, when Liza had seen Eddie and Nash ensconced together in the study at his party?

It was further confirmation that she hadn't really known him at all.

"Well. If there's no chance you might be with child, that makes things a lot simpler."

"You do not seem upset," said Eddie faintly, putting her head in her hands and focusing on the soothing, dependable grain of the wood in front of her. "About any of this."

"You are very young, Edith. But when you love somebody for as long as Nash and I have, you get to know all their faults and foibles—and then when you have a clear idea of the state of things, you assess, and decide whether you can stand to put up with them."

Eddie just stared at her, feeling hollowed-out and exhausted. Clearly believing that these matters had been neatly tied away, Liza cleared her throat and glanced upward.

"I thought I saw some fresh damage to the house on my approach?"

"The ceiling in the long gallery fell in," Eddie said.

"Of course it did." Liza sighed, drumming her fingers on the table, and then stopping abruptly. "Right. I assume you have been eating, even without any staff? Were you planning on breakfast?"

"Er. Yes. I could make . . . Would you like an egg?"

"Best make it two."

Eddie went down to the kitchen feeling as if she were still sleeping. She lit the fire with relative ease, having seen the process demonstrated many times, and then fried four eggs until they began to bubble and curl at the edges. It was easier to focus on them than to think about anything else; eggs were just about the only things that still made sense. She slid them onto a mostly clean plate, located two forks, and then took them upstairs.

When she entered the dining room, Nash was there.

He looked very pale. He had purpling circles under his eyes, and he still hadn't shaved. The overall effect was a little pathetic; Eddie was irritated to discover that she still found it endearing. She glanced him over, looking for injuries, or for any sign at all that he had been involved in a dramatic grapple for his life the night before, and found none.

It was hard to read the atmosphere between him and his wife; Eddie half expected Nash to turn on her and demand that she leave rather than interrupt their private reunion, but he only glanced down at the brown package that Liza seemed to have delivered to his hands and cleared his throat.

Liza took charge.

"Ah, there we are. Thank you, Miss Miller. Nash, the poor girl looks half-dead—you must send her back to town to be revived."

"Hmm?" said Nash. He glanced up at Eddie, his face breaking into a tentative smile. "Yes. Yes, I do think . . . It will be time for Miss Li's wedding soon anyway, will it not?"

"Yes," said Eddie. "Just before Christmas."

"Well, I should arrange to go sooner than that," said Liza. "I will be returning tomorrow. I can escort you."

Half of Eddie's mind immediately fled home to London, and the other half hovered, clinging to Nash and the promise of the letter from his editor. Perhaps all was not lost, if she departed. Perhaps she could have both.

"I have finished my novel," she said, addressing Nash. "If I go now . . . I shall see you in London, when you return? And . . . and when I have pieced my manuscript back together, we will send it to your publisher for review?"

She knew she sounded desperate, completely at odds with the tone of the conversation they were having, but if he agreed to all in front of Liza then perhaps that meant it would truly happen. She would not go home empty-handed.

Liza raised her eyebrows at this, but Nash nodded effusively.

"Of course! Of course. And if this is not quite the right thing, then I'm sure the next thing . . ."

Eddie nodded, placated. They did not have to be the best of friends. She did not have to condone everything he might have done in the past, or the person he continued to be. She felt older, now. Wiser. Perhaps it was *her* turn to set the rules of engagement—to make clear the boundaries, so that there were no more misunderstandings about the nature of their connection.

She would go home to retrieve her manuscript, and have things out with Rose, and eat three meals a day cooked by somebody competent under the roof of a house she trusted not to collapse on her in her sleep. She might have worried that Nash would be angry at her for departing—that he would write her off as a coward, unable to weather the storms of St. Bede's—except that his mood seemed entirely changed this morning.

"Is Henry all right?" she ventured.

Nash glanced up at her and then shrugged, a dismissive roll of his shoulders.

"I'm sure he's just fine."

This did not even begin to answer her question, but as he sat down at the table, Eddie noticed that the silver locket was no longer hanging around his neck.

Perhaps there *had* been a shot, but it had left both Nash and Henry unscathed. Perhaps it really had just been a tree branch breaking. Perhaps all that had happened the night before had been a long, strange nightmare, from the moment she ate those damned mushrooms.

Regardless, it was more than a little unnerving, watching him shrug this off entirely and then sit down at the table with his wife and pull the plate of eggs toward him, merrily tucking into the two that Eddie had, in fact, cooked for herself. Valentine and Kitty came down and betrayed no hint of surprise when they saw Liza sitting at the table. They greeted her amiably, Valentine limped off to fetch more food, and then they indulged in a friendly, polite breakfast, without a whiff of violence or paganism about it.

Eddie watched it unfold in silence, as if it were a play.

"I brought my maid with me," Liza said. "She cannot cook to save her life, but she *can* heat water for baths. I had asked her to draw me one, but Miss Miller, perhaps you would like to . . ."

She gestured at Eddie, who touched a hand to her hair and accidentally set off a small avalanche of dried mud.

"Thank you," she said. "I . . . I will."

The bath had been arranged in the Gold Chamber, Nash and Liza's room, which Eddie had never before had cause to enter; she crossed the threshold tentatively, taking in the ornate four-poster and the sheer volume of gilt in the room. It only looked like Nash at all because of the *mess*: piles of clothes on the floor; empty liquor bottles on the baroque dresser; a colony of books and parchment on the desk, where apparently he *had* put pen to paper at some point. The fire was mercifully lit, the bath tucked behind a silk screen; Eddie felt tears spring to her eyes when she stepped into it and was pleasantly scalded up to her knees.

It was impossible not to think of Rose, sinking down among the curling steam. She would likely haunt every bath Eddie took for the rest of her life. All the anger Eddie had been using to keep thoughts of her at bay had been replaced with utter exhaustion, and thus depleted, she couldn't really find it in herself to hate her.

In fact, Eddie missed her so much that she felt herself start to cry with relief at the thought that she was going home to her, even if they were sure to quarrel. Even if nothing could be as it had been before.

When she was scrubbed clean and hot through, the water murky with the residue of her night in the woods, Eddie stepped out and wrapped herself in the towel that had been left neatly folded on a chair. She felt stupefied and off-kilter, the comfort a shock to her system after being cold for so long, and the dash she attempted to get back to her room without being spotted was more of a stagger.

It was a good thing she wasn't going at top speed, because when she entered her bedroom, she ran straight into Valentine.

Chapter Thirty-two

"CHRIST, BE CAREFUL—I CANNOT LOSE THE OTHER ANKLE, I'll have to slither out of here like a worm."

Eddie was too confused to laugh.

"What are you doing in my room?"

"Um . . ." said Valentine. "You are losing your towel."

Eddie fixed this posthaste. As she did so, she noticed a brown package sitting incongruously on her unmade bed. It had already been haphazardly torn open at one end.

"What's that?" she said.

"Nothing," said Valentine.

Eddie ducked behind her screen to dress quickly, and Valentine used the opportunity to attempt to sidle from the room.

"Stop it," said Eddie. "You are being very strange. Why are you trying to flee?"

"Ah," said Valentine, with a shifty glance back over at the bed. "I would quite like to be very far from here when this incendiary explodes."

Eddie finished dressing and went to see what was causing so much agitation, letting the contents of the package slide gently from the brown paper into her hands.

It was a book. *The Gentleman, Volume One*, by Nash Nicholson.

It didn't make an ounce of sense; Nash had not *written* a book. Eddie would have noticed. He had perhaps had time to write a few pages here and there—she had seen him sometimes, scribbling in corners or going to fetch ink—but she certainly would have noticed if he had been working hard enough to produce something as complete as this. She opened it to the title page, which indicated that this was a test printing, and then flipped through to the first page.

> Delilah Fortescue had not intended to kill her husband—
> but once the unfortunate act had taken place, it felt unforgivably rude not to keep his appointments . . .

Eddie felt shock course through the entire length of her body, followed by a ringing numbness that turned the world around her to static and soap bubbles. There had been some sort of mistake. Nash's editor had somehow encountered Eddie's manuscript—perhaps *Rose* had sent it, meaning well?—and had unintentionally published it under Nash's name.

But, of course, that made no sense whatsoever. Because Liza had brought the package to him. Nash had received it, and not said a word to Eddie about it.

And now Valentine had come to deliver it.

"What is this?" she asked, already knowing the answer.

"I—we—thought you ought to know," said Valentine, with a grimace.

It was no accident. Nash had *stolen* her manuscript.

She held it in her hands, months and months of her life, printed under Nash's name and ready to be distributed to the masses—and suddenly she wasn't the least bit tired.

She felt as if she could have burned the house to ashes with just the force of her fury, and Nash with it.

He had told her that her novel was rudimentary; he had mocked it, said that it was not ready. He had made her feel as if it was worth nothing.

He had lied.

Eddie looked down at *The Gentleman* and turned the pages once more, not realizing she was crying until a fat teardrop splattered across the word *tumescent*, rendering it a blotchy blur. Here was the part where her heroine put on gentleman's attire for the first time and marveled at the rightness of it; here the scene where she accidentally courted a woman, whose smile and deft sense of humor had been painted in shades of Rose.

"I am going to kill him," Eddie said quietly. "I am going to *kill him*." The second time she said it, it came out more like a scream.

"Look," Valentine said urgently. "He is an imbecile, that much is plain. But . . . I'm sorry to say this, Eddie, I really am—you have little chance at recourse. It's already out. So it might be worth—"

Eddie was on the move, fueled by pure, molten rage.

"*Where is he?*"

"He and Liza went for a walk," Valentine said, struggling to keep up on one good ankle. Eddie abruptly changed course, heading for the Gold Chamber. "Eddie, *slow down*, just think for a second—"

The sound that issued from Eddie's mouth could have been accurately described as a snarl. She marched into Nash's room, threw the book down on his bed, picked up everything she could carry in one armful from his desk, and then hurled it into the fire.

It caught easily, the paper starting to blacken and curl at once. It felt wonderful. Eddie wanted more.

She cleared his desk completely and made a start on his clothes, throwing an expensive-looking top hat into the hearth with another scream of frustration. Valentine just stood there, looking very pale, not attempting to stop her.

The fireplace reached full capacity quickly; a vase from the mantel met an abrupt end on the rug instead, and then a small porcelain dog, crunching gratifyingly under her shoe.

"That was Liza's," Valentine said. "Just for the record."

Eddie paused, looking down at the shards of china under her heel, tears streaming down her face.

"You cannot hurt him in any way that matters," Valentine said gently. "At least, not like this."

The door creaked open, and Eddie jumped, expecting to see Nash or Liza; instead, it was Kitty. She took in the scene of destruction before her without so much as a raised eyebrow.

"Ah. I see."

"Did you know?" Eddie seethed. "Either of you?"

"No," said Valentine.

Kitty shook her head. "Not until this morning."

Eddie looked about her at the ruined room, feeling her anger abate and give way to a gut punch of misery.

"*God*. What the hell am I supposed to do *now*?"

There was silence, broken only by the crackling of the fire and the sound of Eddie's breathing.

"I mean it," she said, sitting down heavily on the edge of the bed, feeling as if all of her strings had been cut. "What do I *do*? Valentine? Kitty?"

Kitty considered her.

"I would fight," she said. "Art is everything. It's what truly matters. The people you loved, the politics and arguments, the little things you said and did . . . it all fades away. Art is what's left."

"Yes," said Eddie, picking up the book again, staring down at the hateful name on the cover. "Wait. Actually . . . no. Surely you don't mean . . . You cannot place the value of your art above the value of living your *life*?"

Kitty shrugged. "Art *is* my life."

Eddie took in a breath and then let it out, wetly.

Kitty glanced back out of the door. "Look, I was coming to tell you—you ought to go downstairs. Now."

Eddie was so desperate for somebody to tell her what to do next that she obeyed, going from the room like a sleepwalker.

Downstairs in the entrance hall she met Juno, who was whining at the door; when she opened it, the dog took off at full speed toward the trees. Once again expecting Nash, Eddie stopped short when she saw who was walking up the lawn toward her.

Rose was dressed in a red traveling cloak, her hair tumbling free of its pins. She was flushed and breathing hard, as if she had run all the way up the hill. Just the sight of her made Eddie cry a little harder. In the distance, she saw Albert, in possession of one small trunk.

For one glorious moment, Eddie forgot about everything else.

It didn't matter. Not when Rose was waiting.

It dawned on her, on that threshold, that in addition to her multitude of mistakes, she had been fatally wrong about one last thing.

Because it mattered more to her to see her name on Rose's lips at that moment than it would if it were on the spines of a thousand books. It would never be *enough*, to dedicate every part of herself to the pursuit of that one dream—because she had other dreams, too.

One of them was rushing up the lawn toward her.

Eddie didn't stop running until she was within touching distance.

"I had to come," Rose said, sounding winded, pushing an ecstatic Juno away. Her cloak was askew, and somehow already covered with dog fur. "Eddie, your novel . . . Whatever deal he made with you, whatever he has promised you . . . I have seen it advertised already, and it is being published under his name alone."

"I know," said Eddie, her heart pounding wildly. "He stole it."

Rose's mouth dropped open in horror.

"He *stole* it?" She shook her head, her mouth working. "Of course he did, that *bastard*. Where is he?"

She looked about ready to roll up her sleeves and fight him, and Eddie could not have loved her more. She smiled through her tears, watching Rose look around for Nash, perhaps hoping he might be conveniently within arm's reach.

"Rose, just let me say something, before you hunt him down and punt him into the lake, as he deserves."

"We should pay his editor a visit. Albert will know who he is, we can demand to see him, and then we can—"

"*Rose*. I'd like to tell you that I'm sorry."

"We might have to collect witness statements, I suppose. Do you think Valentine and Kitty would attest to seeing you write it? Dayo would, I'm sure of it. Wait . . . You want to do what?"

"To apologize. To make things right between us. To tell you that I have been a boundless fool, undeserving of you. I have ruined everything."

Rose looked confused. "Well . . . Yes, that is all very well, but—"

Eddie cut her off with a shake of her head. "Rose, if it helps to make things clearer—it has come to my attention, somewhat belatedly, that I am very much in love with you."

Rose now looked beautifully perplexed.

"You're . . . ? Eddie, are there not more pressing matters to attend to?"

"Actually, no," Eddie said, stepping in close and taking Rose's gloved hands in hers. "I don't think so. Not at the minute."

"Oh," said Rose, finally shutting up.

It had begun, very gently, to rain.

"Will you listen to me now, you maniac? I love you. I mean, you know that, I have always loved you—but I mean, I love you in a way that will need to be . . . presented before the board, for approval."

"What on earth are you talking about?"

"I'm not entirely sure. But, Rose . . . I know that I mean it. Look . . . you said before that I've always known exactly what I want and who I am, and *I* certainly believed that was the case, but these past few weeks have been . . . revelatory, to say the least.

A lot of things make sense to me now. Of course I never really looked elsewhere for romantic diversions! Of course I saw no need to marry! You have always been everything I needed, and more. It was too much to look at directly, so I've been skirting around it for months—no, sorry, what am I talking about, for *years*—but I'm brave enough to see it, now. To see all of this for what it really is. You have always been there for me, even when I *certainly* did not deserve it, and if you'll let me . . . I'd like to try to make it up to you. To give back what you gave, and more and more and more. The home you want to make for yourself in London—I want to be a part of it. If I am too late, if I have hurt you too much with my pigheadedness and my ignorance, I understand . . . but if there's any chance you might still love me just a little, I'd . . . well. I suppose what I'm saying is, that information would be of great interest to me."

Rose looked stuck halfway between tears and wariness. Eddie supposed she couldn't blame her.

"And you really are sorry?"

"I really, really am. I have been an ass of monstrous proportions."

"And . . . and you aren't going to make a fool of me? Because you are on your last strike, Eddie. There's only so much idiocy a person can take."

"The only person I intend to make a fool of is myself."

"Well, that's a given," said Rose. "You're not drunk? Or . . . delirious, from the cold?"

Eddie let out a sigh of a laugh.

"If you are *not* going to strike me down, would you just let me kiss you? I promise we can discuss the ins and outs later, but I am so full of fire right now that I either need to kiss you or find a stick to hit something with, and I'd rather—"

Rose rolled her eyes, pulled her in by the sleeves, and kissed her. Eddie couldn't help but laugh quietly into her mouth before drawing her in close, her hand finding the back of Rose's neck and cradling it, Rose's arm steady around her waist.

It *was* real. Undeniably so. It always had been. She wasn't going to mistake it for anything less ever again.

"Right," she said, when Rose finally pulled away. "Now, about the other thing."

"He really stole it?" Rose said, pink and breathless, one hand going to her hair where Eddie had made a bit of a mess of it. "You had no idea?"

Eddie grimaced. "I sort of thought . . . that maybe *you* had taken it. Nash said . . . and I shouldn't have *believed* him, of course, but I was upset, and . . . Are you about to wallop me?"

"I am seriously considering it," said Rose. "You thought *I* had taken it?"

"I was wrong," said Eddie. "As it turns out, I often am. Again . . . *very* sorry."

"As you should be," said Rose, straightening up with a sigh. "So. What's the plan?"

"I just want to go," Eddie said, glancing over at Albert, who was now sitting on the trunk a respectful distance away, scratching Juno behind her ears. "I don't want to be here for a moment longer."

"Good," said Rose. "Let's get you home."

They went upstairs to pack, Albert following behind. With all three of them together, they accomplished it quickly, and then Eddie ducked behind the screen to change into her traveling clothes, ignoring Albert's look of horror. At the last minute she added Valentine's coat on top, reasoning that she could return it in London, and feeling as if she needed a bit of armor. The rest of her manuscript fitted nicely, folded into the inside pocket.

"I will take this down to the dock—the boat is waiting for us there," said Albert, lifting her trunk.

"Thank you, Albert," Eddie said, giving him a quick kiss on the cheek, which made him so flustered he just nodded in reply.

"Please do not harass my fiancé," Rose said, giving his arm a squeeze. "He is the one you have to thank for hearing news of Nash's supposed book, and for insisting that we come here at once, before I had even opened my mouth."

"Albert," Eddie said seriously. "Thank you. I . . . I give you my blessing, to marry Rose."

"Hmmm," said Albert. "I am not entirely sure you have earned *mine*, after all the tears I have had to dry these past few weeks—but I will take it under consideration."

"Fair enough."

It was raining harder now, as if to befit the occasion, and they had to bow their heads against it as they walked quickly across the lawn and into the safety of the trees. Eddie chanced a look back at the house, magnificent and decrepit, one strong gust of wind away from total collapse, and only walked faster in the direction of the dock.

Captain Perkins was standing at the prow of his boat, looking irate; Albert reached him first, and carefully deposited the trunks.

"Oh, *God*," said Rose, her eyes fixed on something over Eddie's shoulder. "Whatever you do, Ed, do *not* turn around."

Eddie turned around.

Nash had just cleared the trees, and was making straight for them.

Chapter Thirty-three

"WE CAN JUST CAST OFF AND GO," ROSE SAID URGENTLY. "Eddie?"

Eddie took a deep breath and then shook her head.

"No," she said. "No, I rather think we need to have a little talk."

Nash slowed down as he approached her, and then did a few ridiculous adjustments of his hair and collar, as if they had not seen him at full sprint just a few moments ago and might imagine that he had strolled here with perfect composure.

"Edith," he said when he reached them. "Eddie. You weren't really going to leave without saying goodbye?"

Eddie just stared at him, open-mouthed and disbelieving. His audacity was truly something to behold.

"Well, yes, all right . . . Valentine told me what you . . . Look, let's just get this over with, shall we?"

"Get this over with?" Eddie shouted, any trace of *her* composure abruptly taking its leave. "You *stole my manuscript*, Nash! You watched me work myself to the bone over it these past few months. You acted as if it was second-rate, as if I needed your help to make it worthy of anything at all—and all the while you planned to *steal* it from me, to pass off as your own!"

Nash was already shaking his head.

"All the while? No, no . . . Good Lord, you greatly overestimate my powers of forethought. It was only once I had started helping you, giving you guidance . . . Really a lot of it *was* my work, by the end, if you—"

"You barely even *brushed* a pen against it! You gave me a handful of notes, on *one* occasion!"

Nash rubbed his eyes with great agitation, as if he had somehow imagined this conversation going much better.

"Edie, look—"

"*Eddie.*"

"Whatever. This is just . . . It's wasted energy. We both worked on this novel. And not to be crass, but honestly . . . there's nothing you can do about it now. Who would believe you? I *did* make some further changes to some of the language before I sent it to town—everyone will recognize my flair, my style. It is a change of direction for me, obviously, but there is enough of me in it to prove I was involved. I don't say this to insult you, but . . . nobody *knows* you. Everybody knows Nash Nicholson."

"Good God," Rose said faintly. "You did *not* just refer to yourself in the third person."

"Are you not embarrassed?" Eddie demanded, impatiently wiping away the rain that was threatening to blur her vision. "Do you care so little about your *art*, the thing I thought you valued above all else? That you would just take mine, and make a few changes, and pass it off as your own?"

"Listen," Nash said, his tone suddenly cotton-soft and confidential, reaching out to touch Eddie on the arm and then retracting his hand when she flinched away. "I know this is dreadful. Believe me, I had no desire to do it, but I was in a bit of a tight spot with my editor and this seemed the only solution . . . You *must* understand that people do things they would never normally consider, with the threat of financial ruin hanging over their heads . . . Look, Edie—Eddie. There is nothing I can say to fix this, but let us be practical and look forward, instead. This is just the first volume. We can work together on the rest, and I will make sure your credit is added; that we coauthor the second and third. Your name will be everywhere—whatever you write next, my editor will be desperate to publish. Just *think*, before you throw all of that away."

Eddie could see it so clearly: *The Gentleman, Volumes Two and Three, by Nash Nicholson and E. Miller.* Her nom de plume stamped in gold, displayed in the window of every bookshop, just as she had always dreamed. She was a hair's breadth away from being a real writer; she could have it *now*, almost at once. The past two months of upheaval, sleepless nights, blood, ink, and tears would be worth it.

Her name, however, would be inextricably linked to his. People would always assume that he was the real talent, and that she had been his *student*, his protégée, only published at all because of the kindness he had shown in teaching her his craft. Everybody would think that he had *made* her, when the truth was that here on this island with him, she felt that he had almost unmade her. She imagined having to go with him to dinners and parties; having to stand next to him and smile, always pretending.

It was unendurable. If she was going to do this, she would do it *right*. Even if the road was more difficult. Even if it took her the rest of her life.

"Eddie?" Rose said uneasily; Eddie realized she hadn't spoken a word for perhaps five long seconds. The rain was pummeling the surface of the lake.

"Come," Nash said, relaxing now, already sure that things had gone his way. He held out a hand to help her off the dock and back onto the shore. "Come in out of the rain, and we will rest, and then we can start back to town tomorrow and work this out in a way that benefits us all."

It *was* tempting, for a moment. But only for a moment.

"No," said Eddie. She was struck by the thought that he was not used to hearing that word. The appalled expression on his face made that clear. "And also . . . fuck you."

Rose let out a single "Ha!" of triumphant laughter behind her.

"Damn it, Edie. You are . . . You are just feeling upset and *reactionary* right now," Nash said, shaking his head. "It is entirely understandable, but just . . . Christ, just sleep on it, and you'll see—"

"No I won't," said Eddie. "I have quite made up my mind. In fact, here—" She reached impulsively into the pocket of Valentine's coat and pulled out the rest of her manuscript. She took one last look at it, and then held it out to him. When he only stared at it, she gave it a little shake to encourage him, as one would a dog. "Take this. I do not need it anymore. Frankly, you have ruined it for me . . . too many cooks, you know how it is . . . and I know you would struggle to finish it by yourself, as you have not a single original idea left in your head."

Albert laughed from the boat and quickly turned it into a dignified cough. Nash stared at the manuscript for another few seconds, clearly torn between his desire to take it and the fact that doing so would mean accepting Eddie's insult as fact, and then snatched it from her.

"You are making a very childish decision," he said, trying to sound dignified even as he scrambled to tuck the pages away in his pocket out of the rain. "And you will live to regret it."

"Ah, well," Eddie said bracingly. "If it is childish to choose to be happy, then I suppose I am. Good luck with everything, Nash, really. You are certainly going to need it."

She went to Rose and took her hand. They started down the jetty toward the boat, but Eddie found herself tugged to a stop as Rose broke away and turned back to Nash.

"You are a miserable man," she said firmly. "And I'm glad to say that you will always *be* miserable, because all you see in other people is what you can take from them. I hope you never write another word, and your house falls down on you while you sleep, and . . . and that you realize that your *dog* is worth a thousand of you. Come on, Eddie. Let's go home."

She took Eddie's hand again, and Eddie squeezed it tight.

She didn't stop squeezing it all the way back to London.

Chapter Thirty-four

THE INAUGURAL MEETING OF THE TREE HOUSE SOCIETY TOOK place on a bright April afternoon; it was the first proper, hopeful day of spring, the cool breeze laced with the heady smell of hyacinths.

When Eddie pushed open the front door, she realized that the reason it had been so difficult to open was that there were two enormous rabbits on the other side of it, barely reacting as they were propelled across the floor. They blinked up at her, little noses twitching, but when she bent to give them a stroke they scattered.

"Rose? Albert? I'm here!" she shouted, hanging up her cloak and then adjusting her waistcoat in the hall mirror.

She'd had to bribe Lucy-Anne with all her puddings for a month when her sister had discovered the small collection of masculine tailoring hidden in the back of her wardrobe; Valentine had insisted that at some point she would be required to give them back, but had not yet come to claim them.

She heard from Valentine occasionally, Dayo often, and Kitty not at all—although one day she had received a small package sent anonymously in the post with a note to only open its contents in private. Eddie had unwrapped it to discover a small portrait that she had never sat for. In it, she was standing back-to-back with Rose, who was looking over her shoulder at Eddie with obvious yearning. Eddie simply looked clueless, gazing off into the distance, her thoughts anybody's guess.

It was perfect. Rose had laughed for five minutes when she

saw it, and then propped it up on the mantelpiece in her new parlor, in pride of place.

Eddie and Nash had not exchanged so much as a letter, although she saw him everywhere; *The Gentleman* seemed to be selling very well, with volume two on its way any day now. Eddie tried to put her head down and walk very quickly past all the bookshop windows it dominated, but it was somewhat difficult to ignore. Occasionally, when she was feeling particularly content and charitable, Eddie told herself that it was good that it had done so well—she was a published writer, even if nobody else knew of it. People loved her book, even though they had no notion that it was hers.

It was enough. For now.

She was writing again, slowly but surely. Sometimes she worried that her finest work was contained in *The Gentleman*, that she would never manage to produce anything like it again, but Rose reminded her that this was tripe and nonsense. That she would only get better, with practice; that the best of her writing was ahead of her, unencumbered by miserable poets with dastardly motives.

"Guess what I've got in my pocket," Rose said now, approaching Eddie from behind and kissing her on the neck, glancing up to meet her gaze in the mirror and winking.

"I have no idea why you insist on continuing this game," Eddie said, turning around to kiss her properly, being careful not to crush the aforementioned pocket. "Because it is *always* a rabbit."

"Incorrect," said Rose. She removed her hand from her pocket, cupping a pale bundle very carefully, and then unfurled her fingers to reveal something that had absolutely no business being so small. "He is a *baby* rabbit. So technically, a kit."

"Technically, you are insane, so it is best we do away with technicalities altogether," said Eddie. "He is very lovely, though. How does nature even make anything this small? You'd think the particulars would get lost. They'd forget to put in a lung or something."

"His name is William Wilberforce."

"You cannot name a rabbit after a Member of Parliament, even if it is one we like at the moment."

"Yes, I can. Dayo met him recently, did he tell you?"

"Well, be sure to tell him about the rabbit and have him pass it on. I'm sure Wilberforce will be thrilled."

Albert came wandering into the hallway and scooped up the two rabbits on the floor, waving one of them absentmindedly at Eddie.

"Good afternoon. How is Trix enjoying Bunty?"

Bunty was a rabbit sent straight from Hell, with razor-sharp teeth and a thirst for blood; Albert had given her to Beatrice as a gift after they had met at a dinner party and been loath to part with each other.

"She has taught her to attack Lucy-Anne on command," Eddie said grimly. "Nobody is quite sure how, but Lucy-Anne has had to take to carrying around pocketfuls of carrots to throw at her in self-defense."

"Oh dear," said Albert, as he went to deposit the rabbits elsewhere. "Tell your mother and father how very sorry I am."

Eddie and Rose went into the cozy drawing room, which had been populated with a number of extra chairs to accommodate their visitors. The Tree House Society had only been formed a month prior, but once they had started putting it about that they were creating a literary salon for young artists and enthusiasts that encouraged everybody who was *not* a wealthy gentleman to apply, the guest list had grown rather quickly.

"How many are we?" Eddie said, counting chairs and frowning.

"Twenty, I think," said Rose. "Although Isabella Cliffe might be bringing a lady friend."

"All right, well, we should just about manage it, as long as you and I stay standing."

There was a tentative knock at the door. Rose and Eddie exchanged an excited glance, and Rose made to go and answer it—but Eddie grabbed her by the waist to stop her and pulled her in for one last, lingering kiss before their guests descended.

"Are you ready?" said Rose, straightening Eddie's collar for her.

"Absolutely not, but I suppose we shall just . . . start small, see what sort of thing people are interested in discussing, and then perhaps . . ."

There was another knock at the door, more insistent this time; Rose glanced over at it quizzically and then went to open it.

Ava Forester stepped inside. She was pink-cheeked and looked slightly nervous; the fact that Eddie was staring at her, completely aghast, probably wasn't helping matters. She exchanged pleasantries with Rose before coming to join Eddie in the living room.

"Miss Miller," she said, with a curtsy. "I hope you're well. I was so thrilled when I heard about this, we have all been talking of nothing else for a week."

"But," said Eddie. "You're . . . Are you *lost*?"

"I don't think so," Ava said, shrugging. "The invitation said you were open to all with an interest, is that not correct? I am primarily partial to Shakespeare myself, and I have tried my hand at some of my own sonnets. I think they are rather terrible, but Sophie says they have merit."

"Sophie," Eddie said blankly. "Wait . . . Sophie *Newport*?"

"Yes! I think she'll be along any minute."

There was another knock at the door. This time, when Rose opened it, three ladies came in at once. And then a person in a top hat, who removed it and gave a deep bow.

Rose went to close the door, but found she couldn't, due to the sheer volume of people who were now streaming in, laughing and talking in hushed voices, introducing themselves to Rose and to Albert, who had come down the stairs still holding one of the rabbits and looked completely astonished.

"If you will all just . . . hang up your coats," Rose called above the noise, which was quickly rising to a hubbub, "and then go to the drawing room, where my partner will . . . *Eddie*," she hissed in an aside, "we aren't going to have enough chairs."

Eddie was speechless, watching as far more than twenty people piled into the room and took their places on chairs, sofas, and footstools, cramming onto every available surface and then happily sitting down on the floor when there were no more seats to be found. Albert came rushing back in, this time sans rabbit, with some of the garden furniture. Six people took up residence in the wide archway into the drawing room and the hall beyond. Sophie Newport, with her perfectly coiffed curls, was one of them. Eddie caught Rose's eye again from across the room, and for a moment they just blinked at each other, Eddie wrinkling her nose to prevent herself from getting misty about the eyes.

There would be time for that sort of nonsense later.

The room gradually went silent and all eyes fell on Eddie, who put her shoulders back, cleared her throat, and then grinned around at them with her heart full of a fierce, determined hope.

"Thank you for answering our call," she said. "Now . . . let us begin."

The London Review, 20 April 1838: ... Mr. Charles Marsden, a promising poet from Hampshire, cites Mr. Nash Nicholson as one of his greatest inspirations. Mr. Nicholson's first novel, *The Gentleman,* was considered his last great published work; although he published two further novels and has returned to poetry in later life, critical acclaim has continued to elude him ...

City Gazette, 15 September 1899: Pictured: the Tree House Society of London celebrates the eightieth anniversary of its inaugural meeting. The meeting took place in the house of Rose and Albert Rednock, who took in a number of wards over the years, many of whom are still members of the Society today. The salon was cofounded by the author known as E. Miller, a lifelong spinster, who moved in shortly afterward and stayed as a guest of the Rednocks for the rest of her life. The Tree House Society celebrates voices often unheard in literature, and has produced many prolific and successful artists throughout the nineteenth century.

Women Writers of the Nineteenth Century, by Alice Racine: E. Miller published an astonishing fifty-six novels in her lifetime, and became a cult favorite among certain groups in society. Five of her novels were banned from production, and had to be reproduced and distributed in secret. Every one of them was dedicated to a mysterious *R. L., chairman of the board*, whose identity remains a secret to this day.

Acknowledgments

WRITING THIS BOOK WAS SOMEHOW BOTH A MARATHON AND a sprint. At one point I was so caught up in edits that I forgot about my own birthday party. If you interacted with me at all between the summer of 2021 and the spring of 2022, please consider yourself gratefully acknowledged, and also: I'm sorry.

While the characters in this book are fictional, Rose's father, Mr. Li, was inspired by the man known in the UK as John Anthony, the first Chinese person to become a British citizen, and there are hints of Anne Lister and Isabella Norcliffe in Miss Bella Cliffe.

Now for the specific thanks! I'd like to thank my agent, Chloe Seager, for changing my life (gross, so earnest), and everybody else at Madeleine Milburn. Thank you to my editors, Sarah Bauer, Katie Meegan, and Sarah Cantin, along with the rest of the incredible teams from Bonnier and St. Martin's who worked so hard to get this bad boy turned around. Thanks also to Sarah Shaffi, and to early readers Zhui Ning Chang, Dervla, Peter deGraft-Johnson, Lisa, and Alice. Miranda: you were a lighthouse (derogatory) during the final push to the end.

Big smooches on the forehead are due to my sister, Hannah; my parents; Rosianna; and my partner, Nick, who sits and listens when I talk at him about plot when he could just get up and walk out of the room. Thank you to my unofficial but very enthusiastic street team over in New Zealand, and especially to Barbara, who is sorely missed. Thank you Gladstone's Library, MUNA, The Beths, and Classic FM. Thank you to my cat, Fliss, for not getting poop on the manuscript (although she did get poop on everything else). Love and Success Rats to the Hellions.

I am so lucky that Louisa Cannell and Sophie McDonnell got the band back together for the beautiful cover, and I am so grateful to the readers, reviewers, and booksellers who shouted about *Reputation*. It's your fault that they're letting me write more books. Hope you're proud of yourselves.

About the Author

LEX CROUCHER is the author of *Reputation*, *Infamous*, and the forthcoming young adult novel *Gwen & Art Are Not In Love*. Lex grew up in Surrey reading a lot of books and making friends with strangers on the internet, and now lives in London.

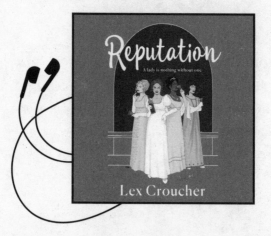